THE RISE OF SAINT FOX AND THE INDEPENDENCE

Corin Reyburn

Published by Unsolicited Press
www.unsolicitedpress.com
info@unsolicitedpress.com

Unsolicited Press Books are distributed by Ingram.
Printed in the United States of America.

Attention schools and businesses: for discounted
copies on large orders, please contact the publisher directly.

Editor: S.R. Stewart
Editor: Sarah Keen
Cover design: Erin B. Lillis
Author photo: Jose Perez

ISBN: 978-1-947021-23-5

Contents

Prologue

THIS MEANS WAR

Janus Jeeves was ready to detonate, and had been waiting to do so for three-and-a-half lifetimes.

In this lifetime, at the tail end of the bleak and prepackaged 2030s, he built himself a network. The network was called the Arcane Society, its members the Arcana: a quotient of lost geniuses—misfit students, professors, musicians, astronomers, arsonists—those who could never quite find a proper place to hide in the transparent world in which they found themselves. Jeeves and the Society designed a set of laws on how best to conduct themselves in this thoroughly trussed-up civilization. And the Eight Laws of the Arcana were these:

1. Thou shalt never purchase anything using credit.
2. Thou shalt have no outstanding debt to any institution or to thy neighbour.

3. Thou shalt not purchase a replacement item when the original item can be repaired.

4. Thou shalt disregard any and all current trends—they are temporal, and impossible to keep up with. Build thy identity outside the moment.

5. Thou shalt boycott processed foods to the fullest extent thy pocketbook can handle.

6. Thou shalt not obtain a license for marriage. Love is not a business contract. Let your yes be yes and your no be no.

7. Thou shalt not be a member of any guild, union, club, or organization other than the Arcane Society.

8. Thou shalt evade thy income tax.

First born at the turn of the Industrial Revolution, Jeeves crawled out from beneath dusty streets into a putrid cloud of factory smoke. There he toiled night and day, working on newfangled metal contraptions for a few pence to buy bread and clothes to keep his modest family—a sweet-faced wife and two pale-faced children—warm and fed. Jeeves died suddenly at the age of twenty-nine when the sleeve of his workman's shirt got caught in a bread-slicing machine.

He resurrected a full-grown man in America in the year 1920, shortly after their Eighteenth Amendment prohibited the sale of alcohol. He immediately offed himself using a corkscrew he found in a rubbish bin.

The third incarnation of Jeeves appeared in Scotland and was coddled as a child, thereby never learning discipline and acting up at school, from which he was frequently sent home. His parents then allowed him to homeschool himself through colour television and gramophone records, making sure to ignore him most of the time, focused as they were on not going bankrupt.

The telly and tunes made young Jeeves very silly at first. A skirt chaser, a celebrity in his own right, with dreams of being both a film star and an entrepreneur.

When Jeeves turned sixteen, he realised it had all been a distraction technique, a tall tale designed to make him want something which wasn't that great anyway and that he wouldn't be able to get his hands on without selling his old soul. He didn't want to be like his parents, working all day to earn a dollar only to die prematurely from butter and cigarettes.

Jeeves grew angry through the rest of his adolescence and into young adulthood. He smashed a lot of shop windows. He went out and drank too much at pubs, wandering the streets yelling insults at posh buggers. He got arrested frequently. He developed and overcame heroin addiction five times.

The sixth time, he overdosed.

The spirit of Janus Jeeves then floated for several years before being born again in London, into a body made of spare and surplus parts—wires, feathers, and nicotine stains. He arrived at some point during the 1980s, right before everything really started going to hell but no one knew it yet.

In this life he became a professor, so he could spend all day talking about the things he loved. His favourite class to teach was a course called Neurotic Poetry: 17th–20th Century, and focused on the works of some of his former mates and heroes—Wilde, Plath, Poe. Coleridge, Shelley, Dylan Thomas.

And then, Janus Jeeves was sacked.

The university needed to cut expenses, and the first place they started was the Arts and Humanities department. He and his kind were replaced by a small army of bright-eyed, cost-effective graduates, and his courses replaced with ones more current and digestible such as Suprasocial Media and Contemporary Vlog Critique. Classes that could easily be self-taught, something Jeeves himself had done. He liked to keep up to date with the pulse of the nation, what the youth were into these days.

Now, he bided the free time he found on his hands. He lived on adrenaline, on the abstinence of his vices, on the injustices that had been done to him throughout the centuries, on books and classical music. Jeeves had read books stoned, sober, sauced, sweating, and sleeping, had absorbed them all in their entirety, and now he knew the truth.

The children were our future.

Jeeves would rally them to his side to make the future into something new.

And so, in this lifetime, the Arcane Society was born, straight in the middle of London—the pancreas of the so-called developed world. Jeeves watched as the Ministers and CEOs of Great Britain drove around in one of several luxury vehicles they owned, while the rest drove beat-up cars with no hubcaps, fenders smashed, broken LED indicators, parts slapped on at random, make and model irrelevant. The Ministers and CEOs lived in estates worth millions, owned vacation homes and islands, while for everyone else the housing market was in tatters, and homes were systematically foreclosed upon to become the property of yes, the government, who were in league with the banks, who had written the bad loans in the first place. The Ministers and CEOs drank single malt scotch equal to the price of a month's rent, and the rest drank the cheapest bitter they could find to forget that the rent was due.

Did they know, the children, of the disparity they took for granted as status quo?

They must, surely, for it was staring them straight in the face.

And if they did not, Janus Jeeves would make it known. The Arcane Society would grow.

It would grow enough to save the nation.

Chapter One

WELCOME TO THE JUNGLE

Janus Jeeves had cultivated yet another disappointment in Julian Starr.

Cameras recorded the failure for posterity as the young man trounced around the rented studio, blue eyes blazing. He had already destroyed two set lights, irritated the film crew into dashing out for a smoke break from which they would not return, and sent an antique tea set sailing through an open window. Julian's hands shook with pent-up fury from somewhere else—resentment towards his parents, perhaps, a strict schoolmarm, a lover who'd hurt his pride.

Jeeves exhaled loudly through his nose, frustration mounting. It was not him who deserved this rage. The unfortunately positioned red-upholstered chaise that Julian had stumbled into, bruised his shin upon, and was now kicking with the heel of his suede leather boot also did not deserve it. The leading man who would lead no one gave the chaise one more lashing for good measure, then turned on his mentor.

"Go ahead and laugh, old man. I know you want to," said Julian, running a hand through his hair and glowering at his director.

It was not amusement which Jeeves felt. Frustration, perhaps. Exhaustion, definitely. His directorial dreams dissipating into the depths along with the entire plan. He would have to sack Julian, sack the films, sack everything, just as he'd done so many times before.

Back to square one.

He needed to grow the Arcane Society by exponential amounts, that much was certain. A series of films with an irresistible hero, subversive intent—it seemed the best solution, the best way to plant the seed, to get the message out.

To grow in numbers.

Should have been, he thought, as an apple that moments ago resided in a pig's mouth went sailing through the air. Just another discarded item on a long list of things once lovely that had been destroyed. Jeeves glanced over at the glamourous spread laid out on the dining table at the far end of the room and had to laugh. Though most of the fancy tableware and mouthwatering delicacies—clove-laden curries, golden serving spoons, granny's pewter goblets, a pilfered Christmas goose—were discards collected by his fellow revolutionaries amongst the Arcana, it seemed that he, too, had now contributed to the world's massive waste cycle.

"What a messssss…you're making," he said to Julian, who wasn't listening. Jeeves sat perched upright in a tall director's chair, his silk-draped limbs crossed every which way. A man with impeccable flair himself, Jeeves never failed to catch an eye, though not always the ones he wanted. His own eyes were mismatched, one blue and one yellow, one row of teeth smoke-stained and the other pearlescent white, the disparate features set inside a narrow face that peered out from beneath long strands of stringy brown hair. On his arms he wore silver bangles, and his thin body was draped in loose-fitting fabrics dark and bright, black and crimson, oily and iridescent.

If only the timing were different; if only he'd figured it out sooner. Back in the seventies, perhaps, when freaks like him were lauded instead of shunned. Oh, then he would have had his chance. He would have taken the world by storm.

Now, it was too late for him. He was an Ana, as the kids would say. Short for analog. Someone from the past ought to stay there.

What he needed was someone digital.

He thought he'd found his answer in Julian, a lad so current he attached himself to a fad in practically the same moment he rejected it. They'd met by the river one night and the boy was gorgeous, so gorgeous in fact that he mistook Jeeves' intentions, a situation commonplace amongst the beautiful. But Jeeves had been interested in his face for one reason, and one reason only.

To bring more followers to the Arcana.

Julian had complied easily, aimless as he was and enthralled by Jeeves' reptilian words, promising to make him a star. He was energetic about anything new and too dumb to ask questions.

But Jeeves had miscalculated. Julian equals minus one key factor for the ultimate revolutionary star—

A kind heart.

Dreams dying now as Julian acted out his last performance for his audience of one. The words "I quit" froze on the boy's lips as the words "You're sacked" fell from Jeeves'.

At the verbal crossover, Julian howled. "How're you going to make your little propaganda films without me, huh? What are you gonna do, crawl back to your sorry flat full of reject geeks and losers? Gather more trash in the name of 'rescuing' it? Have those two-bit hackers of yours break into the CCTV feeds so you can perv on people wanking?"

"Julian," Jeeves said, with more patience than was deserved. "We use everything we find, and our hackers are the finest in the land. Why, Benson graduated top of his class."

Julian shrugged.

"And the chaise you're currently embattling is a Giatalia," he added.

"I don't care," Julian said, gathering his things in an exaggerated huff of departure.

No one does, thought Jeeves. Irony, irony in having to hang his hopes and fears on someone so young.

"I hope you find another gullible sucker to dangle from your rod. I hope you find him real soon," Julian said. "And when you do, I hope he doesn't just help you break the system. I hope he breaks your heart."

"Why do you hate me so much, Julian?" Jeeves inquired in earnest.

"Because you remind me of my father."

"Farewell, Julian." Jeeves drew his spindly limbs closer to his body, creating the appearance of a cocoon with his long fabrics draped around him.

As the door to the rented studio slammed, the thrice-reincarnated Janus Jeeves began to mentally sort through his mind box—a box containing items from his previous lifetimes, a box containing memories. A worn grey scrap of fabric from his first wife's dress, an empty syringe, Elvis' first Sun record, the corkscrew Jeeves had topped himself with during Prohibition. Some items he remembered and some he didn't. Some people he remembered, others he thought he remembered, but had maybe made up. Stories he told himself about his past lives were perhaps just that, stories.

Or perhaps not. Quite possibly the feeling in his bones that remained always was indeed his beacon of truth. He knew, oh he knew that the same sort of thing had happened too many times. That people with money told lies, and people with less believed them, and wound up with even less. That humankind too often manifested the darkest parts of themselves that overshadowed the light—but that amongst them, sometimes, there were bright and shining jewels whose sparkle and magnetism pulled the weight of the world off-kilter until just, if even for a moment, the dark world shone bright, too.

He folded inside, and waited for one to arrive.

~

"Let's get pissed," Sam Numan said to Sailor, his best mate, flatmate, and only person who really knew him well enough beyond what his favourite brew was.

"Someone's a bit tense," Sailor teased. "You should go to bed with me, will take yer mind off things."

"Bad idea. We'll traumatise Binky." Binky was an imaginary dog Sam used sometimes to distract Sailor. It almost always worked.

Sailor sighed, dramatically flopping onto the worn suede couch in their tiny flat. "Don't think about the rent," he said in a Northern accent. Sailor was from a collegiate family in Exeter, but spoke like he was from either Manchester, Scotland, or Texas depending on his mood that day. Young and loud, with a tall, lanky frame and wide round eyes like an anime heroine, Sailor was both a loyal friend for life and an airheaded flake who could never make it on time for scheduled appointments. He and Sam had become best mates after meeting six years ago at Glastonbury, both having lost the friends they'd arrived with after ingesting hazardous amounts of booze and mind-twisting party favours.

"If I try not to think about the rent, it's all I'm gonna think about. Can't believe that shyster raised it again. Who the bloody hell does he think he is—the King of England?" Sam ran his fingers through his wild hair, turning away from Sailor.

He stepped outside onto the low balcony overlooking Brixton Hill. Only a few cars passed by, one or two every thirty seconds. Sam stood on tiptoe and leaned over the rusted balcony. A light mist hung in the air, painting spotted reflections across the shabby blue curtains in their balcony window. The flat was sparse, almost utilitarian. Two lads who couldn't afford much in the way of décor, the flat, in shades of blue and grey by default, was brought alive by stray pieces of clothing and the cold England light that bled in from the wide North-facing window in ghost-shaped patterns.

"Looks like rain again," Sailor said, joining Sam on the balcony.

"Acid rain," said Sam. "Always acid rain."

"You should let me give you a haircut soon. S'getting shaggy 'round the edges again—you look like a tosser from the seventies." Sailor slid along the railing till their sides were touching, reaching his arm up to dance his fingers through Sam's messy mane.

"Time's it?" Sam asked, playfully batting Sailor's hands away.

"Pub o'clock. And time for you to get a new cleverband. Can't you just check your wrist and tell what's up like everyone else?"

Sam sighed. "Jules, time and date." The occasionally functional hologram's genderless form materialised before him in shades of blue and steel. An older model—glitchy, response-lag, the 3D wasn't as good as some—but Sam didn't have the funds to upgrade, and didn't much care whether his gadgets had features like diamondsphere sound or whatever was in vogue this week.

"Five thirty-three p.m. April twenty-ninth, two-thousand-thirty-eight," the drone voice informed about five seconds after he'd given up on it.

"Well, there you have it. Pub o'clock, just like you said," Sam announced. "You're buying the first round."

"With what, my arse?"

"If the trousers fit."

"Maybe they'll slash the rent if we cut out the pet deposit." Sailor moulded his face into a cartoonish frown. "Go on now, Binky, get! Off with ye into the wide, cruel, world. We can't care for ye no more. Mummy and daddy can barely afford a pint."

Sam laughed, clasping a firm hand around Sailor's lanky shoulders. "If only Binky were real, and not a product of your drug-addled imagination."

"Sacrilege." Sailor stuck his hand into Sam's back trouser pocket. "Binky's as real as you or I."

They made sure to leave a light on for him when they went out, electricity costs be damned.

The Tube was late again.

Sam and Sailor stood on Platform 3, waiting to board the train for Oxford Circus. When it finally arrived, they crammed into the last car along with the rest of the blank-faced commuters, pressed together like cardboard cutouts, half-finished sketches, virtual avatars piloted by their users at home. They interacted with their cleverbands and no one smiled. Dressed to impress in the latest fashions—bright pops of orange, white, and green, the cute mass-manufactured woolen caps that were a must this year, sensible and stylish boots for city or country that came up to the knee with designer jeans tucked inside. Most had gone into debt to maintain this season's current look. All looked fabulous, yet no one looked at one another.

Ten years ago, we had one of the smoothest running subway systems in the world, Sam thought. Now it's just like any other metro in Europe—smelly, covered in graffiti, failing to show up. He stared mindlessly out the window while Sailor rested his head against his shoulder.

Sixteen stops to Oxford Circus. Sam disliked Oxford Street, but they were only stopping there to pick up his mate, Benson, and the pub they were headed to in Soho wasn't nearly as precious as most in the area. Armloads of shopping bags, too-sweet snacks, screaming tots, and ladies dressed to the nines. Luxury shopping for trivial goods was the side product of the Exchange's distribution of profit and loss.

London in the 21st century was a poker game of bits and bytes. The stock market soared or plummeted based on a series of digital entries made by faceless assistants. The free market soared or plummeted based on carefully controlled, artificial values created by those with strong wills, weak constitutions, and no liabilities.

Sam was fourteen years old when his parents lost the house, and had lived on his own ever since. He didn't want to worry his mum by telling her he'd just lost his fifth job this year. He was always on time for work, and his managers recognised that he went above and beyond to see that customers were happy. But Sam liked to work for small businesses, and small businesses were never able to afford the rent for very long, so he found himself unemployed more often than not.

He told himself he wasn't attached to anyone, thinking himself a bit of an orphan, and made a habit of never asking for much of anything, save for maybe a couch to crash on from time to time. Even then, he made up for favours in trade—he bought the beer, made dinner, tidied up the place.

Still, people tended to grant him favours he'd never asked for.

After exiting the train at Oxford, they rode two escalators and climbed twenty-six stairs to the crowded street above. Sam and Sailor did their best to evade the mass of shoppers, weaving through the area's side streets until they reached Urbani, a high-end camera shop where Benson worked. Sam knew a thing or two about photography—he'd even snapped a few photos on film with his father's old camera, caught landscapes and architectural planes and people unaware. Unfortunately, the few places where one could get them developed cost a fortune. Even Urbani failed to offer film processing, and sold only digicams that claimed to have all the capabilities of any outdated analog model ever to freeze-frame the earth.

They entered Urbani and spotted Benson Bridges, a 22nd century geek, standing behind the wooden counter against the far wall. He was scrutinizing components of a homemade circuit board under a magnifying lens through his ridiculously narrow eyeglasses—Sam couldn't imagine how he managed to actually see through them. From bottom to top they were no taller than a slice of bread on its side, and the lenses were thin as a razor. Benson said he absolutely needed them to see; he couldn't do his work without them. All his clothes were black and faded from fastidious washing, and his always serious face was paper pale in contrast to the rough shock of dark hair that sprouted from his head like a patchwork of burnt weeds.

"Oi, Bezza, you ready?" asked Sailor, ready to get properly trashed.

"I'll be done in five," Benson said, without glancing up from his work. He was hand-soldering tiny chips under a brightly illuminated lens. "They've got shittier cameras in America," he said. "Exactly the same, but shittier."

Benson closed up shop and they headed for the pub. As they walked, Benson lit up several fags and left them dangling between his fingers without ever taking a drag, letting them burn down to their ends.

"You're wasting tons of money," Sam said, a confused grin on his face. "Why would you do that when a pack costs twenty quid?"

"That's exactly why I do it, mate. It's in line with the Society's rules, I think. Also, I'm saving some poor sod from getting lung cancer. If I kill this here little pack o' fire sticks, well then no one else can smoke 'em, can they?"

"And they call you a genius," said Sam.

The last vestiges of the sun dissipated, fading the sky from blue to black. Benson took a drag from one of the cigs, then coughed for about three minutes straight.

"We're here, my lovelies," Sailor said, holding the heavy wooden door open for the others.

Sam stopped in front of Sailor, bowing to him cheekily before waltzing through the door like he owned the place.

"Let's make tonight a night to remember, lads."

Chapter Two

THE JESTER AND THE KING

The pub in Soho was not quite Sam's idea of a perfect pub. The locale itself was not guilty of any grievous errors—minimalist décor in warm strokes of reclaimed wood and rust orange, plenty of comfy seating in a stripped down atmosphere where the ale was cold and crisp. And the clientele were colourful enough, a mix of characters both savory and unsavory—blokes in suits, vagrants, blokes in feathers and derbies and stripes, disgruntled West End queens, disgraced literature professors, those who were all of the above.

Still, Sam felt uneasy inside the pub's four walls for some reason he could not put his finger on.

Sailor arrived at their table with a round of drinks, sliding into the booth beside Sam and across from Benson.

"Say, what are ya, Bez? Glaswegian? Korean? Californian?" Sailor teased, having only met Benson recently through Sam.

"All that and more, probably. My parents were both mutts so by the time I was born, no one knew what the fuck I was. Was born in Suffolk but grew up in Florida. Then I came back here an' been movin' around the city. I'm in a new flat 'bout every month. Soon as they ask for the rent, I move." Benson fiddled with his glass, avoiding eye contact.

"Must be why I can't figure out your accent. Usually I'm spot on," Sailor said.

Sam steepled his hands together, elbows resting on the wooden table. "Speaking of rent, we're past due again. Sailor and I are about one step away from whoring out our arses down by the docks."

"I tried that once," said Sailor with a dismissive wave of his hand. "Made a decent chunk of cash but blew it all straightaway. Besides, it made me feel dirty."

"I have a tough time believing such acts are below your moral standards." Sam smirked behind his beer, earning him a smack against his ribcage.

"You're hilarious. I'll have you know that my moral standards are perfectly in line with the times. Now, I came here to dance. You coming, smartarse? Bezza?"

"I'm good here," Sam answered as Benson shook his head. Sailor disappeared behind a crowd of impeccably dressed lads and ladies moving in liquid-slow motion.

Sam tipped his head back against the booth. "All kidding aside, mate, I'm skint this month. You know anywhere I can find work? Is Urbani hiring? I know some stuff about cameras."

"You don't need to know anything," Benson said, eyes solemn behind his thin specs. "The cameras operate themselves, practically. I think the shop's gonna fold soon. I mean, we basically deal in antiques."

"Then what'll you end up doing?"

"I do some hacking on the side for this group. Might start doing it full time."

"The Arcana, right? Grassroots anarchists and shyte?"

"Something like that."

"You're a braver man than me," said Sam, grinning.

Sam knew a thing or two about the Arcane Society. Bits he'd gleaned from Benson, stuff he'd watched on vlogs. He knew they thought credit was a farce. They shunned large cities, yet were usually found in the heart of them. They minimised patronisation of corporate-manufactured goods and services, were known lawbreakers, non-participants, many without any family or formal identification, though authorities tried their best to tag and file.

The Arcana wanted to reset the balance of monetary power. For the U.K. at least, globally if it were possible.

They'd been called radicals, anarcho-capitalists, even terrorists, which Sam thought was a bit extreme—it wasn't like anyone had gotten hurt, at least according to what he'd heard. No one knew exactly how they intended to achieve their improbable goal, and their actions thus far did not fall outside the range of any similar organization—protest rallies, setups to recruit new members in artsy public locales, minor theft and vandalism of targeted corporations.

Benson had asked Sam once or twice if he wanted to join. Sam always laughed and said he'd think about it. He'd sign on for something eventually. He just hadn't gotten around to it yet.

Sam grimaced as the murmur of the pub was overpowered by the sound of bad karaoke—if there was anything that murdered a good buzz, it was the murder of a good song. A wailing rendition of Pulp's "Common People" by some wasted ginger bloke had him cringing.

"Blimey, gives new meaning to the term 'misery rock,'" said Sam.

"You can do better than that, can't you Sammy?" asked Benson. "I've heard you crooning on the Underground with your eardiscs in. You could kick that guy's arse."

Sam drummed his fingertips to the beat as a grin spread across his face. "Challenge accepted," he said. "Sign me up."

In the darkest corner of the pub, Jeeves watched the crowd with quick-darting eyes, obscured by the changing shadows of young people moving to and fro, and they did not notice him because he wished it so. This was no small feat considering his unusual appearance, how his very being vibrated with centuries-old electric energy. The young people slid against one another with laughter on their lips and false promises in their eyes.

In his private corner booth he sat and watched and learned, quietly sipping his scotch. A very attractive young man with a microphone in his hand currently held the attentions of almost everyone in the pub. He was perched up on the small wooden karaoke stage, and though his voice was silky and sweet, this was not the aspect of him that alerted Jeeves to the presence of someone valuable.

The young man held the audience's focus because he was making them laugh. For his song choice he had selected "Subterranean Homesick Blues" by Dylan—Jeeves' old mate from his third lifetime. The lyrics were a mouthful.

"...wants eleven dollar bills, you only got ten," the boy sang, letting out a self-deprecating laugh every time he ran out of breath or tripped through the landmine of lyrics. The crowd laughed along with him, charmed by his grinning antics and the way he hit his stride when he got to the chorus.

Aha! And there it was. A new plan. A plan to grow in numbers, a better plan than all his plans before. Better than Julian and the films. Films were too long, anyway. People have trouble paying attention these days.

The best pop songs are only three minutes long.

The lad on the stage had style. Like Dylan himself, it wasn't about vocal prowess. It was there, that intangible somethin'-somethin'. The way his voice curled around the words, sang 'em like he knew 'em, like he'd been there.

Jeeves grinned as he sipped his drink. *Look out kid, you're gonna get hit.*

Sandy brown hair, almost the same colour as his. It would have to be dyed, something much more vivid, Jeeves thought. Bright red, perhaps, like Ziggy. The lad's clothes were offensively lackluster, torn-up jeans and a Jack Daniels t-shirt—he would need more flare, clothes that were much tighter. He was in pretty good shape, but might need to lose a few pounds in order to achieve that shaking, shimmering, starving musician look.

There was something else about him. Something in his large, watery eyes that threatened to awake dormant memories. This was not the first lifetime in which they had met. The boy, of course, had forgotten, but Jeeves would always remember.

The young man finished the song with a little ragman dance, bowing low at the edge of the stage and receiving friendly cheers and back slaps from patrons before returning to his mates. He slid into a booth across from a man Jeeves knew well—Benson Bridges, coder extraordinaire.

The lights in the woodsy orange pub brightened a tad. Janus Jeeves straightened his spine and crooked his bowtie as he emerged from the shadows.

He waltzed over to the boys' table, where Benson and the karaoke singer sat drinking and chatting. Jeeves clasped Benson round the shoulder with a silver-bangled right hand.

"So, you do come out of your blue-lit computer lab," he said, startling the young programmer.

"Jaysus. Didn't see you there, appearing out of nowhere like that," Benson said, hiding behind his specs and fiddling awkwardly with his pint glass. "I don't go out much. I only know about this spot 'cause you and some of the guys dragged me here once."

"Yes, yes of courssse." Jeeves said, drawing out his S's like a snake. "Who's this?" he asked, openly appraising Sam.

Sam introduced himself, extending his hand before Benson had the chance to answer.

Jeeves was suddenly seated next to him when a moment ago he'd been standing on the other side of the table.

"So, bet you've heard all about us," he sang into Sam's ear.

"You're the bloke who runs the Arcane Society," said Sam, meeting Jeeves at eye level and looking curious enough.

Jeeves' lips spread into a wide, all-knowing grin. "So, you *have* heard. Has Benson here told you much about our little group?" He slung a silk-clad arm across Sam's shoulders. "Not so much a group, more like a Movement. An Idea. A Militia. Heh, heh, a New World Order, of course."

The pub lights had dimmed again and Jeeves couldn't make out whether this Sam kid was keen on hearing his bit, but continued anyway. He drummed his fingers against the dark wooden table, peering curiously at Sam through strands of stone brown hair that fell in strings across his face.

"So, Sam, was it?" Jeeves asked, leaning close. "Our little society could always use more members. Tell me, son. Are you good at getting people to like you?" He raised an angular eyebrow, interlacing bony fingers together.

The expression on the lad's lovely face grew thoughtful as his gaze returned to Jeeves, index finger circling the rim of his glass. "I think so. Not much to it, really. Just got to get to know 'em. Most people have got something going on underneath once you get them to open up a bit."

"That's right, babe, that's right," Jeeves said. "What I need is bodies, Sam. Lots of bodies. Live ones, of course. Dead ones do me no good."

"What do you need bodies for?" Sam inquired.

Jeeves leaned in close, touching heads with Sam. "To build an army. An indestructible one. To turn our way of life into, 'Life!'" he said with a starburst motion of his hand.

"I'm not usually up for joining any kind of club or society," Sam said, pulling back minutely. "But the Arcana...you guys are different. I believe in leveling the playing field. Not sure how I'd be of any help though. I ain't no one special—not a whiz-kid coder like Benson or a great speaker or anything like that."

"Oh, no," answered Jeeves. "You're much more than that. Have you looked in the mirror lately? Your face! Your face can help me, baby. Yer arms, your legs, your wedding tackle. Annnnd, most importantly, you've got natural charm, and a real pretty voice on you. I saw you singing up there. You had everyone's attention."

Sam watched Jeeves through squinted eyes, regarding him with a mix of skepticism and curiosity.

"So, how would you like to front a band for the Arcana?" Jeeves asked. His grip across Sam's shoulders tightened.

Sam glanced over at Benson. Jeeves recognised that look. It was the *What the fuck's he on about?* look.

It had never deterred him.

"You're it, Sammy. I just know it, can feel it in my bones. I look at you, and I know. Benson knows, don't you grandmaster Bridges? You must have brought us here together tonight. It must be fate."

"I gotta take a leak," Benson said, leaving Jeeves to his prey.

"You ever thought about playing music before? Gaining thousands of adoring fans?"

"I've fooled around, played a little guitar," Sam said. "But it's hard to get things going these days."

"You let me worry about getting things going," Jeeves said. "Getting things going is my specialty. I like your voice. You sound like a male Janis Joplin. We'll write honeysuckle words, we will. We'll write 'em together. I'll make you a star, make you a god, make you a martyr—the story of success since the dawn of time—it's an oldie but a goodie. You can't go wrong with the classics."

Sam set his glass down on the table. "I don't know," he said, sliding out from under Jeeves' heavy arm. "I don't think

I'm your man. You'd need someone with more talent than me to pull off whatever it is you're planning."

"You might not see your own potential, but I do." Jeeves leaned back in the booth with a knowing look on his serpentine face. "You just need time, and you have a little. Come with Benson the next time he visits my kingdom. We'll talk again."

Sam let himself smile a little. "We'll see. I'm not making any promises. Now, if you'll excuse me, I'd better find my flatmate and make sure he hasn't caught himself a new STI in the last twenty minutes. The worst things happen when I lose track of him," he explained.

"Suit yourself," said Janus Jeeves, receding into the shadows. He was not concerned. Once he hatched a plan, the plan would commence. The players cast would play their roles, the pieces would fall into place. It was only a matter of time.

The tide would turn, the scales would balance, and Janus Jeeves would have justice—in this life, or the next.

Chapter Three

BREEDING GROUND FOR ADVERTS

The toilet lever was broken again. Tied string, rubber bands, and duct tape had failed to provide an economical means of repair, and now Kit had to call the landlady, a task she dreaded. As per usual there was no one at the receiving end, just the loathed automated voice instructing her to leave yet another message.

"Hi, Mrs. Harrow, this is Kit Alysdair again, from downstairs. It's about the toilet, again. Please call me back."

The girl's flat was falling to pieces. Bits of carpet coming up round the edges, chipped paint on the shutters, anything with a pipe hell-bent on leaking, squeaking, or busting. The lamps were shoddy and the upholstery on the chairs was torn and over ten years old, but replacing them was out of the question. Every few months, items cost a few more quid while salaries remained the same.

Kit imagined a sad Russian symphony, a bowl of ripe berries with clotted cream and a shiny new tabletop—dark lacquered cherry wood. She then scorned herself for her idleness and superficiality. Before her parents had passed, they'd taught her better than to waste energy pining after trivialities.

She typically left eight minutes late for work, and would be even later today. Four different transfers on the Tube—all the way across the city, to sit at a desk and exchange a barrage of phone calls and emails with ignorant, demanding customers. Every day she swore she'd find a way to get out of I.T. but she was trapped—her C.V., as with all others, offered only one path, and taking time off work to go back to school would make the high cost of even the most frugal lifestyle nearly impossible.

Everyone does it, she told herself. Everyone does it.

Another Monday afternoon found her stuck in front of a coworker's station, fighting with their virus-ridden OS while the hours dragged slowly, as they do at VipTech.

"Got time for tea?" her office mate, Jim, asked.

"Not really," she said. "This one's a tricky bastard." She swiped away another barrage of pop-ups on the outdated holo monitor in front of her.

"S'always time for tea."

"Right. Gimme a sec."

"'Ey, how come you never wear skirts to work? Something wrong with yer legs?"

"How come you never wear a skirt to work? A little pleated schoolgirl number would suit you well," she remarked, a steady gleam in her eye.

"Alright, alright, fair enough. See you downstairs," said Jim.

The number of people gathered in the kitchen made the break less enjoyable—backs crowded up against countertops smelling of Dettol surface cleaner—and they were out of PG Tips. And spoons. VipTech ran near empty on most things, from food and office supplies to funding and new clients. Kit had narrowly escaped being a casualty in a redundancy sweep three times in the past thirteen months.

"Mr. Dottier, I quit," she said quietly into her teacup.

At twenty-six years old it seemed her path was already decided—and that said path lay buried in the digisphere like the fate of so many others. Pretty but not pretty enough for London—her hair too dark and frizzy, the curves of her body slight and slender, the bright, pale face of a neglected doll. Smart but lacking ambition—above average in a world where average was exalted whenever it was accompanied by insatiable drive and a set of fake tits.

She didn't want to wind up bitter, afraid she already had. Yuppie whites working in tall office buildings had so much, and still there were endless complaints. The nonstop wandering eye of the too-complacent, the lifelong search for the next bit of entertainment when too much leisure time is afforded by way of everyday labor assigned to apps and washing machines. If she'd had to work out in the fields all day just to put bread in her mouth, she might not wonder what if, because then there was no what if, only what was.

It used to be different.

She used to play before thousands, under bright stage lights.

Kit placed her teacup in the sink.

"I'll see you later, Jim," she said. I'll see you later, VipTech.

Or never again, as it were.

~

It had been years since any member of the Royal family had stepped foot into the Palace of Westminster for any reason other than a cup of tea. While the people were thoroughly absorbed with their every move, and stories about them filled the tabloids, each year the dwindling connection they had with Parliament grew ever smaller. Referred to still as His Majesty's Government, though the King of England was more often spotted in attendance at football matches than within the halls of Westminster. He now supported Arsenal, to everyone's surprise, though not surprising in light of the fact that his oldest son played defence for the indomitable club.

The King did not meet on a regular basis with Prime Minister Harold Waterman. Prime Minister Waterman seemed to everyone the kindest accidental tyrant one would ever meet. He was unusual-looking for a politician, in good shape and ineffaceably young-looking. A good 1.87 meters tall with brown hair and blue eyes, yet somehow his face did not seem either handsome or memorable. It was this, the having of all the correct parameters, plus the tendency to fade from people's minds, that made him so successful at his job.

Prime Minister Waterman's office looked like something out of a posh catalogue—everything was expensive and nothing appeared to be uniquely indicative of the room's occupant. Not a speck of dust to be found, a personal trinket in sight, a stack of paper askew, or an article of clothing tossed carelessly over the back of a chair. Everything was in its right place.

Seated now in his Italian leather armchair, the Prime Minister removed his tie, leaned back, and reached for his glass of Polish vodka—two shots on the rocks.

Just as he was starting to relax, his assistant poked his silly blonde head into the office. "Sir, your wife is calling," he said.

Waterman had been an investment adviser before he became a politician, and like all investment advisers, he was a wizard at insider trading. He was part of a secret social network of brilliant mathematicians and general right-place-at-the-right-timers, a global community whose deep sense of philanthropy caused them to provide support to one another by sending hired hands to mop up each other's shyte on a regularly scheduled basis. Outwardly, their philanthropic hearts manifested themselves in displays of large charitable donations, which were of course, tax deductible, and often did not find their way to the actual charity at all.

It was not Harold Waterman who'd created the old boys' rules. He simply conformed in the manner which was expected, as generations before him had. What else was there to do?

"Sir. Mrs. Waterman on the line," his assistant repeated.

"Tell Amelia to stop fretting; I'll be home at eight," Waterman said, dismissing the man by touching an icon to rotate his chair around 180 degrees.

Harold Waterman went home at eleven-thirty, after some time spent at the Windsor Club having drinks with the special advisers on his staff he could stand to be around. Amelia would hardly mind. They'd been married twenty-two years; she barely noticed his absence as she noticed his presence, unless something he did was not to her liking.

Harold Waterman ruled His Majesty's Government with a light hand; a well-oiled machine needs not much tinkering. He controlled your salary, he controlled your rent, he controlled what you ate and how much you slept. He controlled your girlfriend and he controlled where you called home. He did it all from his armchair, with a remote control. He did it all using his cleverband, and you didn't even know.

Chapter Four

THE MUSIC OF THE ARCANA

Any metropolis was a utopia and a cesspool, an unavoidable 24-hour broadcast of the ever-widening gap between men who spent three hundred quid on a haircut and thought nothing of it, and men who could not keep a roof over their heads and froze in the streets at night, who ran like dogs through alleyways chased by bookies, trails of smoke and dust and racial slurs left behind in their wake.

Sam found himself on the cesspool's edge, somehow managing to tread just above it. No one was better or less than Sam, everyone just made choices and had to stick by them. He was a good listener, a man who always saw both sides of the coin, who could always see your point.

Sam would soon see the world through Janus Jeeves' mismatched eyes.

Jeeves conducted business in his deceased brother's flat on the fourth story of a building whose three lower floors had already collapsed, the fourth floor held precariously aloft by weathered beams and perhaps the sheer force of will of its lone occupant. The place was accessible via rope ladder; groceries and the like were brought in via a pulleyed freight lift with a max allowed weight of twenty kilos.

"The duffel bag's not gonna make it," Benson said, staring forlornly at the lift.

"What's in it?" asked Sam, tapping his foot impatiently.

"Just spare parts, man. Stuff for building contraptions. No big deal. The boys'll bring it up later." Using all his strength, Benson pushed the bag behind a large cement post.

"Just spare parts? Not an electromagnetic explosive?" Sam joked.

"EMPs aren't this heavy," Benson said. He gripped the bottom rung of the ladder and started climbing. Sam followed on Benson's heels.

For the past few days he'd been hard-pressed to think of anything but Janus Jeeves' strange offer—what it might mean, where it would lead to, if it was for real. Maybe the Arcane Society was just what he was looking for—a chance to make something happen, escape from the endless monotony of adverts and Dot purchases and overpriced coffees.

Inside, the place smelled of fire and spices, liquid metal and black witch incense. Window coverings were a mosaic of stitched-together scarves in bold colours and abstract patterns. Not a single piece of art or furniture matched; it was as if all locales and time periods had been mashed together, a Postmodern Renaissance Baroque Art Deco yard sale.

Sam followed Benson into the kitchen, where a pair of twin young men dressed in clashing paisley sat at a wooden blue picnic table eating chicken masala, yellow dal, and some fire-red mystery dish.

"Did I miss supper?" asked Benson. "This is my mate, Sam. Where's Jeeves?"

The twins only stared while shoveling in spoonfuls of food at a steady, alternating pace. The sound of a low D on a squeaky piano resounded from the adjacent room, effectively answering his question.

"Have a seat and have something to eat," the twins said together.

"Jeeves'll be out in a mo' I'm sure," Benson said. "He takes a while to get into the right headspace."

Sam extended his hand to the twin on the left. "Chuffed to meet you," he said, smiling.

The twin stood, clasping Sam's hand in both of his and shaking it vigorously. "Well chuffed indeed! I'm Jack-of-all-Trades. An' this here's my brother, James." The pair linked hands, waving their joined arms together like a pair of connected marionettes, then resumed their meal.

"Can you really do all trades, mate?" Sam asked.

"No, I can only flip burgers and build explosives. We work for Jeeves," James said.

"He's our father," Jack added.

"And our mother," said James.

"He lets us stay here for free."

An ominous melody drifted in from the sitting room. A black sound, a crashing storm, a dissonant dirge you only wanted to hear once, yet were sure you dreamed of it almost every night since.

Sam and Benson turned around in their seats.

Janus Jeeves was seated crossed-legged at an old wooden piano. The keys squealed and cried as he banged on them in turn, and his hands moved so fast it seemed there were six of them.

The song ended with a bang. Jeeves dropped his hands to his sides. He swiveled around on the uneven piano bench, leveling his gaze directly at Sam.

"Everybody out," he said quietly. "Except for the newcomer."

"But we haven't finished our supper," James protested, though he was already grabbing his bowl, linking arms with his twin and ambling into the next room.

"This could fix your money problem," Benson said to Sam over his shoulder as he left with the twins.

Jeeves sauntered into the kitchen, all bright-colours, twitches, and flowy sleeves. He grabbed a bottle of red wine and two glasses. "Come," he said, motioning for Sam to follow.

Sam followed Jeeves into another room as red and gold and hideous as the rest of the flat he'd seen so far. It had a high-vaulted ceiling with shelves of books on two adjacent walls, and was decorated with large-scale maps, old tapestries, ancient artifacts from the Bronze Age, the Industrial Age, the New Age, and the Age after that. His study, Sam realised. The Arcana's leader was certainly intriguing—a gangly, odd professor type who seemed to vibrate with frenetic energy.

The former professor, former addict, former factory man seated himself in a red leather chair by a tall window. He poured two tall glasses of wine, squinting at the amount of liquid to make sure they were equal.

Sam received the proffered beverage, sitting on the floor near Jeeves' feet, a willing pupil for the time being.

"Do you want to be a rock star, Sam?" Jeeves asked, one of his long legs dangling over the armrest of the chair.

"Who doesn't?" I've only dreamed of it all my life, like every other lad, Sam thought. He took a deep breath. "So, I think I have some idea what you guys are about. Been reading stuff…looked up more about the Arcana after that night we met."

"Oh?" Jeeves steepled his fingers together, looking inherently pleased.

"I can see where you're coming from. I mean, we're told it's a free market when it's far from it; it's custom-designed to benefit a privileged few. The lot of us may be warm enough, fed enough, but so are pet rats. Keep us in a cage, give us a wheel to run on, let us think we're accomplishing something when we ain't going nowhere. I get it." He took a tentative sip from his glass, watching Jeeves out of the corner of his eye.

"You're speaking my language, baby. We need a war, Sam. To set things right, you need a war. That's how it goes. But…I am anti-violence." Jeeves pressed his hands together solemnly like a monk. "I'm not able to gain enough followers for the Arcana as a grassroots society, Sam. But tell me now, what *would* gain me a massive following?" he questioned with a gleam in his eye.

"A witty BitBit account?" Sam joked.

"A killer rock band, Sammy. The big bold bombastic kind, the likes of which haven't been seen in over forty years, the over-the-top outrageous ones a kid like you's only heard about from his granpappy. We'll give 'em the ol' razzle dazzle, we will. With stars in their eyes and fire in their hearts, with the right words and the perfect thrash-squeal of steel strings—we'll have 'em—we'll promise to make good, and then we will—oh, how we will. The boys and girls of the future, the hungry kids waiting to be fed, willing to follow where we lead 'cause we make their hearts sing in ways almost forgotten in this dead-end century. We'll give 'em what they need, what they didn't even know they needed before we sparkled and shook our way into their veins. That's how we do it. That's how we build our loyal army." Jeeves' speech was all hands and eyebrows. He seemed everywhere at once, perched on the edge of his chair like a raptor.

"What sort of army?" Sam asked, eyes darting back and forth with growing interest. "We start a rock band. Get a ton of fans, recruit them to the Society. Then what? Massive protests? Organised arson?"

"Do you want the job or not, kid?" Jeeves asked, suddenly dismissive. "If you don't want an opportunity like this, there's plenty of lads who do. It's a chance to make music, to make a difference. A chance to be somebody. Not just another face in the crowd."

"Now hold on a minute, I didn't say I wasn't interested. This gonna help me pay my rent?" he asked.

"It'll help everyone pay their rent," said Jeeves. He paused, drumming long fingers against his chin and considering for a moment. "You wait right here. I'll be back in just a tick. Don't you go anywhere."

Jeeves soon returned with a small group of people in tow. His Arcana—an attractive, intelligent bunch, most younger than he was. They spilled into the room like decorations, adding pops of colour and light to the historic-looking study, lounging against bookshelves and chairs and one another, and looking like just the kind of people that were Sam's kind of people.

Jeeves waved his chiffon-sleeved arm across the room by way of introduction. "These are some of the fine men and women you'd be helping. This here's Ada, she used to own a fabulous Greek restaurant down at King's Cross, but had to close up shop due to constant raises in rent. James and Jack-of-all-Trades here are reconstructionary artists, of course brilliant, but can barely afford a decent meal. And you know Benson. One of the smartest techheads in the world, but with all the red tape involved in getting his inventions to press, his genius is at a standstill."

Their eyes were all on Sam, as if he was already in on the secret. Did they, like Jeeves, think there was something he could do to help them? How could he? There was nothing he could do about any of those things.

"You've got a good voice, Sammy. Why not do something with it?" Benson offered, coming forward to stand beside Jeeves' chair.

By nature, Sam was not an angry young man. Quite the opposite, in fact. Other boys had been cruel to animals, cruel to one another, vacant, unfeeling. Even so, Sam had always felt they were victims of their circumstances. They'd just been dealt the wrong set of cards.

And lately it seemed everyone he knew had been dealt losing hands. The ever-elusive "they" always found a way to take more. Every year taxes went up, food cost more, housing, power, water, gas, electricity, transportation, raw goods and processed goods and whiskey and wine and hairdos and health treatments, waxing-waning-slicing-dicing-pulling-pushing, eliminating hairs, dead skin cells, dust and debris, excess fat, dangerous molecules in the air, dangerous molecules in the water.

Eliminating everything but debt.

Jeeves asking Sam to be the poster boy for his cause seemed like fate finally smiling upon him. He wanted this to work, because what else was he going to do? He didn't think he could endure becoming an avid watcher of programmes like *Strictly Come Dancing*, sitting at home on his couch and gaining five stone while pretending the world around him wasn't unravelling.

Jeeves might be maniacal and eccentric, but at least he gave a shit and seemed clever. He was a professor, after all, and all these people were on board with his movement.

If the Arcana wanted bodies, if the Arcana wanted a war, then Sam wanted it, too.

Jeeves smiled knowingly at Sam, his eyes gleaming bright in the afternoon sun pouring in from the study's lone window. "So, whaddya say, son? Join us, play a song or ten, remake the world?"

Sam watched the boys and girls in the room as they watched him. Blue hair, hemp jewelry, smart eyes, nervous energy, They joked around, conversing with earnest smiles and casual touches like they'd known each other for lifetimes. The type who ask you questions about yourself when you meet them, who don't tell you what it is that *they're* about until you ask.

He already was one of them.

A crooked grin spread across his face. "Okay. Why the hell not? Let's sing so loud we put the Exchange out of business," he said, raising his glass.

Jeeves clasped his hands together, springing from his perch. "Excellent! We start immediately. I've got musicians here, lots of 'em, a few good ones even. You'll be playing onstage at Wembley Stadium before you know it."

Sam stood up, swaying slightly, the wine now having gone to his head. "Freedom," he mused. "What does that even look like?"

"What kind of freedom do you want, Sam?"

"The free kind," Sam said. Flashes of light shone in his eyes. "The free kind of freedom."

"This one won't cost you a cent," Jeeves promised.

Chapter Five

I'M YOUR MAN

Montreal wasn't a natural-born singer; he became one for the soapbox and the ride. Prior to rock superstardom he'd been a poet, a carpenter, a wax-worker, a demon, an MI-5 officer, and a faithful husband. Faithful in deed, that is. Montreal had wandered in his heart many times.

But he was not alone in his transgression. His wife, a ballet dancer, had up and left him one summer for a half-mad philosophy grad student named Janus Jeeves.

Montreal became a rock star on his thirty-seventh birthday. His body had felt already too old, but his eyes sparkled like someone twenty years his junior, and he had no choice but to follow where they led—into the spotlight. Despite the inability to sing beyond a range of five notes in his gravel-laden voice, he knew how to work with what he had. In the rock n' roll game, it was more about attitude than raw talent.

He possessed a fine-tuned vibration that lived under his skin like a live wire, an indeterminable itch that couldn't be scratched. It had provided him with what he'd needed in the business—attitude by the shitload. Back then, he'd gotten arrested so many times the local coppers named a cell after him. Now, new recruits who'd never met the namesake were instructed to "Throw 'im in Monty's block."

After Montreal's ex-wife became Jeeves ex-fiancée, they'd become tentative mates—trading barbs, insults, and bedroom stories. Jeeves saw Montreal as the powerful commodity he was, for both his experience in the music industry and his ties to the military.

Montreal put up with Jeeves because the old dog tickled him pink and told fantastic stories.

Sam met Montreal when the former rabble-rouser was almost dead—thirty years after fame and fortune had lifted him up and plummeted him back down.

Meeting one of the few young men in the city with fire still in his belly gave Montreal life again.

Jeeves sent Sam to Montreal to teach him everything he knew, from moving beyond basic chord progressions to slithering across the stage like an acid glitter monkey love snake. What Montreal lacked in vocal range he made up for in guitar technique, and Sam was a fast pupil, adding Montreal's variations on twelve-bar blues and the easiest way to write a riff to his basic knowledge of open and power chords.

At Montreal's request, Sam had stopped eating and started shaking. He was just trying it out—an experience to draw upon so that he could fake it later. Anything for the cause. Four days without food. He'd lain for hours on the roof of his building, staring up at the billowing clouds while hunger pangs and delirium brought new words to him, along with a frenetic, manic energy unlike anything he'd ever experienced.

He'd written ten new songs in those four days.

The sun was setting on a cold spring evening outside of Montreal's two-story townhome, the few leaves on the neighbourhood trees yellowing and withered, dry and spotted from inconsistent watering. Sam and Montreal sat on the steps out front, taking a breather from rehearsing with the rest of the band who had taken up semi-permanent residence in Montreal's garage.

"So, what have you been doing with yourself for the last thirty years?" Sam asked the older man as they sat out front, sipping cold beer and watching the sky darken.

"Not drinking, not smoking, and writing words no one will see," Montreal said, a sad-sweet look shimmering in his pale blue eyes. "Now I'm drinking and smoking again. Still writing those words though."

"Think Jeeves would have liked to teach me himself, but he don't know a thing about playing music other than how to massacre Beethoven on the piano by ear alone. He's a ruddy genius in his own right, but he's never been a rock star."

"Nah, Janus's been through a lot of things, but he ain't been through the business." Montreal set his beer down on the step between his feet, folding his hands together and facing Sam. "So then, my dear boy, let's see what we've learned today." Montreal leaned forward, hands on his knees and a crooked smile on his lips. "What, pray tell me, is Rule Number One?"

"Rule Number One," Sam stated, noting a bit of irony in the constant memorizing and repeating of rules associated with a freedom movement. "Rule Number One is…everyone who says they're your friend is a liar."

"I'll bet it was nothing but A levels in school for you, my friend."

"True. Not that it's done me much good." Sam stretched his arms out behind him, leaning back. "You see the obvious problem with Rule Number One though, don't you?" he said, grinning. "That would make you a liar. And that would, in fact, make Rule Number One itself a lie."

"Ah, but I never said I was your friend." Montreal smiled so his eyes squinted, character-affirming laugh lines showing on his weathered face. With the darkest hair, the lightest eyes, and a lean physique, he could pass for a much younger man from a distance.

"But I also never said I wasn't a liar," Montreal cautioned.

Montreal's a closed book with half the pages torn out, thought Sam. He was brilliant though, and terribly funny. Sam thought he ought to front Jeeves' movement instead of himself. The job would probably be his if only he were forty years younger. "Fair enough. What's Rule Number Two?" Sam asked, sipping his lager.

"Always wear a coat of arms."

"Do you have one I can borrow?"

"I have one you can have."

Everything in Montreal's wardrobe was black and more than half of it was leather. The wardrobe sat on four wheels, one of them cracked. It leaned against a rust-coloured wall covered in tan stains. Like the rest of Montreal's South London townhome, his bedroom was sparsely furnished and mismatched. An emerald green vase housing a nest of twisted bamboo reeds sat atop a scratched wooden nightstand. His bed was along the far wall, and reminded Sam of some kind of civil war hospital bed—sunken-in mattress, grey-white sheets, and a short, sterile-white bed frame.

"Most of these are too small for me now," Montreal said, sorting through his various black jackets. "Here, think this one'll fit you just about right." He took out a short-cropped black leather coat with a high collar, pointless zippers and buttons decorating it from bottom to top in perfect asymmetry.

"Oi!" A lanky man with a plectrum between his teeth appeared in the doorway, leaning against the frame. Twenty-year-old Muzzy was Sam's new bass player and synth master, the son of a black British banker and a South Asian schoolteacher.

"So, while you guys have been in here shopping, we finished rewiring the setup to feed through the V90. Everything's good to go," Muzzy said.

Muzzy looked the part of the quintessential dreadlocked bass player minus the dreadlocks. Tattoos, laser piercings, ill-fitting clothes, plus a short crop of bleached blonde hair that looked like it'd been cut by his mum. He stood a couple inches taller than Sam, but would seem smaller on stage a meter behind him, partially hidden behind his silver Rickenbacker.

"Let's not keep the lads waiting," Montreal said, as Sam slid on his old jacket.

It was a perfect fit.

They returned to the garage, and Sam picked up a sheet of paper on which Muzzy had scrawled the bare bones of one of their new songs.

"Can we try it in G?" Sam asked.

"You always want to do it in G," Muzzy complained. "What's wrong with D?"

"Yeah, well G's my sweet spot."

"Oh, you want me to hit yer G spot, do ya?" said Muzzy, raising an eyebrow.

"You're such a juvenile," said Sam.

A frantic drum fill with too much high-hat interrupted their ribbing. Montreal looked up from where he sat on a wide amp, studying some scribbles of songs Sam had asked him to look over.

"Hey kid, what's your name?" he asked the drummer.

"Seth." The slight, dark-haired boy grabbed the cymbals to mute them, twirling a drumstick in his other hand and dropping it. He could be sixteen, seventeen, spots still on his face and a beard just barely managing to make itself known;

Sid Vicious if Sid had been an introvert and had parents who were software engineers.

"You can't be just 'Seth,'" said Montreal. "What are we going to call you?"

"No more animal names," Sam said. "Jeeves is callin' me Fox. Saint Fox. I tried to fight it at first, but I kinda like it now."

"How bout 'Bongo'?" suggested Muzzy.

"Piss off," Sam smirked, tossing a cigarette butt at him.

"Zephyr," Montreal said. "We'll call him Zephyr."

"That's bloody awful," Muzzy said.

"This coming from a man named after a fuzzy green cartoon character," said Sam. "Anyway, Jeeves'll love it."

"The more ludicrous, the better, right? Ain't that how it goes?" asked Muzzy.

"It is," said Montreal. "It absolutely is." Montreal squinted at Seth, giving him a thoughtful once over. "You're awfully scrawny to be doing much damage on that thing for hours at a time—but then again, some of the best ones were."

"He's a bloody machine," said Muzzy.

"No more dicking around guys." Sam plucked the low E string, then modulated his whammy bar till everyone got annoyed and paid attention. "Let's play some music. We've got a show in less than three days."

Chapter Six

WORKING CLASS HERO

At home behind other broken dream memorabilia, Kit kept one black-and-white Telecaster and a practice amp. Staring at them now, deep pangs for her one and only true love reverberated, a love she'd abandoned for practicality and a habit of feeling comfortably uncomfortable in her own skin. Running her hand over the smooth, wooden neck, she gripped the Telecaster and brought it against her chest, cradling it like a child.

When Kit was seven, she began learning how to play the electric guitar—a glitter-red and half-sized Strat that her father, a blues musician, had custom-made for her. She was very good by age twelve, and by fourteen she was excellent. By sixteen she had a record deal, and by sixteen-and-a-half she had managers and producers telling her to lose weight, dye her hair, take her clothes off for photo shoots. Write catchier tunes about dark nightclubs, obsessive crushes, partying, and the naughty naughty things she dreamed of doing to men.

She'd tried to compromise in her own way. Wore quirky outfits that showed a little skin but nothing she'd be embarrassed for her mum to see her in, dyed her hair Japanese pop-star violet, wrote a couple tunes with simple, crunchy, three-chord progressions.

The songs weren't catchy enough. Her top could be cropped shorter, breast implants were obviously necessary. She should be photographed out with Darin Flynn, a hot young singer-songwriter just like her, with black eyes and the impossibility of walking through a metal detector without incident—except unlike Kit, Darin barely contributed to his own songs, and strummed two or three power chords while his band did the rest. He was cute though, and management was insistent, and so she had agreed to dinner, during which he was nice enough, and after which he was not.

At eighteen, Kit gave up being a pop star, sold most of her equipment and applied to uni. Fell into computer tech so she could still play with wires and make electric equipment do what she wanted it to do.

It'd been years since she'd sung. Her voice was clear and luminous, but no one heard it anymore save for the pets and plants she occasionally looked after for neighbours. Kit's sweet voice belied her chronically malcontented soul, so she had to get her aggression out through her guitar. The shredded-to-bits fuzz distortion and army of pedal effects she used created an alarming dissonance with her appearance—slight, unassuming, only wildly beautiful at a certain angle to those with an eye for unusual aesthetics— her eyes too large, her legs too thin, sticks and stones pasted together with craft glue at awkward angles. Men came to her in between relationships; they thought she was unique, some sort of mystery, different from their wives and girlfriends who played head games and asked for too much. But when they couldn't crack the code, they left, returning to their familiar, mapped-out lives. An independent woman, a used toy, she kept a smile on her lips during the day and saved her melancholy for the night.

She tuned her guitar quickly, deftly; it was terribly out of tune from years of neglect and would need new strings. Within minutes she had plugged the amp into the wall, plugged the guitar into the amp. She struck chords at random, hitting the strings wildly with her thumb as off-key squeals rang out through the tiny flat, the distortion on the amp turned up too loud to allow any pleasant noise to come out.

She played one of her old songs, found her voice had a new quality, a maturity previously lacking. Just a touch of gravel, a mockingbird with an injured wing.

The tenants in the flat next door banged against the wall. She turned the amp up and played the opening riff to an old song of hers that once upon a time sat at the top of the charts. A long dead dream coalesced in her mind, the colours still faint, the image still fuzzy, not much more than a warm feeling in her throat and her gut. Still, it was there, and it wouldn't be leaving anytime soon.

She had learned from her mistakes—she would do things her way, stay out of sight, out of the stranglehold of the lizards and pigs who'd once ran her like a business. She would sing again, and she would play whatever she wanted.

The cobblestone streets twisted wide and narrow, the smell of day-old bread and grease hanging loosely in the evening air. Kit's worn, three-year-old suede boots made no sound on the stony ground. She never wore dresses and never heels—black pressed trousers and a white gossamer-thread top would do for tonight. It was not a fancy dress occasion anyway.

Kit had done her share of travelling, to big cities and smaller ones, in all sorts of countries and climates to play for all sorts of people, and they were all different and all the same. London was the same as any other city. It was large and vacant, cool and comfortable, judgmental and welcoming—you just had to know where to go and who to avoid.

Her mate Lindsey had rung up and invited her to a party, saying there would be some other musicians there tonight she might like to meet, and that it would be good for her to get out and socialise before she forgot how.

Having no better offer, she agreed.

She arrived early, and was immediately whisked away by a girl named Delia, one of those girls who plays at being your best friend the minute they meet you, usually for no apparent reason. The girl will make your life more interesting for the time being, but she will also steal part of it. Absorbing your identity into her own, she would grow more colourful as you grew more bland. Kit had met plenty of girls like her before and kept her guard up, and yet, Delia had good taste in music and laughed in what sounded like earnest at her jokes, so she couldn't help but like her.

"See anyone you fancy here?" Delia asked her in a conspiring tone, the dyed ends of her red-blonde hair brushing against Kit's shoulder.

"Not really. So far no one here seems my type."

"And what is your type, love?"

Kit scooted closer to her on the velour-covered bench, finishing off the last of her third lager. "Don't know, really.

Someone clever. Pretty. But not stuck-up, vain, or rude. So hard to find one without the other. The one everyone in the room falls in love with while he's completely oblivious to it. I guess what everyone wants, really."

"You'll have quite some competition, then," said Delia. "Let's hope we get lucky tonight."

Kit rolled her eyes but allowed the briefest smile to cross her lips. Delia linked arms with her and dragged her along to grab another drink. The hosts' three-story home was decorated like the future began in the sixties, which of course, it did. Homemade radios and toaster ovens, Indian rugs and posters from the F-Punk revival at the start of the decade. Different boarders every month, and the place paid off by generations of kindness and good luck.

"You're shy, aren't you?" Delia asked Kit as she popped open a bottle and handed it to her. "You fake being sociable when you want to though—you're good at it. But the shy ones always have something to hide," she said with a grin. "Do you?"

"Yes," said Kit, though she felt it was a lie. By sin of omission perhaps others assumed she had some dark secret hidden away. Everyone else seemed to wear if not their hearts, their carefully crafted personalities on their sleeves—

like Delia, for instance. Perhaps there's something I can learn from her, Kit thought.

Delia flipped her hair behind her shoulder, laughing loudly, insincerely, at a comment made by a lanky bloke standing beside them.

Perhaps not.

Chapter Seven

HOW TO WIN MATES AND INFLUENCE THE BORED

"You're coming with me to a gay party," Sailor said.

"No, I'm not. Have to finish this book." He held up the cover for Sailor to see. *The Rise and Fall of Nitro Winchester and the Self-Stable Apocalypse* by Janus Jeeves.

"'Here, I'll tell ya what happens." Sailor swiped the book from him while Sam waved his arm around uselessly in the air. "He gets reincarnated into a toad at the end. You see, what most people don't know is that toads live a pretty good life. They don't have to buy groceries or petrol or get a job or get married or divorced. They just eat insects and slime on things. Fuck me, I'd like to be a toad."

"Those are two separate requests, and thoroughly incompatible with one another," Sam said from his prone position on the couch.

"You don't have to come as my date," Sailor said, his voice fading as he headed towards the loo.

"Oh, I wouldn't dare. Anyway, I've already got plans. My band's playing at this party tonight, at this couple named Lindseys' place. We've been gettin' pretty good I think—might even be up to your saccharinely deplorable music tastes…Are you listening to me?" he hollered over the running tap.

Sailor's head popped round the corner, pink suds in his crayon yellow hair and a green mud mask circling his wide brown eyes. "That's it, that's the hooley!" he said. "At the Lindseys'. We leave as soon as I'm done getting ready, which could be anywhere from one to five hours, so you'll have time to finish yer book. Just make sure you're scrubbed and plucked and polished and shiny, yeah?"

"Yeah, I'll be nice and shiny," Sam said. He paused for a minute. "Hey, why'd you invite me along to a party you already knew I was going to?"

"I just like hearing you turn me down. You know what they say, comfort in repetition." Sailor winked and disappeared back into the loo behind a flurry of river-blue satin.

After spending half an hour getting dressed, Sam stood in front of the narrow full-length mirror in Sailor's room. Aviator sunglasses. Check. Tattered black jeans. Check. A blue, yellow, and violet top in metallic criss-crossed patterns that Liberace would be embarrassed to go out in, check. Dark hair purposely disheveled, skin glowing, stretched taut across his architectural cheekbones, shoulders, elbows and hips. Scented like a girl and just a hint of pale grey eyeshadow that made his water-brown eyes appear even more sunken in.

Sam attracted women, men, and those both or neither, but had few serious relationships to reflect upon. The girl would move. The girl would break his heart. He would fall in love again within a week, or at least be under the impression that he was until the shine wore off the new penny. He never wanted to let her know though, didn't want the guilt; he'd just go silent until she went round and round in her head with suspicions and ruined it.

He'd probably never been in love. Love might merely be something invented by advertising execs to sell more rubbish at Asda.

"Are ya ready to 'ave the time of your life?" Sailor asked from the doorway in bowtie and leather chaps.

Sam stifled a laugh. "You bet. The night is young."

Sam and Sailor arrived at precisely 10:30 p.m., late enough so that they were fashionably late and everyone was already drunk, but not so drunk as to be incoherent.

Sailor always started the evening off with a whiskey and ginger in one hand and the other clasped around Sam's shoulder. He and Sam chatted with the hosts of the party, a man and a woman who were both named Lindsey. The Lindseys were the sole local distributors of rare upper class goods—handmade commodities from places like Paris and Milan had become a scarcity and would usually cost a small fortune.

The Lindseys gave them away practically free. Exchanged them for odd jobs like car rides and laundry.

"Charmed," the female Lindsey said as Sam introduced himself. She had thick pale lips, oak-coloured hair, and wore vivid violet eyeliner too bold for her unassuming features. "So, you're the singer. What sort of singer are you?"

"A motivational singer," Sam said.

"Indeed. And what do you sing about that motivates people?"

"I want to get people to take what turns them inwards, and get them to turn it outwards."

"That sounds very inspiring. If only we had more pretty boys like you trying to get people off their arses." She reached up to run a mannish hand covered in rings through his already-mussed hair. "Follow me."

"I'll catch up with you later," Sam said to Sailor, who was currently engaged in a heated debate with the male Lindsey on a topic both of them clearly knew nothing about, supercars or some such nonsense.

The Lindsey woman led Sam into the den to show him where he would perform, in a wide, elevated alcove cut in black marble—gorgeous acoustics, no doubt, made for displaying prominent works of art and doubling as the perfect stage. A mic stand remained from the start of the evening—a soprano from Barcelona had attempted to move the guests to tears with her aria while they were arriving and the first drinks were being poured.

"How's this for your debut?"

"It's perfect," Sam said. "It's just what I need for people to hear me."

"Sweetheart, I'd like for you to meet Delia and Kit." Lindsey led him over to a pair of girls, one bouncy and feminine, the other tomboyish and angular. "Both these girls are so talented. Musicians—like you."

"Oh, I'm more of an actor than a musician. Just backing vocals for friends' bands sometimes, and I can strum a few chords, but that's about it," Delia said, her eyes shining at Sam.

"And our Kit here's a wizard on the guitar," Lindsey added, squeezing Kit's shoulder fondly.

"I'm not sure about that," said Kit.

She was pretty, in an odd sort of way, Sam noticed. Not pretty in a way you'd notice right off, like Delia. He had dirty thoughts about both of them immediately, which he pushed to the back of his mind for the sake of making conversation.

"I've just been playing since I was young," Kit continued. "I learned enough technique so that I could break the rules is all."

"Got any projects going at the moment…anything I've heard?" asked Sam.

"Maybe. I haven't put out anything in a while. Been working in I.T. for the past few years, but...I just quit my job."

Sam raised an eyebrow. "Working for the man finally get to you?"

"Something like that. It was time for a change," she said, internally chastising herself for the trite statement. "I'd like to get back into music."

"Sounds like you could teach me a thing or two. You into effects?"

"Yeah, my pedal board weighs more than I do."

Sam laughed, flashing a genuine smile.

"I'm excited to see you perform," Delia interjected. "You've gotta be brave to put yourself out there like that."

"It still scares me, to be honest. I've only just started, but I'll get used to it."

"What's the band called?"

"We don't have a name yet."

"Maybe I'll think of one while you're playing." Delia widened her lips into a smile, running her vermillion-painted nails along the rim of her glass. Kit was staring off at the stage, sizing up their gear, perhaps.

"Sold to the highest bidder, darlin'. Well, I'll see you girls after the show then. Cheers."

A group of fine, fabulous young men and women had gathered in front of the marble stage, relaxed and euphoric with the late hour of the night and drink coursing through their bodies. They discussed everything salacious and incendiary except for politics while Sam and the band set up.

"Excuse me," Sam said into the microphone, and was greeted with feedback from the sound system. "If I could have your attention, please."

His voice, soft yet commanding, did not belie the tension he felt. One would have to pay close attention to notice his eyes moving rapidly back and forth across the crowd of people, his nervous fiddling with the guitar strap.

Behind him, Muzzy and Zephyr stopped adjusting their instruments, turning towards him with quiet interest. Some in the audience did the same. "Just a few moments of your time, ladies and gents, then I'll let you get back to your conversations. I'd like to start a conversation with all of you tonight, just a little food for thought."

Sam bent his head, placed his hands on the strings, and began to play. The first song was a folk song with hints of blues and electronica, and went like this:

Rally your troops and test your weapons
For you, my friends, are the enemy
Laughing the night away, wanting for nothing
While millions struggle to make ends meet
Come closer now, my darlings and hear me
I am the face of what you ignore
No more protests, and the songs will be few
I'll be your action man, you can be sure
So rally your weapons and test your troops
First, remove the ones who need handling
We come like death, like a thief in the night
And we won't leave a' one of you standing

When the song ended, Sam gazed out into the audience, making eye contact with the ones who were paying attention. More than half, he noted.

When the set was through, he stepped off the platform with a confident smile on his lips, and found himself face to face with the fashionably later-than-late ringleader.

Or had he been there all along?

"That…was most excellent," said Jeeves, placing his hands on Sam's shoulders.

"It was, wasn't it? Quite the adrenaline rush—just a little gig like this," Sam said, jittering up and down with post-performance energy.

"This is just the beginning, Sammy. Just you wait. You think they're eating out of the palm of your hand now—come now, come! Let's go thank the Mizz Mister double-Ls, shall we?" Jeeves directed, leading him over to the Lindseys. "Aha! There they are. So, what do you think of my boy?" he asked, all eyes and gestures.

"He has a beautiful voice," the female Lindsey gushed, turning to Sam. "Why darling, I'm practically in love with you after hearing you sing. But isn't that always the way it is?" She stroked her hand along Sam's arm, toying with the material of his garish shirt as the male Lindsey clasped him round the shoulder.

"You know, a university mate of mine is a music producer," the male Lindsey said. He was tall and slender with grey messy hair, and wore a suit that was somehow both ill-fitting and expensive-looking. "I see fame and fortune in your future, young man. Let's go outside for some air and discuss it further. You must see our garden."

"And you must remember us when you're well on your way," the Lindsey woman said. "So many do forget."

As the male Lindsey led Sam outside, he turned his head to glance back at Jeeves.

But it seemed he had already disappeared.

There was something in the way Sam performed that held hints of the former greats—the jut of his hips recalled Mick Jagger, the hair in his eyes Kurt Cobain, the commanding twinkle in his eye and slitherine movements tricks that any junkie jiver would be proud of. Kit knew the protocol, knew that if you put anyone semi-good-looking on stage who was semi-decent at playing, they were immediately the object of sexual desire to everyone in the room. Whether at a party in someone's flat or in a stadium full of thousands, it was merely a matter of numbers. There was something deliciously mind-numbing about it; you were a slave to your own desires, ridiculous fantasies accumulating in your head despite tugging notions of boring reality. This was what rock n' roll sold—a tried and true formula. A formula which, for years, had been abandoned in favour of regurgitated beats with one watered-down lyric laid on top of it repeated over and over ad nauseam. Nothing you could really get excited about, nothing you could get behind. Nothing that would wake people up.

This was different.

This was the rock n' roll she knew and loved, stripped down to its core. She recognised it clear as day.

She wondered if the band even knew what they had, knew that they'd touched upon that intangible magic. Not only were their songs lyrically solid, but the music was at once reminiscent and new, songs that—with a little work— would become instant hits. Smart enough to appeal to smart people. Catchy enough to hook everyone.

Could use more guitar, she thought wryly. Her mind had already begun dancing hooks and phrases on top of the crunchy chords and simple riffs. Sam's guitar sound was good—clear, crisp, and loud—but she could teach him a thing or two about effects that would instantly liven up his sound to make it even sweeter.

She let her gaze wander back to Sam. The frontman's disheveled hair and lithe frame said *protect me, care for me—*

the last laugh of all rock stars—tiny, effeminate outcasts, mercilessly picked upon in school, stealing girls from the bigger boys by playing on both their maternal instincts and promising they were man enough to treat you badly. An irresistible dichotomy.

When the set was over, Kit watched the gently brazen rock-star-in-the-making take care of the room, moving from one misty-eyed new convert to the next, all smiles and easygoing charm.

I'm a silly girl after all, Kit thought as she watched him. No different from the rest.

Chapter Eight

YOUR PULSE IT RACES WITH MINE

The Lindseys' garden was a paradigm of nostalgia, of a time when common people took leisure, strolled through parks, cultivated their own veggies for recreation. Conifer trees stood proud and askew, their branches reaching in between neighbouring plants of blue, purple, and gold, touching soft white ferns and skimming above surreal patches of ground cover—black leaves with multi-coloured sterile berries. Greek marble statues and bronze angels hid behind tree trunks and gushed fresh running water over unripened blossoms. The Lindseys sauntered hand in hand wearing silver gauze and blue chiffon, regaling their guests with the proper names of rare species and the blooming cycles of the vast array of green growing things, many of them in full bloom of their fruits and colours as they embraced the cusp of the season.

The evening was dying down as Kit watched Delia and Sam through the entrance to the garden—an onyx black gate wrought in sundial patterns. The night air had a rough chill to it, dancing around and defying the edges of the approaching summer, and Sam gave Delia his coat.

She accepted his outdated chivalry with a tilt of her chin and a wide smile on her warm, red lips, sliding Sam's hand into the pocket of his own coat that she now wore. They sat down together under green-black trees on a wooden bench, momentarily commanding each other's full attention. Sam activated the holo keypad on his cleverband and began typing—a number, an address, a plan. A plan for seeing each other again soon, certainly.

Kit hesitated at the gate, wondering if she should join them outside. Delia's laughter drifted through the air, false laughter meant to flatter. The sound had Kit turning away. She shrugged on her coat and gathered her things in a slow-motion gesture of leaving, then headed out alone into the dark night.

They probably stayed on that bench for hours, talking about nothing at all.

About an hour after Kit arrived back at her flat, her cleverband chirped a two-second sing-song as she prepared for bed. She popped open the holo display. A message from Delia.

Kit snuggled deep into her double bed and pulled her white down comforter around her tightly. She can have him, she thought to herself. They're better suited for each other anyhow, I'm certain of it. I'm happy as I am, and it's wonderful to have made a new friend. Simply wonderful, she thought, as she faded from waking to dreaming, and in her dream-state dreamed of wrong and forbidden things, things she had forgotten, things she felt she didn't deserve. Things bright, luminescent, and loud, people she could kiss and touch and hold if only she would reach out. She did, and it was warm and brilliant.

Then she woke, and just like that, it faded away.

~

Sam and Sailor came home drunk at quarter past three.

"You sang beautifully mate, beautifully. Just gorgeous, you were," Sailor crooned. "I'll buy whatever you're selling, man. I'll fight for whatever cause you're fighting for."

"It might require you to get out of bed before noon," Sam said.

"I'm out, I'm out!" Sailor exclaimed. "You'll have to go on without me. I'll put scarlet-coloured roses on your grave." He collapsed like a ragdoll onto their worn blue couch.

Sam sat atop his knees. "How'm I supposed to save the world without my best man?" he asked.

"Aww, you know I'm not your best man. I'm your worst man. But I'm your only man."

"That isn't true, my dizzy love. Got lots of men. Gonna get more."

"C'mere," Sailor said, reaching for Sam's waist.

"Don't start that again. You're drunk."

"But very good-looking."

"Only in the right light. In our low-watt house lights you're beautiful, in others you're grotesque."

"That's what you like about me, you sick bastard." He slid his hand underneath the back of Sam's hideous multi-coloured top.

"One of these days I'll grow weary of resisting your very unique charm," Sam said, leaning down to kiss him briskly on the lips. "But I've still got a bit of fight in me yet. G'night, Sailor." He got up, smacking Sailor on the thigh as he left the room. Sailor muttered vague insults at the loss but was dead asleep moments later.

Sam's room was down the hall, to the left, and had nothing in it—a twin bed with navy sheets, a used wooden desk he'd brought in from the curb, a Joy Division poster—his, and a Jimi Hendrix print from the previous tenant. He lay down on the bed the wrong way around, dropping his head onto his crossed arms.

Sam wasn't a fool. He knew the world as it stood was based upon an all-encompassing, nearly impenetrable infrastructure, a faceless giant nearly impossible to destroy in an over-information age where every word was questionable and almost nothing could be traced back to its original source. People were made to function in society like clockwork components, and those whose gears did not fit were marginalised. Those who tried to go against the structure in any significant way were eliminated one way or another.

He knew that Janus Jeeves and the Arcane Society were idealists, dreamers, men with hope and goodness and soul food in their hearts. Men with big ideas who rarely had the means to follow through with them.

War was the opposite of what Sam wanted. The last time he was at Jeeves' he'd listened to him and Benson talking about starting a war by stopping one, disarming them before they even had a chance to fire, leaving them castrated, limp. Take them by surprise and take 'em down when they were unarmed and frantic, lost in chaos and pissing their trousers as their virtual bank accounts drained, hit zero as imaginary numbers left them with nothing in their hands.

Whatever *that* meant.

Freedom. That's what he wanted. He thought back to his first time at the Arcana's headquarters, how Jeeves had promised him that their brand of freedom "wouldn't cost a cent."

Tomorrow Sam would go again to Janus Jeeves' flat, bring him more bodies, write more songs. Tomorrow Sam would help Sailor nurse his hangover, tomorrow Sam would take Binky to the vet. Tomorrow Sam would help build a better tomorrow, but tonight he was alone in his bed, half-asleep and drunk on cheap vodka, lucid dreaming of choral melodies winding around crunchy distortion, while a girl with full pink lips left electric whispers along his collarbone, under his navel. Tonight he would dream, and enjoy it, because tomorrow had not yet come. Tomorrow would do something about tomorrow, and Sam would be there, too.

He would sing and he would fight, but oh—wasn't it
better to just lie still in this blissful, quiet night—and dream?

Chapter Nine

TAXLOSS

The people were just waiting to be chopped up, chewed, and spat out. Toughened and sedated by years of stale 12A-rated films and not touching one another for the past century. All craved emotions could be bought, yours with just the swipe of a finger.

The Dot made it easier than ever—a small magnetic disc about 3mm across, that everyone, save for the technically obsolete, had embedded in the top pad of their right index finger. The technology began with the integration of magstripes once used in credit cards into a stylus for use with electromagnetic digitiser touchscreens, more accurate and sensitive than their capacitive touchscreen counterparts. Users, however, still preferred the convenience of using their hands. The next step in accessibility was obvious—install the stylus in the body.

The Dot could easily be installed at various kiosks found throughout shopping centres, grocery stores, ATMs, and underground terminals. The miniscule device felt like nothing at all a few days after installation, and took less time to acquire than a cup of tea. The process was simple; it was much like having one's ears pierced.

Once it was made available on the market, its time and space-saving properties and its growing popularity amongst the young and savvy turned it into a necessity. The next step up from making purchases via cleverband—it was more secure, storing banking information inside oneself rather than in an external device. The Dot made people feel their wallets were protected, a personalised system beyond the reach of the cleverest cloud hackers and identity thieves.

The Dot allowed one to make secure purchases from any touch-sensitive device or point-of-sale terminal by simply swiping their finger across a designated spot on the display, typically a peach or mint green-coloured box. Only a handful of shops in the countryside still accepted payment the old-fashioned way—credit card terminals had gone the way of the compact disc, and almost no one carried cash.

With the Dot a ubiquitous part of the human body and personal assistant devices as wearable as pants, technology had come a long way in providing the ultimate convenience.

Janus Jeeves saw it as the ultimate opportunity.

～

The sun set outside Jeeves' collapsed flat as two new members were brought into the fold.

"Come in, come in!" He motioned grandly for Kit and Delia to sit down next to him and Sam on the swirl-printed, shagpile carpet.

Jeeves liked Kit the minute he met her, due in no small part to him recognizing her as that one teen pop sensation from a few years ago who had actual talent.

And she would like him back.

Straightaway he buttered her up with compliments, showing off his knowledge of what real rock-pop was, regaling her with tales of his experiences either personal or metaphysical with The Sweet, Mansun, Sugarpop Hideaway—bands that anyone worth their salt knew about.

"You ought to teach Sam a few things about being a rock star. Make sure he stays outta the traps, like you did, you smart thing," he told her.

"I'm not anyone's nanny," she said gently, a wry smile folding her lips.

"Of course you're not." Jeeves dismissed the notion with a wave of his hand. "You don't worry about none of that. You just look after you."

Jeeves glanced over at Delia seated on the carpet next to Sam, leaning against him and laughing probably more than he deserved. Good, Jeeves thought. He's already attracting groupies.

But Sam's head all dizzy from dames was not what he wanted. This one's got to go, he determined, switching his attention back to Kit, who was talking about the Bowie album *Diamond Dogs*, how the band could take a page from its revolutionary war cries.

This one's got to stay. She might be a key player.

"Make sure you come to the show Friday night," he said. "Now come on and have a look at our first vidcast, see how foxy our new saint is."

Jeeves motioned for them to gather round. He perched on the arm of his white faux-fur couch while Kit and Delia sat on either side of Sam. Benson walked in carrying his tablet.

"Check it out," he said. He set the device on top of the coffee table, touching Play.

The camera's eye zoomed in on Sam, from a blurry swirling mass of colours it focused into the sharp planes of his face, lips glistening, smears of charcoal across his eyelids. He wore a powder blue suit, his hair standing on end in angry spikes. Sam's honey-textured tenor drilled deep, hit primal chords, awakened electric signals long dormant within the listener's psyche. The video focused on his delicate hands against a white background, plucking the strings of his black Stratocaster. The other band members appeared in soft flashes as if they were figments of his imagination, floating waiflike things, men from a different time and place.

It wasn't long after christening Sam as 'Saint Fox' that Jeeves dubbed the band Saint Fox and The Independence, having conjured up the name in an endorphin-induced haze brought on by rapid movement throughout his flat and advanced homeopathy. Jeeves had pieced together the band by hand-selecting from amongst his followers the prettiest and most musically gifted, then sent them off to his old friend Montreal to learn the tricks of the trade. Now, he sent the lads out into the stratosphere to conquer the hearts and minds of the young men and women of England.

"You're gonna go viral, baby," Jeeves said. "Your velvet acid voice, your yearning eyes, your somethin'-somethin'. It's all coming together."

Sam looked downwards and away, eyes unfocused as a small smile played across his lips. "Thanks," he said softly.

"You sound so good there," Delia said. "You look really good, too—god, the whole band looks just smashing. Benson did a great job directing."

"Sam did all the work. All's I had to do was point the camera," Benson said.

"So, whaddya think, love?" Jeeves asked Kit, sidling up real close. Wisps of her dark hair fluttered against her cheek in response to his perfumed breath. He smelled of cloves and plumeria, was dressed in zebra-striped rags and gold-plated jewelry. Kit drew back from him almost imperceptibly, his presence all-encompassing. That she found his energy magnetic no one would guess from the wide berth of space she kept around her. Not quite standoffish, but as though a part of her was always somewhere else.

"I think it's brilliant. The video's stunning and the band sounds fabulous, very tight. Catchy chorus," she said. "Can't believe you've practically just started, you're oozing confidence like an old pro," she told Sam, her eyes drifting to the mesmerizing image of him on the screen.

Sam smiled crookedly. "It's just the leather jacket. Or 'cause I watched the Stones' 'Rock n' Roll Circus' the night before."

"Just be careful not to let it go to your head," she said. "Things can go from naught to a thousand in the blink of an eye."

"That's right, you were once a little Miss rock n' roll star yerself, weren't ya?" Sam grinned.

"More or less. Times have changed though. Record companies are dead. Maybe that puts you a little more in control."

"Just making good music," said Sam. "And making lots of friends. Then we'll see."

"Oh, we'll be in control," Jeeves interjected. "Let's watch it again, let's see our new messiah do his thing." He touched Play, smiling with all his teeth. Sam rested back on his forearms, languid and content.

"So," Kit began when the video had finished a second time. "How…how exactly is turning Sam into a rock star supposed to bring down the credit system?" she questioned, eyeing Jeeves with a look that was both eager and suspicious.

Jeeves had to admire her curiosity, and managed to keep all but a tad of irritation from his voice. "Don't be so short-sighted, baby," he said, rising to stand. His gangly body began spinning circles around the group, long arms rising and falling as he spoke. "We need the fans, darling; it's all about the fans. You, her, him," he pointed to Kit, Delia, and

Benson in turn. "You'll spread the word, won't ya? Every one brings ten. Every ten brings a hundred. Ten thousand. All sixty-five million. They'll follow him anywhere, yeah? Look at this face." He gripped Sam's jaw in his wide hand, pinching until he puckered, then slapped a short, exaggerated smacking kiss against his lips. "Follow him anywhere."

Delia nodded with false wisdom in her eyes, she would. Would little Miss wild-haired former teen rock star follow him down the rabbit hole? The girl seemed uncomfortable in her own skin. What was she afraid of?

The fun had only just begun.

On Benson's announcement that he'd gotten the app Jeeves had asked him to build up and running, the maestro disappeared with him into the next room in a flurry of printed fabric, the slender developer barely visible between the waves of Jeeves' silky sleeves.

This left Sam on his own for the moment, seated between the two girls. Benson's tech-jargon and Jeeves' questions, which he answered himself in two different voices, drifted into the main room without enough volume for them to hear what they were saying.

"Do you know what he's on about?" asked Delia.

"Sometimes," said Sam, scratching the back of his neck. "Other times yeah, I wonder, but still, I trust him more than the other guy, you know? He's a pacifist, like me, and now I get to do what I've always wanted to do but could never make happen."

"Become a famous rock star?" Delia asked, her eyes staring brightly into his.

"Become a musician," Sam corrected. "I've messed around with it before, but the guys I'm working with now are really clever, really talented. And motivated."

"Well, Jeeves must be doing something right, all the 'cool kids' I know have heard of you already." Delia uncrossed her legs and stretched her arms back, smiling hazily at Sam.

Kit's hands were folded in her lap. "How much did you look into Jeeves and the Society before accepting his offer?" she asked.

Sam didn't get a chance to answer. "Saint Fo-ox," Jeeves sing-songed as if on cue. "C'mere and see what our Bezzy has done."

Benson motioned for Sam to sit down beside him on the blue-painted picnic table while Jeeves hovered over them like an eagle, wings spread. "Check out this app, Sammy," said Benson. "Here, I'll put it on your cleverband for ya."

"What's it do?"

"It's a way to interact with fans; we're calling it FoxDen. See over here? That's where you intertalk. And this is LyrikCafe. This here's where all the user profiles are—I've already started one for you. Check it out...yer photo's that one I took of you against the bricks behind Urbani when the sun was out the other day. Whaddya think?"

"Yeah, brilliant," Sam waved his fingers through the air, navigating the app's interface. It was impressive, he had to admit. Great communication features, 3D avatars displaying in hyper-realistic form within the holospace. "It says I've already got 73 messages," he said, after poking around for a while. "How's that possible?"

"Don't worry," Benson said. "I've set up an auto-responder based on a series of algorithms that replies with a 'customised' message. You'll be able to interact on a massive scale."

"I don't know, doesn't that seem a bit dishonest?"

"Sammy, if you wanna save the world, you've gotta cut a few corners. Now give it here," he motioned for user control.

"What for?" Sam asked. He switched the controls of his cleverband's holo display back over to Benson with a few fluid motions.

"Finishing your profile. What's your favourite band?"

"The Clash. I have to say that, don't I?" he said with a grin.

"What's it really?" Benson asked, glancing away from the display and peering at Sam over his thin specs.

"I rather like John Mellencamp."

"Out!" Jeeves exclaimed, spinning away from the table. "I've made a terrible mistake."

"I'm just pulling his leg," Sam defended. "Actually, I do like a bit of Mellencamp, nothin' wrong with that, thanks very much; he fought authority after all. But favourite? Tom Waits, of course. Can't beat it."

"Americans," Benson muttered. "Such a shame when practically all the decent bands that ever were are right here at home. I'm putting The Smiths."

"I actually ain't that into The Smiths. I mean, I like 'em and all, but sometimes Mozza's a bit much. You're the one that's mad about The Smiths."

"Shut up or I'm putting Oasis," said Benson.

"Don't you dare."

"Okay, you're all set." Benson returned the cleverband controls to Sam.

James and Jack-of-all-Trades entered the flat then, a horde of eager-looking misfits straggling behind them. They found places to sit—beanbags, mismatched velvet furniture, spread across the floor in front of the two girls.

They were young. Pale-faced. Enthusiastic. Kind eyes. The type who could hold their own in an intellectual debate. The type that sewed their own clothing, made their own jewelry. The type that gave things away just because they decided after a split second that they liked you.

"All right, street team!" Jeeves rallied. "The wheels are turning. The game is afoot."

Heads turned to face the ringmaster, members of the Arcana—his colleagues, friends and followers that Jeeves had met along the way. And today there were new faces—some new fans of the band, others scenesters just along for the ride.

Around thirty bodies present and accounted for.

They would need many more.

"I've gotta go meet up with the guys at practice," Sam announced, grinning apologetically at everyone. "Listen to this man," he said, clapping Jeeves on the shoulder. "He knows what's up. See you dolls later." He slid into his rock star persona on the way out, moving like a cat, with smiles and kisses for the whole gang as he made his way to the lift.

He's perfect, Jeeves thought to himself. Absolutely perfect.

Jeeves clasped his hands together. "Let's go out and spread the word, shall we?" he said, mismatched eyes full of firelight. "A star is born from ash and fire, times are tough and the situation is dire.

It's all up to you and me. Learn to love thy neighbour, for he shall be your only means."

Chapter Ten

ELECTRIC BLISS

The Electric Ballroom smelled of piss, sweat, and white euphoria. A streak-thin hiss hovered in the air, akin to a wave of panic that when turned on its side became utter bliss. Bodies and blackness so thick you could barely see a foot in front of you. A line outside the door that extended down and around King's Cross square. The Arcana had been busy all week promoting the show, making sure anyone who was possibly interested became definitely interested in a show they absolutely couldn't miss.

The floor was loud and packed, each person pressed up against strangers, bare arms touching one another, shifting their feet to get a better view. They spoke to each other by shouting over the music that blasted between sets or kept themselves busy with their cleverbands, but stilled, silenced, and gazed up as bright blue lights flicked on to full blast up on the stage.

From fog and steel a figure emerged, wrapped head to toe in a silver cape. On cue of the low rumble from Muzzy's strings, the cape pooled at Saint Fox's feet, revealing the frontman wearing Montreal's tight black leather jacket and even tighter black trousers, posed with his arms to the sky. He strode over to where his guitar sat waiting—red, with a black and white union jack painted across it in smooth lacquer. He slung it across his shoulder, and hit the first chord as the crowd cheered. The stage lights faded from blue to red, bathing him in an eerie pink glow.

"You all feeling good tonight? You look beautiful," Sam's voice echoed throughout the crowded venue. "This one's called 'Money Dance'."

With that, the band erupted. The first song surged, the second pulled, the third made them almost mad. Electric distortion squealed through the crackling air, a sound that should have been a bloody offence to their ears but it was sweet, sweet and sad, striking something utterly lost and ready to be moulded inside each individual in the crowd that night, sending reverberation back and forth between spectacle and spectator, a string of nervous tension vibrating on a wire, an entire audience of hundreds holding one breath as they stood captivated, each one silently pledging their hearts that night to Saint Fox.

Watching from the side of the stage along with Sam's flatmate, Sailor, Kit was almost caught up in it, or was completely if she were honest with herself. Sam's songs were flawless, full of rally chants as he channeled disillusionment into action, coupled with some of the catchiest guitar riffs she'd ever heard. They were technically simple, yet sounded complex and were easily memorable. Sam's guitar rose to a frenetic crescendo as he beat against the strings with all the theatrical flair he could muster, seeming everywhere on stage at once, sliding to his knees, dark hair laced with silver glitter in the pulsing strobe lights that billowed upwards to form a sort of alienesque halo.

The fist-pumping anthems were interlaced with slower, darker tunes, an ominous promise for revenge wrapped in electricity and light. Zephyr's war drums and Muzzy's low vibrations ran from the audience's feet, up their jelly-filled legs, and straight into their hearts, beating an eternal presence there.

"He's fantastic, isn't he?" Sailor shouted to her over the music.

"Yeah, he is. Makes me miss it," she said.

On stage, Saint Fox and The Independence took their fake-out bows to wild cheers before disappearing, then reappearing for the encore. It ended with Saint Fox and Muzzy crashing into Zephyr's drum kit, knocking everything over while the guitars hissed feedback and cymbals crashed to the floor. Squares of black and silver glitter rained down from the ceiling over the band and audience, coating everyone's hair in streaks of shimmer.

"G'night, everyone! We'll see you soon! Thanks for coming out to see us; it means the world. You know, we are The Independence—all of us. Brothers in arms. We love you…we'll see you next time!"

Kit and Sailor caught up with the band backstage. "That was bloody fabulous," Sailor said, effortlessly falling into step beside Sam. He threw a purple towel over Sam's hair and ruffled it, a mix of sweat, glitter, and pomade soaking the fabric. "That was like watching Iggy Pop perform. Or Elvis. Shyte man, you even brought me to tears at one point. You made my mascara run." He slung an arm across Sam's shoulders as the frontman grinned, vibrating with post-show adrenaline.

"You were his first groupie long before he was even in a band, weren't you," Muzzy slapped Sailor on the back, sending him stumbling forward a few steps.

"Oi! Watch the hair, mate," Sailor said.

"Hey, has anyone seen Jeeves?" Sam asked. "Didn't think he'd miss our first gig playing to over a thousand. Sweet and intimate, but just big enough to be a mob. So, where is the mad genius?"

"He was here for the first half of the set," Kit said, right in step with the band. "Said he had something to attend to."

"What would that be, I wonder?"

"Dunno. He sort of...babbled some tech-sprinkled word salad and moonwalked out of the club."

"Figures. Where's your blonde friend?"

"Amsterdam," she answered, toying with the bracelets on her wrist. Delia seemed to be always flying off somewhere with someone new, this week to Amsterdam with two girls she'd met last Thursday at a club, next month to Singapore with an ex-boyfriend she was 'absolutely just friends with now.' Kit pegged her as one of those people with plenty of money to travel despite the fact she seemed perpetually unemployed. Even back when Kit had been making industry money, her paychecks weren't big enough to afford many luxuries after everyone and their brother had taken a cut of her profits.

Kit could practically visualise the loose threads of her friendship with Delia already unraveling, a broken cord that had never been plugged in all the way. Still, it had gotten her here.

To Sam, to Jeeves. To the music.

"Well, we've got everyone we need right here," Sam said, slinging his arm around her. "We've done ourselves proud. This calls for a drink or eight."

"Here, here," Muzzy chimed in. "Let us partake in the spoils of electric war."

Once they were settled backstage, Sam raised his bottle high in the air. "To rock n' roll," he said. "To fame, and an impending lack of fortune."

The group clanked their drinks together with unanimous cheers. Muzzy bluestreamed a demo of a couple new songs into the speakers, the sweet strains weaving dark earth, light, and magic throughout the greenroom.

"What's this one called?" Kit asked.

"'Love Junkie'. What do you think?"

"I like it," Kit said. "Lots of layered guitars."

"Yeah, well, in the studio you can layer on as many as you like. I'm not sure how we're gonna work this one out live though, but you know we've been talking about finding another guitar player," Sam said, staring pointedly at her as a lazy smile spread across his face.

"Got anyone in mind?" she ventured.

"'Ey, well there's a certain curly-haired guitarist I've got my eye on, and I'm not talking about that guy from Guns N' Roses who just kicked it." He slid an arm around her shoulders, squeezing her close. "Do you know someone who fits the description? Think she'd be up for it? I've been listening to her stuff and from what I've heard, she's a way better player than me, though to be fair that'd be just about anyone..."

Kit slapped his arm. "I'm sure she finds it a very interesting proposition," she said, "though she might be wondering if your all-boys club can handle her."

"We can definitely handle her! We'll handle 'er all at once," Muzzy called from his corner of the couch, where he was gesticulating wildly in some inane conversation with Sailor.

"Woooo," Sailor said. "You'll have to beat them off with a stick, love. Or just beat them off." Sailor had become somewhat indiscernible from the grey leather couch he was seated on, covered head to toe in a skintight jumpsuit resembling an emergency blanket. He receded into a tight ball, inhaling from the electronic joint he rarely parted with; tonight it'd been making the rounds between Sam, Kit, Muzzy, and himself, Seth refusing in favour of his own pack of Sterling Evergreen.

"Enough of that," Sam said. "No pissin' her about, all right? You've heard her albums, she plays better than most folks out there, man or woman."

"Thanks, love, but I don't need you to protect me from this lot," she said, jutting her chin forward. "I can rumble with you lads any day. Bring it on." She turned to Sam. "You sure your ringleader won't mind?"

"To be honest, I've already discussed it with Jeeves. He's all for it. In fact, it was sort of his idea. But this is a democracy, so let's take a vote," Sam offered, eyes scanning the room. "Who says 'aye'?"

"Aye," said Seth, tipping his beer bottle towards her.

"Aye-yi-yi," said Muzzy.

"Ayeeeeeeeeee," Sailor slurred from his human cocoon.

"You don't get a vote," Sam told him.

"Why not?"

"'Cause you're not in the band! You don't even play any instruments."

"Doesn't matter," said Sailor. "Besides, I blow the horn."

"Speaking of, I gotta take a leak," said Sam.

"Coming with ya," Sailor responded. He extracted himself from the couch, skip-running to catch up with the quick steps of his flatmate.

The toilet was about fifteen degrees colder than the backstage lounge. Two out of four stall doors broken and flecks chipping off the tile in zigzag patterns, an odd contrast in comparison to how the lounge was kept, decorated in faux leather and stocked with plenty of designer drinks.

Sam stepped up to the second urinal, Sailor to the third.

"So I guess you're on the road to bein' famous now, 'eh?"

"Sailor, I'm just trying to have a nice, quiet piss. Can't you shut it for one second?"

Sailor leaned in, kissing him sloppily on the cheek, too high and happy to notice the abrupt change in Sam's demeanor or contemplate its indications.

"Oi! I said give it a rest, will ya?" Sam pulled away, tucking himself back in and storming over to the sink.

"The pressures of fame gettin' to ya already, Sammy boy?"

Sam scrubbed hot water over his hands and face. "Maybe."

"I'd say I know how to take the edge off, but I can tell you're not in the mood."

"Correctamundo. Maybe some other time."

Sailor joined him at the sinks, preening a bit and pulling faces in the mirror. Sam had to laugh.

"That's what I'm talking about," Sailor said. "Anything else I can do to lend a hand?"

"Nah." He watched the tap run for a bit before facing his reflection in the dusty mirror. "Just—what if I'm not cut out for this? I mean, playing music is brilliant, and the fact that so many people came out to the show tonight is great, but..."

"But...?"

"But, I don't know. Jeeves, and the Society, it's just...turning fans into an army. An army of what? He speaks in riddles, he's half crazy. Sometimes I wonder if he has a plan at all."

Sailor placed his chin on Sam's shoulder, matching his frown in the mirror. "Put it this way, mate. What else ya gonna do? World is shyte. At least he's tryin' something, or thinks he is. An' he had no small part in promoting this gig tonight. That's something."

"Yeah, I know. Thanks, Sailor." He reached up, scritching his hair. The Sailor in the mirror smiled.

"You know Sailor's not my real name, right?"

"Yeah, I know. But every time you're pissed you tell me it's something different. You gonna tell me tonight?"

"Not tonight," Sailor said, grinning wryly. He gave Sam a friendly smack on his bicep and pulled away.

"Fair enough."

"C'mon, let's go see what those other stoner revolutionaries are up to."

Sam and Sailor headed out into the hall, back into the fray.

Chapter Eleven

WAITING FOR THE MIRACLE

Benson Bridges finished primary school at the age of eight. By sixteen, he had created twelve unique technological inventions which he'd never bothered to patent. Some would say Benson had thrown thousands of pounds down the drain. But he loved creation, hated business, and didn't mind if his flat was forty square meters and a complete mess.

He preferred to work at home most days, but today was stuck working at Janus Jeeves' obscenely decorated flat. The man insisted. He wanted biweekly updates, said it was part of Bez's duties now that he'd been promoted to 'Magician,' his formal-informal title amongst the Arcana. Jeeves had gifted him the title immediately after Benson had brought Sam over that first night.

"Is it ready?" Jeeves asked, his face mere inches from Benson's across the communal table currently serving as workspace. Customised widescreen tablets light as a feather designed by Benson himself, with decacore i21 processors and upgraded memory capacity, lined the table in either direction, staffed by his own little team of quiet-as-mice programmers. He was now a manager.

"Shove off, these things take time," Benson said. "Jayla, any luck?" he asked the girl across and two screens to the left from him.

"No joy," the dark hair girl responded.

"This sequence keeps throwing an error; he don't like anything I've been feeding him. Gotta keep tweaking it 'til it bypasses these permissions," said Benson.

"I know baby, I know, I just want to see the program in action," said Jeeves, punctuating his words with a few spazzy thrusts of his hips.

"Can you go away? Your weird dancing makes it hard to concentrate. If you want us to finish this on time, you gotta give us some space."

"Suit yourself." Jeeves strutted away from his kitchen table with moves somewhere between modern dance and tango.

Five minutes later he strutted right back in.

"How's it goin'?" His black and yellow chiffon sleeve covered half of Benson's face.

Benson swatted him away, annoyed. "Remind me again why'm I doin' this, eh mate? You harass me all the time and you don't even pay me, except in curry. I quit a decent paying job at that camera shop, dull as it was, to sign on and do this full time, you know."

"You love curry, baby. Must be your Korean blood. I once had some Korean blood in me," Jeeves mused.

"First of all, this curry ain't nothing like Korean curry; it's Punjabi and you know it. It ain't all the same."

"I know that, Bezzy-Bez. I've been everywhere. I get spices no one but the rich can afford." Jeeves crouched beside him, breathing the aforementioned spices in Benson's ear. "I get them illegally."

"Is that one of the laws?" Benson asked dryly. "Thou must obtain one's spices illegally?"

"Don't be absurd," Jeeves said. "But yes, it falls in line with the rest of it. You know that. And you *know* why you're doing this. Tell me now, tell me extra quickly. Why *are* you doing this?"

Benson sighed. "Because I believe."

"Because you believe!" Jeeves exclaimed with his whole person. "Because you know. And because you got the big maths computer brain, baby. Only way to take down a computer is with a computer. That much is obvious." The maestro took a deep breath, calming a tad. "And I believe in *you*," he told Benson, fixing the lad with an earnest look. "Why, you're the key to this whole thing."

Benson ignored the compliment. "It's gonna be brilliant when it's finished," he said. "Gonna be mayhem, but the kind we need. I just hope Sam can rally together enough people."

"Have faith, my son," said Jeeves, crossing himself like a priest. He folded his hands and bowed down until his head touched the picnic table. "Fan army grows as we speak," he said, popping back up.

"So, when we set this thing off...what about people who don't have the Dot? I mean, I know there's not many of them, but they're out there."

"Ahhh. Those people are already on our side. They don't even have to listen to Saint Fox and The Independence. They're ready to play. Been doing it this whole time." Jeeves put his hands on Benson's shoulders and squeezed, squinting at the display like he understood the lines of code.

While Benson's baby continued to throw SQL errors, Janus Jeeves sat on the floor and thought about the world. This would work. It wouldn't be like last time. The people would rise up—unified, and follow them singing and dancing into the light. He was doing the right thing. Previous attempts in previous lives had only been practice. This time, with Saint Fox by his side, this time it would ricochet around the globe, pinging and ponging until all were almost free, until this time ran straight into next time.

Two hours later, Benson shouted eureka. "We're in! Finally."

"Yeehaw," said Jeeves. "Sooo...is it ready?"

"Only 1,051 more sequences to go," Benson said. Jeeves slapped his hand to his forehead, spinning dramatically before crashing to the ground.

"If only the revolution relied on art instead of maths," he said from the floor.

"If only," Benson said, returning to his work.

~

Kit had to change trains four times across seventeen stops to get to Sam and Sailor's flat in South London. Between the District line shut down for maintenance and the nonstop pouring rain that amplified the paradoxical aggressive zombie nature of crowds, the trip took over an hour.

Still, she was only ten minutes late, and Sam Numan did not seem to mind at all.

The flat was just as sparse as she'd imagined it, a place for eating, sleeping, drinking, and writing music. Amps crowded up one side of the room, and papers with chords, licks, and lyrics written in biro were scattered across the floor. The air smelled of afternoon rain, vodka, burnt tea, and damp.

"You can close the windows if you like. I know it gets cold, but it helps me think." Sam sat on the ground in front of a stack of amps with his Stratocaster across his lap. The wind blew his hair—recently dyed crayon red to complete the alien rock star look—across his face as he scribbled on a piece of paper held down by a mug. He wore dark blue faded jeans, a T-Rex t-shirt and his leather jacket. He looked up at Kit, grinning crookedly.

"I'm not cold. Been trapped on the Tube for what feels like hours, so fresh air is nice," she said.

"Hope you didn't have any trouble getting here," he said, placing the end of the biro he'd been writing with in his mouth, letting it hang like a cigarette.

"Not really. What're you working on?"

"Pop song. Crunchy. Easy. Three chords. Ya know, the stuff they like."

"Yeah, I know." She smiled and picked up one of the papers lying on the floor. Despite knowing the transient nature of the heart revealed in a pop song, she read his lyrics through the rose-coloured illusion that they were about her.

"Come here, I'll tell you a secret," he whispered conspiratorially, motioning for her to move closer. She sat down beside him, their knees touching.

She couldn't think properly when he was near. Equally strong was her desire for him to recognise how clever she was and for him to think her pretty, the latter of which she internally chastised herself for.

"What's your secret?" she asked on a quiet breath.

"I'm going to add a fourth chord to this song," he said, eyes glowing. "Nobody can know."

She broke out in uninhibited laughter, shoving at his shoulder. Kit reached over to open her own guitar case and gently took out her baby, the black and white Telecaster. She was dressed to match—black boots, black stockings, black skirt, white boyish blouse. Her kinked black hair was free and loose, curling inwards and outwards at the nape of her neck.

"Let me show you how it's done," she said.

After tuning up and plugging in, she got straight to work at impressing the trousers off Sam Numan. Her fingers danced across the fretboard with prowess and grace, some licks recalling celestial refrains, others rumbling up straight from the gutter. Each frenetic riff speeding down the neck, each note held and bent obscenely, showed on her face in flashes of light, sparks of intricate intensity. She and her six-stringed instrument bled together in perfect harmonious discord, a whirlwind of angst turned into joy via steel and electricity. When she played the guitar, she played the angelic whore.

When she finished, her eyes slowly lifted to meet Sam's. She smiled almost shyly, one eyebrow raised.

"Show-off," said Sam. His eyes were glittering. "Knew I was right about you."

"Right about me how?"

"That you're fecking brilliant. That you'll complete us." He leaned in close, grinning, their faces almost touching.

Kit shifted positions, accidently smacking Sam across the forehead with the headstock of her guitar.

"Sorry!" she gasped. "Sorry, sorry...are you alright?"

"Yeah, I'll be fine," Sam said, rubbing his forehead and grimacing.

"I'll go get you some ice."

"Nah, it's fine, hey, settle down." He grabbed her hand to stop her from rushing off, pulling her down to sit beside him again.

Kit sucked in a tense breath, pulling ever so slightly away from him even as she wanted to surge forward. She knew better, knew guys like Sam. He uses people, she thought. He probably doesn't even realise it.

Doesn't mean I have to end up being used, she told herself. I can use him right back. We can use each other.

But not just yet. Better to draw it out.

Sam was trying to get a good look at her, but she wouldn't make eye contact for more than a second. He grinned sideways, tilting his head down and deciding not to push her for the time being. Anyway, they had work to do. He rummaged around for his cleverband, finding it buried in a pile of Rolling Stones tabs. Sometimes it made him feel a little freer to take the damn thing off. Most people never did, so used to having the ultra-comfy, waterproof, stainproof devices strapped to their wrists that they never thought to remove them.

"Hey, check out this lyric submission I pulled from the FoxDen app. Think we can work around it? If we do, this kid wins this lyric contest thing we're running." Sam showed her the set of words glowing on the display in neat black type:

If I am cruel I have cause to be
You lied when you said I was free
If we are cruel we have cause to be
They lied when they said we were free

"There's a ready set rally chorus in there," Kit recognised.

"Yeah, that's what I thought, too," Sam said. "Four chords?" he said.

"Yeah, four chords. I'll come up with a solo that teases off the melody of the verses."

"Perfect. And I'll wear purple at the next show to match the shiner on my forehead," he said with a pout.

"Don't start," she smirked. "You're a fighter; you can take it."

"I hope so," said Sam. "I'm sure to take a few more hits along the road."

Sam and Kit worked late into the night, writing words and melodies of candy and bliss. When the sun set and the air blowing through the open windows turned bitingly cold, neither of them noticed, too engrossed in their songwriting which flowed freely and easily. Down in the streets below, the workforce praised high heaven that the day had ended, and retreated to pubs, to restaurants, into the storybooks of the modest 84-inch televisions inside their flats. The new composing duo of Saint Fox and The Independence were hard at work preparing to gift them with another dream—a dream of freedom and equality, a dream of expression and light.

A fool's dream, some might say. And only a dream.

Chapter Twelve

ARMY OF ME

If you were counted amongst one of the supposedly carefree and spoilt generations who had never seen war, and had not been corralled into earning degree, you held a retail job. You lived in a flat with one or two other people and together you drank, smoked, laughed, and watched a telly that one of you owned until you sold it for rent money, then you watched telly on your holo display in your individual rooms. You woke up at six a.m. and rode the crowded Tube lines for forty-five minutes until you arrived at your ubiquitous everything-you-need-chainstore, at Tesco, at Argos, at Asda. You stood on your feet for ten hours a day with one half-hour lunch and one fifteen-minute break, smiling at people who were rude and demanding. You stared at the clock as the minutes dropped off like water from a broken faucet.

Janus Jeeves was collecting data. He collected data from a database connected to an app created by Benson Bridges. The data was collected through tracking cookies and surveys; the data was then parsed into charts which Janus Jeeves poured over wearing ruby red horn-rimmed spectacles with no lenses in them. The data showed that ninety percent of Saint Fox and The Independence's fan base was in the lower twenty-five percent income bracket, which despite current reported statistics, accounted for about fifty percent of the population.

Janus Jeeves correctly assumed that this meant a significant percentage of Saint Fox and The Independence's fan base worked at Tesco, at Argos, at Asda. They were there when the shops opened, they were there when they closed, they were there when you swiped the Dot across *Pay Now* on the P.O.S. interface. Their shoes were new and their cleverbands were up-to-date, and these were the chosen luxury items of the younger generation who fed on ramen noodles, slept on secondhand furniture, and were peripherally aware of the discrepancy between their wages and the rate of inflation, but powerless to do anything about it. They watched Mr. and Mrs. Designer Suit buy bottles of imported wine that cost a hundred and eighty quid and swallowed their envy, knowing they'd been cheated. So they killed time laughing and drinking and playing with their cleverbands, and sometimes wondered whether someone would come along and offer a solution for why—no matter how many hours a day they stood on their feet—they still could not get a leg up.

They put their eardiscs in and turned the volume up.

~

Harold Waterman's study on the second floor of his three-story home was nearly identical to his office on Downing Street. Both contained: A beautifully finished, antique desk large enough for a family of ten. A name brand, Korean-manufactured 17K-pixel SO-LED monitor—the same one anyone who knew anything about technology owned, or so his man in I.T. said. The most comfortable and ergonomic office chair money could buy, and, of course, a fine selection of top-shelf liquor housed along the wall in crystal decanters.

Waterman sat quietly in his study on a Thursday evening, hoping no one would disturb him. No such luck. A relentless knocking was followed by his wife's voice drifting in through the door, the tone of it lifeless and hollow.

"Harry? Are you in there?" she inquired in an admonishing tone that reminded him of the director of administration back at Eton, a woman who bore a physical resemblance to his wife as well.

Amelia was a shapely woman with chin-length brown hair and a full, round face. She was a wonderful philanthropist to various social causes, a doting daughter to her widowed mum, and a picture-perfect mother to their two children, Stephen and Felicity, who were away at very posh boarding schools most of the time.

She was a terrible wife to Harry. Or so, this was the story he told himself.

Condescending and cold. Forceful and demanding. She chewed him out at every opportunity, and if there wasn't one, she'd create it. They'd not had sex in six years. In fact, Harold Waterman believed she'd turned him off sex forever. Women and their sweet smells and their soft hair and exquisite breasts were forever associated with demands and long lists of inadequacies. The sight of a naked woman now turned his stomach. She'd ruined that for him, too.

"Harry, have you spoken with Stephen yet? He still hasn't taken his car to the shop. It's dangerous. This is the third time I've had to ask you. Do something about your son."

The Prime Minister sighed, staring blankly through the large holo monitor in front of him while leaning back in his chair, a half-empty glass of vodka in hand. As far as he was concerned, life was a constant string of chess games where the opponent's moves were all rumor and nothing ever actually happened. Home life, Downing Street—it made no difference. The most powerful man in the country, slave to the banality of the 21st century. What a boring time to be alive. Sometimes he wished for a great travesty; it would give him something to do other than tread these tepid waters. Of course, there were actually a great number of things to be done. Healthcare reform. National security. The ongoing financial crisis. Didn't Amelia understand that he had more pressing matters to consider?

Harold rose from his seat, unlocking the door. Amelia stood on the other side with one hand on her hip and the other raised as if she were about to knock again, wearing a look of surprise which quickly schooled into apathetic disdain.

"Harry, how nice of you to show your face." Hers was impeccably manicured, like a well-cared-for Ming vase.

Waterman stared at his cuticles. "I heard you the first time, the second, and the third. I will deal with Stephen and the car when I deal with Stephen and the car." As he gazed at her, a cold look adhered itself to his forgettable features. "Now, if you'll excuse me, I've other important matters to attend to, such as running His Majesty's fair kingdom."

Amelia was unimpressed. "Well well, such a convenient excuse for whenever you don't want to tend to your own family. I don't care if you're in the middle of an intertalk session with the King himself. Tell your son—who takes after you—to get the damn car fixed."

"Oh Amelia, the King most likely doesn't even know *how* to use intertalk. He's far too busy following the earth-shattering drama of the latest footie match." He closed the door on his wife, who called him a few choice words through the door before turning on her heel, and would most likely forget about the whole thing in a matter of days once she found a new cause to get up in arms over.

Waterman returned to his desk, attending to one last trivial matter before he could retire for the day. He swiped through the messages on his holo monitor and confirmed a meeting next Monday with the President of the United States, a Mister John V. Ellis. A man of the old world order like him, a sixty-three-year-old Caucasian with Rockefeller money and a ludicrous salary for himself and those who'd gotten him into office. Waterman, however, did not readily welcome comparisons between himself and the American President. There were few, and none of substance, as far as he was concerned.

Relations between Great Britain and the United States had gone from cautiously polite to painfully strained to hanging by a thread, years of resentment and dependence giving way to alienation and outright disgust. British corporations that were mutant Siamese twins, joined at the hip to their sister American corporations, were suffering separation surgeries by the hundreds, the steady plummet of the American dollar a drain on anything tethered to it. America simply didn't have much to offer Britain these days, and since Britain's economy was only faring marginally better than her sister's, the most logical progression was to amputate. She had no desire to drag around the weight of a country she could fit inside more than fifty times over, one that treated you like a mistress you were happy to ravish under cover of night, but denied ever enjoying the spoils of her pleasure in public.

The slow but steady divorce proceedings that happened behind the curtain hurt Britain, but they hurt her sister more. Wall Street scrambled to create new connections and solidify whatever old ones remained. With a finger-light touch against a shimmering display, they sold their souls and their second sons in order to secure secretive and lucrative alliances with any country who would still have them.

Great Britain grew more isolated every day. Truly an island nation.

Harold Waterman rubbed at his temples, sick and tired of attempting to get a hold of the President for a conversation that was nothing more than a formality. He glanced longingly at his brandy decanter, but would not allow himself to partake until after six p.m.

Americans were bloody fools, everyone knew that. Still, dealings with them were occasionally necessary. They had an incredible weapons supply, for instance.

British banks and businesses would recover, and ultimately benefit from the growing schism. The military, however, was a different story. In case of crisis, America was unlikely to come to Britain's aid—not solely out of spite, but because they simply couldn't afford to. Though their debt expanded by the hour, they spent money they didn't have equipping and deploying troops to every pocket of the earth. Reckless use of natural and human resources had caused both to wear thin. Rumor had it that some sort of covert draft had even been instated to compensate for recent drops in the number of voluntary recruits.

Even so, America's motto of "We're Number One" continued to ring loud and clear as far as armed forces were concerned, though Britain, despite its size, trailed at a respectable fourth place, and remained well-protected from outside invasion. On the matter of what was inside, well, that was kept under control by an optimum level of surveillance that was so invasive some likened it to unscheduled prostate exams.

Operate within the system, however, and one went virtually undetected.

Chapter Thirteen

TWO MEN AT SEA

Montreal of Middleton Park and Janus Jeeves were playground buddies, war buddies, went into foreclosure together, and had once loved the same girl. Between them there was mutual trust and respect, but not much love. Jeeves saw Montreal mostly as an asset; he saw most people as assets. Not that there wasn't plenty of love in his heart—no, in fact, quite the opposite. That love just manifested itself through his lives' purpose—to rebalance the equation, to set things right. Things *must* be set right—through any means possible.

He hoped the children would understand.

Janus Jeeves used his assets wisely. Montreal was no joker—he knew people, had connections. His pal Montreal was ex-MI-5 and somehow still maintained top-level security clearance, which would someday prove useful, very useful indeed.

On a Tuesday afternoon in early winter, Montreal and Janus Jeeves sat across from each other on Jeeves' secondhand colour-clashing couches with cigars in hand, trying to out-smoke one another. Jeeves blew rings within rings of smoke, rings that spun around 360 degrees before shrinking and sliding through the middle of a larger ring. Montreal blew long, slow puffs which dissipated steadily, the colour fading from grey to white to nothing.

"So, what do you think of my boy, Saint Foxy?" Jeeves asked.

"You mean Sam?" said Montreal. "He's a quick study. And he's wiry, like you." The gravel in his voice made it sound like an insult, but it wasn't meant as such.

"I'm talking about his stage presence. The bing-bong boy's got what it takes, right? You seen him on stage. Got 'em eating right outta his hand." Jeeves' left leg twitched impatiently like a dog's tail.

"I think he does. He got a sweet, silky voice, an' he moves like he's transparent," Montreal said, flicking a spot of ash off the pale red sofa. "Still, there's something about him that worries me. D'ya know what I mean, or am I gonna have to try and find the right words to explain it?"

"I know it," Jeeves said. "My kitty's got an itch. They'll give him pills for that."

"Just make sure it's the right ones."

"There are no right ones." Jeeves stood. A faint cloud of smoke and glitter dispersed through the air, temporarily obscuring the vision of him in his faux magenta-dyed ermine fur coat and his five-inch pleather boots. Jeeves sat back down next to Montreal, but not too close. He leaned back, returned the cigar to his mouth and spread his arms out along the back of the sofa.

"You remember when we was in Russia?" he asked, extending his S's.

"No, I don't. I don't remember being taken prisoner and I don't remember gettin' questioned. I don't remember being starved, beaten, mind-fucked, or any other kind of torture."

"Nah, don't remember any of that, brother. Just remember Sarah," Jeeves said, exhaling slowly. "You still think about her?"

"Course I do. Think about her all the time. You remember her gams?"

"I remember her gams, man. I remember her gams."

Jeeves took a long drag, choking the smoke out through his nose. "So listen, man, I'm going to need your assistance..." he began with his drawn-out S's.

"Oh, you need my assistance, do you? More than what you've already asked for? I thought perhaps you just wanted to spend some quality time with an old mate," Montreal chided, eyebrow raised.

"Last time I asked the former rock star for help. This time I'm asking the former military man." Jeeves grabbed Montreal's arm and forced it into an awkward salute. Montreal pulled his arm out of Jeeves' grasp without much effort. He had quite a bit more strength—in body at least, than the serpentine, idea-crazed apparition beside him.

"I'd say I'm not up for anything illegal, but we both know that's not true, and we both know those are the only kind of favours you ask," Montreal said.

Janus Jeeves grinned with all his teeth. "You still got a man inside?"

"Nah," Montreal said, stubbing out his cigar in Jeeves' garish pink crystal ashtray. "A woman."

"Brilliant," said Jeeves, "I like dem tough as nails chickadees."

"Tough as nails on the outside, soft as a lamb inside."

"So get in there, mah brotha. Get me information." Jeeves tentatively slung a silky sleeve across Montreal's shoulders, then immediately retracted it in response to the withering look he received.

"What do you need? And why should I help you get it?"

"The ol' gov'ment screwed you over pretty bad while you was in there, didn't they? Sticks in your craw pretty bad, don't it?"

"Yes, they did," he answered with a dark sigh. "And yes, it does."

"Revennnnnge!" Jeeves hissed, seeming to multiply before him in multi-tonal, erratic display.

"Yeah, I could just about go for that, any way you wanna cook it. What kind of information are we talking about here?"

"Aha!" Jeeves clasped his hands together, shaking them in front of his heart. "My man Benson will hook you up with the details. We need to get innnn places only they can get innnn..."

Montreal chuckled. "Ya know, I never get caught. They never suspect me for some reason. Must be this honest face of mine. Now, back to the gams. Who's got the best legs of anyone you've ever pulled?"

"Why, Tina Turner of course."

Montreal laughed. "Full of shit as usual. What? You went out with her when you was a baby?"

"Something like that, man. Something like that."

⌒

The pub was a relic from a time of trendgasmia, everything from the furniture to the kitschy old glassware to the geezers tending bar past the age when they could have retired. Forgotten old things belonging in a place where nothing belonged, three-legged wooden chairs, plywood tabletops, every wall painted a different colour—rust orange, pale yellow, brick red, cadet blue. An inoperative video game machine stood in the far corner. The bartender's name was Mack or Teddy or Gene, an Irish import who'd been left behind when people started migrating back home to where a job was just a job and not a life sentence. Two pool tables— one regulation size, one a bit smaller. Mismatched shades of red and yellow balls rolled across a scuffed-up surface that threw the game, though the lads and lady of Saint Fox and The Independence were too drunk to care.

"C'mon, I set that shot up for you. How'd you miss it?" Sam teased.

"I'm slow-playing you, obviously," Kit said. "Gonna take all your money, Saint Fox."

"You can have it, darlin'. Corner pocket," he said, placing his cue at an angle. Thwack!

"Nice shot."

"Your turn, rock n' roll princess. Show me what you got."

Kit pressed forward against the billiards table, cue in her left hand. She missed, then sunk three in a row on her next turn.

"Told ya," she said, grinning.

"She's better at guitar, she better at pool, don't yer masculinity feel threatened, Sammy?" Muzzy inquired from his barstool vantage point, gulping his third pint of bitter.

"Nah, I'm all about women who can do things better than men. I bet there's a ton of women out there who can do most things better than I could. Like rule the world for instance." Sam lined up his next shot, potting another red ball, then scratched on the next. "Hell, Miss Kit here oughta be fronting this movement instead of me."

"It wouldn't work," she said, sinking her final shot and ending the round. "Male-dominated society and all. We've come a long way though...or have we? It's hard to tell sometimes. Women in positions of power still make a lot of people uncomfortable."

"That bug you any?" Sam asked, leaning against the billiards table.

"Not really. I work with what I've got, show 'em they're wrong when I can. Otherwise, pearls before swine, as they say. Why waste my energy if they ain't gonna listen?"

"They'll be listenin' soon enough, darlin'," Sam drawled in a poor attempt at a Southern accent. "We'll be too loud for 'em to ignore."

"Damn right," Kit said, smiling. "I'm gonna grab another pint before last call. Anyone else want anything?"

"Bitter," said Muzzy.

"Same," said Sam.

Kit ordered, waiting by the bar until the drinks were ready. Would they really be the ones to bring a new kind of independence to people? she wondered. Last week she'd talked with Benson for the better part of an hour, and figured at this point she knew more about the movement's goals than Sam. She knew that Bez was developing an electronic weapon. She knew it was biochemical in nature. He'd gone on about how few people realise just how much we have in common with electronics—*After all, our bloodstreams conduct electric currents too*, he'd said.

The key lay in the deployment, Bez had explained, in the army. The entirety of Saint Fox and The Independence's fan base was made up of disgruntled dreamers, people looking for a leader to rescue them from their mundane, advert-laden existence. Switch flippers, Benson called them. An operator within every half kilometer of every major borough.

If people wanted to make purchases, there would be a price to pay, higher than the cost of goods plus the insane VAT rate of thirty-five percent remitted to the government.

"Guinness and two pints of bitter, love," the bartender said, shaking Kit from her thoughts.

"Thanks. Hey, is there any form of payment you take besides the Dot?"

The bartender, Mack or Teddy or Gene, scratched his head. "Think I have an old-fashioned card machine around here somewhere. Ain't workin' right now though. Outta paper."

"What about payment that isn't tied to the Crown? Some sort of trade, like washing dishes or something?"

"There's only one other form of payment I'd accept, darlin'. An' I expect you ain't up for it with an old codger like me." He winked, gently grabbing her hand and placing it against the pay pad. She touched her index finger to the green-coloured square underneath the text that read *Pay Now*.

She swiped the Dot slowly downwards across the surface of the screen.

"Thanks for your payment. No Receipt." the screen read, defaulting to her preset option.

"Cheers," Kit said to Mack, Teddy, or Gene, as she took the tray of drinks.

She returned to where Sam and Muzzy were engaged in another game of pool. Not one ball potted yet. Muzzy shot and missed.

It seemed they were both losing.

A young man with bright ginger hair who was likely in the midst of his gap year approached Sam as he was exiting the loo.

"Hey man, just wanted to say I love your music. Really brilliant stuff," the kid said.

"Thanks mate, glad to hear it." Sam glanced over his shoulder at Kit and Muzzy, who had taken up the pool game he'd abandoned.

"You're really...you're like a hero of mine," he said, his Irish accent coming through thick and pronounced. "I've been to 'alf a dozen of your shows, slamsounded the EP as soon as it came out, can't wait for the first album to drop," he rambled, wide, dark blue eyes boring deeply into Sam's.

"Er, cheers, man. Thanks for the support." Sam glanced over at his friends again, shifting his weight from foot to foot.

"So, when's the album coming out?"

"Well, we've been really lucky, only started playing this year, but things have really taken off, solid promotion or something I guess, people like you getting the word out. It uh, we've been working really hard, it should be coming out soon," he shrugged, giving the lad's shoulder a friendly squeeze. He made his excuses and wandered off before the boy could ask him any more questions.

Jesus, it was working. Jeeves' plan to skyrocket them to stardom seemed to be happening at lightning speed. One minute they were playing in dirty bars and coffeehouses, the next thing he knew they'd put in countless hours at practice, in the studio, were headlining their own little tour around semi-local venues, bypassing the part where they were someone else's opening act almost completely. He didn't have a chance to blink, was too busy being Saint Fox to even know what was happening half the time, his cleverband constantly bombarded with messages from Jeeves telling him where, when, who he needed to be.

And who was he? What the hell was he even doing? For a moment he wished that he could freeze time here in this pub, just drinking and shooting pool with his mates. But he was in this now—in for a penny, in for a pound as they say, and the sort of revolution he'd only vaguely coalesced in his mind in pale shades of blue and grey was exploding into reality in vibrant red, fueled by Jeeves' inexorable puppeteering.

Over by the pool tables, Kit was joking around with Muzzy, doing that thing girls do where they flip their hair over their shoulders and tilt their heads coyly to the side. It drove him a little crazy. She probably doesn't even realise she's doing it, he thought. Would probably scold herself for being all flirty and silly. He noticed her long legs for the first time as she leaned against the table to take her shot. Or maybe it was just the boots making him notice her legs. The boots and the stockings, transparent black with criss-cross patterns. I bet there's a name for that pattern. Not fishnets, but something like it. Christ, now she's looking at me. Caught me staring. Some smooth rock star I am, can't even pull my own bandmate, he mused.

His cleverband rang twice. The first time he ignored it, the second time he answered.

Sailor's face popped up on the holo display. "Hey there, Saint Foxy-fox. So…I'm not gonna be home tonight. Just wanted to remind you to feed Binky," he said.

Sam smiled. "Shyte, mate, I ain't home either. Poor li'l mutt's gonna starve."

"Isn't that just like you," Sailor said in a teasing tone. "Putting your band or your revolution or whatever before our child."

"I know, I know. It's because I'm selfish," Sam said, feeling absurdly guilty.

"Ain't that the bloody truth."

"Well, where're you at? Out at some cosmopolitan dildo party or god knows what?"

"I'll have you know I'm on my way to a very proper gathering. The crème de la crème of society will be there," Sailor said.

"At the cosmopolitan dildo party?"

Sailor responded with a sly grin and raised eyebrow.

Sam laughed, grinning widely at the 3D image of Sailor floating in front of him. "Alright, well I'll try not to get back too late so I can at least give Binky a midnight snack. You play safe, you hear me? I'm not taking you to the emergency room again."

Now it was Sailor's turn to laugh. "Yeah, alright, I hear ya. Kisses." He made an exaggerated kissy face.

"Night night, Sailor."

"Nighty night, Saint Sam."

Sam ended the call, minimizing the display. Kit bounced over to him, her cheeks flushed from drink.

"I'm knackered," she said. "Going to call it a night."

"Need a lift?"

"Nah, station's 'round the corner and I'm just a couple stops away. Goodnight, Saint Fox." She wrapped her arms around him, squeezing him tightly before letting go. She smelled like cider and rainwater. He watched her leave.

Three drinks and four pool games later, Saint Fox headed out into the cold night air and walked home alone. As he walked he sang quietly to himself, a new song he'd been writing about the rising price of petrol and unrequited love. He was convinced that one begat the other, though he couldn't say which had come first.

Chapter Fourteen

THE PRINCE OF THIEVES

The media were vultures, preying equally on bloodlust, scandal, and the lifestyles of the incidentally rich. Magazines and newspapers printed on paper were archaic forms of communication, noteworthy news was instantaneously retrievable at the touch of a fingertip. There was no room for common decency where there was money to be made; the climb and clamour to be the first to report was as vicious as it had ever been.

There were currently seven different inaccurate stories circulating about who Sam Numan from Saint Fox and The Independence was dating. *The Sun* insisted it was the Prime Minister's daughter. *The Mirror* insinuated an illicit affair between Sam and fourteen-year-old rising sensation Gabby Miller. *The Daily Mail* had a source who swore they'd spotted Sam in a three-way between a top-earning supermodel and a recently out-of-the-closet footballer.

More than half of the stories had been called in anonymously by Janus Jeeves, who believed in the old adage 'there's no such thing as bad press.'

True fans knew the stories were fabricated and didn't pay them any mind. People who gobbled up tabloid trash like bags of crisps wondered who this dashing young man seen with their favourite tartlet was, asking their children and their hairdressers if they'd heard of a band called Saint Fox and The Independence. Now the suburbs knew his name, and everyone had heard one or two of the more popular songs in grocery stores and football stadiums. The kids— kids being any fan under the age of thirty-five—tended to mistrust a band once they were famous enough to become tabloid fodder, but the music continued to be good, their style and their shows continued to beguile, and Sam continued to interact directly with the fans through the app Benson built as their fame and popularity grew.

Touring over the last few months had been relentless. *Taking over the nation is taking over the world*, Jeeves had said. *Your house at home looks even bigger when they know you've gots others homes elsewhere.* Sam couldn't count the number of countries they'd been to, waking up in a different time zone every morning, completely disoriented. It was both wonderful and terrible, and Sam found himself jonesing for the takeoff, for that moment when the plane left the earth and they were off to somewhere else he'd never been.

He was disappointed that they hadn't been to America yet. Jeeves had hired a touring manager, some skinny bloke with too much hair named Bob or Rob, Sam could never remember. He'd asked him when they were headed to the States. *Travelling's fuckin' expensive. Janus's practically funding this tour on favours and willpower alone,* Bob or Rob had said with a derisive laugh. *Keepin' it this side of the Atlantic's what makes sense for our bankroll, where we're wanted, and for Janus's plans. We ain't big enough in America.* He said there was so much red tape getting over to and booking venues in the States that he'd just as soon hang himself with it, that if they wanted to join him there was enough for them all to hang themselves with; he'd be happy to share.

Sam decided not to push the issue.

Today he woke up in Berlin—cold and grey and blonde and black. Clean and warm and filthy and dark. The venue they were playing at tonight housed about a meter of concrete in any direction, pieced together in symmetrical, architectural perfection. Sam said it looked like a very beautiful prison, and Kit agreed with him. They sat at the edge of the stage amidst dust and wires, legs dangling over a very straight row of red LED lights.

"See those fixtures joining the roof to the walls?" Kit said. "One degree off and the whole thing would collapse."

"That's not really true, is it?" asked Sam.

"You know the Germans don't allow for inaccuracy," she said with a smirk.

"Tsk, that ain't fair," he said. "In fact, I find them very warm and friendly. Why, just last night I was dancing with a girl who was absolutely not concerned with inaccuracy at all. I'd say you're more of a perfectionist than she is."

"Fraternizing with the groupies again?"

"Gotta do what I can to spread the word," he said, a boyish smile on his face. His hair was perfectly tousled, and he had on that black leather jacket with all the zippers that he always wore and more jewelry than Kit was used to seeing him in, layers of silver rings and bangles. It appeared Jeeves was rubbing off on him. His cheekbones were more pronounced, jutting upwards towards the slant of his colour-changing eyes. Eyes that today, looked like they were hiding something.

"Lucky girl," Kit said.

"You jealous?" he teased, leaning into her and knocking the toe of his boot against hers.

"'Course not." She looked away, sucking her lower lip between her teeth.

"Well, nothing happened anyway. Not that it would matter if it did," he said, his hands making vague patterns in the air, "but it didn't."

"Makes no difference to me," she said, though the idea of Sam with some nameless groupie twisted her stomach in knots. She would use it in the performance later that night, channel her aggression into her guitar. It would express for her what words couldn't.

She had watched him night after night, one eye on her guitar and the other on the man to her left in profile, watched as he slithered, shook, crooned and screamed, breaking hearts and gathering new recruits. She thought Jeeves had chosen his frontman well—Sam was certainly a fast learner. He was hesitant to admit it, but he'd learned quite a bit from her in the past few months; she'd been able to use the experience of her formative years as a teenage rock icon to gift him with tools of the trade. He picked up everything like a sponge, from songwriting techniques to what to say and not say to the media.

Just because he learned something didn't always mean he applied it, but she believed he tried his best.

"Well," said Sam, slapping her on the knee, "I'm starving. Wanna get a bite to eat?"

"No thanks, love," she said. "I've got to work on the solo from 'Unbreakable'. Didn't you notice how wonky it came off last night?"

"Thought that was on purpose," he grinned. "I know how much you love dissonance."

"True, but like you said, only purposeful dissonance, not just random bad noise."

"You're such a control freak."

"I am not," she said defensively, without any real bile. "Don't know where you got that idea from."

"S'not like you're trying to control everything that's on the outside. You're controlling everything on the inside," he said, tapping his finger lightly against her sternum.

"Ha ha, Saint Fox, you think you're so clever."

"Indeed I am. Seeing into people's souls is part of my charm."

"What about your own?" she asked.

He jumped up from the stage and onto the floor below, tracing a lazy circle across the floor with one foot before boxing her in, his arms on either side of her dangling legs.

"The secret is," he said softly, staring at her with his head cocked to one side, "The secret is...I don't have one."

He backed away from her, dancing reptile-like across the dusty floor.

"My soul belongs to Janus Jeeves now," he said. "It does whatever he wants me to do. It feels whatever he wants me to feel."

"I thought you wanted him to use you like a cheap toy," she said, grinning.

"Oi!" He stopped dancing and glanced up at her, a look of mock offence on his face. "I like the old man's ideas. He wants peace, freedom. Who doesn't? As long as it puts the fat cats outta business. Still, sometimes I feel him draped over me like a shroud. Like I'm not me—I'm him. I'm Jeeves with a younger face and a guitar. Avatar Jeeves."

"You know much about what he's planning?" asked Kit.

"I'm off in search of a schnitzel," Sam said.

He shuffled a few more ragman dance moves across the floor, spinning and disappearing through the red-lighted exit.

Kit thumbed at the edge of her boot where he had lightly scuffed it, feeling the weight of him in the room after he'd gone. How much had Jeeves really told him? she wondered. How much does he know? Kit had done this before—at least the rise and fall of the rock star bit—knew the ephemera of it, the flightiness of people's loyalty. Still, there was nowhere else she'd rather be. Best to wait and see. This plan of Jeeves' could really turn out to be something.

She swung her legs back over the edge of the stage, stood up, and went straight for her Strat—she would sort this guitar solo out once and for all. Sam Numan was just one of many silly boys she knew, and he would have to figure things out in his own time.

~

Janus Jeeves selected Sam Numan as the frontman for Saint Fox and The Independence because he had the following three qualities he looked for in descending amounts: good looks, malleability, and intelligence. That is to say, he was a good-looking piece of clay who was smart enough to learn fast and adapt easily to new situations, but not quite smart enough to examine another's motives too deeply or predict the future based on the present, or so Jeeves thought.

Lately Sam had started asking questions, his arms crossed and a jittery little twitch-twitch in his eye. Jeeves kept a close watch on him and he loved the way he walked, but wasn't sure he loved the way he talked. Sam would ask questions like *How many fans are enough fans? When are we going to take a break from touring? Is anyone going to get hurt?* Jeeves would answer with a lightning fast barrage of words that didn't really mean anything, which had the intended effect of either confusing the recipient or causing them to forget what they had asked about in the first place.

Janus Jeeves loathed deception and loved transparency, but the twitch-twitch in Saint Fox's eye meant he could only reveal to him small tidbits of truth at a time.

Too much and he would break.

Jeeves sat in a sparse, utilitarian greenroom backstage, posed like a king atop a chair that was actually just an upside down rubbish bin. He sat with his legs crossed, smoking a cigarette that wasn't there, alone backstage while the band went through soundcheck. His hair was all tied in knots and he wore an eyepatch over his right eye with a black-and-white target print on it, rubber-spandex-gold-alligator trousers, and a white mesh top that once belonged to Madonna. The Independence rarely needed to shop for stage clothes anywhere other than Jeeves' wardrobe.

I've got to get Saint Fox a girlie, he thought. Keep him distracted. He fancies Kit, that short little minx who plays guitar like David Gilmour crossed with Thurston Moore. Band romances usually ended in disaster, but it would only be for a little while, just long enough to draw his focus. The band isn't designed to last anyway. And it's obvious I'd be doing them both a favour.

Time to play matchmaker.

Jeeves sprung from his perch, one hand extended, fingers splayed. He lifted the eyepatch to sit across the center of his forehead.

"Love is in the airrrr," he said to no one in particular.

Kit entered the room then, her guitar slung over her left shoulder. She wore a black and red zigzag patterned jumper and an A-line black leather skirt, her hair frazzled in electric waves.

"What are you doing back here all by your lonesome?" she asked. She began sifting through piles of gear, searching for something.

"Making, calculationnns," Jeeves said.

"Oh, really," she smirked. "And what are the results of these calculations?"

"I've determined...that we'll run out of petrol in approximately 8.25 years, the following month will be four degrees hotter on average, and Saint Fox is in love with you."

Kit laughed, a musical sound that was uninhibited, the warmth on her face bringing her subtle beauty to the forefront. "You're wrong on at least one of those accounts," she answered, finding a capo amongst the pile of equipment she'd been searching through and clipping it to the headstock of her guitar.

"You may be right," said Jeeves, walking towards her in a slinky criss-cross pattern, one foot in front of the other. "We'll probably run out of petrol sooner than anyone expects."

"You're quite the joker."

"I'm quite, serrriouss," he said, taking the direct approach. "I've seen how he looks at you."

"He looks at everyone like that. It's probably a medical condition."

"You make jokes, but you're invested. Look at your face." Jeeves stroked her cheek gently with the back of his hand, an overly familiar gesture, one of many forgiven him due to his eccentricity.

"Yeah, well, I don't know about all that. I'm just here to play music."

"And how excellently you do play, and how you do shine," he said, smiling fondly. "I'm sure you don't want to get your delicate little heart broken, but isn't it sometimes worth the risk?"

"Vapid platitudes. Excuse me, love, but I've got to get back to business," she said, her voice wavering like the steel strings of her guitar.

"Indeed." Jeeves watched her go, scuttling backwards like a duck until he was once again seated on his perch.

Excellent work, he thought to himself. The seeds I plant, they always grow.

Chapter Fifteen

ANARCHY IN THE U.K.

Black dirt, red sky, white t-shirts stained with sweat. Thundering war drums, electric metal wailing loud and clear, rising to the heavens, plummeting into the gutters. Words like a shot to the heart. The crowd shouting protests along with the band in perfect harmony.

One body. One mind. Thousands upon thousands of parts.

Glastonbury Festival took place across acres of wide field, but every inch below the Pyramid Stage was packed to the brim with fans here to see Saint Fox and The Independence, whose performance included a green-grid laser light show, four outrageous costume changes, and six-and-a-half screeching guitar solos.

Bodies crunched so close together you and your neighbour were practically the same person, and the stench of it was beyond unbearable—none of the festival goers had bathed in several days and were subsisting on a diet of grease, sugar, and lager, and today the temperature broke record as the hottest and driest Somerset had seen in the past decade.

But though they'd been on their feet for hours pasted into the thick of it, pain was no factor in the face of love. Enthusiasm only grew as the band neared the end of their set, still bleeding out the same force of energy they'd possessed at the start.

The adrenaline singing in Sam's brain was full to bursting. Up on stage he was invincible, gravity-defying. Sam and the band were in top form, the music never tighter—Saint Fox, Kit, Muzzy, and Zephyr working as one perfectly imperfect machine.

Today, Sam played the rock star so well that he was buying his own act. Dressed in white feathers, black leather and makeup so heavy he barely recognised himself, he soared across the stage, spun in circles, his guitar crying out sweet, crunchy chords in perfect time with the band. His voice was more powerful than ever, chanting out rally cries that echoed back to him from the crowd. It felt like heaven and he never wanted to come down, he was whole and wanting for nothing in the golden moment.

Off stage, he sometimes sank like a stone.

Not today though, he told himself as he stood in the wings, sizzling red and high on adrenaline and electric fumes as he waited to go back on stage for the encore. Today he would give everyone exactly what they wanted. He took a sip of water and glanced around the side stage, starting at Jeeves suddenly standing beside him.

"Hey," he said, offering the maestro a big grin. "We're doing good out there, yeah?"

"You're knockin' 'em dead, Sammy boy." Jeeves removed his top hat, placing it on Sam's head instead. "You're showing 'em proper, Foxy, showing 'em how it's done. We ain't like dem good ol' boys dressed in black just staring at their shoes, we sparkle and shine and seize their hearts, twist 'em up real good. Saint Fox flying through the air on silver shoes, Miss Kit wailing her geetar like a spurned lover, our boys Muzzy and Zephyr keepin' time like a heartbeat about to burst through their chests," he said, the fervor rising in his voice. "Proper rock n' roll! It's been too long and these kids here, they didn't even know they could have it like this."

"I guess rock n' roll ain't dead after all," said Sam, still grinning.

"You hear them screaming for ya? That's your cue. Get back out there, kid," Jeeves said, giving him a gentle push towards the stage.

Sam was riding high as he approached the microphone. "We can't thank you enough," he said, his voice a booming echo for miles. "We'd be nothing without you guys. It's you—beautiful people like you—who make all the difference. Who will change the world."

Sam's face shone with white radiance as they launched into their final song. He played, sang, shook and shimmied, imagining he was channeling the rock gods from lives and worlds past, present, and future.

They were one. The crowd was one. Completely enraptured.

But as the first notes of Kit's frenetic guitar solo hit the air, something shifted.

The cries from the audience changed in tone; he heard gasps and exclamations. Down in the pit he saw movement, people spreading away from a small area like schools of fish. It was over near Muzzy's side of the stage. He couldn't see what was happening, really.

Then he smelled the iron-rich scent of blood in the air. Someone had been hurt.

Sam stopped singing. "Hey—hang on, wait a minute," he said into the mic. "Can we get some help over here? Something's happening down there. We need security."

A few stretched-out minutes where the air hung heavy passed. Soon a voice came through his earpiece.

"All clear," the PA operator said. "We're a-ok. Let's get this show back on the road."

"You sure?" Sam replied quietly. "It's under control, everyone safe?"

"Just keep playing," she said in a voice that couldn't be argued with.

And so he played, finishing the performance to deafening cheers and applause, pushing from his mind the young girl's face in the crowd he'd barely managed to glimpse before the swarming mass of bodies reformed into its usual shape. He made himself forget and finished the encore, clasping hands with Kit and Muzzy and taking a bow.

If only he could stay on stage forever.

But the show, like all good things, must come to an end.

Backstage, avid young blonde journalist Joanne Fairweather pushed her way to the front of the pack.

"Sam, Sam Numan, Saint Fox! Hullo, how are you, that was amazing!" she rambled out in a half breath, eyes wild. She shoved a large silver microphone towards him. "How does it feel to play Glastonbury, the best festival in the world?"

Sam opened and closed his mouth, initially failing at a response. "Feels like jumping out of an airplane," Muzzy said, leaning over Sam's shoulder to speak into the microphone, a wet towel draped around his neck. Kit and Zephyr chatted a few steps behind, sweat on their brows and glow in their cheeks.

"Sounds fantastic!" Joanne Fairweather trilled. The cameraman zoomed in on her and Sam's faces in a close-up—hers radiant, Sam with his lips set in a straight line and his eyes glazed over. "And what did *you* think?" she questioned again.

"I think we almost had a riot out there during 'Cause of Cruelty'," Sam half-muttered, half-spat, his expression distant as if he were still up on stage, gazing out over the crowd as singing and dancing turned to shoving and shouting. "There's power in rock n' roll, and that can feel great. But there's a responsibility, too, I...I just hope no one was hurt. I've got to go check on something with the crew, if you'll excuse me."

Joanne Fairweather turned to face the camera. "And that, ladies and gentlemen, is just like Sam Numan of Saint Fox and The Independence, his first concern is always the fans, as well it should be. But they put on a great show tonight, didn't they?" Now she held the microphone out to Kit, addressing her as if she were an outside spectator rather than the studiously energised axeman who'd performed the most technically difficult parts of the performance.

"It was great, yeah," she answered. "At one point I botched it up a bit and had to improvise, but I don't think anyone noticed." She smiled, somewhat forced, but still buzzing with enough post-show energy that it felt authentic.

"I sure didn't notice," Joanne verified. "Now tell me, what's it like being the only girl in the band? Do you have all the lads fighting over you, you lucky thing?" she teased.

"No, it's not like that at all. We're like family," Kit said, ever the polite girl she strived to be, not one who lashed out with venom when presented with antiquated social constructs. "I don't think being a girl in music makes me any different than anyone else in music. I'm just doing my job."

"And what a great job it is that you do..." Joanne's sycophantic rambling faded out as the entourage made its way past her.

In a closed-off area round the back, away from the din, Saint Fox slid down against a divider made of green tarp and metal poles, hidden by stacks of blue plastic crates and cardboard containers. He pulled his leather jacket up over his head, arms still in his sleeves. The festival noise lowered to a white fuzz, words thankfully indiscernible, just the distant hum of another universe, one fading rapidly from his reality. He focused dully on his surroundings—yellow patches in the green grass, bits of rubbish blowing in the wind, the worn edges of his trainers, anything that was tangible, solid, made up of atoms, pieces of matter that didn't matter.

But that only helped for so long. His mind went back to the ugly mob scene that had broken out in the pit—looking down and seeing that girl, not more than fifteen, with dark blood trickling down the side of her mouth.

They were just kids, he thought. Just kids. Whether they were his age, younger, older, it didn't matter. It was the blind mentality of the follower, the chaos of the adrenaline-filled rock show mob, unwittingly going along with whatever was happening at the moment, all individual wills meshed into one. That was the mentality they sought. That was the army. That was the mindset they were taking advantage of.

Sam took a sip from a flask he'd started carrying around—silver, leather, and full of Irish whiskey. He used it to wash down two round, white pills he'd found in Sailor's stash, probably methadone, oxycontin, whatever, some housewife heroin pilfered from some lounge queen in curlers and a kimono.

The booze worked instantly, the pills would take around half an hour. He shouldn't mix; it would make him sick, but immediacy was key.

What am I even doing? he thought, scrubbing his hands roughly over his face. The air smelled of stale food and banality.

He needed an escape.

Kit found Sam slouched on the ground behind one of the smaller stages. She watched him slowly raise his gaze from her two-toned, shiny leather boots to meet her eyes. His own eyes were glassy.

"Whatcha doing, Saint Fox?"

He held out the flask to her. She took a sip before handing it back.

"Just thinking," he said.

She sat down beside him on the grass and began braiding the green blades into knots. "It wasn't your fault," she said.

"Wasn't it? Ain't we just the same as them, sugar?" He swallowed another lengthy sip of whiskey.

"As who? People who commit violence for violence's sake? The greedy corporate bastards who run the machine?" She paused, playing with the laces of his shoe. "I choose to think we're not."

"When's Jeeves gonna unleash his secret weapon or whatever, anyway? I feel like I gotta move, go to Thailand or Fiji or go climb Mount Everest or something. There's too many people feckin' starin' at me. I only wanna be Saint Fox up until the system crashes. An' hell, afterwards there'll probably be no means for rock stars anyway. At least not for a while."

"You can always stop, you know."

"I can't. Something about momentum. Once I get going, I can't stop. Gotta see it through." He took another swig. "To freedom," he said.

Kit sighed, resting her head on his shoulder. "To freedom."

"Kiss me, pretty girl." He wrapped a long arm around her, nuzzling at her cheek.

"You're drunk." Just this once, she told herself. Only to comfort him.

He kissed her soft and slow, his hands coming round her waist. She felt the desperation in it, sex as a means to avoid feeling.

Still, her back had hit the grass and his hand was up her skirt before she found the will to stop him.

"Wait...wait," she said, pulling back. "People in bands shouldn't sleep together. It fucks everything up. Don't you know anything?" she teased gently, a sad-sweet smile on her face as her fingers softly trailed his cheek.

He stared hard at her for a moment, his features forming various unreadable expressions before deciding which mask he wanted to wear. "Yeah. Yeah, okay." He stood up abruptly, wobbling a bit. "You're right. You're amazing. You're an amazing guitar player. Guess I want that more than I want in your knickers." He wiped the back of his hand across his mouth. "Hey, I'll see ya later, alright?"

"Okay. Later, Sam." She straightened her clothing, looked down at her knees. Watched him walk away in long, uneven strides.

She knew Saint Fox would bed the next dumb lucky bitch who caught his eye.

Chapter Sixteen

BROTHERS IN ARMS

Sam was face down on a makeshift bed in the private cabana reserved for Saint Fox and The Independence at Glastonbury, fingers trailing over patches of dead grass beneath him, when Sailor entered the tent, wearing feathers and body paint and not much else.

"Oi, Saint Fox!" Sailor slapped him on the bum, then made a cushion of it.

"Leave me alone," Sam moaned. He buried his face in a round pillow as Sailor tried to explain to him how the smoothie he'd purchased for seventeen pounds at an organic foods stand over in William's Green had more hallucinogenic properties than the shrooms he'd eaten a few hours ago.

"...s'all about the enzymes," he was saying.

"I can't right now, Sailor, I really can't. Just go off somewhere and let me sleep."

Sailor pouted, bringing his wide eyes and feather-crowned head into Sam's line of vision as he crouched by the bed—white and green linens with matching pillows strewn haphazardly across a bean-filled mattress. A white sheet was pooled around Sam's hips, his jacket and t-shirt discarded with his jeans unbuttoned and halfway down, the furthest he'd gotten to undressing before passing out. Sailor stared for a while, his tongue nestled in his cheek, lips parted.

"You're such a tease, you know that? Here I am, high as a kite, admiring the planes of your torso as per usual. Saint Fox, you sly dog. I'll take care of you, you know. You don't even have to move a muscle..." He crawled on top of him and began messing about like a kitten, nuzzling his face. The feathers tickled Sam's nose, beads hanging from suede fringe whacking him across the chest.

"Hey, cut it out," Sam said half-heartedly, batting him away.

Sailor paused, sitting back on his heels atop Sam's shins. "God, you're such a twat sometimes. Why do I even bother with you? I'm sick of you, I'm moving out, I'm leaving," he said, managing a wounded and judgmental expression despite the dilation of his pupils. "Fuck you."

"Fuck you," said Sam.

"No, fuck you," said Sailor, poking him in the chest. He swung his legs off to the side, making to leave.

Sam groaned, "Hey, wait. I'm sorry, okay? Don't go. My head is killing me. Can't we just sleep? Come on." He patted the space beside him.

"Tell me you're sorry," Sailor insisted.

"I just said it, you tweaker. But for the record, I'm sorry. For what I'm not sure, but whatever. I'm drunk and exhausted and I keep taking your downers, you know? I think that's what I'm sorry for, taking your damn drugs."

"Sneaky bastard," Sailor said, making a show of reluctance as he crawled up the mattress next to Sam. "Your fans don't know you like I do."

Sam barked out a laugh. "You're weird, mate." He wrapped his arm around Sailor's shoulder, letting him rest his head against his chest, but not before removing the feather headdress so it wouldn't tickle him.

"I know you better than that Kit girl," said Sailor.

"Leave her out of this. And you probably know me better than I know myself." Sam paused. "Maybe there's not much to know."

Sailor, with his black doe eyes, paint smeared across both cheeks, and pouty coral lips was as good a distraction as any. Sam kissed him on the mouth, tentatively at first, then pulled back a fraction, his eyebrows raised in question. Sailor answered by closing the distance between them and kissing him dizzy, hands tugging at hair and slipping roughly across skin.

"You want me to know you a little better?" Sailor asked against his cheek, unable to hide the smugness in his voice.

"What's your name, Sailor?" Sam asked, voice barely above a whisper.

"My birth name's Dave, but my friends call me Sailor."

"Hello, Sailor," he said, closing his eyes.

"Hello, Saint Fox," Sailor said against his lips. "Is this part of the V.I.P. package?"

Sam laughed, maneuvering Sailor onto his back and hovering above him. "Yes, it's complimentary, along with a psychedelic smoothie and this." He pressed lengthwise against him, tit for tat, pinning his hands above his head against the bean-filled mattress.

"Careful now. Don't break my heart; you know how fragile it is," Sailor said, breathing shallowly as Sam's hips rotated an evil dance above him, moving like the reptilian rock god he played on stage.

"I'll do my best," Sam answered. "That's a promise."

～

Kit had watched five different bands play in the past three hours. She abandoned analyzing the technicality of the bands' performances as a choice and allowed herself to get lost in the music, letting melodies at the right frequencies soothe nerves in her brain, a pain-free electroshock treatment.

The frontman of the group onstage now was a Saint Fox wannabe, blue glitter eyedust smeared across his lids, dancing a fearsome shimmy and shake across the stage in a secondhand leather getup. Kit grinned and lifted her cigarette to her lips. One of the sure signs of making it was when copycats started to appear.

Maybe this kid should have been Saint Fox. She saw what it was doing to Sam, the weight of fronting a band serving as decoy for a mysterious cause, everything moving too fast. He'd been created to float in the in-between spaces, drifting unseen through crowds, perhaps a shadowed figure on the underground platform at night who you thought just might be your soulmate—except you didn't really get a good look at him and crafted him mostly from your imagination using his shoulders, his shoes, and the colour of his hair.

Kit understood that the spotlight shining so harshly exposed too much, made one want to flee, exacerbated that 'look at me'/'don't look at me' dichotomy that so many performers possessed. Celebrity was simply a freak show instituted to cast blind spots on the even freakier components of the world taking place in the shadows.

The Sam-a-like prancing around on stage winked at her; she wondered if he recognised her or was simply flirting with the entire audience, much like Sam himself. She tried to push the thought from her mind that Sam was one of those people who was incapable of having any genuine feelings for another person, some kind of defence mechanism, brain dysfunction, the truth about all of us.

Maybe she and Sam needed regular jobs, somewhere out in the country, something outdoors they could put their backs into, reaping and sowing and sweating and earning. It wouldn't be much different than now, she thought, and anyhow she couldn't really picture it, could never picture what stability looked like—a house, kids, marriage. Someday a woman would probably marry herself to Sam without him realizing it, some model or socialite who seemed extra understanding at the right time and then bam, married, and a few months or years later, bam, divorced.

Maybe it was okay to do none of the above. Okay to just look after herself. She hadn't signed on to be anyone's wife or mother because she didn't need to.

The music transcends everything, she realised. Transcended what counts as him or her or anyone else. Together, apart, it didn't matter because—

Because they *were* the music.

Kit wandered away from the Sam-a-like show, tossing her half-smoked, burned out cigarette into a nearby rubbish bin. Not looking where she was going, she almost ran feet first into Sailor, who was headed away from their tent area. His hair was a disaster and his cheeks held a high flush.

"What have you gotten yourself into?" she asked, smoothing tangles of hair behind her ears. "You look like you've been having fun."

"Blimey, Miss Kit, I have. I have indeed," Sailor said, stretching his limbs like a colt. "Been partaking of the festival's delights."

"Yeah, I can see that. Have you seen Sam?"

"Darlin', I've seen all of him. Which bits did *you* want to see?"

Kit smirked wryly, one side of her mouth curling upwards. She didn't know it, but she had started grinning just like Saint Fox.

"Just the general shape of him will do. The last I saw of him he wasn't at his best, so to speak. I hope he got some rest."

"Oh, he's out like a light now," Sailor said, grinning with his arms folded across his chest. "Should sleep like a baby after the workout he's just had."

"Yeah, performing usually gives you that jolt of adrenaline for a few hours after, and then you crash. Anyway, Muzzy says I gotta go check out this trance/thrash/lightshow act he swears is allowing him to hop dimensions. You wanna come?"

"Nah, I've done enough dimension-hopping for one day, love," he said, eyebrows raised. "You enjoy yourself. And don't take candy from strangers."

"Don't you worry, I never do," she said. "See ya later." Black boots, black shirt, and black hair faded into a crowd of colourful festival goers.

"Later," Sailor echoed.

"Too late," he said quietly to himself. He headed off towards The Unfairground, intending to blend in with the freak show and get thoroughly off his tit but never made it, stumbling across one of his favourite sugar pop dance bands playing a secret show in Silver Hayes, and there were far too many other distractions along the way.

Chapter Seventeen

LOVE SONGS IN THE KEYS OF U AND I

The network of the Arcane Society was spreading exponentially in line with the rise of Saint Fox and The Independence, an ever-growing fan base who were all instantly accessible at the touch of a button.

On a Tuesday evening, Janus Jeeves sat cross-legged on the floor of his living room, his cleverband at the ready, its inner chips and wires protected by a poorly designed orange-and-white striped waterproof silicone slipcase that didn't quite fit around the edges. A full, pink moon was high in the sky; he watched it through the purple folds of his semi-sheer curtains as it watched him. It was a quiet night in South London and absolutely everyone else was at home eating supper in front of their tellies.

"Chief code monkey," Jeeves addressed his partner in crime.

Benson Bridges was balanced precariously on a kitchen stool, daydreaming in SQL. He responded with a grunt, not having slept for the past forty-eight hours.

"Is it time?"

"Up to you, doc," said Benson. "Told ya. Broke through, we're in. It'll work."

Jeeves' grin spread across his face in increments. "You're a good lad, Benson." He touched his cleverband and opened the FoxDen app, signing into the admin account.

New Post. Visible to: All Members.

Hello, my Independents. The time has come for you to emancipate yourselves. Be prepared to sync your devices tomorrow. You will receive a gift from us, complete with instructions on when and how to use it correctly.

If you've been following our regularly posted updates, then you've been expecting this! More to follow.

Love on and love well,
Saint Fox and The Independence

Janus Jeeves hit Post.

50,000 Likes in less than an hour.

~

Sam Numan awoke with a massive headache, upside down and tangled in blue sheets. The flat was eerily quiet. Outside, a grey rain beat an irritating pattern against the pavement.

Sam groaned, grabbing the pillow from the proper end of the bed with his feet and squashing it over his head.

Things had not gone well at Glastonbury following his tryst with Sailor. As soon as his flatmate had left the tent, Sam panicked, immediately bedding the next pretty blonde girl he came across. He didn't know her name. Eyes bloodshot and his mind wild and reeling, he'd patched one destructive bandage over the next to try and snuff out the feeling of being responsible for anyone else's happiness. She'd tasted of cheap beer and oranges, and she'd screamed and screamed, trailing scratches down his back with long, tiger-striped nails. She's a better performer than I am, Sam had thought.

After an hour of staring at the ceiling, he got out of bed, pulling on a black t-shirt and some army green track bottoms that barely held onto his slim hips. He passed Sailor's room on his way to the kitchen, noticing that the bed hadn't been slept in. Sailor's narrow floor length mirror was awkwardly propped against the far end of the room. Sam's reflection grinned at him sideways, running a hand through his tussled shock of bright red hair. The reflection threw out twin rock horns and started headbanging. Sam groaned and looked away.

He needed coffee badly. Or if he was lucky, he hadn't actually drained the bottle of vodka he'd opened last night.

In the kitchen Sam frowned at the vodka bottle, which was indeed empty. So was the bottle of wine beside it, some godawful rosé shyte that belonged to Sailor—he would pour it in a martini glass and prance around in his frightfully short turquoise satin robe with curlers in his hair pretending to be a nagging housewife, telling Sam to trim the hedges and take Binky to the groomers and why don't you ever notice when I wear a new frock? until they both failed at the roleplay and collapsed in fits of laughter.

It would be coffee, then. At the back of one of the cabinets behind dozens of unsorted tea bags, he found a tin of instant down to its last grounds. It would have to do.

He hadn't been to the shop in ages, hell, he hadn't been home in ages, touring the country instead of doing normal things like going to the grocer's or doing the laundry. He put the kettle on and began humming to himself, soothing, low vibrations to try and quell the pain in his head. It seemed he always had a headache or some other sort of ache these days, probably the fault of some pill, though impossible to pinpoint which, there were so many. Pills to make you sleep, pills to keep you awake, pills to make you lose weight, pills to make you happy, pills to make your cock hard, pills to make you feel, pills to stop you from feeling anything. He wondered how anyone kept track.

The coffee was bitter and stale. There wasn't any sugar left in the house except for baker's sugar, and too much came out of the large box when he tried to pour some directly into his cup. It tasted even worse now, but he would gladly eat ashes if it would make his head stop pounding.

Sam sat down on the understuffed couch and flipped on the telly—"news" programme, "news" programme, gals gossiping about celebrities programme—he hoped they weren't talking about him; he hadn't been able to walk down the street lately without people staring.

BBC Two was playing some dreadful game show where the contestants competed to be the next host of the show by humiliating the current one in creative and twisted ways. He left it on the game show. The poor bloke serving as today's host was having his hair cut and dyed by one of the contestants. Shaved on one side, spiky and green on the other. He looked quite the sorry muppet.

That pathetic bastard's just like me, he thought. Trussed up like a Christmas goose and on display for all the world to see. He felt bad, then. His mother would say he was ungrateful. Nah, he thought. It ain't really like that. It's been a brilliant ride so far, it's all just happening too fast. I just hope it all amounts to something. Sets things right, makes everything fair and square.

His cleverband rang. An image of Janus Jeeves in light-coloured sunglasses and a stovepipe hat appeared on the holo display.

Sam activated the display and the face sprung into motion. "Good morning, Saint Fox. Good afternoon? Good evening?"

"Good-fucking-early," Sam protested weakly. "What's up?"

"We are on the brink...of success," Jeeves' face said, his mouth spreading into a flat grin. "It's time to deploy Bezzy's little mechanism. The foxhounds are ready. Thought you'd like to know."

Sam rubbed at his temple. He knew he must look like shit. "You promise no one's going to get hurt? Just no more buyin' and sellin' for a little while?"

"No one is going to get hurt," Jeeves said solemnly. "We're a peaceful protest. Pacifists. Radical, technological, transcendental pacifists."

"If you say so," said Sam. "Anything I need to do?"

"Yesssss. Get your lovely, hungover, scrawny arse over here."

"What for?"

"It's time to record...the advert."

"Brilliant," Sam said. He downed the rest of his coffee in one go and left the room to get a refill.

"Don't keep me waiting," Jeeves' face said, though the phone call had been abandoned, Sam's cleverband left on the arm of the couch. "I've waited long enough."

Chapter Eighteen

HOW SOON IS NOW?

Janus Jeeves and Montreal Maybury stood in the back alley behind a Tesco on Marlborough Road at 7:27 a.m., the dawn before the storm. From within and without Tesco, nothing appeared out of the ordinary. The barest trickle of shoppers came and went. This particular store was open twenty four hours. *A waste of electricity*, Jeeves had said, *keepin' all them meats cold that nobody's gonna buy.*

Montreal's nerves showed on his face, lips set in a thin line and shoulders hunched up to his ears. Janus Jeeves, giddy as a schoolgirl, was unable to keep himself from moving this way and that, the gleam in his eyes obscured by the dark, oversized sunglasses he wore. The pinkish light from Belisha beacons reflected off his shades, creating a ping-pong effect off every nearby reflective surface.

"Yer bloody sunnies are blinding me," said Montreal. "Watch where you point those things. Why're you wearing those anyway? It's dead dark and cold out here. Sunrise is slow this morning."

"Ironic words from a former rock star," Jeeves said. "Anyway, the light in Tesco hurts my eyes. I know we aren't inside, but just being near it is bad enough."

"You're a kook. A kook who's about to singlehandedly take down the financial system."

"Not singlehandedly!" said Jeeves. "Oh no. Each member of our little family played their part. You, Bezza, Foxy, Jack and James and Jill and Joseph, Johnny and Jimmy and Shortie and Tallie. Everyone's worked together for this moment."

"Yeah, and I wonder how everyone will feel once the repercussions of what we've done come trickling down," Montreal said, leaning back against the wall. "Wish I had a cigarette right about now."

"I thought you quit," said Jeeves from atop a bicycle rack, the big bright heels of his shoes balancing precariously against rusted metal.

"I thought I quit, too," he said. "But then they pull ya back in."

The brick walls in the alley were red and grey. It smelled like burnt sugar and alkaline; it smelled like a sewer. It sounded like dead eerie quiet save for the two veterans' cold breaths. The street lamps above them illuminated dust particles in the silent air.

"So, why this method? Why force them to make the switch?" asked Montreal.

"You'll see," said Jeeves. He stood on one leg in an ungraceful arabesque, then dismounted in a loud leap from the shaky bike rack.

"This seems more like a statement than a solution," Montreal said. The shadow he cast on the pavement was big and looming, twice his stature.

"The two aren't mutualllly...exclusive. We're just giving them a little shove in the right direction. The rest is up to them." Jeeves' shadow was narrow and shifting, a thin wisp of tightrope walker.

"The fans. The Arcana. One in the same?"

"They read our laws as soon as they log in. They log in as soon as they hear the music. You know nothing about kids, do you, old man?"

"Lot of blind trust, all I'm sayin'." Montreal crossed his arms over his chest to block the cold.

"What do you think people are doing when they pay their taxes? Send their kids to school, leave 'em with a neighbour, make purchases? Pray to god?"

Montreal sighed heavily, a stilted expulsion of air. "Maybe you're right. You usually are, god knows why. Let's head back soon; I'm freezin' my arse off out here. No one but you would loiter at the scene of the crime just for kicks. We're probably about five minutes from being arrested."

"CCTVs will be off soon," Jeeves said. "As you well know," he said in a quieter voice. "Coppers are useless without 'em."

"Can't see anything from here, anyway. No people screaming, no alarms going off, no central banks collapsing to the ground before our eyes."

"I just like the feeling," Jeeves said, offering no further explanation. "Indeed, there is work to be done back at headquarters. Foxy'll be over soon."

Jeeves rocked back on his heels, feeling like fire and electricity. Soon, retribution would take place. Soon, the tide would turn. Soon, the oppressed masses would rise. Soon sorry bastards would be sorry bastards and his army would rocket to the surface in a blaze of cobalt flame, no longer hidden in dark cellars behind LED-lit screens. Soon vague notions would burst forth into 17K-pixel clearer than a bug's eye 8-dimensional sapphire-screen red-ray plasma A.I. UltraTouch so unfucking-believably real you're too turned on to even salivate corporeal vision.

Finally, finally, finally. The time was now.

◠

Whoever's on shift during opening hours worked a near empty store. Any customers were either solely focused on the mission of finding whatever it was they needed to buy, or else had no reason to be there whatsoever and were merely hiding from the outside world, killing time wandering the aisles, distant and lost in a fog of too-bright lights, pre-packaged meals, and cheap plastic toys made in China for ages four and up.

Access codes were given to sixteen-year-olds who'd been employed for less than twenty-four hours. When supervisors' backs were turned, an employee could pretty much do whatever he or she wanted as long as he remained invisible to the eyes of the CCTV.

At 8:06 a.m. that morning, a universal override was provided to all subscribed members of Saint Fox and The Independence's fan base via the FoxDen app. Those members then hacked the WiDi displays of the CCTVs where they worked—at Tesco, at Argos, at Asda. The CCTV feeds began playing footage from exactly the right time, exactly the right day—one month ago, with an altered timestamp. Ninety-nine percent of the footage was of empty aisles anyway.

At 8:23 a.m., Tim Easton, an introverted, intelligent young man with an encyclopedic knowledge of mafia films, stared at his cleverband's holo display, waiting for further instruction. Tim was a solid and devoted fan of Saint Fox and The Independence. He worked part time at Asda on Whitechapel Road to help pay for university, though his education was mostly funded by student loans he would later regret. There were only two customers at his Asda this Monday morning—an older gentleman wearing some sort of fishing hat who'd been staring at packaged luncheon meats for the past fifteen minutes, and a woman in the home bedding section who couldn't decide what style of throw pillows she wanted—the ones with the tassels or the ones in sheeny satin. Neither of them noticed Tim Easton connecting his cleverband to the P.O.S. system through the network profile settings on his device, using passcodes that may or may not have been provided by one Mister Montreal Maybury.

Once the connection registered on his holo display, Tim didn't have to wait long before receiving his next instruction. It came in the form of a personalised text message:

Hi, Tim! Tired of working the grind at Asda? A thankless mission, to be certain. It's time your customers learned that we are all equals. The next step is easy...touch the big red icon below!

Underneath the message, a shiny, round icon pulsed up and down in ultra-photorealistic 3D animation. Tim couldn't resist touching it. He was dying to see what would happen, and he believed in The Independence. The band thought like he did, were of his kind, their messages rallying against the one percent, those pulling one over on the populace for their own power and financial gain. Sam Numan had risen above the murk, the monotonous and mundane to shout "You're not alone, they killed your dreams. Gimme your hand and we'll make a scene."

When he touched the red icon, a little trill rang from his cleverband. The P.O.S. terminals at Asda on Whitechapel Road went black, and began to reboot.

Tim's cleverband trilled again. A new message.

Congrats, Tim. You've never been more brave or brilliant.

Now remember, whatever you do, don't use the P.O.S. terminals to make purchases yourself from here on out.

If you need anything, come to us.

Sincerely,
Saint Fox and The Independence

Chapter Nineteen

STRANGE MAGIC

At 9:01 a.m. on a Monday morning, shortly after the CCTVs went out, your regularly scheduled programming was interrupted by Janus Jeeves, appearing alongside Saint Fox from Saint Fox and The Independence, on every satellite channel across the nation.

Jeeves wore a black and white Renaissance frock over a pair of too tight burgundy corduroys. Before they were all set to record and transmit, he'd donned a top hat and monocle as well, but the accessories had been vetoed by his colleagues. He did want to look respectable, and so he appeared tame as a kitten to his own eye, albeit still a dandy eccentric to others, with his stringy, long brown hair and New Romantic wardrobe.

Saint Fox wore his signature black leather jacket—now swimming on him, and dark circles underneath his eyes.

The broadcast occurred straight from Janus's Jeeves collapsed flat in South London, though Benson had rendered the source untraceable. The two gangly figures stood side by side in Jeeves' living room, against a wall papered all in black.

Jeeves stepped forward, a little too close to the cleverband cam operated by Benson, who transferred the live feed to every home in the country via the emergency broadcast system that had been child's play for him to hack.

"Greetings, and warnings, and heed me carefully, all ye young and old and about to be compromised for your own good..." Janus Jeeves began.

Sam placed his hand on Jeeves' shoulder, halting him from his potentially confusing diatribe. When Sam had finally arrived here this morning he'd checked himself in the mirror. He'd looked alright—after all, strung out was how rock stars were supposed to look. Now he gathered his courage, momentarily filled with a sense of purpose—or maybe it was just his mind playing tricks on him, whatever meds he'd taken last kicking in. It didn't matter now. Right now, he really and truly cared. He'd been rehearsing for this moment, had all his lines memorised just like his lyrics, was itching to say his piece. He practically vibrated with excitement, or else just had the junkie shakes, out-twitching even Jeeves. Anyone watching might blame it on a handheld camera, but it was just the men.

Between half-answered questions batted to either Jeeves or Benson, Sam had finally managed to learn enough about their initial act of war to feel like he was onboard the rollercoaster, albeit with a faulty seat belt. The upset to the current financial system was a long overdue necessity that would be a temporary struggle for some, an overwhelming disaster for others. But the human instinct is to survive. They would survive. And to do so, they would have to learn to trust one another again.

Jeeves raised one eyebrow, staring expectantly at his young protégé. Sam cleared his throat and began.

"Hi everybody. I'm Sam Numan from Saint Fox and The Independence. Today I've got some good news and some bad news. Not sure how you're gonna take it. Some of you will probably be delighted. Those that know me, that listen to the band, probably won't be surprised. Many of you even helped, and you've helped us without knowing exactly what you were getting into, and we thank you for that. We thank you for trusting us enough to help us out and we just hope we're doing the right thing."

"We arrrrre, indeed," Jeeves chimed in beside him with a wave of his arm. "Listen to this boy carefully."

Sam glanced over at Jeeves, swallowed, then focused his attention back at the camera. "I'll give it to you plain and simple, no beating around the bush. You can't shop anywhere that takes the Dot anymore. Any shop that uses a Dot-sensitive sale terminal—Tesco, Argos, The Gap, pretty much all major and most minor retailers, online shops, the holo display on your cleverbands. The Dot is useless now. Not only that, it's devastating." He paused for effect, taking a deep breath.

"If you do use it to make purchases at any of these terminals, you're going to get sick."

Sam held up his index finger. A circular brown scar remained where the small magstripe had been removed. "We should never have had these installed in the first place. The sale terminals have been reprogrammed. If you use them now, it'll alter your DNA in ways I don't care to describe. Do not—I repeat—do not use the Dot."

Beside him, Janus Jeeves pointed an accusatory finger at his audience, slowly shaking his head back and forth.

"If you need anything, you can come to us. We're called the Arcane Society. We've put together some things to get you started, but the success of this really depends on you— the merchants and the consumers. The government has been interfering in your private business for far too long. It shouldn't be like that. Just two entities exchanging goods and services—that's it, that's all there should be. Why should fat cats get a cut for work they didn't do, things they didn't make? Come to us. Bring what you've got and we'll help get you started."

"We've got a new system to replace the old one," Jeeves said. "It's verrrry basic. See this here?" He activated the holo display on his cleverband while Benson zoomed in. The display showed an app called GiveNGet, an image of a green coin with a happy face on it. "Download this app. If you already have the FoxDen app, open it now and you'll see a link to it. GiveNGet is an app that starts everyone out with the same amount of cryptocurrency. 10,000 GGcoin. Everyone starts with 10,000—all the same. An even playing field, baby."

"Multiple layers of encryption. Completely hack proof," Bez mouthed quietly from behind his equipment.

"Right," Jeeves said. "Multiple layers of encryption. One hundred percent hack proof. You decide the cost of whatever goods and services you can offer. For those who are self-employed, this won't even make much difference, except now you get to keep all the money you've earned instead of forking over a heavy chunk to a government that doesn't serve you anymore. If you work for a large corporation, well, your boss is having a coronary right about now, and now's the time to brush up on any of those skills you learned that you never thought you'd use."

"We realise some people might risk choosing to stick with the current financial system if they can't work it out any other way," Sam continued. "Here's a list of some of the early symptoms of the viral program TAKEBACK embedded within the P.O.S. terminals: Headache, nausea, stomach cramps. Memory loss, disorientation, fatigue. Weight fluctuations, weakness in the extremities. Eventually you won't be able to get out of bed." Sam shifted from foot to foot, left hand in his pocket. "We don't want this to happen to anyone. We want you to come to us."

"Quite simply, if you buy, you will die," said Janus Jeeves, managing a solemn expression. "Not right away, but slowly, as the virus takes hold."

"Come to us," Sam repeated. "Let's build again from the ground up. The only people this is really going to hurt are the people who've been stealing from you your whole lives. They'll be coming after us, too, so join us, and help us defend the right to live freely."

The feed cut out. Shocked individuals seated in their living rooms heard the cheery strains of the intro theme to *Good Morning Britain* fade in as they turned to one another in bewilderment, trying to reconcile what they'd just heard.

Many figured it had simply been some sort of prank, or perhaps a marketing scheme. Still, widespread paranoia, which had become a cultural mainstay, had them all wondering.

The fan army of Saint Fox and The Independence knew it was not a joke. They were prepared with emergency supplies; they frantically messaged one another on their cleverbands: It's here.

Those who were members of the Arcana's inner circle headed for Janus Jeeves' collapsed flat on Stockwell Road.

On the balcony of said flat, underneath grey skies that parted to reveal a rare burst of sunshine, Janus Jeeves stood with his palms pressed together and his face to the sky, breathing deeply—in for eight seconds, out for eight seconds. To his followers he appeared always confident in his own mad genius, too caught up in manic energy to ever stop and question his own methods; he just kept moving forward at the speed of light.

When Jeeves was alone there were no affectations, no chameleon grins. He stood before the heavens and hoped to a god he had met once or twice that he was doing right by the people of this odd country he loved so much. If so, peace at last. If not, then perhaps he would move on to another century, another world. Start over, again. Or sleep forever.

Sam Numan stood in front of the sink in Jeeves' horrifically-decorated loo, splashing cold water on his face. This'll certainly hurt ticket sales, he thought dryly, not that being a rock star in this day and age was nearly as lucrative as it had once been, back when rock n' roll ruled the world. Their success was a fluke, fulfilling a need the advertising agencies had missed. The caveat was that after paying for studios, crew, equipment, travel expenses, dividing amongst the band members, and putting money back into the Society, they had barely broken even. Sam still needed this revolution just as much as anyone else. He would keep a low profile while chaos ran loose just outside the door, would take a break from playing the rock star and align himself with the Arcana, learn how to survive and thrive within this new paradigm they had created.

He smiled crookedly at himself in the mirror, and swallowed two round, white pills with water from the sink, his second dose today.

A reward, he thought. A celebration.

Chapter Twenty

TEENAGE RAMPAGE

For once the sun was shining in beautiful London. Janus Jeeves took one more deep inhalation of the free free air, then stepped inside to check on his crew. He found Sam and Benson at the kitchen with bowls of curry in front of them, Benson scanning his ever-present tablet and Sam eating his meal with a gold-plated spoon.

"What's the word, hummingbird?" asked Jeeves.

"It's all over the news," Benson said, activating his tablet's larger holo display to show him. "People are panicking. There's riots and mayhem outside of every Tesco right now."

Jeeves was over the moon. "Excellent! A bit of mayhem gets things back in order before the dust settles. First things first—we have to move. Then, we will celebrate our victory. Have you found a place?"

"Here," Benson said, waving his hand to switch to another screen. "More than a stone's throw away, but records say it's been occupied by the same couple for decades, and I have it on good authority that it isn't."

Jeeves grinned, rubbing his hands together. "Sounds like the place has style. Our guys and gals will be over in a tick to help move everything. Foxy, you coming?"

"Yeah," Sam answered around a spoonful of curry. "Why wouldn't I?"

"That curry's about eleven times too hot for most people," Jeeves said. "You'd better be careful."

Sam raised his eyebrows, defiantly sticking another spoonful in his mouth. "S'good," he said, as his face grew red and his eyes watered.

The scavenger army, led by James and Jack-of-all-Trades, arrived and immediately got down to the business of relocating. There was much to be done. In addition to Jeeves' books and garish furnishings, there were loads of emergency rations strewn about that ranged from the essential to the ridiculous. Litres of water, cans of baked beans, jars of Marmite, tins of curry, boxes filled with cups, silverware, vinyl records, jewelry, cloth napkins, sheets, soap, shampoo, garlic presses, paintings by the ringleader himself, rubbish bags, ciggies, boxes of PG Tips, Twinings, Tetley. Egg cups, trousers, Wellingtons. Scarves, hats, understuffed teddy bears. Jump ropes, playing cards, a lightshow disc copy of Mr. Bean's Holiday.

All of these items had been found, discarded and practically brand new, most of them in the Chelsea district of London. James and Jack-of-all-Trades led a determined army of young Arcana, the first kids on board when Saint Fox and The Independence broke onto the scene, misfit and luminous in their winter scarves and hemp bracelets. They collected, tore down, and built up Jeeves' new circus in a matter of hours.

The Arcana's new headquarters was situated above a footwear shop in Morden that had been empty for ages.

Jeeves clasped his hands together with childlike glee, practically somersaulting.

"This is it," he kept saying. "This is it. I love this place. It has even more character than the last one."

In truth, the flat above the shop had decidedly less character than the collapsed flat that had formerly belonged to Jeeves' deceased brother. In its bare bones state it was just white walls and wooden beams, a wide and narrow space. Still, the windows, which were soon decorated in sheer and beaded curtains, let in a good amount of light. With furnishings both new and old, plastic and wood, digital and analog, it began to feel like home again.

Janus Jeeves was perched in an old blue velvet chair he had positioned along the center of the back wall like a throne when Saint Fox and The Independence arrived, the remaining three of four—Kit, Muzzy, and Seth, carrying bongos and acoustic guitars.

"Children!" Jeeves welcomed them. "Come in, come in! Have you come to play us some celebration tunes?"

"Of course," Kit said. Jeeves detected a note of false enthusiasm in her voice. "Where's Sam?"

"I'm'ere," the frontman said, raising his face slightly from where it had been buried in a pile of mismatched cushions on Jeeves' bright green couch. He gave a weak wave before spotting Kit out of the corner of his eye. "What's up, little Miss rock n' roll?" he said with a lazy grin.

She sat down beside him. "Look at you all lying about. Shouldn't you be jumping up and down like your leader here? We just started a revolution."

Sam leaned against her shoulder and sniffed her hair as she put her arm around him.

"Okay, lovebirds. Let's get this party on the road," Jeeves announced as more bodies began streaming into the main room. Kids and adults, some of them colleagues from his professor days, some of them with spots and crayon-coloured hair, some he recognised and some he didn't. But all of them he loved.

"Hey, Sam," Muzzy nudged him with a guitar. "Let's play 'Action Man', the first song we played that night at the Lindseys. You remember?"

"Yeah, I remember," said Sam. He reached for the guitar. "Give it here."

He placed his fingers against the strings, people once again gathering round to hear what he had to say. Jeeves looked on with a bizarre expression on his face, both fond and pensive. Sam, Kit, and Muzzy strummed the opening chords. The sound melted into the room, rich and warm.

Rally your troops and test your weapons
For you, my friends, are the enemy
Laughing the night away, wanting for nothing
While millions struggle to make ends meet
Come closer now, my darlings and hear me
I am the face of what you ignore
No more protests, and the songs will be few
I'll be your action man, you can be sure
So rally your weapons and test your troops
First, remove the ones who need handling
We come like death, like a thief in the night

With percussion made of anything—ottomans, tabletops, spoons and one another—and a mixed chorus of those who could carry a tune and those who couldn't, the Arcana sang a chorus of Saint Fox songs, of old folk songs about sailors lost at sea, of families with no money and too many mouths to feed. They sang late into the night and the music was pure and sweet, to Jeeves' jubilant ears more so than anyone's.

As the night bled into day, Janus Jeeves surveyed his domain with pride. A few diehards remained awake, including of course, Saint Fox himself. The lad had indeed proved himself useful.

"A toast," Jeeves announced to those who had managed to stay up alongside him until dawn. He lifted his glass, a teal-green goblet filled with gin and grapefruit juice. "To Saint Fox and The Independence. To our Foxy little saviour here, whose delicate charm gathered thousands of bodies to our cause. To the new paradigm. To the future!"

"Hear, hear!" they echoed, as Sam and Jeeves' looked at each other with smiles on their faces.

The Arcana raised their glasses to father and son, and to the dawn of a new morning.

They were not the only ones celebrating that night. The fans, the foes, the children of mayhem ran through the streets, setting off smoke bombs and throwing bottles at windows. They were happy and free, because whatever happened to the middle and upper classes affected them not at all. They would go on living, drinking beer pinched from their dad's fridge in the den, sucking up helium at the party shops where they worked and floating on cloud negative nine. They didn't care that international phone lines were jumbled together in wireless disaster as cabinet ministers and CEOs dialed one another in fits of panic, didn't care that stocks at the Exchange would plummet to their lowest point in decades. They went on with their lives as usual, with only a bit more arson and petty vandalism.

Others however, cared very much. Enough to pack up immediately and head to the train station, enough to put a gun to their heads. Enough to decide that enough was enough, and that terrorism must be stopped, once and for all.

~

Asda on Whitechapel Road burned like a plastic sun, the night air thick with smoke and fog. Rows of bodies lined the streets behind lines of tape reading *Do Not Cross*. Some preached doomsday, others held signs, *Viva the Independence!*

Cops with their billysticks and their modern electric weapons did their best to keep folks in line, a swat or a volt of lightning to anyone who wouldn't jump to the beat. People who were just watching, people who didn't fit into their narrow profile of nice, middle-class white folk, even those who came to the store thinking they'd just pop in and grab a 24-pack of toilet roll were quickly swept into the chaos. Two long-haired young men with tattoos reading TAKEBACK underneath an X'd out pound symbol slung a rubbish bin over the head of a dull-faced cop as they seized his plastic club and threw it into the bushes.

Shouts of protest or hallelujah could not be discerned amongst the din, and as many coppers that showed up there were twice as many rioters, men and women yelling that the pigs would never steal from them again. There were too many of them, and the Metropolitan Police were ill-equipped to handle it—there was no specialised riot force to call upon. The people were more organised than the police, united by a common drive—to withdraw every ounce of faith from a dollar and a system they had lost belief in decades ago.

The workforce of Asda on Whitechapel Road had fled out the back way as rioters used cigarettes and lighter fluid to set outrageously low-priced goods aflame. Motor oil from one department spread fire to all others—the electronics department, toy department, grocery department, home department. Cheaply-made jumpers and mass-manufactured boxes of cereal and 800-thread count bed sheets for half price and vacuum cleaners and scratchy bow ties and undersized yoga mats and oversized pantyhose and scrunched polyester hair ties and giant stuffed teddy bears burned, burned, burned, till they were ash upon the shiny, scuffed white floor.

"You're all fucking sacked!" Tim Easton's manager, a Mister Gerald Batts, had shouted at his employees when he'd noticed the altered display flashing on the P.O.S. terminals—a question mark, warning and red—at the same moment the smell of smoke entered his nostrils.

Tim Easton had only smiled secretly to himself with his hands behind his back, covering the cleverband on his wrist with his palm. Mister Batts never paid him any mind. To him, Tim Easton was invisible. He was completely clueless to the fact that it was Tim who had played a key part in sabotaging his store.

Tim Easton stepped outside the flaming superstore into the smoky night to sweet sweet sounds, the shouting in the streets like so many rally cries in Saint Fox's songs—the screech of tires like the squeals of the electric guitar, the sound of glass shattering like a chorus of wind chimes. Tim was not a violent young man, but he knew the violence was necessary and he knew the violence would pass—he'd seen enough films and even read enough books to know this was what revolution looked like. He walked home towards his tiny flat on the South side where he could barely afford the rent, his hands in his pockets and a skip in his step, whistling a tune to himself that now, everyone was singing.

Chapter Twenty-One

FOR PENCE ON THE POUND

Charlotte Piebald was a skeptic, a narcissist, and a mother of two—two 'best in show' Corgis, that is. A thoroughbred herself, with tight alabaster skin and small bright hazel eyes that were a bit too far apart, a figure kept in good shape by smart eating and a custom-designed exercise regimen of cardio and Pilates. Her doctor once told her she had the body of a twenty-five-year-old, a fact she took much pride in being that she had just recently passed the dreaded forty-year milestone.

She kept quite busy with spa appointments and entrepreneurial pursuits—her father had helped her start up a handbag line of her very own, and now *Charlotte P.* was a high-end brand name found in every major retail shop worldwide. The bags were all either ridiculously small or as large as a suitcase, made of Italian leather in white or apricot, with tiny bronze embellishments spaced evenly across diagonally quilted patterns.

Charlotte Piebald rarely cooked. She had a personal chef who came on weekends and three out of five weekdays to her fourth generation estate in Holland Park. On the occasion she did prepare food for herself, it was simple meals with fresh, organic ingredients—mixed field greens, smoked Coho salmon, herbed goat cheese.

It was a Tuesday afternoon. Charlotte's personal chef Elise would be off tomorrow, so she needed to do a bit of shopping, for tomorrow's two-and-a-half meals of two 500-calorie and one 200-calorie portions, no more, no less.

She'd seen the adverts—some skinny maniac decked out in more chiffon than she owned and a junkie rock star claiming doomsday. Trying to stir up panic with their absurd announcement. A scare tactic. A joke. A performance art piece. Whatever it was, she'd brushed it off as something that simply didn't concern her.

"Left-wing to the very edge," she'd said, turning off the television set as she headed out the door.

Her white patent leather heels click-clacked against the hardwood floors as she entered Cherry Pickers Green Grocer. The shop was rather less crowded than usual. The manager, a Mr. McKenzie, wore a strained look on his face.

"Mr. McKenzie," Charlotte greeted him, "how's business?"

"Lousy," he answered, picking at his teeth. "Those radicals seem to have caused quite a stir. Frightened away a good number of my customers. People trying to pay in whatever cash they have left. We don't take cash here! Haven't in years."

"Well, at least there aren't any riots out front like they're having at some of the major shops. Anyhow, I'm not afraid," Charlotte said, her head held high. "What they're claiming sounds impossible anyway—creating a virus that can be transferred through the Dot. People aren't machines."

Charlotte ran a perfectly manicured index finger around the edges of the P.O.S. terminal at Mr. McKenzie's register.

"Aha, see? Not a scratch on me."

"You're a brave soul, Ms. Piebald. Now you just go ahead and grab whatever it is you need, I'll make sure this little machine here don't hurt ya. We've got some lovely local vine-ripened tomatoes just in."

"Brilliant. Be back in a jiffy."

Charlotte roamed through the green grocer's, stocked to the brim with freshly baked wholegrain breads, grassfed beef, local and organic produce from the countryside. She gathered ingredients to make two large salads and a corn farfalle version of kasha varnishkes.

"Well, I'm all set, Mr. McKenzie. Ready to take the plunge."

"That'll be 128.57£. Go ahead and swipe, if you dare," he chuckled.

The mint-coloured swipe box was now coloured red, and the text beneath it that used to read *Pay Now* had changed to *Pay At Your Own Risk*. These childish pranksters must think they're clever, she thought. Still, she hesitated— an irrational fear, an imagined phantom crawling across one's shoulder that was never even there. She squared her shoulders and pressed her finger to the screen.

"A girl's gotta eat," she said.

~

Sam woke up face down on Jeeves' velour couch, his fingers trailing the shagpile carpet that had been laid down the night before. When he realised where he was, he grinned to himself, remembering Jeeves' toast from last night. They'd had a proper celebration, and he now had the hangover to prove it. Turning his head to the side and squinting to block out the daylight, he saw Mister national orchestrator himself before him, seated cross-legged on the carpet.

"How we feelin' today, Foxy?" Jeeves asked, a wry expression on his narrow face.

"A bit shyte," Sam admitted. "Had quite a lot to drink last night. Hard to keep up with you." He groaned, pressing his hand to his forehead. "So much has happened these past few months. It's making my head spin."

"Hmm..." Jeeves stroked his chin. "Pressures of being a messiah must be gettin' to you. Don't you worry, relief is at hand. You're more than welcome to take a break, Foxy—your work for now is done. You got the bodies. Now the fox is free to scamper off back to his lair and nurse whatever wounds he feels he may have incurred," said the maestro with a quiet lilt in his voice.

Sam raised his eyebrows. "You sayin' I should leave?" he asked.

Jeeves sucked his lips in between his mismatched teeth. "Just looking out for you—you must be tired. You did what you set out to do. Now it's on to phase two. Might as well skittledeedo."

"Last night I was a revolutionary hero," Sam said, his jaw setting in a defensive live. "Besides, if I go back to my flat now, I'll probably be arrested, or worse."

"Oh, dear me, I didn't mean for you to go off where anyone could *find* you," Jeeves said. Sam found the concern on the maestro's face disingenuous, a painted-on drama mask, but maybe that was just the hangover talking, a trick of the light.

Jeeves stretched his palms out in front of him and stared off into the distance, frozen in place as the wheels in his head turned. He lowered his hands and sighed. "When you're right, you're right, Sammy boy. Who knows what direction things will take! I may have use of you yet. You gotta hide out from all the King's men, or Watermen's men, rather. You *must* be kept safe, and we should be the ones to do it. From now on, you'll stay with me. Hell, some people out there think that you're my own son. Must be the good looks." Jeeves grinned widely, clasping his hands together, the motion causing his long black sleeves to fly across Sam's face.

Sam frowned and moved away from him, sitting up. "We don't look anything alike," he said.

"I've got to go check in with Bezza. Now you just rest up your pretty head, take some paracetamol or something. Oh, what in god given hellfire will happen now that we've flipped the switch? The show begins!" He left the room in his usual tornado of fabric.

What if I'm just another cog in a new machine? Sam thought. Jeeves had promised the rebirth of a nation and the start of a brave new world, chanting hallelujahs and other discordant hymns until they had all believed. Right now, Sam couldn't picture what this perfect new world looked like. How much does a pint of bitter cost with GiveNGet? he wondered. He was glad he'd recently bought a bag of Black Jacks, his favourite candy, at Tesco. He would not be shopping there for a while.

Saint Fox, our rock n' roll saviour, he though derisively. What am I now? A revolutionary, a traitor, a refugee? Sounds like the ol' ringleader don't even need me anymore.

He reached into his jeans pocket, taking out the saccharine sweet medicine that would wash his doubts away.

Chapter Twenty-Two

BANKROBBER

Benson Bridges was directing a wireless circus. A virtual roundtable would soon take place, a chance to intertalk over the new trade.

He and the other techheads were busiest of all, readying to open up Q&A to the public. They brought methods from the deep web to the surface, making privacy and anonymity available to everyone. They would hide in plain sight, layers of shade in place to block any traces, IPs switching every second. They were in Mumbai, then Auckland, then New York. Even the cleverest hacker could not outhack Benson Bridges and his team of pale-faced, lightning-brained women and men.

Protocols were in place to try and stem the massive flow of users. Intertalk sessions were now open in shifts, restricting the number of users allowed in at a time, transcripts visible to all, updating live so that people could see the answers to questions that others had already asked— how to use the GiveNGet app, what TAKEBACK was, and why it would eventually prove lethal. They would explain how any merchant or individual could keep running their business free of interference—as long as they only accepted the new currency. Everyone had questions—the keen conspiracist, the close-to-the cuff skeptic, the follow-the-crowd youth, anyone who was invested in what the Arcana were doing in some form or another. Now they had no choice but to invest—their lives were at stake.

The overall response had been surprisingly positive, at least from where Benson was standing. When he'd mentioned this to Jeeves, the ringleader had simply declared, *The music's that good. They believe in their Saint.*

Benson straightened his specs as he attacked the latest barrage of tedious queries from his current group of users.

Martin110101: So everyone starts with 10,000? No matter who they are? There's no secret society membership, no Platinum club if I sell my firstborn child to u?

GlassEyeAS: Everyone gets 10,000. Take it and turn it into more. Keep what you earn. Just head over to the site to set up your GGcoin account and download the app. New users instantly get 10,000. Don't try to set up multiple accounts; it won't work. App requires a retinal scan—money's in your eyes.

Martin110101: Sounds simple enough. Better than the "designed to make you lose" system we had.

Z3_Freddie: What about taxes?

GlassEyeAS: They can't have 'em.

Z3_Freddie: They'll be pissed…won't be able to leech off us anymore. They'll come after you. Shut it down.

GlassEyeAS: If everyone's using the new system, what can they do? We just need to outnumber them. Just keep doing whatever it is you're doing, but bill in GGcoin.

Martin110101: So 10,000 GGcoin's all I got to my name now. I got 60,000 quid in savings. That's just gone?

GlassEyeAS: We're working on a conversion system so that those with savings will get a fair percentage of 'em back. There will be a cap though. If the amount in your bank account's in-fuckin-sane, the cream off the top is coming off.

In real-time, Benson waved his fingers around in a mimic of Jeeves' dramatic swishes, imagining cream-off-the-top money disappearing into thin air.

METAL_MACHINE: Going to the grocer's is a problem. Everywhere's a mess. You can't get in, let alone find out if they're accepting any alternative currency yet.

GlassEyeAS: They will, but we've got a network of members delivering care packages throughout all the major boroughs to tide you over in the interim. Drop-off locations will appear in the app once our delivery people are safe. Or use the

Benson cracked his knuckles as a stream of new users were allowed into his intertalk session. It was going to be a long day.

Sam, meanwhile, felt like a right tit. He'd been assigned to smile, flirt, and give out foodstuffs to the few inner circle members who'd been informed of their new location. He felt like some godawful beauty pageant queen, smiling and waving and repeating words someone else had scribbled on a cocktail napkin. People stopped by to tell him how much they loved the music, tell him how brilliant he was. He gave them his trademark grin, played the humility card, loaded them up with jugs of water and boxes of nonperishables.

Everywhere he looked, there were people congratulating him—older gents he didn't know, like Jeeves' mates, or crew members who'd travelled with Saint Fox and The Independence. They gave him accolades for his cleverness and bravado, for saving them from their straight-jacketed 21st-century existence. The crew made him feel particularly awkward. They were his mates, people he joked around with, drank with, and now they were putting him on some sort of pedestal like he weren't just one of the boys. He'd even used their words in some of his songs—most of the crew were also fans, and some had submitted lyrics through the FoxDen app. Where do I end and they begin? he wondered. Like it couldn't have been any one of them instead, if only they'd come across the mad orchestrator at the right time.

"Excuse me, darlin'," he said to a girl whose name escaped him, a pretty brunette in a polka-dotted head scarf. "Just going to pop into the loo."

He shut the door behind him and leaned against it, feeling the solid wood behind his back. The mirror above the sink was broken, the remaining pieces of glass sitting haphazardly within the frame. His face reflected back at him in shards, cracks, and slivers.

A song was stuck in his head. One of his own, a new one, the melody rough and dissonant, a mash of frenetic guitar notes at war. The lyrics in his head repeated something about being invisible, about disappearing.

Would he ever sing again in front of thousands, now that he'd played his role in Jeeves' grand design?

He reached into his front pocket, taking out the tin cigarette case he now kept on hand at all times. A scratch-marked Bettie Page pin-up adorned the front cover. Written across her, barely legible, was the word TITS in black permanent marker—Sailor's handiwork. In fact, it was his cigarette case.

It'd been at least a week now since he'd seen him, maybe two. Sam was almost certain he was shacked up somewhere with some petty old queen, someone who was bad for his health and even worse for his mental state. He really hoped that everything between them wasn't completely fucked. Being best mates who flirted a lot but never did anything about it was an arrangement that worked well for Sam; he got emotional gratification out of it without having to get too close.

Sam wanted to pretend that what happened between them had never happened, and just go on with their lives like before.

He missed his friend.

Ringing up Sailor's cleverband only got him the male-voiced auto-recording again.

"Sailor, Sailor, Sailor. You've got to come home sometime," Sam reprimanded his voicemail. "Anyway, I've got some big news. Your money's no good here. Ha ha, get it? Yeah. Jeeves pulled the trigger. I'll fill you in on the details if I ever see you again." He ended the call, staring blankly at the cleverband on his wrist.

Sam took out three round, white pills—methadone this time, sickly sweet and procured from a clinic on the pretense that he was trying to get clean. He'd worn translucent brown sunglasses and a hoodie over his bright red hair. No one at the clinic had recognised him, or at least he told himself as much.

He swallowed the pills with water from the tap, wiping the back of his hand across his mouth, his other hand pressed against the medicine cabinet. When he slid his hand downwards, a piece of the broken mirror glass cut him. He cursed, sticking his finger in his mouth, the taste of iron mixing with the bitter residue left behind by the pills. His grin in the mirror was twisted, his eyes two black daggers shooting backwards into himself.

Soon there would be no bright colours or exclamation points in his mind, no phantasmagoria, stage lights, or fireworks. No pound signs, dollar signs, green GGcoin circles with smiley faces. Just a warm, warm feeling in the pit of his stomach and in his head.

Someone knocked at the door.

"Oi, busy," he managed.

"Sam, man, it's Bez. Hey, I only got a second. You've gotta get back out there, people seem less nervous when they can see you. Just hang out, pick your nose, whatever."

"Just give me a minute," Sam said. He swallowed dryly. His reflection squared his shoulders back in the shattered mirror, then hunched over again of their own accord.

"You okay in there? Can I come in?" asked Benson.

Benson entered on a no-reply. "Jesus, man. You look like shyte."

"I just need a nap," Sam said, sliding down against the wall beside the tub.

"You're on some sorta junk, aren't ya? Took this rock star thing too literally." Benson peered at Sam cryptically through his specs, edging closer to him in the cramped loo.

"Thought that was my role in this whole thing. Some pseudo rock n' roll messiah—but just a fake-out, a trick of the light. Something you toss aside when you don't need it anymore." He tasted chalk and bile on his tongue.

"You're full of shyte," Benson said. "C'mon." He hauled the lanky and uncooperative frontman up by his arms and led him back out into the hallway. "Things are going good, man. Everyone's happy—this is what we wanted. People who weren't so sure about it are feeling better with the info and hookups we're giving them. People who want to see our heads on spikes with our intestines twined around them in flower-shaped bows, well, they're still out there looking for the spikes."

Sam's face twisted into a grimace. "You know, my songs...some of the best lyrics came from the fans. Or Kit. She's like a songwriting genius or something." He waved his arm around aimlessly. "All of them out there, all of you—you made me look good. Smoke and mirrors." His throat was dry as he swallowed. "There anything to drink?"

"Grab one of the water bottles from the supply kits, but drink it in the kitchen," Benson said. "Jesus can't be seen eating his own loaves and fishes. Now plaster on that grin of yours and get back to saving England."

"I'm going to bed." Sam said, leaving Benson to his more important work. On shaky legs the rock star made his way through his devotees, his pain washing away by the second into a white, warm fog of dull bliss, where he lived on a cloud, and didn't owe anything to anyone.

Chapter Twenty-Three

REBEL, SWEETHEART

Wildly conflicting reports of what is being called the Dot virus continue to abound. While some sources are reporting the whole thing to be a hoax, others claim that the initial symptoms of the virus have already taken hold.

Meanwhile, the top technicians in the country employed by the Dedicated Dot Crime Unit are working round the clock, analyzing P.O.S. terminal tech to try and determine the nature of the threat. Remaining resolutely composed in the face of bioterrorism, the DDCU has stated that the primary aim in their investigation is to disarm.

"So far, every attempt to remove the virus has been thwarted due to the program's overwhelmingly complex level of encryption," claims Yasmine Mattoo, a DBA specialist employed by DDCU. "Technicians on our staff and experts who have been

brought in have gone sleepless for nights attempting to extract the virus from the system. But like any smart virus, the more it's attacked, the more it mutates and grows. The dreaded red question mark is spreading—it's showing up now on cleverbands, tablets, vending machines, any touch-sensitive surface that extracts payment from the Dot.

There is no way to remove the virus without damaging the technology it runs on," Mattoo continues. "This would, in turn, harm the entire network through which all the nation's electronic data systems are connected. Everything runs on the same interlaced frequencies, and shutting it down would mean a nationwide technological blackout."

The little silver dot as ubiquitous a part of the human body as one's belly button is now the Achilles' heel of the nation. Within a few short days, the virus has gotten in everywhere. It started at various locations where members of the ubiquitous Saint Fox fan army were employed—at Tesco, Asda, Argos, Sainsbury's. Spidering its way across the electromagnetic stratosphere, it has spread across the entire country, so far appearing limited to frequencies within our national borders.

Safety warnings have been issued. Police forces are stationed around every corner, though it appears that they are not yet authorised to take any particular action. Presumably, the authorities do not yet know what action to take.

People are refusing to leave their houses. Those who have long ago prepared for doomsday are going into their bunkers, unearthing their emergency rations. Others, however, are going about their business as usual, rolling their eyes at the latest nationwide scare that can't possibly be true. And though many major stores have temporarily closed their doors, your odds of finding your milk, sausages, and whatever else you need improve if you're willing to travel a little further to a less-populated neighbourhood, or patronise a smaller shop.

There, at these shops that are staying open during the mayhem, shoppers swipe despite the risk. They swipe right across the big red question mark that is the Pay Now

square, and go on with their lives as before. The price they
pay for their bravery or foolishiness?

Nothing. At first.

Then, the symptoms begin.

Dr. Christopher Wender, a top neurologist at Saint
Thomas hospital, had a few words to say about our
newest epidemic:

"The beauty of the disease is in the psychology of it.
It starts in the mind, slowing things down just a tad
but increasing sensitivity—to loud noises and light,
in particular. Many afflicted have reported that one
of the first symptoms they notice is that they 'hear
things'. They start to believe the adverts are talking
directly to them, they hear their names shouted in
the streets on their way to work, while sitting alone
in coffeehouses, on satellite radio programmes.
Their minds fill with things that simply aren't there.

Memory is soon affected as well. The transfer of
information between short term and long term

memory becomes a broken bridge. Important dates, names, and places fall through the cracks. People misplace things, forget where they parked their car, forget to turn off the stove, forget about appointments they've made.

Some of the physical symptoms reported thus far are nausea, headache, congestion, indigestion, constipation, diarrhea, insomnia, dry skin, fatigue. Weight loss in some, weight gain in others. The stomachs of some refuse to hold down food, while others are compelled to feed themselves constantly.

We've speculated that the virus is a sort of synthetic biotoxin, a series of electrical sequences that the body recognises as its own. A touch to any P.O.S. terminal transfers the virus through the Dot. The electrical signal then continues its current through the bloodstream, and in rapid-fire time to its intended destination—the brain. Once there, neuronal activity causes strand breaks in DNA, altering the genetic code in a way similar to Alzheimer's, mimicking symptoms of various known disorders along the way so that it's hard to pinpoint, and even harder to treat."

The latest reports show that approximately 1 out of every 50 citizens is infected. Every hour, reports flood in of new incidents, and new symptoms. Doctors have begun turning patients away, as too many are coming in at only the mildest onslaught of symptoms, fearing the worst—that the disease is in fact fatal, though the first fatality linked to the virus has yet to be reported.

There's been talk of returning to cash exchange, at least temporarily. This would be fine for small items, but makes major transactions impossible, considering that when the country switched over to the Dot, the recycling programme that was simultaneously put into effect—cash for electronic credit—means that hardly anyone now owns more than a few bills, save for those they kept as souvenirs.

As the country reels in chaos, those who have a moment to spare to collect their thoughts all seem to be asking the same questions:

Harold Waterman waved his hand, closing the holo window displaying the article, frowning with as much disdain as he could muster. Up in his ivory tower he sweated and drank, but in front of others, he maintained a carefully crafted appearance of composure.

"Sir, you have a phone call. It's President Ellis."

"Thank you, Ben. I'll take it in my office." Waterman sighed heavily. He was exhausted, his face drawn and sallow. This morning his wife had been sure to point out that the grey in his hair was starting to show again; he would have to dye it soon.

"This is Prime Minister Waterman. I've been waiting for your call, President Ellis."

President Ellis cleared his throat. On the other end of the line, the university football game he was watching on his 4D-Interact MAXDEF TV with stadium surround sound had been muted—his alma mater was playing. Ellis reclined in his mahogany leather-upholstered chair as far back as the seat would go. He swept his fingers backwards through his full head of chestnut blonde hair—regenerated hair, lab-crafted from a follicle of his teenage son's and grafted onto his underpopulated scalp in a one-time surgery that guaranteed a lush landscape of locks for life.

His video feed for the call was switched off. Waterman saw only an image of the official seal of the President of the United States. An aggressive-looking bald eagle behind a silly-looking shield in the colours of the American flag.

"Terrible. Terrible what's happening over there, Waterman. If there's anything we can do," President Ellis said.

"There certainly is," Waterman answered, not bothering to mince words. "Send emergency supplies, water and non-perishables. Send reinforcements immediately. We're going to stop these terrorists with brute force, take a page directly from the American handbook. We will not tolerate terrorism. Their university-dropout hacker technology will not stand in the face of our armed forces."

"I'm sure it won't. Just terrible what's happening," Ellis repeated, holding in a cheer as his team scored. Hologrammed players ran past him in line, slapping his outstretched palm with high-fives.

"How soon can you get here?" asked Waterman.

"Well, Harold, the thing is, as you know, we're treading water post-economic collapse here. We're barely staying afloat. The unemployment rate just passed eighteen percent—we ourselves are reliant on goddamn Mexico for almost all our food. Our military's powerful, sure, everyone wants a piece of us, but we've got to think about defense first and foremost. Hell, the same thing that happened to you could happen to us, probably some basement-dwelling techhead has already bought or been handed the technology. To tell you the truth, I wouldn't be surprised if we ended up being the real target. You guys were probably just a test run."

Prime Minister Waterman gritted his teeth as the colour drained from his cheeks. "So, it's look out for number one then, is it?"

"I wish it weren't so, I really do. America simply can't afford to come to anyone's aid right now. I mean, I know the history, but you know as well as I do that our countries' 'special friendship' has been in name only for a long time. Just don't tell the kids."

"They're not children anymore, I'm afraid," said Waterman. "They've grown up, and they're very angry."

"I've been prayin' for ya. So has my wife. We're all praying for England over here."

"Then God help us all," the Prime Minister said. He touched End on his console. His brow furrowed intensely but his hands did not shake. He would not waste any more time. There were other important calls to make.

~

Kit bit nervously at her thumbnail as she waited in the alley behind the club, checking her cleverband for texts.

"C'mon, Sailor. Where are you?" Her breath ghosted puffs in the deathly cold London night.

As if he'd heard, her cleverband vibrated and the text indicator lit up.

It's a madhouse! I'm inside already, the message read.

Kit grinned crookedly, leaning back against the wall. She tapped the heel of her boot against the brick, feeling the thump-thump pulse of the music through its layers, the war cry bass and the thundering kick drum that was too loud even for her. She edged towards the door, running her fingers along the exposed brick.

She knew Saint Fox had been missing his little friend lately. She'd taken it upon herself to find Sailor and try to remedy the situation. It seemed like everything Sam did lately was forced, like he was Sim Sam, puppeteering himself from some remote location. He needed someone, that much was obvious, and if it couldn't be her, it didn't matter. It might as well be anyone, as long as it delayed him doing something stupid in a drug-induced haze. So when Sailor texted her tonight asking what she was up to, she'd put down her guitar and put on her dancing shoes.

The club was called Visionairee. She peeked inside, taking in the electric blue lighting, the soft, gauzy white fabric strewn across the ceiling, the black and white posters of famous revolutionaries and cult heroes—Che Guevara, MLK Jr., Malcolm X, Angela Davis, Gloria Steinem, Phoolan Devi.

A large-scale poster of Saint Fox, in a very James Dean-esque pose, was positioned near the front of the club.

Thwack! A dart landed on the poster of Sam, inches away from his crotch.

"Almost hit a bullseye there, 'ey love?" Sailor, clad head to toe in white leather, sauntered towards her with oversized drink in hand, no doubt something disgustingly sweet, she noted, as she caught sight of at least six rainbow-coloured cherries drowning in the bright purple liquid.

"'Ello, Sailor," Kit greeted him, lifting her chin. "So what's a nice girl like me doing in a place like this?"

"Thought this'd be your scene," he said, eyes sparkling. "Thought that photograph of Patty Hearst over there with her big gun was you for a second."

"There is a resemblance," Kit said, smiling.

They made their way over to a more sparsely populated area of the bar where people could actually hear what their mates were saying. Sailor hopped up on the barstool, his trousers squeaking against the leather cushion. A wubwoof remix of "Neon Angels on the Road to Ruin" bled in bells and whistles across the soundsystem.

"So. How is he?" Sailor picked a blue-coloured cherry stem from his drink, tying it into a knot with his tongue before chewing it into a stringy pulp.

"Not great. Think he misses you. He...I don't know what's wrong with him," she finished. It was the truth. Though having convinced the masses he was a rock star revolution hero, it seemed he was faltering in the wake of everything they'd worked for coming to fruition.

"He's drinking more, ain't he?" Sailor took a sip from the sugary violet monstrosity that was his drink and winced.

"He should try this, would put him off alcohol for at least three days."

The bartender set a gin and tonic down in front of Kit.

"Cheers," she said, lifting her index finger, ready to swipe.

The bartender simply raised a tattooed eyebrow.

"Oh. Oh, how stupid of me. Hold on." She lifted her cleverband. "GiveNGet," she spoke into it.

"First drinks are on the house tonight. After that, we're a GGcoin-only establishment."

"Of course," Kit said, feeling foolish. "Sorry."

"No worries, love. Drink up." He slapped his large palm down on the bar next to her drink, smiling a black-toothed grin before walking away.

"Easy mistake," said Sailor, leaning forward against the bar. "Instinct. We're all doing it."

"Yeah, but I of all people should know better," Kit said, running the thumb of her other hand over the Dot and wondering if surgical removal really was as painless as everyone said. "How'd this place get up and running again so fast?"

"Independent. Did you not see the posters?" he teased. "Markus owns this place, the big guy with the black teeth who just served your drink. Don't got ties to no big corp or nothing. Keep what they make, except for taxes. Now, they keep what they make."

"It almost seems too easy," she said.

"Yeah, for now, until they come after us with bulletproof metal hounds and start ripping our faces off."

Kit laughed, raising her glass for a toast. As the clink of glasses dissolved into the strains of whatever Post4-punk song was playing, she wondered how long it would actually be before the dogs arrived.

"You should talk to him," she said. "Maybe he'd clean up his act a bit if you guys patched up whatever's gone wrong between you." She paused, taking a sip of her drink. "Actually, what has gone wrong between you? I don't even know."

"Doubt you wanna hear it. But if you must know, he broke my heart a little."

"Think that's kind of his M.O.," she said quietly, glancing at him out of the corner of her eye. "Why'd you wanna talk to me about it?"

"Don't know," Sailor said, leaning forward on his elbows. "Was drunk. You're nice. You don't bullshit. My cleverband thought your name sounded like 'cab'."

Kit let out an uninhibited laugh, which proved to be contagious. The laughter between them died down and was followed by a comfortable silence. A K-pop cover of Ani DiFranco's "32 Flavors" played, barely audible Minnie Mouse vocals strung between tin can drum snaps.

"Well, I'd better be going," she said. "Can I tell Sam you said hi?"

"Depends. When you gonna see him next?"

"Tomorrow. Band practice."

"That still happening? Thought the band was just for the revolution."

"I don't know," she said, smiling with her eyes, "if we stop playing, they might stop revolting."

"Tell him whatever you want. Or you could tell him the truth, that I said he's an arsefaced twat, and I'm stopping by the flat later to get the rest of my stuff."

"I'll tell him the second half of that, though he won't be there. He's hiding out at Jeeves'." Kit hopped off the barstool. "Now, don't drink too many of those, or eat too many of these." She picked up a bright orange maraschino cherry, popping it in her mouth.

"Oi! Markus says if I eat enough of those I'll turn into a princess," Sailor protested.

"You already are one, my dear. The prettiest princess I ever knew."

"Yeah, yeah. Get outta here, go on with your bad self and make love to your fiddle."

"Best lover I ever had," she said, blowing him a kiss. With a flurry of black skirts and blacker hair, she was gone.

Chapter Twenty-Four

GOOD LOVE IS HARD TO FIND

Sam walked down Brixton Road, past a graffitied wall that read, YOU BUY, YOU DIE, in rough, red lettering. Another one in green further down the street read TAKEBACK. He saw signs of the usual rebel chaos—overturned rubbish bins, petty vandalism, cherry bombs thrown through broken shop windows. The work of the kids. They were the first to use the cryptocurrency, started trading it amongst one another for decals and patches with GiveNGet printed on them, for blocks of code and gear, motherboards, circuits, amplifiers and synthesisers, for packs of ramen and bottles of Lucozade.

He'd heard through the grapevine that the new system was working on a larger scale, that many businesses had taken to it with surprisingly little provocation. Everyone seemed to be on board.

Around the next corner, a look from two kids smoking cigs against a dirty wall said recognition to Sam. He thought he saw them gesture to him, stand up from the wall, and make their way towards him.

He put on his sunglasses and broke into a run, however short-lived—his endurance was shot from drugs and lack of sleep. He'd taken to chopping up his pills and snorting them; it felt godawful but it got them into his bloodstream faster. A half-hour fully aware and waiting was too much.

He needed to get out. Away from bloody England. He halted his run, resting his hands on his knees and catching his breath.

Were the authorities looking for him? Were airlines accepting GGcoin? What was happening on a global scale? Surely there had been widespread panic at the Exchange, on Wall Street, the entire bloody interconnected web of fuckery. What were they all doing right about now?

Probably covering their asses with their own imaginary currency, he thought. Type in a number and it's real.

Where would I go if I could? he wondered. I'd go to an island, to Fiji. No one will look for me there. I'll lay in the sun all day and eat lots of fish and bananas. I'll get clean and I won't even notice because there will be no reason to get high—no pressure, no wondering if I'm gonna get arrested around the next damn corner, no eager young faces staring at me like I have all the answers, waiting for me to give them a sign.

Saint Fuckin' Fox, fine and dandy. Left his heart in a bowl of candy. Was a total blam blam, didn't give a damn, he fucked off to an island, watched everyone drown in the sand.

Sam composed his final Saint Fox and The Independence song in his head. It would end with a whirling guitar solo by Kit, the notes spiraling down, down, down into a frenzied abyss, the lights cutting out on the final note, the audience left in darkness.

Kit. He wondered if she would go to Fiji with him.

Nah, she wouldn't, he figured. She's a true revolutionary, wants to see this thing through, I bet.

Left my heart in a rusty tin can, did it all just to prove I'm a man. When all's said and done, I do what I can. Just like anyone. Just like any man.

Do what you want Foxy, don't make a sound. Do what you want, get out of town.

~

International trade was shot. Nothing coming in, nothing going out. Automobile enthusiasts were positively suicidal, driving their Maseratis off the nearest cliff, no doubt.

They were cut off. For many it was business as usual, for others it was a total disaster.

Lucas Norcoford of Primary Illusion Industries had twenty-two billion pounds tucked away in foreign banks that he currently could not access. To acquire his favourite kosher foods he'd sent out various assistants to the shops—some took the risk of using the Dot, others used GGcoin, both currencies in circulation at different levels. Ma and pa shops began accepting GGcoin seemingly overnight, several medium-sized businesses were hybrids for the time being, larger stores like Tesco were still on the old system, or shut down in many areas as they tried to figure out a solution. Signs popped up in shop windows—"GGcoin Only," "Still Open – Virus Free," "Open: Buy at Your Own Risk. No Liability."

Either way, any purchase these days was paid for in faith.

Lucas Norcoford himself had utilised the Dot just last week to purchase a pack of Stop Smoke nicotine pins. Running out of them was not an option. He needed at least four of the damn things poking into his skin for them to have even the slightest affect.

His assistant Tom had acquired the GiveNGet app and showed him how it worked. Norcoford was not impressed. What was he supposed to do with 10,000 units of imaginary currency? He had been on the phone for five days straight, demands growing hotter and hotter, words like *outrageous, unacceptable, lawsuit,* falling from his lips, while a maddeningly calm voice on the other end of the line told him *Just taking necessary precautions, I'm sure this is only temporary. The money is safe—just on hold.*

Foreign banks, foreign corporations, the United States—all seemed to be under the impression that the British pound was currently worthless. After all, it stood to reason that whether a London merchant attempted to transfer pennies or millions, he could not do so without risking infection.

Rage sat in Lucas's gut like a stone, his blood pressure rising by the minute. Today he had inserted six nicotine pins at recommended acupuncture points with help from Cindy, his personal wellness therapist—two in his temples, two in his feet, two at the intersection between neck and shoulders. The ones positioned there left him unable to move his arms.

"Cindy!" He yelled for her over the com system.

She appeared as summoned, dressed head to toe in yellow-green linen—the colour chosen to promote the most soothing aura to Mr. Norcoford's psyche, as was the colour of her hair, dyed a greenish blonde, just three shades darker than her uniform and cut in a loose, asymmetrical bob.

"Yes, Mr. Norcoford? What's it you need, love?"

"A fucking twenty-two billion GGcoin, apparently," he said. "Like I worked this hard for nothing. Who do these radical morons think they are?" He gritted his teeth, grinding down hard enough to do damage to his nano-diamond bridgework. "Other than that, take these goddamn pins out, I can barely move."

"Of course. I'm sorry they aren't working out for you, would you like them in another location?" The scrub-style shirt on her was loose-fitting, and as she leaned over him, Norcoford was sorry to discover she'd worn a bra today, flesh-coloured and unexciting. He inhaled sharply through his nose.

"Stick 'em in the back of my left hand," he said. "Only use the right one anyway. Then find Michelle, tell her I need to see her." Michelle was his personal assistant, and *she* knew how to dress, skirts in either black or red with a tight fit that showed off her ass. She had this one little red miniskirt in animal-friendly leather that practically made him weep when she bent over. He kept his filing cabinets low, filled with obsolete duplicate paper copies of everything.

"That'll do ya," Cindy said. "Your hands feel a little dry. Want me to rub some of that Vitamin X cream on them?"

"Later," Norcoford said. "Go get Michelle."

Cindy exited the spacious office, replaced only moments later by Michelle.

"You rang?" she asked, her hands on her hips and a knowing grin on her lips. Her ruby hair fell in loose waves across her face, only half of it her own, and her black dress clung to her figure like paint.

"Hey, baby," he said, running a sweaty hand along his designer-clad thigh. "You've gotta do a better job organizing these contacts, I couldn't find my own mother in them." He gestured through the projected dashboard—17K-pixel SO-LED resolution and ninety inches wide, dancing on thin air above his cordovan cherry-stained desk.

"Oh, Norc, I've explained it a dozen times. It's all very simple." She walked over to stand between him and the display, leaning forward. "You touch here, wave to the left, then slide down here for alphabetical. You want categories? Wave twice to the left and slide your hand down."

Norcoford smirked, his small eyes narrowing. "Touch here," he repeated, placing his large palm against her waist, "and slide my hand where again, exactly?"

"You know where," she said, leaning forward to give him a better view as he thoroughly groped her ass.

"You're right," he said, "very easy."

"I hope this latest crisis doesn't affect that raise you promised me last week," she said as he slid his hand between her thighs, feeling the ribbed stripes of her stockings.

Norcoford grunted, really getting into mauling his sexy assistant. "Won't affect it at all. Don't you worry."

"Good, that's what I like to hear." Three years ago, Michelle had been repulsed by his nonstop come-ons, by his small, too-close together eyes piercing through her, his freakishly smooth skin, his once swollen gut now clamped firmly into place. Now, she got off and got off quickly from her manipulation of him. Men were so easy.

"I actually did need you to show me how to use my contacts," he said, slowly pulling her stockings down to her knees. "Anyone who steals from us is gonna pay."

Chapter Twenty-Five

A RUSH AND A PUSH AND THE LAND IS OURS

"How many of *those* messages have we received?" Jeeves inquired of Benson Bridges, seated on opposite sides of a folding table at the new headquarters of the Arcana. Benson's nose was buried in several screens as Jeeves milked him for the latest information.

"1,861 death threats, 5,793 general fuck-you-up threats," Benson said, slumping down further in his chair, exhausted from continuous sleep deprivation.

"And how many of these are we taking seriously?" Jeeves propped his feet up on the table, his crossed ankles twitching with nervous energy.

"It depends. Some were sent anonymously and I haven't been able to get past their VPNs yet, but we're working on it. I've got an alert set up for anything that hails from an IP within a five-kilometer radius of Westminster."

A loud beep from Benson's tablet startled the two men, both snapping their heads up like puppets.

"What was that?" Jeeves screeched.

"Oh, just needs an update," said Benson, his eyes scanning quickly across the display. "I gotta change the alert sounds on this thing."

"They're watching us," Jeeves tittered nervously.

"Course they are. That's what they do. But we're watching them, too. Plus, it's been this long, and still no one's shown up."

"They may be slow in gearing up, but they'll come," Jeeves said.

"They're calling us bioterrorists, you know. Next thing you know they'll get King Billy to sign a proclamation declaring us traitors to the Crown."

Jeeves closed his eyes, placing a thin cigar between his lips. His nerves popped and sizzled, a fact he wouldn't share with young Benson. The bastards had to pay, but he hoped the kids wouldn't. They would be fine. They had enough people on board, he knew it. You can't fight the masses.

"I'm sure they'd like to arrest everyone using GGcoin," Benson said, "but it's been catching on so fast they probably don't know where to start."

Jeeves sighed, holding onto the table by his feet and leaning so far back in his chair that it was only luck or incredible balance that kept him from falling. "They'll arrest Foxy first," he said. "Make an example of him." He dropped his legs from the table, the weight of the chair landing against the floor with a hollow, reverberating sound. "See that all members of our inner circle are present and accounted for, and that no one leaves without taking proper precautions. Especially Sam."

Benson pressed his specs against the bridge of his nose. "I'm a programmer, not the fucking underground railroad."

"You're getting cranky," Jeeves said, waving his fingers around in front of Bez's face until he swatted them away. "You need yer sippy cup?"

"Is this all a game to you? People we care about could die because of what we did." He paused. "Because of what I did," he added quietly.

"You lack faith, baby," said Jeeves, holding his own pointy chin in hand with his arm twisted at an impossible angle.

"Stop calling me 'baby'. I know it ain't exclusive to me but it's feckin' weird." Benson cracked his knuckles, kicking his chair in as he stood.

"Where're ya goin'?" Jeeves asked.

"To get some sleep," Benson gestured vaguely at his various holo displays. "Nothing's even making sense anymore."

"I never said you couldn't take a break." Jeeves smacked his lips in the air, placing his head atop tented fingertips. Benson left the room in silence.

By Jingo, it's not like I want any of these kids to suffer, Jeeves thought. The youth of this generation. You give them a little hard work and they crumble. Look at all we've accomplished! I couldn't have done it without them.

But this was war. Sacrifices had to be made. It was unfortunate, of course, indeed, it hurt his very soul. But he didn't make the rules—it was the law of the jungle.

Still, he worried. He saw their minds getting dark, and he saw them blaming him. Blaming him for giving them a purpose, these lost children who weren't there to see all the times the world spun round and then fell on its ass again.

He supposed it couldn't be helped. They were a product of their generation, after all.

~

His Majesty's Armed Forces contained 260,000 men and women who were children willing to die for King and Crown. They enlisted for all the wrong reasons. They enlisted because it was what their dads and grandads had done and they wanted to make them proud. They enlisted because they believed the adverts promising greatness and heroism.

They enlisted because they wanted to kill.

Prime Minister Waterman did not bother to pretend that he didn't have sovereign control over the Armed Forces, any phone calls to the King were made after orders had already been executed.

What affected the city of London affected the nation. The virus was spreading, reports of it popping up in York, in Manchester, in Devon, in Glasgow. While the city police scrambled around aimlessly trying to tame riots or Sherlock out the location of the terrorist movement's leaders, Waterman was preoccupied with arming his troops, preparing to fight technology with technology. A ragtag group of individuals held loosely together by strings of downtrodden camaraderie was no match for personnel armed with VLe .410 electronic smartguns.

Now he just had to wait. It wouldn't be long before these little terrorists made a big mistake.

His cabinet ministers agreed. The government was eighty-five percent funded by London banks. It was paramount they protect their investment, and everything else belonging to them.

"Prime Minister," Waterman's assistant said over the com system. "A Mr. Norcoford here to see you."

"Send him in please, Ben," Waterman said.

Lucas Norcoford entered the Prime Minister's office on shaky feet, dressed impeccably in suit and tie. His eyes were bloodshot and his hands clenched, fingernails digging into his palms.

"Norcoford," the Prime Minister's forgettable face schooled into pleasantry as he greeted the CEO.

"Hello, Harry," Norcoford breathed out, sinking into an oversized leather armchair opposite Waterman's desk. "Looks like you've done quite well for yourself. Most likely to end up P.M. indeed. The lads back at Eton got it right."

"Not much choice. It was either politics, or wind up CEO of some big corporation like you. I'd rather serve my country." Waterman ran his fingers across the smooth surface of his desk, his gaze of no discernible expression directed at his former schoolmate.

"Full of rubbish as usual, Waterman. We both know you're useless without people like me—everybody knows. Hell, that's why you called me here, isn't it? It isn't to talk about the good old days. We never were very good mates, after all."

"Of course." Waterman leaned forward. "Down to brass tacks, you know. Primary Illusion has always been key in funding our troops. And now, with everything at stake and these wolves amongst our sheep, you choose this inopportune moment to withdraw your support. I must ask why."

"Honestly, Harry," said Norcoford, his whole body pinched together as if in a vice, "you'd think they could get someone brighter than you to run the country. What kind of blockage have you got in your head that you don't already know the answer to that?" Norcoford pressed his index finger to his forehead, made impossibly smooth by botox and custom-manufactured ointment made from sheep's bladder.

"Guess I just wanted to hear you say it," said Waterman, crossing his long fingers. His expression seemed almost pleased. "You're money's locked up."

"Of course it's locked up. Switzerland won't make any transfers to London right now. Utterly ridiculous, really. They're not the ones who are infected. It's all one big scam. Deploy your fucking soldiers, Waterman."

"I'm about to, Lucas," Waterman said. "But the Chancellor wants to see the numbers add up. Your contribution is one we depend upon."

"Then make them add up." Norcoford ran a hand over his bald head. "You've been doing it for years, I'm sure. What do you want—my permission? Go ahead. Annihilate those mingebags."

Waterman, all business, produced a form on the display interface integrated into his desk. "Sign here," he said.

"What's this, an IOU?" asked Norcoford.

"Something like that."

"You'll have the money when I have it, old mucker." Norcoford hastily signed the digital form with his finger. "If and when you blast those bastards into their primordial particles."

"Thank you, Lucas. You can go now."

"That's it, eh? You're not going to offer me a brandy or cigar for old time's sake? To extend the royal hospitality on behalf of His Majesty?"

"We are at war, Mr. Norcoford," said Waterman, touching icons on his oversized display to organise and transmit. "Perhaps some other time."

Norcoford rose to his feet, his recently-shined shoes squeaking against the marble floor of Waterman's office. The tense set of his shoulders sat parallel with the lines of Waterman's display screen, rapidly displaying and analyzing numerical data.

"Good luck, Lucas," said Waterman as Norcoford strode towards the door.

"Same to you, Harry," he said over his shoulder. "Just like when we were kids. It's kill or be killed."

"It's not so bad as all that," said Waterman, adjusting the data with precise hand motions. "At least now we're the ones holding the rod."

"Spare the rod and spoil the children," Norcoford said as his hand clasped the brass doorknob.

"Don't you worry, Lecherous Luke," Waterman replied. "They shall not be spared."

Chapter Twenty-Six

FOLLOW THE COPS BACK HOME

D.I. David Ewan Thomas beat an ominous rhythm on the door of Sam Numan's flat at a quarter to two.

"Police! Open the door," he shouted.

Sailor, dressed in a teal green robe and white fuzzy slippers with polar bear heads on them, slid the metal door partway open, wide eyes taking in a pair of stocky and stern-looking officers.

"He's not here," he said. "Neither will I be in a moment. Just grabbing the last of my things, taking one last bath in the ol' tub..." He was cut off as the cops shoved the door open the rest of the way, barging past him into the flat.

"Where is he?" barked the second officer, a short man with a heavy brow.

"Hell if I know," Sailor said. "Saint Fox has scampered off. Either of you lads like a cold beverage?"

D.I. Thomas scoffed. "He could still be here. Search the place."

"Don't you need a warrant?" Sailor protested, but was thoroughly ignored as the officers stormed through the flat, emptying drawers and upending furniture.

"He ain't in the medicine cabinet," Sailor called out. "Surprisingly enough," he murmured to himself.

"What's this?" The detective held up a sandwich baggie half-full of white powder.

"It ain't baker's sugar," Sailor said, "and it ain't mine. You know how musicians are."

Detective Thomas handed the bag to his partner to tag and file. "You the flatmate?"

"Ex-flatmate. But you lads already knew that, right? Got all our photos in a spreadsheet somewhere next to our NI numbers, what our favourite flavour of ice cream is, whether we take it up the arse, and whether or not our dads or uncles or nans ever killed anyone."

"Keep talking, Margaret. One way or another, we're arresting a bioterrorist today."

"I ain't no bioterrorist," Sailor said. "I recycle."

The other officer, the one with eyebrows to spare, pushed an upended chair out of his way and grabbed Sailor roughly by the throat, shoving him against the wall.

"Tell us where Sam Numan is," he demanded.

"Your guess is as good as mine!" Sailor shrieked. "I ain't seen his slick self in weeks. Now let go of me."

"Not so easy," Eyebrows said. "That group. The inane Arcane. Bet you know where we can find 'em."

"I swear I don't," said Sailor, struggling weakly in the officer's grip. "I'm just here for me trousers and me bath beads. I've no idea what those revolutionaries are up to. Cross my heart and hope to wear plaid and stripes on the same day."

"Cheeky bugger," Detective Thomas said, striding over. "You use GGcoin?"

"Don't you?" Sailor asked. "You wanna risk infection?"

The officers shared a glance.

"We're wasting our time," said D.I. Thomas. "He don't know nothing. Let's get out of here."

They left as ungraciously as they had entered, leaving Sailor slumped against the wall, rubbing his neck. He glanced around the wrecked flat, his former home.

"We were sorta happy here for a while, weren't we, Sammy? Things sure got turned around. Stupid," he said, unsure if he was talking to himself or to the friend that wasn't there. Afternoon light streamed through the washed out blue curtains, the left one tattered at the edge where Binky had chewed on it. The worn blue couch where they'd spent many a night passed out on top of each other when they'd had too much to drink was flipped onto its back, mismatched cushions strewn across the navy blue carpet like forgotten islands.

Sam's things were gone. He'd packed up his guitars, his various array of garish women's blouses, his scribblings of song lyrics and funny little limericks he'd written on scraps of paper. Sailor knew Sam wouldn't be there when he stopped by—it wasn't safe. Still, a nonsensical part of him had hoped to run into him, although he'd told about a dozen people that he hoped to never lay eyes on that egomaniacal cokebrain again. Now the flat was a ghost house, just an empty unit in an overcrowded building, soon to be snatched up.

"Viva la revolucion," Sailor said.

~

"Come with me to Fiji," Sam Numan said to Kit Alysdair on a Friday night. They were standing in the stage wings shrouded by black curtains, moments after playing a secret intimate celebration show, so secret that the venue had changed seven times and the crowd was exclusively limited, but it would have to do. Jeeves had decided that the kids needed *a bolt of lightning to remind them to keep on keeping on*, as he put it. They would record the show and share it through the airwaves afterwards, though he lamented that a secondhand show on a sad flat piece of fiberglass was less than one hundredth as exciting as being present for a live performance.

It was enough for Sam. He was more than happy to play the rock star again, if only for a night.

Saint Fox was decked out head to toe in leather and lace. Black glitter on his eyelids and white lightning coursing through his veins. The show that night was as sweet as it had ever been, in a club so small and obscure it felt like the first show they'd ever played. Sam shimmied and shook like a fallen prince, a junkie love slave. His vocals screeched and soared, his guitar squealed and sang, almost as if it were trying to get away from him, terrified of his mania as it flew high on the frontman's coattails.

Kit had noticed the extra surge of energy Saint Fox possessed tonight, waves of adrenaline pouring out of him in cascades and whips. He had more lung capacity, leapt through the air in defiance of gravity, was stronger, faster, harder, better, fucking sexy if she had the balls to admit it.

And terrifying.

Sweat poured down Sam's neck and he dabbed at it with a towel, most of the liquid escaping to trail down his clavicle into the V of the ridiculous shiny charcoal vest he wore with no shirt underneath. He jogged circles backstage, trying to shake off the excess energy.

It wasn't cutting it.

Sam wrapped his hand around the back of Kit's neck, twining his fingers in her wild hair and pulling her firmly to him, kissing her without shyness or pretense.

She placed her palms against his chest, her own post-show adrenaline coursing through her veins and making it nearly impossible to stop. Kissing Sam felt like playing her guitar in front of tens of thousands, like plugging into a live wire. Her long list of reasons for turning him down that usually played in the back of her mind were silent.

"Been waiting forever to do that," Sam said. His hand trailed down her arm to hold hers as he led her towards the dressing room.

She didn't say anything, but her eyes never left his and her hand gripped his tighter. He pulled her into the dimly lit dressing room, clothes and makeup scattered everywhere, and shut the door. Within minutes he had her up on the vanity countertop and her skirt pushed up to her waist.

"What was that you said about Fiji?" she asked breathlessly.

"We're going. Right after this," he said, dropping to his knees.

"Why would we do that?" she asked with a laugh, bracing her hands against the counter.

"Just need a little break," he said, running his tongue along the inside of her thigh. "Come with me. It'll be great." His breath quickened as he slid his hands inside her stockings, yanking them down to her knees.

"Wait, wait," she said, grabbing both his hands in hers and hating herself a little. "We can't go to Fiji. Even if there were any reason to do so—the airports are a disaster right now. You might think they'd let you on a plane 'cause you're a celebrity, but well...you'd have to be any celebrity other than you."

There's gotta be a way," Sam said, standing abruptly and rubbing his fingers together like he wanted a cigarette. "Commercial flights might be on hold for the time being, but someone's operating somewhere. Hell, I'll bet Montreal knows a guy."

Kit sighed, wishing they could go back to three minutes ago. "We've just set into motion a plan to solve the problem of economic disparity right here, on our home soil, and you want to leave?" Her voice was a sing-song, a lyrical breath against the skin that hardly sounded like admonishment.

She wanted to be angrier at him, the righteous indignation she displayed primarily for show. Mostly she just felt a horrible mixture of turned on and sorry for him, that foolish, inescapable sexual-maternal paradox that men inevitably evoked. Damn his girlish face and gaunt cheekbones, his big watery eyes that could never decide which colour they were. Damn him.

"Come with me, darlin'," he insisted, breaking out his sideways smile and placing his hands atop hers on her knees, letting his fingers play with hers. "We don't have to take responsibility for none of this. Let Jeeves and them deal with whatever comes next. It's his revolution anyway, not mine. Hell, if he didn't have a tendency to rub people the wrong way he wouldn't need me at all, could have done it all himself, could have been Saint Fox. He is Saint Fox."

Kit considered his proposition while simultaneously chastising herself for doing so. "You're crazy. Everything's fine, it's all fine. You're overstimulated. You just need to rest for a week or so. I'd tell you to wait until this feeling blows over, but I'm afraid that meanwhile you'd just ingest whatever mind-altering substances you can get your hands on."

"That's an excellent point," he said, taking a step back. "Where's the booze?"

"Fuck's sake," she said, handing him a fifth of whiskey from the myriad of half-empty bottles littering the vanity she was sitting on. She pulled up her skirt and stockings. "I'm an enabler is what I am. Look at me."

"I'm lookin'," he said, letting half the bottle's contents pour down his throat.

"Yeah, well don't," said Kit, scrubbing over her face with both hands.

"This is Glastonbury all over again. What's a guy gotta do to get into you, huh?" His eyes were dancing firelights and that stupid smirk was still on his face.

"Not think he's entitled to, for one thing." She tried her best to look stern, channeling her sixth form maths teacher, crossing her legs and straightening her spine.

Sam continued to grin wickedly, smiling around the bottle as he downed the rest of the whiskey. "Come to Fiji with me." He walked towards her again, bracketing his arms around her against the countertop. He stared over her shoulder at himself in the mirror, admiring their reflections. "We're such a fucked up, beautiful rock star cliché right now."

"Why do you want me to go to Fiji with you?"

"'Cause I like ya."

Kit shook her head. "That's not good enough."

"What would make it good enough?"

"I don't know. Just…stay. See this thing through. The fans are counting on you, everyone is. I know it's rough with everything up in the air right now, but if you take off out of the blue, it'll just make things worse."

Sam leaned his forehead against hers, shutting his eyes. "You're always right, aren't you?" he said, touching her cheek. "Yeah yeah, I know. I know, I know, I know." He punctuated each 'I know' with a slap of his palm against the countertop.

"Good, saves me the breath," she said, leaning back against the mirror. The bright bulbs cast her in a yellow-white, incandescent glow.

Sam pressed up against her. Kit thought he was going to kiss her again. Instead, he traded his empty whiskey bottle for a shyte brand of vodka two-thirds full. "Well, if you're not interested, I'm out of here," he said, swigging from his new bottle. "Cheers, little Miss rock n' roll."

Her pretty lips parted, then closed again as a retort failed to surface. The door to the dressing room clanged shut behind Saint Fox. She unscrewed the top from another of the bottles beside her. Silver tequila.

She took a long drink. The acrid liquor only made the
blood in her veins burn hotter.

Chapter Twenty-Seven

THE DRUGS DON'T WORK

Charlotte Piebald was running a fever of 37.7 degrees. She'd been checking her temperature regularly on the hour—it hadn't changed much in the past three days.

Doctor Wender would be by any moment now—the Piebalds were one of the very few who could afford a family doctor that made house calls. Charlotte propped herself up in bed, her shoulder-length, chestnut-coloured hair fanned out against a small mountain of damask-patterned pillows. She wore a set of peach-coloured Nancy Miller silk pajamas, a lavender and rosemary-filled sachet pillow resting gently against her forehead. A lightweight crystal glass of electrolyte-enhanced water and a bottle of paracetamol were within arm's reach atop her antique solid oak nightstand.

Dear god, I'm dying, thought Charlotte. Never in a thousand years would I have guessed I'd become a victim of terrorism. How naïve of me.

Besides the fever, numerous symptoms had begun to manifest over the past few days. All-over body aches, particularly in the shoulders and lower back. Her stomach refused anything other than consommé and cabbage. Her skin was dry, her hair and nails brittle. She'd spent a small fortune on hydro-synthesised essential oils and Nuvo-Botanica intensive therapy products before coming to the grim realization that they simply weren't having any effect.

The confusion was the worst for Charlotte. I'm nothing if I don't have my mind, she thought. My business will be ruined. It'll end up in the hands of my cousin Reagan, that little Scottish bitch. She'll take my lovely designs and turn them into something tacky and dreadful, all metal studs and garish, bright colours. And rhinestones, god forbid. It seemed Charlotte couldn't hold onto a thought for longer than a few seconds. I haven't had anxiety this bad since university, Charlotte realised, as a cold tremor ran down her spine.

A knock at her bedroom door broke her out of contemplation.

"Ms. Piebald?" The doctor's soft voice sounded muffled from outside the door.

"Yes, doctor?" Charlotte managed in a thin voice. "Please come in."

The doctor entered quietly, removing his coat and hat and placing them on a seat near the bedroom door. Doctor

Wender was thin-haired and forgettable-looking, and spoke in an even voice that never housed alarm no matter how grave the situation. He picked up a floral-upholstered chair, bringing it over to sit by Charlotte's bedside.

"How are we feeling today?" he asked.

"We…are feeling absolutely dreadful," Charlotte said, coughing a bit for good measure. "You've got to get online right away doctor, and use your connections to get in touch with whoever's developed a cure."

"A cure…I'm afraid it's too soon to talk cures, Ms. Piebald."

"Charlotte," she said.

"Charlotte. I'm afraid it's too soon to talk cures. All we can do for now is treat the symptoms, which we discussed previously over the phone. Have you noticed any changes since then?" The doctor activated his cleverband, switching its recorder to 'ON'.

"Well, the headaches have gotten worse, for one. Paracetamol simply isn't cutting it anymore; you'll have to prescribe me something stronger. And I've been having terrible insomnia."

"I have a couple scripts for you that should help—my staff has already forwarded them to your account. Just open up our office's app at any chemist's and they'll be able to fill the order for you," the doctor said, without so much as taking his patient's temperature.

"Thank you, doctor," said Charlotte weakly.

"Remember to get lots of bed rest," Doctor Wender said, rising to leave. "And drink lots of water. One of the scripts I gave you is for Vitalica, something I've been prescribing to all my patients who've shown symptoms of the Dot virus. It should give you enough energy to perform your day-to-day activities, buy us some time while we search for a cure."

"That'll have to do, I suppose," said Charlotte. "Is there any way of knowing how advanced the disease is? Aren't there some tests you should be running?"

"Unnecessary," the doctor answered, scratching his chin. "I can tell just by looking at you, and from the symptoms you've reported. You're likely in Phase II of the Dot virus. This isn't cause for alarm. Our projections are that patients ought to be able to lead normal lives for years in Phase II, with no guarantee that they will ever progress to Phase III. Of course, no one knows yet what happens in Phase III—all we can do is speculate. It's simply too soon to tell." The doctor put his arms through his long grey overcoat, then reached for his hat.

"I've heard the disease progresses slowly," Charlotte said. "Have there been any fatalities?"

"That information isn't available at the moment," said Doctor Wender. "It's hard to obtain accurate data, you know, special interest groups wanting to set the death count artificially low. My guess would be that there are far more fatalities than reported. The elderly, for instance, anyone with a compromised immune system would deteriorate rapidly, as opposed to the disease's typically slow progress rate. But, Ms. Piebald, as I said before, we simply don't have enough information. Take the medicine prescribed as instructed by your chemist, and get lots of sleep. Best of luck to you." He tipped his hat, exiting the room.

Charlotte lay back against her mound of pillows, quickly sending a message via her cleverband to tell her assistant to head to the chemist's right away. It seemed all her staff were now using that new currency, avoiding infection. Streetwise survival skills of the working class. As for her, it didn't matter if she kept using the Dot to make purchases—she'd already been infected—what difference did it make now? Charlotte knew how diseases work. Once you catch a virus, you can't catch it again. It was like chickenpox, which had sent her home from year two at the academy for almost a month and caused her to fall behind.

She wasn't sure how payroll and reimbursements were currently being handled, trusting that her accountant was capably managing the upheaval in her absence. She was simply too ill to attend to business matters right now.

Doctor Wender was looking a bit poorly himself, thought Charlotte. Poor man. I wonder if he knows.

~

Sam sat up in a hard bed that wasn't his, tangled in green plaid sheets that smelled like daisies and cheap perfume, in one of several bunk beds where Jeeves housed any Arcana who needed a roof over his or her head. The noise from outside, where Jeeves ring-led the circus's hustle and bustle, was no match for the pounding in his head.

He'd been in the middle of packing a bag for Fiji, then Benson had burst in sounding urgent and paranoid, telling him that under no circumstances was he to leave Jeeves' flat, and he'd been too high and too apathetic to protest. It seemed he'd been in this miserable bed ever since. A sad A-minor melody wove through his head, something about dying young. He tried to think of something else to rhyme it with besides 'son of a gun'. He couldn't think of anything.

It was like being an insect at the bottom of a vacuum cleaner, he thought. More dirt and dust and debris keeps getting sucked in, and you choke. You don't see the light.

You think of just a few seconds ago when you were on the outside, but it's pointless to think of that now, because you are trapped, and all you can do is wait to be thrown out with the rest of the trash.

Sam buried his head under a bright red pillow with too much stuffing. Despite his best efforts to drown out the clang of pots and pans, the *bee-boop swish!* of electronic devices, and half-heard conversations, a voice sounding like a panicked train conductor announcing that no one would be getting off at the next stop broke through the din.

"...and then they just came in and demolished the flat," he was saying. "Those berks barely had time to throw a few unimaginative insults at me in between smashing things up like gorillas."

"Did you ever think...that they might have followed you here?" Jeeves' shrill trill was unmistakable. Sam visualised glitter and feathers flying through the air in a spastic rage.

"I waited a while," said the messenger, who was obviously Sailor, Sam realised as some of the noise in his head cleared. "No one followed me here. Besides, I changed before I left, made sure I blended in. Look how I'm dressed, ugh!"

"It is rather bland, baby," Jeeves admitted.

"Anyway, I just wanted to warn you all, let you know they're after 'im," Sailor finished. "He here?" he asked, looking around.

"Nappy napping," said Jeeves, "but I bet he's wakey woken now. He's in one of the cellar bunks."

"I'll just...pop down and make sure he's not dead, shall I?"

"Suit yerself, baby. An' tell him nap time is over, we need to rally."

Sailor tiptoed down to the cellar quiet as a new bride, thinking maybe Sam would be passed out cold and he'd just stare at him for a bit, then leave.

No such luck.

"I can smell you and hear your twinkle toes from 'ere," Sam mumbled. "You smell like burnt sugar and that godawful aftershave."

"Nice to know you still recognise me by scent alone," Sailor said, stepping into the streaks of light filtering through the blinds, casting his face in shadowed stripes. "But you probably heard me upstairs, too."

"Yeah, I heard you and Jeeves clucking. What's this about coppers at our flat?"

"They want you bad," Sailor said, staring at his fingernails. "Must be super fans or something. And it ain't our flat anymore."

"I thought I only had one super fan," Sam said, sitting up in the bunk and hunching over so he wouldn't hit his head. He scratched at his stomach, having fallen asleep with no shirt on in a pair of ill-fitting jeans.

"Not anymore. The spit and polish have come right off you. Just blow on it a little and all the sparkle fades away." Sailor stood with his hands on his hips, looking uncharacteristically menacing in a black zip hoodie and dark grey jeans, no makeup decorating his angular face. His big, dark eyes blinked steadily and his hair was coloured straw blonde today.

"Why am I always apologizing to you," Sam moaned, placing the heel of his hand against his forehead. "I swear, you get put off more than anyone I know. You're good at making other people feel like things are their fault."

"It is your fault," Sailor said with a jut of his chin. He walked over to stand by the bunk, leaning an arm against one of the wooden posts. "So, you want my tips for how to survive in prison?"

Sam groaned again, dropping his elbows to his knees and burying his face in his hands. "My head hurts."

"If you're angling for a backrub, you're knocking at the wrong door," said Sailor, drumming his fingertips against the bed frame. "You gonna hole up here for a while?"

"Ain't got much choice. Where're you staying at?"

"Was staying at Ron's. You remember him...that creeper from Lancaster with the big muscles and wonky eyes."

"God, I knew it," said Sam. "Don't go back there. He'll murder you in your sleep."

"I might die at his hand by erotic asphyxiation. That would be fun, wouldn't it?"

"Just stay here, you loon, and don't cause any trouble. There's plenty of room."

"Why, you miss me or something?" Sailor cocked his head, looking smug.

"I told you, I'm just trying to keep you from getting murdered."

"You do care!" Sailor exclaimed, throwing his arms out in an exaggerated display. He sat down next to Sam in the bunk, tentatively reaching a hand out to rub slow circles against his back. "Come on now, I'll give you that backrub. Just don't tell anyone I've forgiven you already."

"Secret's safe with me," Sam said, breathing out and relaxing into the massage.

"You've got to lay off the party goodies a bit, mate," Sailor said.

"I must really have a problem if you're the one telling me that." Sam yawned, feeling the need for yet more sleep wash over him.

"Uh uh," Sailor said when he saw that he was drifting. "Jeeves said nap time's over. He wants to go over phase twenty-seven or whatever of his master plan."

"It's not like he actually needs my input," Sam said. "Why don't you go? You be Saint Fox."

"How about you be Saint Fox..." Sailor's right hand drifted down to squeeze his bum, "and I stick my hand up your arse and work you like a puppet! Then you won't have to do anything."

Sam squirmed around, laughing. "That sounds brilliant, and also terrible."

"Just trying to help."

"You already have," he turned around, kissing Sailor on the nose.

"Glad I could contribute to the cause." Sailor hesitated momentarily before placing his hands at Sam's waist, dancing fingers along the waistband of his jeans. Sam hung his head low, catching Sailor's lips before pulling back and looking at him with a cheeky grin, one eyebrow raised.

Needing no further invitation, Sailor crawled into his lap, licking at Sam's neck and deftly undoing the button on his trousers.

Someone in the doorway cleared their throat. Alarmed, the two men quickly shuffled away from each other, Sam hitting his head on the bunk above.

"Ow, fuck!"

"I see you two have kissed and made up." Kit stood in the doorway, drumming her fingertips against the frame.

Sam quickly buttoned his trousers, smoothing his hair back with his palms and resting them behind his neck. "How long have you been standing there?"

"Long enough to notice you're not wearing underwear," she said, glancing down and fiddling with the strings on her bracelet.

"S'cause I usually do his laundry," Sailor said, leaning his head against Sam's shoulder.

"Well, I'll leave you boys to it then." She smacked her palm against the doorframe, turning to leave.

Sam stood up. "Wait, hold on a sec."

"Where'ya goin'?" asked Sailor, pulling at a loose thread on Sam's trousers.

"Just stay here. I'll be back in a second," he said, hurriedly pulling on a t-shirt.

"Suit yerself." Sailor flopped back onto the tiny bed, humming "Love Junkie," his favourite Saint Fox and The Independence song to date.

Kit was trying and failing to light a cigarette with a finicky lighter when Sam caught up with her round the back of the flat.

"Here, lemme get that for you."

"S'fine, I got it," she mumbled, finally managing to light it on the next try.

"Hey, so um, what you saw in there, that was…"

"It's fine, really," she cut him off. "What, you think I didn't know?" Her eyes were hooded as she stared off into the distance, arms wrapped around herself to keep out the cold.

"Know…what do you know?" Sam asked, shivering a bit and hopping up and down as the trickling rain outside grew to a steady pour. "Know that I'm gay? I'm not. I'm bi, I guess, I mean if you have to put a label on it. It's just…like, people, not gender, right?"

"I know." The wind picked up then, blowing mist from the rain in their faces that clung to their hair and the tips of their eyelashes.

"I like you, too, you know." He removed the cigarette from between her lips, taking a drag.

"I know," she said again. "I told you, it's fine. I wasn't just saying it. It really is fine."

"Yeah?"

The street lamps flickered on as the sky grew dark. Kit saw their light reflected in Sam's eyes as she at last made eye contact.

"So… no Fiji?" she asked, a small smile on her lips.

"No Fiji," he said. "Anyway, I'm sick of planes." He closed in on her, sheltering out the rain with his back and bracketing her in against the brick wall. He kissed her twice. Tentatively at the first, then slowly the second time, sucking her bottom lip between his and pressing closer. When they broke apart she breathed in, smiling softly with her eyes cast downwards, watching the drops fall against the pavement.

"We good?" he asked.

"Yeah. We're good."

And they were. It truly didn't bother her, the Sam and Sailor thing, at least not by much. She wondered if maybe it should, if her jealousy deficiency made her somehow less human. Was it because Sailor was a bloke? It didn't matter either way, she decided. Sam wasn't the kind of guy you kept in a gilded cage. She wasn't the kind of girl you kept in one.

Love is always a gift, and one should be open to receiving as much of it as possible.

The rain slowed to a trickle as the sun set in hues of orange and gold. It was as though the weekend had arrived, and felt, for a moment, that it was here to stay.

Chapter Twenty-Eight

LULLABY

Benson zoomed the camera in on a tight shot of Janus Jeeves, looking abnormally solemn and refined. He was seated upon his blue velvet throne, jewelry and makeup kept to a minimum, classy shit—a black and silver pinstriped suit, brass bangles on his wrists, a thin pair of stainless-steel-rimmed specs, wing-tipped shoes, and the faintest smudge of charcoal eyeliner. He sat with both his feet on the ground, back straight, hands on his knees. He did not shake and he did not shiver.

Saint Fox stood to his left just out of frame. It had been Jeeves' intention to have Sam as the focus of the advert, but the lad looked like he was feeling about as under the weather as those he would promise to cure. He'd lost weight and was sweating a bit, thin beads misting on his forehead and upper lip. Jeeves had given him a few lines to speak, hoping he could handle as much.

Keeping Sam at the forefront of the movement was in the Arcana's best interest. After all, it was his face that people recognised. Honestly, it was a bit of a blow to Jeeves' ego that he still needed the rock star, but kids these days have such short attention spans, and it's best not to disrupt them from the familiar. Besides, he liked the lad.

At least Sam looked the part. Eyes wide, glittering and earnest, tight black trousers, hair slicked back, a techy-looking black denim jacket with rivets and bolts he had borrowed from the past lives of Montreal.

Time for the second act.

Janus Jeeves focused his attention at the camera.

"Ladies, gents, and those both or neither, have you been feeling a bit poorly lately? Everything not right as rain? Do your side effects include nausea, heartburn, swelling, rapid heartbeat, ulcers, weakness, jitters, rapid weight gain, rapid weight loss, confusion, memory loss, depression, anxiety, altercations with loved ones? Some of the above? All of the above? At least one or more of the above?" He leaned forward, cocking his head to the side. The camera zoomed out to reveal the king on his throne, his knight in shining leather by his side.

Sam spoke in a strong, steady voice, summoning his stage presence through shattered nerves. "We're not heartless. We don't want to hurt anyone. The goal of our mission is not to terrorise, it's to revolutionise. We never meant to cause any harm, but drastic measures were necessary."

Jeeves patted Sam's arm, staring up at him sagely. "The lad speaks the truth. And today, we're here to tell you that we don't plan to leave you high and dry. The virus...it was never meant to harm. It was meant to heal. And heal you we will," he finished with a wink.

"We have the cure," Sam announced. "We're giving it out on a first come, first serve basis, but supplies will never run out. Members of our coalition will be dispensing the cure at various locations listed on our portal."

Jeeves crossed one leg over the other. "Now, I know what you clever clogs are thinking. But, as the saying goes, 'Fool me once, shame on you. Fool me twice, shame on me.' The cure only works once. A reinfection will synthesise differently, and this patch will be unable to counteract it, so don't reinfect yourselves by using the Dot again once you take the cure. We invite you to get clean, and join our system of equality. Don't waste time. Log in now. Be safe. Be healthy."

"Never use the Dot again, never get the virus again. It's that simple. Our network grows by the hour. Millions are using GGcoin. Join us and be free," Sam affirmed. He looked straight into the camera, and held his shaking hands behind his back.

Benson touched the Stop icon on the recording.

"Well," said Jeeves, immediately dangling off the chair sideways at an impossible angle now that the camera was off. "How d'ya think it went, Foxy?"

"Fine. God, how's Bez able to create an epidemic *and* a cure? He's a bloody programmer, not a doctor."

"Aww baby, you know human bodies are all hardwired now. He can create a virus, he can create anti-virus software. He just writes infinite loops, equations, stop commands, dontcha Bezzy?" Benson was waving fingers across his holo display, shutting down camera mode and uploading the video through his network of virtual hiding places.

"Yep, I'm a regular Dr. Frankenstein," Benson said. Today his black strawman hair was unwashed and unruly.

Sam hunkered down onto the floor, the back of his head hitting Jeeves' footstool. "Right. So how's the cure administered?"

"Same way it was put in, really," said Benson. "App on the cleverband. See? Touch the display here. Transmits an electric signal, carries through the bloodstream. Distributes antibodies to block the initial virus. Users should show improved results within a few days."

"Wouldn't it be easy for others to get a hold of it?" Sam asked, crossing his long legs at his ankles. "Start distributing it amongst themselves without our help?"

"No way, man," Benson answered. "Only way anyone can get it on their cleverbands is if we put it there. Only authorised members of the Arcana have distributor access codes."

"We got enough guys to get this done? This thing is everywhere now."

"And so are we. Just like the movement—it starts with us. It grows as it needs to grow," said Jeeves definitively. "You gotta trust the motion of the ocean." He punctuated his statement with a corresponding dance move.

"Better hope we don't have a mole or something," Sam said, closing his eyes and leaning back. "You know how these things go."

"There are no moles in our home, baby. I look into their eyessss, every single one of them. If they ain't one hundred percent sincere I knows it, can feel it in my blood, can hear it singin' between my ears, can feel it tingling in my nether regions."

Sam and Benson exchanged pained glances.

"No one will betray us," said Jeeves.

"This could go fuckin' wrong," Sam said, his voice raspy. "Just putting our boys and girls out on the line like that? It's completely dangerous."

"It's phase two, baby," Jeeves said, standing tall on the tips of his toes, bracelets jangling on his outstretched arms. "There were always gonna be risks. We've gotta expand the community… and even though they're suckers, we gotta get the squares on board, 'cause I suppose at the end of the day, they're people, too, made of blood and dirt just like us. We just about outnumber them now—the baddies." He ran piano fingers through Sam's hair, twirling gelled bits into little twigs. "And you just wait and see what happens when they show up. Don't you worry your lovely head about our boys and girls. We safeguard our own."

"Let me guess," Sam said, eyes growing unfocused as his gaze floated between Jeeves and Benson. "Dr. Frankenstein invented something which does just that."

"Correctamundo," said Jeeves.

～

Jack-of-all-Trades and his brother James went to the Women's Refuge on Leicester Road, hope in their hearts and the remedy in their hands. The refuge was barely used as such anymore—funds had been cut so drastically that only a few diehard champions of the organisation remained. They opened their arms to the Arcana readily, offering to help wherever they could, setting up plastic chairs and tables, tea and biscuits, for the guests about to arrive.

Already, the line was out the door.

"You nervous?" Jack-of-all-Trades asked his twin. Today they wore clashing plaid jumpers, green and orange, each sporting the opposite hair colour of their shirts.

"I trust Jeeves and Benson," said James, wringing slightly shaky hands together.

"They've never lied to us," Jack-of-all-Trades agreed.

"How does this thing work again?"

"You just launch the app, then have 'em touch here where it says GET CLEAN," Jack-of-all-Trades demonstrated, patting his twin solidly on the back.

"Well, then. Shall we open up shop?"

As the doors opened, a stream of people entered in systematic fashion, successfully funneled by volunteers who guided the anxious and tittering arrivals to the appropriate stations as though organizing a soup kitchen. The first group let in were mostly day jobbers from a variety of backgrounds. Luckily, Jack-of-all-Trades spoke all languages.

"Kanagatu venna epa," he spoke to a woman in Sinhalese. "Safe, no worries, see?" He touched the display himself to show her.

Fear and resentment were abated by the fact that people would try anything to get rid of the Dot virus' symptoms. Some of them had even become fans of Saint Fox and The Independence post facto, jumping on the bandwagon a second too late after swiping across *Pay Now*.

"So, Saint Fox himself has officially endorsed this method?" asked a tall, well-groomed blonde man in a powder blue shirt and sports coat. "He endorses it as a cure for the Dot virus?"

"If you mean does he approve of it—yes, he does," said James. "Like you heard them say in the video, our organization never meant to harm anyone. Think of this as a reboot. A reboot of the financial system, a reboot of your health. Tomorrow's another day. Brand spankin' new world."

"Well, I've got to do something about this chronic fatigue I've been having. It happened right after the virus was dispersed, when I purchased a bottle of milk thistle extract at Boots. My employer's not happy with my decrease in efficiency, to say the least. Which brings me to my next question," he said, placing his index finger on the bright blue GET CLEAN square.

"My employer has the virus, and he couldn't make it down here today. Perhaps you've heard of him? Lucas Norcoford, of Primary Illusion Industries. I've got to bring him the cure right away."

"I'm afraid that's not possible," said James, glancing wearily at his twin, who was conversing with a couple in Swahili. "This app can't be transferred to other devices. It can't be purchased. He'll have to come to us."

The blonde man smiled falsely, drawing a gun from his coat pocket.

"That won't be necessary," he said.

James froze, the colour in his ruddy cheeks fading from pink to ashen white. "What the—how did you..."

"How'd I get past your so-called security? Entered through the fire escape. You boys really should be more careful."

"Jack..." James looked to his twin.

Silently, Jack-of-all-Trades raised his cleverband. He spotted the app he was looking for, one installed just two days ago by Benson Bridges— 'Code Red'.

The blonde man aimed his gun squarely at James' forehead.

"First casualty of the cause," he said. "Maybe now you boys will learn not to mess with the men in this country."

He pulled the trigger.

Nothing. An empty click.

He fired again—once, twice. Nothing save for the hollow clicking mechanism that refused to launch a bullet.

Bewildered, he stared at the gun like it was a foreign object. He aimed the gun at James, then at Jack-of-all-Trades, pulling the trigger furiously.

"What have you done?" he demanded, angry and confused.

"Stopped you from committing an act of violence," Jack-of-all-Trades said, walking over to stand beside his brother.

The man glared at the twins, tossing the gun across the room. The cold metal object hit the wall with a heavy sound. He looked to his colleagues, another man and a woman with grim expressions and similar pedestrian attire. They drew their weapons and fired, only to encounter the same malfunction.

"Nice trick," the man said, his knotted brow smoothing as an eerie calm crept across his face. "We'll see how many more you've got left. You'll run out soon enough."

The next moment, he and his colleagues were out the door and through the crowd of frightened onlookers, people frozen to the spot.

"What just happened?" James asked his brother once his breath had returned to him.

"Electromagnetic weapons disruptor," Jack-of-all-Trades answered. "Freezes the bullets in their barrels. Wouldn't have worked ten years ago, but all guns are electronic now, so..." he took his cleverband off his wrist, cracking it in the air like a whip.

"Fuck, man," said James. "I thought I was a goner."

"I'd never let that happen," Jack-of-all-Trades said, linking arms with his twin. "Our father and our whizkid brother would never let that happen."

"Does this mean we've accomplished world peace?" James asked on a shaky exhale.

"I wish that were true, but you never know. Maybe this is just the calm before the storm."

Jack-of-all-Trades turned to face the people. Some had fled immediately following the incident, but others remained, watching and waiting to see what would happen.

"So, who's next?" he asked.

Chapter Twenty-Nine

MAP OF THE PROBLEMATIQUE

Sam Numan was dreaming a cycle of four lifetimes. In the first one he was a tired old folk guitarist, busking in subway stations and hoping to earn enough for a kidney pie at Paddy's down the street. In the second, he was the head of a multi-million-dollar corporation; he drove a black Lamborghini and fucked a ginger-haired girl with impossibly long legs while high out of his mind. While the girl gave him head, he crashed the car into one of the warehouses that stocked what he sold—military tech.

In the third life, Sam was himself, but not himself. Flitting between jobs and treading water, playing in a band, but he was much less famous. There was no Arcane Society, no Janus Jeeves. One night he came home to his flat and Kit and Sailor were there—Kit was a man in a smartly tailored suit and Sailor a daft bird in silver high heels—he found them on his couch doing the horizontal tango. When they invited him to join them, he refused, headed straight into the kitchen and opened the refrigerator, which was stocked with car batteries. He kept taking the batteries out and stacking them on the countertop, figuring there must be a beer in there, somewhere. Soon he was trapped on all sides by an impenetrable fortress of batteries. He could hear Kit and Sailor shrieking and laughing from beyond the wall, having a grand old sexy time.

Suddenly, he spotted what he was looking for in the back of the fridge—one final can of Boddington's. Just as his fingertips brushed the aluminum surface, he fell into the next cycle of the dream.

In the fourth life he was falling, falling, falling, through darkness both instant and limitless. People say that you wake up before you hit the ground. That wasn't true for Sam. He hit the ground, and then, he kept on falling.

He awoke in a suffocating sweat, laying in stark post-nightmare paralysis for a while. It was dark by the time he wandered out into the main room, where everyone was talking and laughing with drinks in hand.

Kit and Muzzy sat against the wall in a couple of wicker chairs, debating the pros and cons of different guitar models. On the other end of the room, Jeeves was animatedly talking to Sailor about the Arcane Society's evolution over the course of many years. Sailor's eyes grew wider as Jeeves' explanations grew louder and increasingly nonsensical.

In his opiate haze they all seemed distant and sinister. Jeeves was a two-bit salesman who'd traded in his three-piece suit for freakishly-patterned vintage apparel, Benson a soulless sleek-black computer console, Kit a neo-feminist in disguise who wasn't really as okay with men as she pretended to be, his parents part of a beige-coloured generation lost in a never-ending cycle of debt and adverts.

A virus, a cure. A rock band loved by millions. A society, a movement, a militia. A master manipulator, a saviour. Pound signs, dollar signs, digital currency represented by green smiley faces resembling tabs of ecstasy. Electric metal, bass drums, white lights. His best girl and his best man at his side, at arm's length, miles away. Infiltrate. Disarm. Show yourself in all your glittering glory, then run and hide. Snort a pill and go to sleep.

Sam went into the kitchen. At the supper table, Bez was talking tech jargon to the twins who listened intently, something about *the same as disarming a suitcase bomb* and how almost all weaponry nowadays is operated by computers.

There was nowhere to get any peace and quiet. He returned to the front room, intending to save Sailor from Jeeves' madness and his sleeves. On his way he got roped into Kit and Muzzy's gear discussion, his latest predilection being for ESP guitars because they were flashy-looking and easy to play. Kit accused him of being partial to form over function and only knowing how to play three-note riffs, which he copped to because it was true enough. Her voice was teasing and light, a whisper on the wind, but the offhanded jibe still struck a chord.

"You're right," he said. "I'm a sham."

"You are no such thing," she admonished. "You're brilliant, in fact. You just don't realise it."

"Oh, mushy mushy kissy kissy," Muzzy said, standing up from his chair. "Believe it or not, I'm still too sober for a bandmate orgy with you gorgeous, yet irritating lot. I need me another drink."

"Hey Foxy, come here," Jeeves gestured him over to where the ringleader was tormenting Sailor with tales from the past.

"Can you not call me that? At least when we ain't in front of any cameras," he said. "My name is Sam."

"I know your name, baby," Jeeves said, crossing his zigzag print-covered legs. "I know who you are, probably better than you do."

"Oh, and who's that? An unwitting pawn in your national game of chess? Another person to use up like some resource you mine, then abandon once they're empty?"

"I think you're mixing your metaphors, baby."

"Shut it," he ordered. "You use people. I'm not the only one. Look, there's another one of your victims," he said as Benson entered the room, a fistful of cleverbands in one hand and a bottle of scotch in the other. "You use Bez to do all your dirty work." Sam strode over to Benson, placed his hands on his shoulders and shook him. "Don't you feel used?"

Benson's eyebrows raised. "Sometimes I feel like the only clever one around here, yeah. But it's not like I don't believe in what we're doing," Benson said. "Besides, if I wanted to leave, I could." He eyed Jeeves, who was taking it all in with a mixture of concern and amusement on his narrow face. "Anyone could, even you. What's gotten into you?" He slid out from beneath Sam's hands, crossing his arms over his chest.

"I can't," Sam said miserably. "Got nowhere to go." He spoke the last part quietly, almost to himself.

"You're a free man, Sammy," Jeeves said from across the room, his voice lacking the usual frequency of his frenzied tenor. "And you set others free. Don't know why that's such a burden to you. You're welcome to stay—or go. It's up to you." He maintained a relaxed posture, his arms open in passive invitation.

Sam's fists were clenched at his sides, his shoulders raised. He suddenly felt nervous and a bit ashamed, all eyes on him—all eyes on him like they always were.

He'd made it worse.

"I'd better get going," Kit said. She'd been watching from the sidelines as the tension in the room grew, wanting to help, but knowing that any attempt to do so would probably be rebuffed. "It's getting late."

"I'm not going anywhere. You're not going anywhere," he said to Kit.

"Yes, I am. You get your head on straight. Call me when you're feeling better." She pecked him briefly on the lips and gathered her things.

"Maybe you ought to have a bit of a lie-down," Sailor said, standing up and tentatively approaching his friend.

"I just had a lie-down. Been lying down all day. All week," Sam said through gritted teeth.

"And that was better than whatever's happening now," Sailor answered, hands perched on his hips. "Come on."

Sam allowed Sailor to lead him back to the bunks, pausing to glare at Jeeves, whose expression was unreadable.

He crawled back into the lower bunk he'd spent practically all day in. It smelled musty and sweaty and was starkly quiet, like nothing ever happened there. He couldn't stand it.

Sailor sat on the bed beside him, his head tucked low, fluffing and arranging pillows.

Sam placed his hand firmly on Sailor's hip, then ran it across to sit at the base of his navel, pausing to glance at the other man, who had one eyebrow lifted and his shoulders up in a sort of confused shrug.

"What are you doing?"

"How 'bout you make me feel better," Sam said, scratching lightly at Sailor's stomach under his grey t-shirt.

"Would you be looking for a one-way ticket then, mate?" Sailor asked, pulling his t-shirt back down. "We just sold out of those."

"Nah, I'll return the favour. Quid pro quo," Sam said, dipping his head to kiss him.

The kiss was cut short when Sailor barked out a laugh.

"What?" Sam asked, offended.

"Nothin' mate, it just sounds like yer currency app. Give N Get? Ain't that what it's all about? Equality in the marketplace, equality in the bedroom?"

"Sure, whatever," said Sam. "Now shut up and drop yer trousers."

"You're just looking for a distraction 'cause you feel like shyte," Sailor said, running his fingers through Sam's hair and dancing them across the back of his neck.

"You could do worse. Like that weird old bloke you've been living with, Randall or whatever his name is."

"His name's Ron, and don't act like you're doing me a favour. 'Oh, poor Sailor is arse over tit for me anyway. I can screw around with him and my sweet twat hotshot guitarist and it don't matter,'" Sailor exclaimed sarcastically, shuffling back and leaning against the bedpost.

"It's not like that," Sam said, leaning forward.

"Ain't it though, just ain't it? Ain't you the darndest thing, Saint Fox, Freedom Fox, Twenty-Second Century Fox. Good ol' Sammy boy, our own true saviour. Let me bow down to you. Let me kiss your cock." He punctuated with lewd hand gestures, his voice rising into bite and bile.

"You've had too much to drink," said Sam, starting a clumsy wrestling match. He pinned Sailor easily under his weight, looming over him.

"I have not," Sailor defended, trying to bat Sam away with uncoordinated slaps.

Sam gave up the fight and sat back on his heels, closing his eyes briefly. "We should go home tomorrow."

"We can't, you ninny. Don't have a home to go to anymore." Sailor fell back, his head hitting the pillow with a light thud. Dust particles scattered starry patterns in the dim light.

"Fine, then." Sam lay down beside him in an exaggerated heap. "We'll just go to sleep, since you're no fun." He flopped one leg across Sailor's, who let it remain there. "Good*night*, weary Sailor." He closed his eyes, willing sleep to come as soon as possible. It wouldn't be long, his entire body felt dry and heavy.

"Goodnight, Foxy," Sailor said, staring up at the ceiling. "G'night, Sam."

~

Lucas Norcoford was a longtime patron of the Dorchester Hotel. Room 809, The Terrace Suite, was made available to him whenever he wished it. The Dorchester had last been renovated four years ago with brand new appliances, linens, 17K SO-LED panels, and a sixth five-star restaurant added at ground level.

Norcoford sat stick straight in a maroon-upholstered chair that cost eight hundred quid. Streaks of sunlight filtered through gauzy yellow window coverings and reflected off the surface of his perfectly smooth, bald head. He drummed short fingers against the overstuffed arm of the chair in time to the synthesised, repetitive calliope tune that drifted in from the park below.

He waited in the sitting room of his suite for Prime Minister Harold Waterman, who would arrive twenty-two minutes late. Norcoford gazed out of the French windows with disdain at the once glorious Hyde Park, now filled with riffraff and tacky flora genetically engineered in a lab somewhere in York. He'd ordered a gourmet fruit and cheese plate that cost sixty-five quid which he had barely touched; the cheeses were all too bitter, the fruit too sweet. He was staring at his cuticles, irritated that he was past due for a manicure when Waterman entered, flanked by two nameless suits who stood quietly by the door through the entire visit.

Norcoford didn't bother standing up when his guest arrived. "The King's business keeping you from arriving on time, Harry? Or perhaps something blonde, with killer tits," he asked evenly.

Prime Minister Waterman crossed the room in three strides. "This is the King's business," he said. "And I prefer brunettes." He seated himself on the left edge of a damask-patterned couch which could easily sleep a small family. He leaned forward, gazing squarely at Norcoford, who stared back skeptically from underneath waxed eyebrows.

"So," Waterman began, "a ragtag bunch of anarchists fronted by a rock n' roll band have managed to not only disrupt our financial system, they've somehow disarmed our weapons as well. My, my."

"The fault lies with the gunmen, obviously," Norcoford gritted out. "Their weapons malfunctioned."

Waterman shook his head, "Lucas, Lucas. It amazes me how naïve you can be considering all the wicked things you've done in your life. Do you think your men were the only ones we sent after them? We sent men out to location centers all across the developed country. Variations on the same scenario played out at each location. We took no hostages."

Norcoford stood, stepping towards the light and staring out at the remnants of Hyde Park, fingers gripping the windowsill. "Doesn't it make you angry?" he said. "You seem rather glib for someone with so much at stake."

"Of course it does," Waterman answered, running a hand through his thinning brown hair. "I'm completely furious," he said in a voice that neither rose nor fell.

"We're running out of time. The threat of the Dot virus is real—I've been diagnosed with Phase I. My sex drive is shot. I can barely choke down food. I'll end up starving to death and firing everyone."

"How are you even paying for this room, Lucas?" Waterman leaned back against the couch, his hands folded and perched atop his knee.

"The Dorchester isn't doing much business these days. They let me have the room for free, thought having a big shot CEO photographed on the premises might boost things around here. Everyone's desperate."

"I know," Waterman said. His lips set in a tight line, a flash of anguish sparking in his eyes for a brief moment. "My son is infected."

"We have to take this cure by force," Norcoford said, turning to face him. His eyes were black pools with no light in them. "Now that you've got a personal stake in it, maybe you'll finally get off your arse and treat these terrorists like the national disaster they are."

"We've been very much off our arses and more on top of things than you realise," Waterman countered. "We've recovered and analyzed the original CCTV footage from the morning the alteration to the terminals occurred, the recordings they managed to cover up at the time. Do you know who is responsible, Lucas?"

Norcoford merely tilted his head, waiting to be impressed.

"It's the workers," he announced, looking inherently pleased with himself. "Just simple folks working at the damn Asda. They're the ones responsible. They're the ones who originally flipped the switch. Hacked into the system. Leaked it into the main valves, allowing the disease to spread. We now have faces. And names," he said, almost smiling.

"So, you finally learned something, did you? Well, congratulations, good on you, old chum. Now, I don't suppose you have any sort of plan to do something with this information, do you? You're no action man," Norcoford accused.

"I, in fact, do have a plan, Lucas. And the plan is simple. The miscreants are using cutting-edge technology to take us down. We'll simply go the other direction."

"What are you on about?" asked Norcoford.

"The past, Lucas," the Prime Minister said. "We'll go into the past."

Chapter Thirty

FOX ON THE RUN

Sam was certain he was being followed.

He'd snuck out before dawn while it was still dark, when the air in the city smelled of old smoke and new mist, when people who weren't quite awake yet and had hours ahead of them to commute were stacked in neat little lines to get their morning tea or coffee, scone or biscuit. He'd been careful not to wake Sailor or anyone else on his way out, not bothering to change and simply pulling his appropriated leather jacket on over a black t-shirt and blue-green plaid pyjama bottoms.

There were a number of unfortunate tasks scheduled for today that Sam did not wish to attend to. The first of which was an interview with *The Grassroots Telegraph* where he was supposed to play the role of political rock messiah, regurgitating Jeeves' words. Not that it mattered what he said. Even the independent newspapers—still called papers even though they were available in electronic format only—wrote whatever story they wanted and adjusted the interviewee's comments accordingly. Anyway, he knew

Jeeves had only set this up to give him something to do, make him feel better about himself. Keep him under control in light of the little tirades he'd been having, keep him on a leash. He would play the movement's song-and-dance marionette again, only this time with decidedly less fire.

It wasn't that he didn't believe in the Arcana. It was more that their success reverberated only in his mind, and not in his heart. At each triumph of theirs, he had expected to feel something. Some sort of elation, a high, a sense of universal wrongs being righted. Instead, he was merely a tagline-touting, hip-swaying, glammed-up prophesying insect. Buzz buzz buzz.

Tonight Jeeves wanted him to join a group of them planning to hide out and spy on a rally scheduled to take place outside of Tesco on Oxford Street, where things had apparently gotten tense—Tesco was now accepting GGcoin, but the government was demanding remittance of their VAT, although word was they weren't even set up to process it yet. With the financial insecurity night terrors everyone was having, even large businesses no longer wanted to fork over a third of their profit to another entity for doing absolutely nothing.

Excited spokespersons would gather with their signs and their megaphones, their friends and enemies, their hopes and fears. It would turn into a riot, no doubt, one which the coppers would be ill-equipped to handle as per usual. It would be Glastonbury all over again—that teenage girl in the crowd, blood thick and red spilling over her bright, adoring face.

He shuffled along the narrow streets, twisting and turning past shops and cafes, only one out of every five open at this hour to greet the day's first customers. The sun was now bright overhead, but it might as well have been a ball of cold fire. Sam shivered and shrunk down further into his jacket. He thought about buying a cup of tea at the stand on Garth near the edge of the cemetery, but was afraid he'd be recognised.

Instead he wandered into the cemetery, imagining he could hear the dead whispering to him. That faint new melody that had been running through his head came to him again, played on a haunted, out-of-tune piano by the ghost of a man who'd been falsely accused of murder and had lost everything—his wife and child, his dreams and ambition. In Sam's mind the man wore a shabby grey coat that looked like it was made of pigeon feathers. He sang in a hollow, broken voice, words that disappeared into the wind the moment they were uttered:

The cemetery had been beautiful once upon a time—dark, lush, and harrowing, but now it was poorly cared for. Sewage-coloured moss grew in mad patches across the headstones. The flowerbeds which once contained sprigs of bright lupine and lush snapdragons were now covered in rough tangles of weeds, and the few proud evergreen trees that remained in the graveyard were dying from the bottom up.

Sam sat down beside a large headstone resembling a Roman pillar. It said 'BENJAMIN GRAVES – Beloved Father, Husband, and Son. Deus vult.' He didn't know what Deus vult meant. Something about God. God is my vault. God will punish vultures. He imagined the gravestone was his grandfather's. He'd loved his grandfather very much, because he'd died when he was seven, and when Sam was seven he didn't know how to do anything else but love.

He picked at the moss covering the headstone, tossing it aside. "Let's get you cleaned up, grandad."

The moss felt nice between his fingers. Sam wished the pills he'd taken ten minutes ago had kicked in already, then it would have felt even better.

When he'd finished cleaning the headstone, he looked up to find three men in black uniforms standing in front of him, their looming forms blocking the sunlight.

All three had guns trained on him.

"Aww, shit," he said. "Guess you lads didn't get the memo. We're bulletproof now, you know." He reached into his pocket—where he usually kept his cleverband when he didn't feel like wearing it—and found nothing, save for Sailor's cigarette case where he kept his pills.

He'd left his cleverband at Jeeves'.

The fattest of the three men clocked him upside the head with a semi-automatic pistol.

"Ow!" Sam reeled. "Where'd you get that from, a history museum?" He really wished the pills would kick in. Right now.

"You're under arrest, Sam Numan," the fat man said. "For terrorist acts against King and country. Take him."

"Fuck," said Sam. "Fuck, fuck, fuck." He kept saying it as they wrestled his arms behind him and slapped on the cuffs, as they shoved him roughly up against the car and frisked him—finding and confiscating the cigarette case, as they bashed his head against the roof of the car while shoving him into the backseat.

Though he put up only the faintest of fights, he still ended up covered in cuts and bruises. His head throbbed something awful, but through it, a keen warmth washed over him, and the pain began to dull.

At least I won't have to attend that rally tonight at Tesco, he thought.

They drove on for hours, the fat man in the driver's seat and a ginger-haired man on the passenger's side. The third man sat beside Sam with a rifle that smelled of musk and rat dung trained at his head.

"Where are you taking me?" Sam asked, his voice thin. He received no response. The road they were taking was windy and narrow, twisting past a whole lot of nothing— green grass and sheep shit. He started to nod off, forgetting how his arms were uncomfortably wrenched behind him, but every time his eyes closed, the man next to him smacked him in the head with the barrel of his gun.

They drove on in relative silence. Through his downer haze he decided that these were military men, not the local police. They were too clean-shaven, too organised, all seeming to work together on the same rhythm without verbal communication—like bees, ants, attack drones.

His blood vessels constricted as his serotonin soared. Even the rough kicks from the butt of the gun were not a problem; he had to be careful not to smile at the soldier, lazy and uneven. The soldier might fall in love with him, or kill him. Either way, it didn't matter.

"Some leader," the soldier beside him muttered. "High as a kite." He raised his thick eyebrows at Sam's blown pupils and droopy eyelids, his delayed response to pain. The soldier offered a swift kick to his shin as verification. Sam only smirked.

"S'nice, that. I haven't been driven around like this in ages. Being a rock star ain't what it used to be, you know. Limousines and champagne haven't been a big part of my life since this whole thing started. Any of you boys ever ride in a limo?"

"Can you make him shut up?" the man in the driver's seat asked.

"I certainly can," the man beside Sam responded.

Sam felt a tight pinch in his arm. A needle, he realised.

"See what I mean? Cocktails n' everything," Saint Fox mumbled as he drifted into oblivion.

Chapter Thirty-One

HOUSE OF CARDS

Twenty-One Dead Under the Age of Twenty in Vauxhall, the headline read.

Jeeves watched the pixels of his cleverband's holo display dematerialise as he closed the News. Alone in his room he bowed his head low, shedding tears for the fallen. Killing was never necessary. Military men were evil fools in every lifetime. They would never learn.

The war had begun. The old kind of war, the kind Jeeves had seen too many of. The kind he had hoped to avoid, thinking it was possible to do so in this so-called advanced society.

The article was one of hundreds like it mirrored across the country. The King's army had stormed into Tesco, into Argos, into Asda, holding their employees at 20th century gunpoint. Waterman's shoot-to-kill order against those who would not comply had at last come through.

Tim Easton, who worked at Asda on Whitechapel Road, had stood behind his checkout counter with shaking hands, beads of sweat rolling down his back.

"I already told you. I don't know how to disarm it. There's nothing I can do."

A soldier in a black beret and camos held a Smith & Wesson gas-powered semi-automatic to Tim's head.

"Disarm or I shoot," he'd said, as his large hand closed around the trigger.

A hollow bang sounded out as an example was made of what happened to young men who did not follow orders. Fuel for the fire.

A girl who worked with Tim would tell his mother. The colour would drain from her face. She would break down and sob. When she collected herself, she would offer the girl some tea, which they would drink in silence as the sun set on another rainy afternoon.

Enormous chain stores throughout the country were shutting their doors, unable to comply and unable to guarantee the safety of their employees.

Those who had utilised the Dot, contracted the virus, and subsequently been cured by the GET CLEAN app were much fewer in number than planned. Though the cure appeared to do what it promised, its distribution had gone further underground—appearances of disciples carrying magic code in bracelets on their wrists were increasingly rare given the risk. Waterman's military forces had finally crawled out of the woodwork in full fledge, armed with weapons of the dead, and were working day and night to infiltrate a location where they could take the cure by force.

And yet, Waterman's ancient ammunition was not the worst of Janus Jeeves' problems.

He searched behind furniture, in toilet stalls, underneath girls' skirts, in men's trouser pockets.

Sam Numan was nowhere to be found.

Jeeves rattled down into the cellar. Sailor was situated in the top bunk nearest the door, a grim look on his angular face.

"C'mon, Patricia," Jeeves said. "You're the last one who saw him. You telling me you have no idea where he is?"

"Wish I did." Sailor didn't look up, scrolling back and forth through his cleverband texts as if it would make a new message from Sam appear. "I woke up this morning and he was gone."

"I've got a terrible feeling about this," said Jeeves, hands laced atop his bobbing head.

"What's going on?" Benson clambered down the cellar's steps, holding a coffee mug and rubbing sleep from his eyes.

"Our kitty is missing," Jeeves said, crossing his silky sleeves over his chest.

Jeeves should have known better. Experience had laid the warning signs out for him like a map. Still, what could he do? The kid was a free man, but Jeeves knew he felt anything but. The nation was free, and the prince of the free felt he was trapped. He grimaced then, remembering today's headline news.

Freedom came at a price.

Jeeves stomped over to a broken chair shoved into the corner of the musty cellar. It was half covered in faux yellow fur, the stuffing popping out of it. He kicked it with the pointed toe of his shiny black boot until its last leg finally collapsed out from underneath it.

"It's not surprising, being how pissed off he was last night," Benson said. "Figured as soon as he sobered up, he'd bolt for the door."

"Then you should have bolted the door, baby," said Jeeves.

Benson groaned. He sat down on the bunk below Sailor, hiding his face inside his coffee mug.

Sailor sat with his face buried in his hands. "You don't think they caught him, do you?" he said to his knees.

"Speak up, Paddy, I can't hear you." Jeeves pinched the bridge of his nose. His whole body was taut and stretched out like a bowstring, pointed elbows forming the cross of the bow.

Sailor lifted his head. "They got him. I know they did. I can feel it. He's shaking like a leaf in a cell somewhere, vomiting his guts out and hallucinating."

"You're too soft," Jeeves said, shaking his head. "He's too soft, too. I should have known."

"By soft, do you mean queer?" Sailor asked, one eyebrow raised.

"Of course not, baby. Everyone's queer. S'got nothing to do with how tough you are. Maybe soft isn't the right word. Young, I should say, rather. Not used to making sacrifices. This is the first war you all have seen up close. I risked it all on a wee lil' babe. How old is Foxy?"

"He's twenty-three," Sailor said. "Seventeen months older than me."

"And he don't remember his past lives. At least, not while he's awake."

"What're you on about?"

"Life and lives, baby. Our Sammy boy hasn't been through enough of 'em to remember the ones he's over and done with—he's a young soul. Me, I've been cycling through this crap long enough that things start to look familiar. I know I've been here before and before and before—I got bits and pieces of all my lives up in here." He pointed to his forehead between his eyebrows. "Foxy's one of those pieces from sometime, somewhere. He's a piece I remember, even if he doesn't. A shiny, sparkly piece. Maybe from the roarin' twenties."

"You sound like a shaman I met at Bestival," Sailor said. He opened his cleverband display and returned to scrolling through recent messages from Sam, most of which were unfit for the eyes of small children. The last message he'd received from him was a photo of what he thought Binky looked like—a mangy, floppy-eared little thing, black and white fur, with big brown eyes and a portly little belly. Sailor had texted him back No, this one:, a photo of a pointy-eared golden boy with short legs and a pushed-in face. Binky's boyfriend, Sam had replied. Binky can't get a stud like this, poor sod, read Sailor's response.

Sailor sniffed, glancing over at Jeeves who had seated himself next to the collapsed yellow chair. His hands were out in front of him, fingers ghosting over imaginary keys, playing a melody in his mind without making a sound.

"Do you even care about him, about any of us?" Sailor asked.

Jeeves dropped his hands to his sides. His eyes roamed back and forth as if he were reading notes on sheet music.

"I care about all of you, as if you were my own children. But of course, you always want better things for your children. Great things. Impossible things. What do we do to our children when we want something for them?" he asked, gazing forward so that his ancient blue and yellow eyes bore directly into young Sailor's, who slowly blinked at him.

"We push them to succeed?" said Sailor, taking a stab.

"That's exactly right," said Jeeves. "We push them."

Janus Jeeves stared into the neo-impressionist green glass mirror in the corner of his study, propped up amongst the relocated rubble of books and maps, and asked himself for the hundredth time if he might be wrong.

The mirror showed a gloomy black wraith, the fabrics and accessories of Jeeves minus the colour. Long, drab black sleeves, a network of onyx rosary beads, a large hematite cross. Face pale, eyes encircled in black smudges and reddened skin.

Was I a fool? Only a fool would think he could wage a peaceful war, Jeeves said to mirror Jeeves, his hands pressed solemnly together.

This is not the end, his reflection said. *The pieces on the chess board await. Your move.*

A long, jagged crack made its way down the edge of the mirror. In the dark of night, in the black of day, Janus Jeeves sat and recharged, folding into himself like a cocoon, plugging into an ethereal power source like so many before him. The energy popped and fritzed until it became too much. He unplugged from the source once his power had recharged. The image in the mirror was no longer black. Maybe not as vivid and luminescent as it was at times, but at least there were colours. The blues and yellows of his eyes. A golden blush in his cheeks.

The children will build the future, he said to himself, imagining pawns on a chessboard stacking themselves into a tower. The pawns were white and shining.

They were made to look like marble, but they were made of plastic.

Chapter Thirty-Two

I LOVE ROCK N' ROLL

Sam's cot was drenched in sweat, the tiny room ripe with underground warmth and stale air. With nothing else to do, he thought back to the most recent of many nightmares.

Saint Fox, up on stage under bright bright lights—weak in voice and body, unable to keep time with the music. He opened his mouth and sang a beat too soon, he strummed a chord two beats behind. He forgot the lyrics halfway through the song, the rest of the band receding into the background, shrinking into blackness, into nothing. He couldn't hear them playing anymore except for Zephyr's kick drum—harsh, steady, and increasingly loud. Alone on stage, a wide spotlight shone down on him from directly above as he sweated bullets and failed to play his own songs that he knew like the beat of his own heart.

Meanwhile, the audience grew and grew, expanding indefinitely. The bigger the sea of faces got, the worse his performance became. The faces in the crowd all looked the same. Twisted, menacing, mouths set in a straight line. Unforgiving. Disappointed.

He lay down on the cold dusty floor of the stage, naked and shivering.

The ringing of a high frequency siren brought him back to the unfortunate present. It reminded him of the squealing series of feedback strains Kit wrought from her guitar at the end of every show, only less sweet. The lump in his throat made him feel like he needed to vomit, only he couldn't, he tried and wound up merely coughing and gagging over the side of the cot.

How many days had it been since he'd last eaten? How many days had he been locked up in here? Too many, if his stomach was anything to go by. It sat in an angry knot, twisted up like a fist in the center of his abdomen. The dehydration was worse—he ought to drink some water, but any liquid turned to sand in his mouth, any food or drink brought to him by the guards was little better than cardboard and warm piss anyway.

A gust of cold air blew into the room as General Simsworth entered. A man pieced together like he was built out of cement blocks. His fists certainly affirmed that premise.

Sam shut his eyes against the temporary light entering the room. When he opened them again, Simsworth was still there. His face was wide and hairless. No eyebrows even, Sam noticed, whether the result of a genetic defect or overzealous grooming, it certainly wasn't worth the price of finding out.

Simsworth's face split into a toothless grin. "How're we feeling today, Fox?"

"You know damn well how I feel. Or have you not eyes that you can see?" said Sam, for a moment channeling Jeeves and his tendency to misuse biblical quotes.

"You know the way out of this one," Simsworth sneered. "We'll give you feckin' caviar and clotted cream if you tell us what we want to know." His stout fingers grabbed Sam by the jaw, squeezing hard. The mentioned delicacies made Sam's stomach reel, more punishment than reward.

"I've told you before. I've no idea how the technology works," the words shivered out from between his lips in a thin rasp, barely above a whisper. "I'm just a frontman, yeah? The big brains behind the operation is what you want, and I hope for all our sakes that you pigs never catch up with him."

That earned him a hard strike across the cheek. It would join other bruises as they bloomed from red to violet to green, fading to yellow before withering away like they were never even there. The layers of skin and muscle beneath, however, would retain a sense memory of fear and abuse.

Simsworth's too-close together eyes narrowed into angry slits. "You've got nothing to lose, isn't that right, Saint Fox? It's the only explanation for why you're so stupid." Simsworth released him, letting Sam's head fall back onto the cot with a hollow sound.

Simsworth turned to the guard. "He been eating any of the dreck we've been giving him?" he asked.

"Hardly, sir. Going through withdrawal from the smack. Stomach's all fucked I'd imagine."

"Good. If he ever does get around to wanting food, too damn bad. We're gonna stop feeding him. See if he feels like talking when he's *really* starving."

Simsworth exited the room, the metal door clanging shut behind him.

It wasn't food Sam wanted. The guard was right. He needed oxy, norco, methadone, hell, he'd inject heroin straight into his arm at this point, not caring that it'd fuck him up for good, not caring that it made him a cliché. He'd even tried to get one of the 'roid-heads assigned to his watch to slip him some, had tried to bargain with no chips on the table. He'd received only harsh barks of laughter and a few more knocks to the jaw.

On that day and for many days after, Sam Numan wished he'd never become a rock n' roll star.

It was just a silly dream, after all.

~

The landlord's phone calls had gone unanswered. He'd rung up a total of four times in the past three hours, unprecedented for him as he typically ignored his tenants completely, save for when the rent was due. If complaints kept coming in he would have to go down there himself, which would involve putting on trousers, maybe drumming up the lease. He didn't even know the name of the quiet girl who had moved in only a few weeks prior.

Not so quiet anymore.

Ground level flat 147 was a disaster. Glasses and bottles overturned on the countertops. Scraps of clothing in black and white and red scattered about. Leather and lace, spike-heeled boots, chiffon scarves, the contents of a makeup box containing fifteen different brands of black eyeliner spilling out across a sofa that had been recently slept upon. Half-empty plates and coffee mugs, an impressive collection of depleted beer bottles. An island network of papers with riffs and chords and lyrics scribbled on them, *E G A E G A. E B B*

F A. F U. Nobody listens, so nobody stops us when we take over. You're lost in the dark, fallen lonely soldier. A variety of sound equipment that few knew how to properly utilise completed the breakdown mosaic—a lifetime collection of wireless pedals littered the floor, each responding with the appropriate screech, scramble, siren, synth, sin and soundbomb when the angry guitar goddess stomped upon them in turn.

Terrible and terrifying noise to most people's dulled standards, but sweet to her soul. Kit pulled mad, desperate, strangled sounds from the neck of her guitar, feeding it back against her amp stack just to hear its tormented squeal. The dials were turned up as high as they could go for her to still make any sense of the music. She distorted notes until they were ugly, bent strings until they broke.

Sam had been missing for the past six days. Jeeves was trying to sell it as if he'd left of his own volition, *Oh my birdie's flown the coop, should have known, should have known.* Sailor played his own game, pretending Sam was just down at the pub this whole time. *Just passed out somewhere in his own vomit. He'll be back when he sobers up and finds himself sick of himself,* he'd said, though his trembling voice betrayed him. It was bullshit and she knew it.

Though it was certainly possible Sam had simply run away, her gut told her it was much more likely that the authorities had finally taken action, responding with zeal once desperation had sunk in. They'd done a piss-poor job of defending their precious dynasty from the get-go, and now their fat arses had no choice but to get off the couch in a last-ditch attempt to keep the nation locked into slavery in the form of debt.

Their lack of response to the movement's initial strikes must have been typically British, *Oh dear, why isn't that unfortunate.* In reality, it hadn't been that long. It felt as though GGcoin had been in operation for ages, but it had only been about a month since Janus Jeeves pulled Benson Bridges' universal trigger.

If Sam had been abducted, it wasn't as if he could tell his captors what they wanted to know. He'd be just a celebrity bargaining chip, the son taken hostage to lure the king out of his ramshackle castle. If Saint Fox and The Independence's loyal fan base heard that their beloved rock n' roll messiah was being held captive, would they turn on the Arcana? Where did their loyalty really lie?

All she had wanted was to make music, maybe save the world a little. Live life on her own terms, be no one's puppet. Now she wondered if she'd just been fooling herself all along.

Lies on top of lies. There's no such thing as utopia, not here, not amongst the cleverbands and intertalks and Fall fashion trends, not where people have forgotten how to decide for themselves.

We had to make the choice for them, Jeeves would say. Just a little coaxing in the form of rock n' roll.

The door to her flat buzzed three times, but was drowned out by the noise inside. The quick, repetitive pounding on the door finally broke through as a new disturbance that wasn't self-made.

She slid open the door to reveal a jittery-looking Benson Bridges on the other side. He poked his head in, glancing over the flat's wreckage before his gaze returned to Kit who wore black jeans and a Bowie t-shirt, her kinked dark curls standing on end as if she'd been electrocuted.

Benson was equally without sleep and disheveled, eyes darting back and forth, his tongue planted firmly in the hollow of his cheek. He opened his mouth and closed it a few times, trying and failing to make words.

He's looking for the den mother, Kit realised.

"What are you doing here?" she asked, stepping aside abruptly as he entered without invitation.

"What are *you* doing?" Benson countered, his voice nasal and wavering. "It looks like a tsunami hit in here."

"Whatever I want," Kit said. She edged in on him with her arms folded across her chest. "I'm busy. What's up?"

"You haven't seen him either?" Benson flopped down onto Kit's mass-produced couch, its black fabric torn and frayed.

Kit dropped her arms, sitting down beside him. "Did Jeeves send you?" she asked, staring distractedly out the window.

"Nope. Just me, lookin' for him." Benson took off his narrow glasses, wiping them on the edge of his t-shirt before putting them on again.

"Don't tell me you're in love with him, too," Kit said. "That boy has enough admirers."

"He'll have even more if he's dead."

"Dark. Rock n' roll immortality?"

Benson shook his head. "I've always kinda liked ya, you know," he said flatly. He coiled up tensely, poised for imminent rejection.

"That can't be true," Kit said, looking through him. "Smart guys don't like smart girls. They don't like to be challenged." She ran a guitar pick back and forth over her knuckles, eager to get back to playing.

"Well, I like smart girls. And who said you were smart? People throw around the term 'musical genius,' but let's been honest here. They shouldn't do that. That's not what genius means."

"You have a strange way of talking up a gal."

"Thought you might like a bit of honesty for a change. Anyway, if there was such a thing as a musical genius in the simple genre of rock music, you'd be one."

"You're just saying that," Kit smiled, but it didn't quite reach her eyes.

"Maybe." Benson was quiet for a moment. "Do you believe in the movement?" he asked.

Kit thought about it for a moment. Her doubts, she figured, were best kept to herself. "Yeah, I do. I'm not sure it's the best way to go about it, and I know it's hard to trust Jeeves sometimes, but look what we've done so far. Tons of businesses are using GGcoin. They're just that little bit freer. That's worth something, don't you think?"

"I wouldn't be here otherwise. Jeeves drives me crazy, but the reason I worked with him so closely on this was that his ideas made feckin' sense. He's actually really clever. Once he stops gesturing around and gets down to business, he knows what he's talking about, it's just no one hardly ever sees that side of him."

"He's a performer at heart. That's why he acts the way he does. He can't help it. He needs the attention, needs other people's focus to energise him."

"D'ya think Sam's a performer at heart?"

"I think he fakes it well enough. I think he's whatever other people want him to be."

"You think we'll find him?" Benson stared at his knees, fiddling with the zip on his jacket.

"I don't know," Kit said, her expression turning dour. "Look, I don't mean to be rude, but I'd prefer to be alone right now."

"Yeah, yeah, I get it," Benson said. "I'm not him."

"It's not that. I just need some time to process."

"I'll leave you to it then. Just be careful."

"I'll be however I want, genius," she said without malice. "Nighty night, Bez."

She shut the door behind him and set the lock, returning to her stack and turning the volume up two more notches, continuing to drown out everything and everyone with electricity and steel, a tried and true method that always worked. For a little while, at least.

Chapter Thirty-Three

THE MERCY SEAT

Sam drove a stolen neon-green hydroelectric car at top speed, past a sign that read *Next Rest Area: 87 km*. The tires squeaked like wildfire against the pavement and he was low on petrol. The air around him swallowed him up in a warm chill, a barricade, a temperamental prison with its own working mind.

He decided to take a detour down an unpaved road, spotting an old-fashioned American diner in the distance. The car screeched to a halt.

The diner was decorated like the 50s—red vinyl seats, round white tables, a neon sign reading 'Dusty's' and a jukebox. He smelled greasy burgers and chips, heard Roy Orbison playing over the tinny restaurant speakers. The song was Blue Angel—*Oh blue angel, don't you cry, just because he said goodbye,* and Sam ordered a Dusty's Famous Bacon Cheeseburger with jalapeños and barbeque sauce from the busty brunette waitress with killer legs whose nametag said 'Brandi: Serving You With A Smile.'

The record screeched to a halt. A few quiet skips. Then, the song began again from the top.

He waited and waited for his order to arrive. All around him others were being served—a table of jocks and cheerleaders in their stars and stripes, a man and a woman who must have weighed two hundred and thirty kilos each, a lonely little fellow in a shallow-brimmed hat who ate only chips and salad.

His food never came. The patrons around him grew old and grey. The red vinyl seats morphed into uncomfortable aluminum chairs that weighed less than half a kilo and were made for five pence apiece in Singapore. The pretty brunette waitress grew freakishly thin, bones practically jutting through her face, rosy cheeks replaced with pallor. The music changed from Roy's earnest song about loneliness and heartache to a catastrophic din with no melody, just loosely rhyming words shouted over a beat from a 1970s rock song that had been regurgitated and defiled. A fine layer of white dust settled over the furniture, building up in snowlike piles around the jukebox.

Sam exited the desecrated diner, unfed, into the black night. He jogged, he flew, he rode a bicycle. He landed on the moon and played a very special edition of *Celebrity Countdown: Rock Stars on the Moon.* He lost to the resurrected ghost of Ian Curtis, who he tried to argue had cheated by using incomprehensible German words. But the rules of Celebrity Countdown on the Moon were looser, as was the gravity. Contestants and letters floated in vast emptiness, faintly illuminated by fireflies and vertical industrial-sized fluorescent rods.

He awoke in a plush velvet bed. He awoke with naked groupies entwined across him like a spiderweb.

He awoke alone in cold and darkness.

Sam rolled over to his side and fell straight out of bed onto the dusty floor, catching himself on all fours. His palms bracketed against the cold pavement left sweaty handprints.

Here in this prison—wherever here was, physical torture took the form of:

1. Food and light deprivation.

2. Getting tossed around like a ragdoll by men twice the size of him until they drew blood or got bored.

3. Acute opiate withdrawal.

Psychological torture took the form of:

1. Interrogations and accusations, mostly from Simsworth, who asked the same questions over and over, told him he was a worthless piece of shit, pretended to be his friend, then questioned him again, spat upon him, and left him in darkness.

2. Being ignored for long periods of time.

3. Acute opiate withdrawal.

His stomach rumbled a nasty rhythm inside him. He wished someone would feed him something, anything. He thought of the time Sailor had tried to cook a three-course seafood dinner on their meager budget and they'd both gotten food poisoning. It had tasted good at the time, however, and he doubted it had truly been the culprit; it must have been the kebabs they'd had for lunch. He would sacrifice his firstborn son for a kebab right about now.

Tonight, Simsworth had invited him to a banquet. Sam would dine with the Prime Minister himself, he'd said.

What new form of torture could this be? Sam wondered.

He was given decent clothes, shoved towards a basin and told to wash up. From what he glimpsed in the foggy mirror, he had to say it wasn't half bad given the circumstances; he didn't look nearly as horrendous as he felt. He was too thin, and hadn't shaved in weeks, his hair all shaggy in a way that would have Sailor fussing about, threatening to give him a haircut. They'd given him a freshly pressed, dark grey suit to wear. A size too large but still it looked smart, making his eyes chameleon to a green-grey to match the fabric.

Guards led him down the hall to a room that from the outside looked like any other in the building, solid off-white double doors, dirty, painted over several times, reinforced with steel and a security clearance panel—scratches around it on the wall indicating it had been recently replaced—perhaps formerly Dot-operated, now merely a reverse-retrofitted touchscreen.

Inside the room was a transformation, a scene like something out of a Victorian novel. Fine oak furniture, sofas and chairs lined with plush gold velvet. Antique cabinets filled with white China and polished silver. Indoor plants that looked slightly too green to be real sat in blue Oriental pots against the dark hardwood floor, soft yellow light filtering through their artificial leaves. A faint strain of classical music played—Chopin, or Mozart perhaps. Sam wasn't so adept at recognizing his classical composers by ear.

A long, walnut-stained table flanked by eight chairs with high backs and thick cushions sat in the center of the room.

The smell that greeted him upon entering made him slightly nauseated—a dizzying array of roasted meats, freshly-caught seafood, the acrid, delicious waft of alcohol—various libations no doubt aged for decades in oak barrels, in steels casks, with notes of honey and vanilla, juniper and smoke, jasmine and oranges.

Without hesitation, Sam sat down and immediately reached for the nearest glass, a lightweight crystal tumbler filled with sweet, smoky amber liquid. He guzzled down the contents in one gulp, not caring if it made him sick. It made his head spin and his empty stomach turn over itself in endless flips.

"My, my. He dives right into the good stuff, doesn't he?" Prime Minister Harold Waterman entered the room with quiet footsteps, his hair neatly combed, dressed in a custom-tailored three-piece suit. Beside him was General Simsworth clad in his severe grey and maroon uniform. The two men sat down on either side of Sam at the long table where he was seated at the head. Waterman was taller than both Sam and Simsworth, yet somehow appeared the most diminutive of the three whether seated or standing.

Waterman unfolded his cloth napkin and placed it across his lap. Simsworth tucked his napkin into his collar, the crystal chandelier hanging above the table reflecting broken light patterns across his shiny bald head.

The spread laid out before them was magnanimous—a large, spiced, sizzling roast on a silver platter, fishes in delicate sauces, exotic vegetables wrapped in bacon, various culinary delights from around the world that Sam had never seen before.

Waterman reached a pair of silver tongs across a plate of meat, serving a portion to everyone.

"You must try the lamb, Saint Fox," Waterman said. "It's absolutely delicious, my own personal recipe."

Across the table, Simsworth said nothing, opting instead to partake in every aspect of the feast without appearing to enjoy it. He had that ability to consume massive quantities of food without anyone ever seeing him do it. In between courses he would pause to glare at Sam, staring disdainfully as the lithe revolutionary sampled glass after glass of the finest whiskey, gin, vodka, twenty-six-year-old single malt scotch, Sauvignon Blanc, and a pint of dark beer. Sam ate little—only enough to settle his long-neglected stomach so that it could process more alcohol.

"Impressive," Waterman said. "You're a true countryman."

"Why are you feeding me all this good stuff?" asked Sam, "after practically starving me for weeks?"

"A man of your status should be well-treated," came Waterman's reply. "Our early attempts at gaining information from you were obviously unsuccessful. My colleague here, Mr. Simsworth, doesn't understand the nuances of the human psyche as well as I do." Simsworth glared half-heartedly at the Prime Minister, but said nothing as he served himself a large portion of beef Wellington.

"Ah, a bit of good cop, bad cop, then." Sam said, his lip resting on one of his many now empty glasses. "That's the oldest trick in the book. But I can't tell you what I don't know."

"You can tell us where to find Janus Jeeves and his code men," Simsworth spoke, his forehead knotting where his eyebrows ought to be. "As you know by now, we can be very kind, or, we can be very cruel."

Sam chewed bites of food slowly, sampling this and that in between furtive, suspicious glances volleyed between his two captors.

"Do you have any idea how many have died already?" Simsworth asked, folding his hands purposefully and leaning forward, an ugly grin spreading across his face.

"No one's died," Sam answered, after another hearty swallow of expensive liquor. "You're making that up. I don't believe a word either of you gentlemen say. Why, it's practically in both your job descriptions to lie—Mister Prime Minister, Mister General Fuck-U-Up." Sam blinked steadily, mustering his courage despite several of his body's systems beginning to protest their abuse.

"Oh, but you're wrong, Saint Fox," Waterman chided, dabbing at the corners of his mouth with his napkin. "Casualties have begun. We've used relics, you see. Had to practically acquire our weaponry from museums in order to teach you a lesson. I'm sure Mr. Jeeves is positively livid."

Sam swallowed heavily, setting his glass down. "What'd you bastards do, shoot some kids? That makes you right big and bad. I'm sure you're very proud of yourselves." He dropped his utensils on the table and pushed his plate away, no longer hungry. "Tell me something…why do you do it? Why does anyone do it? I mean, I just don't get it, you're paid good salaries, you have enough money, and yet it's never enough, ain't it? Somehow there's always a significant enough portion of the population without any sense of right and wrong, so it don't bother them any. They don't lose any sleep at night if how they increase their annual revenue causes other folks to lose their jobs, takes food out of their mouths, denies them necessary health care, keeps 'em from getting an education, keeps 'em from making ends meet, makes 'em depressed, suicidal—they top themselves, their wives top themselves, their kids are orphans, they become criminals, then you ask taxpayers for more money to fund our prisons to lock up folks who don't need to be locked up and you, you go out and buy a yacht! I just don't get it, don't get how anyone could be that selfish. It's like every year a set number of folks are born with some huge deficit in the humanity department, and those people are always the ones who end up runnin' the goddamn country."

Sam's colour-changing eyes were practically black. They shined with the faint gloss of tears kept at bay by anger.

Simsworth said nothing, but his hand had instinctively moved to the weapon located at his belt. Waterman looked almost impressed, but his raised eyebrows and pursed lips conveyed no true emotion. Sam stood up from the table in one swift motion, hunched over the arm of the chair with dead fire in his eyes.

"Take me back to my cell. I don't care if you bring me wine that costs a thousand quid. I won't help you, I can't. You might as well just let me go, and if you won't do that, at least let me shake and shiver in peace, detoxing on that hard cot, let me sweat and freeze my arse off and cry and vomit but don't give me any more ring-around-the-rosy talk or any more feckin' top dollar ham imported from Spain while you're fighting to keep normal people from exchanging bread and butter in a decent human manner."

"I'm sorry you have such a poor opinion of us, Mr. Fox," Waterman said. "But your perspective is just a bit too narrow, too simplistic. It's all much more complicated than that. It's a very complex system, and it's our job to maintain it. It's what's best for the country. What you and your people have instigated has led to chaos. Why, you can see it for yourself. People dying of a virus you deployed. Shops forced out of business. Riots in the streets. Is this your utopia?"

"If it's all so *complex* that a poor dumb bastard like me can't understand it, it's too complex to serve anyone," Sam said through gritted teeth. "Take me back to my cell."

"Very well." Waterman nodded at Simsworth, who rose from his chair after taking a long swig from a glass containing a colourless liquid. Grasping Sam roughly by the forearm, he hauled him out of the dining room.

Waterman placed his dinner fork on the table, picking up the smaller dessert fork beside it. He resumed his meal, serving himself a lovely slice of lemon bundt cake, a pungent recipe that included the zest of Meyer lemons, his favourite.

Chapter Thirty-Four

BIRD ON A WIRE

Vitalica. Half the nation had been prescribed it to treat symptoms of the Dot virus. Although a controlled Class B drug which could earn a stint in prison if possessed illegally, it was one of many popular street drugs that circulated in seemingly unlimited supply. Previously marketed under different names, Vitalica had been prescribed to treat various conditions from obesity to ADHD.

Most patients with the Dot virus who began taking Vitalica reported improvements in their symptoms within the first week. Fatigue decreased while productivity increased. Some subjects experienced an increase in appetite, while others reported a decrease. Similarly, some patients reported disturbances in sleep patterns while others reported a better night's sleep due to feeling more awake during the day. Overall, it seemed that patients were feeling better, and that the drug made them able to function despite being carriers of an uncharted epidemic.

Though not a cure, it was a welcome bandage. Many were able to resume their normal activities, as if they were in remission.

Some, however, were not.

Charlotte Piebald found herself bedridden—unable to sleep at night, unable to muster enough strength to get out of bed during the day, too groggy and disoriented. She informed Doctor Wender that the Vitalica he prescribed had little to no effect. He'd tripled the dosage and added Somnaquell, a sleep and/or anxiety medication which calmed her nerves for the first hour or so, but ironically kept her awake for most of the night, during which she watched the Ideal World direct shopping channel, its monotonous advertisements oddly comforting. Luckily the Ideal World still accepted 'real' currency, and since she was already infected, it didn't matter if she used their app on her cleverband to purchase gift boxes of triple-milled soap, stackable stainless steel containers, a teapot with the loveliest little pattern of lavender tea roses painted on it.

Charlotte wondered if anyone had attempted to avoid the virus by providing businesses with their Dot serial number manually, by voice, avoiding contact with any P.O.S. terminal, phone, tablet, or computer display—all devices that had eradicated the need to enter in account numbers by hand and potentially expose yourself to fraud—god knows where that information went as it travelled at lightning speed through the atmosphere. She answered her own question by reflecting upon her own experience contacting businesses via voice—recorded messages, an automated response system that guided you through sequences of digits to enter into your keyscreen—and then you wound up swiping the Dot to complete your purchase anyway, rarely was there ever a human operator at the other end of the line. If she required another human being to be present in order to acquire all her goods and services, absolutely nothing would ever get done.

Charlotte touched the call icon on her cleverband's display to alert her assistant. A young woman soon appeared in Charlotte's bedroom doorway. She was dressed in a blue button-down blouse and grey slacks, her thick, brown hair tied back in a firm ponytail.

"Talia, darling. Thank goodness. Do you think you could fluff these pillows for me a tad? They're getting awfully bunchy, what with me just lying around on them all day. In fact, could you fetch me a few new ones from the wardrobe?" Charlotte pulled out a large pillow with a pale yellow ruffled case from behind her head. "Here, replace this one. It's always been too soft, anyway."

"Yes, of course, Miss Piebald," Talia said.

"God, Talia, you're so lucky. This disease is awful—so sinister, so subversive. I can't remember the last time I felt comfortable."

Talia propped Charlotte up with a new purple ruffled pillow and smoothed down her bed sheets. "You look better today," she told her. "More colour in your cheeks. You'll be better soon; you're strong."

"I wish I had your confidence," Charlotte said. She dismissed Talia after the girl brought her a glass of vitamin water, two paracetamol and three-and-a-half white round tabs of Vitalica.

Adverts were playing on the telly again. I swear there's more adverts than actual telly, thought Charlotte. Some of them are rather amusing though. This one with the squirrel and the mop is simply hilarious.

Suddenly, the screen cut to black. Black and white fuzz appeared for a brief moment, frenzied ants darting across the screen. Charlotte had never seen this sort of interruption before in all her years of watching telly.

The picture shivered back into focus.

It was that awful man, in all his tacky feathers and sequins. The one who'd started all this. The one who'd made her sick.

Charlotte glowered at the screen. The effeminate old tosser had the gall to look solemn. She wondered what he was up to now. A new strain of his infectious virus, perhaps? Was she not dying fast enough for him?

The man in the television screen was pleading with the government to stop taking innocent lives, his long face beseeching, dark eyes adopting an expression that was almost human. A crazed cult leader, Charlotte thought.

"You can't fight a war with pleases and thank yous," he was saying. "All you understand is violence and depravity." He held out the tail syllables of words for too long, she noticed. *Depraviteee.* "I, Prime Minister Waterman, I am not depraved, like you lot. You might think I am, but you're wrong. Still, I wouldn't force my hand if I were you." He grinned then, showing off two terrible, unnaturally coloured rows of teeth.

Dear god, how have they not arrested this man yet? Charlotte wondered. I love my King and country, but there's a reason people at large assume our government is completely inept.

Goodness, do I feel faint, she noted, falling back against her harem of pillows. That man is the devil, and he's got the whole world doing his bidding.

Just what would it take to stop him?

Darkness broke in streaks through fog and street lamps, through beer bottles and cigarettes lining damp gutters. The distant shouts of girls and boys echoed as they made their way home from the pub in the wee hours before daybreak, squeezing out the last drops of their collective high before exhaustion took hold. Eyes sleepy and shining, wisps of brightly coloured hair sticking to their foreheads, scented sweet like flowers and stale like whiskey, home to their mums, home to their untidy beds, thinking of nothing but the new loves and old losses found and stolen on the dancefloor only hours before.

How beautiful and bright was the blissful ignorance of youth.

Jeeves scuffed along the trash-littered streets, his shadow on the pavement moving in flashes and stripes in contrast to the unwavering silhouette of Montreal keeping pace beside him.

On this dark morning that felt like eternal night, Jeeves and Montreal returned to the scene of the crime, to the alleyway behind the Tesco on Marlborough Road, to where Jeeves had anticipated the deployment of TAKEBACK in shakes and shivers, pulsing like a livewire in the cold wet dawn of Londontown.

It was raining once again. Not the kind of rain that happens on any given day, light showers in the spring that you can walk through without getting very wet, popping into a café for a pot of tea if it turns heavy, waiting inside for it to let up and the sun to peek out for a few minutes.

This was a torrential downpour. Black sky and thunder in the distance.

Montreal's slick black trench coat was wrapped tightly around him, his gloved hands in his pockets. "It's not going to get better any time soon." he said. "Should stay here under the overhang till it lets up."

Jeeves scuffed the sidewalk with his alligator boot, standing next to Montreal under the canvas awning behind the rear entryway of Tesco.

"It'll get better," Jeeves said, pausing to light a cigarette. "Always does. Just have to be patient."

"Give it here." Montreal reached for Jeeves' lighter and cigarettes. The lighter was fickle, a thick silver thing inlaid with opal that Jeeves refused to part with even though the darn thing only worked half the time.

In between curses, Montreal finally managed to spark a flame, handing the lighter back to Jeeves. "So, I've gone through every channel I could think of. No leads, nothing. No canary I know will sing the song of Saint Fox." He hollowed his cheeks as he inhaled from yet another sworn-off vice. "I can tell you this much though. The fact that we can't find him means they got him."

Jeeves was quiet for a moment. Behind the grey wisps of smoke escaping from his lips, his long face was tired and drawn.

"They're killing 'em dead," said Jeeves, his eyes on the ground in front of him. "Just kids." He dropped his cigarette onto the wet ground, watching as the rain washed it down the street, a bent little submarine. "They'll kill him, too." His voice was barely above a whisper. There was no lilt at the end of his sentence, no frenetic pitch, no exaggerated drawing out of consonants.

"You know they'll stop soon, right? It's a last ditch attempt to scare us off before they accept their fate, calling us bioterrorists, tryin' to convince people that TAKEBACK is aggressive, that their violent demonstration against us is for people's safety. Probably trying to impress the Americans or something, show those bastards we don't need their help." Montreal glanced sidelong at Jeeves, then up at the black sky, exhaling his smoke. "Too many folks are using GGcoin now, whether they like it or not. The money—that's the real battle.

The virus is GGcoin, and when something goes viral, there's no stopping it. The virus takes over. Redefines the system it overtakes. You don't even remember what it was like before." Montreal's blue eyes were bright and earnest like a boy's, a stark contrast to the lines on his face detailing his age and experience.

"No one was supposed to die," Jeeves said. A sick wave of panic had taken up residence in his stomach, but he pressed it down low beneath madness and hope. "War is always messy, no matter what. I should have known."

"Could have told you that," Montreal huffed. "And you did know. You just didn't want to believe it."

"We were supposed to cure everyone. TAKEBACK—*boom!*, then GET CLEAN, rolled out in waves as the usage of GG coin steadily rose—that was the plan. Now we can't even distribute the cure with the goddamn military posted round every corner."

"You could make the cure readily available. Or…you could tell them the truth," Montreal said, casting his eyes skyward.

"Too soon!" Jeeves snipped. "It would threaten the currency." Increasingly ludicrous thoughts ran through his mind like a news ticker. "I wanna help 'em all, I do, but if we time this wrong it'll make all our hard work for naught."

"I know what you're thinkin'. What's my next scheme?" Montreal shook his head. "Ain't always a way out."

"You're wrong," said Jeeves, lighting up another fag. "Always a way out. One way or another, Saint Fox will sing again."

"How's that gonna work?" Montreal raised a skeptical eyebrow.

"He's my boy. I made him once, I can make him again. We'll rally," Jeeves said, nodding vigorously. "Get everyone pumped up again. Teach 'em it's okay to fight back, protect yourself, don't fold yer cards no matter what you've got in your hand, don't show them your belly. Don't sweat and don't break eye contact. Just steady...steady..." he balanced on one foot, arms out in front of him, rain falling between his fingers, "then HIT! Hit 'em where it counts."

"We did exactly that. Hit 'em in their pocketbooks." Montreal pulled his coat closer around himself. "I'll keep digging. Security's gotten tighter, wherever they're keeping him is someplace different from the bases in operation when I was active. Who knows what they're even keeping him for? It's not like the kid knows anything."

"Just what I taught him." Jeeves shifted a tad in his demeanor, so that he stood a little taller and his colours came alive. "Rain'sss letting up. Let's go."

He stepped out into the drizzle, doing zigzag spins past the murky puddles at his feet.

Montreal sighed. "I'll keep you informed, Nijinsky. Try my darndest. I like that boy."

"You do that. We don't want to lose another man. Now come on, I'm in need of one of the other talents on your myriad list of skills."

"Which skills would those be?"

"Your rock star skills, of course," Jeeves said, a smile spreading across his lips as he tilted his face to the wet sky.

Jeeves and Montreal turned their backs on Tesco on Marlborough Road. They walked silently through the water-covered streets, Jeeves dancing in nimble jumps and jives whenever the rain fell lighter.

Chapter Thirty-Five

SCREAM LIKE A BABY

Light slipped into the concrete room through the corridor, and was immediately blocked by the looming, ever-present form of General Simsworth.

"Sleeping in the middle of the day, are we? Just like a rock star," he mocked, stepping in closer.

"I don't feel so good," Sam mumbled. He shook steadily, skin pale and covered with a layer of cold sweat. "Think I need a doctor."

"Is that right?" Simsworth nudged his thigh with a steel-covered toe. Sam shivered, half frozen to death in the stark square prison. His once shimmering days and nights were now spent lying on a cot atop a flea-infested mattress, under a scratchy brown blanket no better than sackcloth, drifting in and out of consciousness and hoping that today would be the last day his body needed to detox.

"Why's it every time I open my eyes I see your disgusting face?"

Simsworth crossed his arms. "'Cause I've been marching over here every couple of hours to make sure you don't get any sleep. Or maybe I'm just dancing through yer dreams," he said, making horrid mocking kissing sounds.

He stepped over to loom above Sam, a bright, sweaty thing casting a dark shadow. "Here." Simsworth shoved a small chalky substance into his mouth with his large fingers. "Chew. Swallow. It'll make you feel much, much better."

"What is it?" Sam choked out, the powder coating his dry throat.

"It's your favourite sweet," Simsworth said. "Tasty smack. Good, isn't it?"

Sam leaned over the cot and spat on the ground, a few pathetic splotches of saliva and white.

"I didn't go through gettin' clean against my will just to get forced into becoming a junkie again," he said.

Simsworth grabbed Sam around the ankles, pulling him off the cot and onto the floor, into his own sick. "You don't have a will anymore, Saint Fix." He spat on the ground next to his face. Simsworth kicked him in the stomach, then exited the cell in three quick strides. A loud metallic clang echoed throughout the room as the door slammed shut.

Sweat ran down Sam's back in wide, thick streams, heat and chills, fire and water, the salt burning wounds that had yet to heal.

Montreal was right, he thought. *Everyone who says they're your friend is a liar.* He coughed and spat hard on the ground, a mixture of blood and bile. The smell in the room was beyond unbearable, warm recycled air and stale piss that he no longer recognised as foul after living in it for weeks.

I'm the King of England, he thought. The kids won't stand for this. When they find out what's happened to me, they'll band together and bust me out of here. My own army of devotees.

But they aren't my army. They belong to Janus Jeeves. They belong to no one. They're just lost kids, like me. Didn't know what the bloody fuck was going on, just wanted something to believe in, something besides superhero movies and cleverly written television shows.

So I gave them a rock band.

All those flashing lights and eyes like so many dead things boring into you, like they wanted to carve out a piece of your soul and cherish it next to their hearts 'cause there was nothing else inside of them.

The beginnings of a killer tune, he mused. Kit would know what to do with it. She'd make it screech and squeal and beg, dip and rise and plummet, leaving the kids high out of their minds and wanting more.

Sam was glad she couldn't see him now. It didn't matter. No snatch, no matter how sweet, could save him. His mind reeled at the thought of sex, of smooth legs and full, red lips, of cunts and cocks and tits and whatever the hell else people had on them these days. He retched onto the concrete floor. The vomit from his near-empty stomach was practically transparent.

For the past three days, seemingly without reprieve, the singer for Saint Fox and The Independence had been beaten, punched, kicked, and cut open. He'd had buckets of freezing ice water thrown at him, then buckets of boiling water. They'd shaved off his hair, through the dark roots grown in underneath the red, not caring how many times they nicked his scalp in the process. *I guess Sailor won't be giving me another haircut any time soon,* he'd thought when it happened.

There were two large, uneven gashes right below his knees, blood seeping through the dark denim of his jeans and soaking it in drabs, the fabric sticking to his skin. His stomach danced in waves and pulses—since the bizarro banquet with Waterman and Simsworth he'd barely been given anything to eat, and so it twisted in knots, neglected and confused.

Sam rolled over onto his side, dry gasps coming from his throat that hardly made any sound. He closed his eyes as much as he could—crusted and swollen as they were, he could only squint them half-closed. Slits of pale light illuminating dust particles swam before him like fireflies.

He imagined he was on a beach; he imagined he was by a lake. He imagined he was a toymaker in a toy factory who could make any child's perfect toy without having to first ask them what they wanted—the joy on their faces set his heart full to nearly bursting. But then, the toys crumbled. The children grew old. The lakes and the oceans dried up.

If my heart did explode right now, it would be okay, he thought. Because I tried, I really did. What else was I going to do? Live like a zombie until the government repossessed my house not long after I signed on for a mortgage I'd never repay in a lifetime? Live inside photographs like some waking digital dream, life in 17K-pixel resolution with a supercar that cost 300,000 quid and a girl who looks like another girl I once knew but is just a proxy, one whose name I can't even remember?

No, he thought. I don't want any of that.

Sam squeezed his eyes shut until even the specks behind his eyelids stopped dancing, and wished away the 21st century.

You are being made sane, you are being made clean. You are being watched, you are being scrubbed, coloured, waxed, spotted and dried. A diamond in the rough, a man stronger than machine, faster than any form of transit, braver than them all.

Sam threw his half-eaten food tray across the room, swill that came at irregular intervals and was barely keeping him alive. The tray made a hollow clanging noise, flat and dead like a butter knife against a hollow tin cup. For days on end now, a monotone female voice—not unlike the voice of Jules, his holographic cleverband assistant—had droned on and on without reprieve. It was all nonsense; it didn't mean anything. Sam felt as though his brain was turning to mush.

"Shut up!" bellowed Sam. He kicked at the sweat-soaked sheet bunched up around his ankles.

The voice boomed at him again, *2 + 2 = 5, soylent green is people. Narcs are drug users, pushers are princes and bakers are thieves. Shame on all the liars, pain and suffering upon them. They are going to reap just what they sow.*

Ten. Nine. Eight. Seven, the voice counted backwards. *Seven. Eight. Nine. Ten.* Before his eyes was now the watery, iridescent face of Janus Jeeves. Now, when the voice from nowhere spoke, it sounded like the father of the Arcana.

I told you, Foxy. I told you this would happen, the hollow vision of the charlatan said, hovering above him. *You weren't paying attention.*

Why? Sam asked, if only in his mind. *Why did you let this happen, if you knew?*

Monkeys gots to keep looking forward, not behind.

Sam held his head between his knees. He shook violently. It had been too long since Simsworth had administered his last dose. He'd started referring to the stone-faced military man as 'Doc' in his head. Where was the doctor with his medicine? Nothing was real.

"You're a horrible bastard," Sam said to the translucent vision of Jeeves before him. "A terrible, horrible bastard. You used me to get what you wanted. Now I pay the price while you enjoy the freedom I bought."

There is no revolution, waxing and waning Jeeves said. *I made it up. I just wanted to see whether it would break a strapping young lad such as yourself. I am mad, after all,* he cackled.

"What about the kids?" Sam exclaimed at the apparition. He removed a leather cuff from around his wrist, now ripped and frayed, and threw it at Jeeves. It went right through him.

Kids are casualties. Can't be helped.

Loud, unbearably irritating dance music beat an unwelcome syncopated rhythm inside Sam's head. It felt like needles behind his eyelids. He looked out and saw crowds staring up at him, their eyes all the same. Arms raised to him, adoring smiles on their faces. They were chanting his name, calling for the band to return to the stage and play their encore.

I'm on my way, he thought. The audience cheered as the sky above them faded from blue to red, from red to black. Their cries and cheers were drowned out by the hollow clanging of Zephyr's war drums, *rat-tat-tat-tat,* like marching on the battlefield. Guitars shaped like his own, Kit's, and Muzzy's were shrieking warbirds flying through the sky overhead, dropping bombs onto the unsuspecting grey world beneath them.

Then Jeeves stood before them all, the general in sparkles and pearls, ready to face the enemy, his army of a million skinny underachievers lined up steadfastly behind him in countless rows.

The battle had begun.

Limbs were severed by deafening blasts, bodies torn asunder. Fourteen-year-old girls blinded in an instant, their wombs made barren. Young men on the battlefield scattered atop the glitter-covered ground, screaming in pain, tears mixing with the blood and ashes on their scarred faces. Chemical fires ablaze throughout London, through the countryside, through the open fields of Glastonbury covered in colourful tents and banners. An orgy of destruction.

You were their leader, Saint Fox. They followed you, not me, said the image of Jeeves. Now he was Dark Jeeves, dressed head to toe in black. No sparkles, no bright colours, no baubles. Nothing but his thin, drawn lips and his razor-cold eyes peering out from beneath a blackened shroud.

Welcome to the future, he said.

Welcome to the present, Sam thought back at him. Goodbye to the past.

Chapter Thirty-Six

LONELY HEARTS CLUB BAND

The flat in Morden was too quiet. The Arcana seemed to have scattered like mice, hiding out in holes where no one would catch them, and Janus Jeeves pondered both the resilience and fear of the human spirit.

He sat in his kitchen eating three different kinds of curry from three different bowls. I'm losing them, he thought. Without a pretty saint to look up to, the little foxes scamper away.

Got to give them something to believe in.

He unlocked his cleverband and began flipping through photos in the FoxDen app, running a finger across each of the band members' lovely faces: Young Zephyr on war drums, lanky and laidback Muzzy on bass guitar, that lightning fast firebrand Kit on lead axe. Saint Fox looked stunning and defiant as always, straight down from the silver streaks at the tips of his flaming red hair to the sharply angled jut of his hips. Cocky, idealistic, sweet-voiced, and up for anything. The boy had been the perfect combination of ingredients.

"It's alright, Sammy," Jeeves said, staring at the 3D image of the lad, moving slightly in animated hyper-realistic lies before his eyes. "Look at you, Freedom Fox. We made the kids sing again. Sing when they'd forgotten how."

Gone were the days when the Arcana were merely a few scattered tatters amongst the many—a smattering of dreamers hosting rallies in parking lots, holding court in bookstores and warehouses, transferring propaganda throughout the digital universe.

They were mainstream now. And nothing kills the mainstream.

They would win the war; he knew it. Reports of shootings had gone down—His Majesty's retroactively armed forces would soon return their weapons to the museums where they belonged. Soon everyone would be using GGcoin; it was the biggest thing to enter the scene since cleverbands.

He tried not to think about the bodies he missed—Sam most of all. He was a good kid. Jeeves hadn't given up hoping that he would return.

Jeeves tapped the display twice over Sam's face, closing the photo. He pressed his palms against one another, mentally pepping himself up. He shouldn't feel grieved or sorry. He must find a way to celebrate, to shout to the world that the kids were free, that rock n' roll was here to stay.

So that's what they would do.

Janus Jeeves signed into the admin account of the FoxDen app, getting straight to work.

GET CLEAN is in the palm of your hand, the sign-in page now read. After logging in, those few who passed through Benson Bridges' security jungle unscathed would gain access to a bit of news that would tickle the pickles of anyone devoted enough to give and get the amount of information required to enter.

Saint Fox and The Independence will play again. Stay tuned for details.

~

The mid-sized club was packed top to bottom with nervous energy. An impressive turnout, considering the headlining band playing tonight was not even on the schedule.

But diehard fans have a way of finding out what no one else knows, at least until the next day when it's all over the news. The night, however—the night is just for them. *Got this from FoxDen. Very hush-hush. Only tell folks you know you can trust.*

Backstage in the dressing room, Saint Fox paced back and forth. His wide eyes, smeared with copious amounts of kohl eyeliner, caught nervous glimpses of himself in the bulb-framed mirror. He wore a faded black-and-white t-shirt with a patterned newspaper print, and very tight, shiny black trousers. Steadying himself with one palm against the vanity, he recited the lyrics to 'Money Dance' under his breath, over and over.

Janus Jeeves entered on a high note, waltzing in and placing two fluttering hands upon the shoulders of his messiah.

"How we feelin', Foxy?" he inquired.

"Terrific, just terrific," Saint Fox replied, inhaling through his nose before turning to face the puppet master. "Now, are you *sure* this is a good idea?" he asked, with more than an ounce of sass and a fair amount of trepidation.

"Silencio, baby," Jeeves said, running his fingers through the frontman's spiky hair and twisting it so it stood even more on end. "Everything's under control."

"It don't feel like it," Saint Fox said. "Feels like we're betraying him."

"C'mon now, shush with that sort of talk. It's what he would have wanted. Keep the movement going. Am I right?"

"Shit, don't say things like 'It's what he would have wanted,' makes it sound like he's dead and he ain't dead. He's just hiding, I know it. I'd know it if he were dead."

"Course he's not dead," Jeeves assured, adjusting Saint Fox's t-shirt so that it hung provocatively off one bony shoulder. "We never really die. Don't you know that?"

"Just...shut it, okay?" he sputtered, hands flailing. "I'm only doing this for him, 'cause before he left he asked me to be Saint Fox, alright? And because I might as fuckin' well, I've listened to his damned music enough."

"Benson's got the PA system all set up. All you have to do is move your lips and shake your hips. Band'll take care of the rest. Crowd won't know the difference with all that makeup on…you're about the same height."

"Yeah okay, fine," he said, brushing Jeeves' fussing hands away from him. "Let's get this over with."

Janus Jeeves guided the rock star out of the dressing room and into the wings.

"Knock 'em dead, Sailor boy," Jeeves cheerleaded, squeezing his shoulder.

The lights in the club rose from dusk blue to sunset orange. The drums sounded the alarm, raising incrementally in volume and intensity.

Saint Fox appeared from the shadows, sauntering out onto the stage. He raised his arms wide and lifted his chin to the sky, bold and defiant.

The crowd roared its approval.

Kit Alysdair had played horrendously tonight by her own standards. Guitar solos botched, backup vocals off-key, fingers ghosting the wrong chords, picking out the wrong riffs. Even her guitars had protested—wrong tuning, broken strings, amps squealing feedback against her will. Even if no one else had noticed, it didn't matter. She'd noticed. She knew how poorly she'd performed.

I need a drink, she thought, not for the first time today, wanting badly to fuzz out the decision-making centers of her brain. Thankfully, there was always plenty of alcohol backstage. She stared at herself in the mirror of a vanity with more makeup and sequins littered across it than usual. Sailor's stuff he brought from home, she realised. In the mirror her own eyes were sunken in and black, hair frizzy, lips red, the skin on her face sallow and stressed. She thought about how she would look in another thirty years—grey frazzled hair, thin puckered lips, eyes with no life light in them.

Stupid girl, she chastised. Superficial. She unscrewed the cap from a bottle of Jim Beam and took a long swig. It burned like sweet heaven on the way down, lighting a fire in her gut that felt like tears kept at bay, twisting them into something else—anger, lust, aggression. Anything else. Anything other than how she was feeling.

She wanted to be angry at Sailor for taking Sam's place, angry at Jeeves for orchestrating it. She couldn't quite manage either.

Another long sip of whiskey.

It was Sam she was mad at. She saw the way he'd been self-destructing before he went missing, hell, he'd probably gone and done something stupid to get himself caught, probably turned himself in during some drug-inspired epiphany where he figured it was the only way to clear his conscience, save his soul.

Maybe I should have gone with him to Fiji, she thought. At least then I'd know he was safe.

"Selfish bastard," she muttered. She downed about a quarter of the bottle, then wiped the back of her hand across her mouth, smearing her red lipstick.

"Are you talking about our dear Sammy boy?" Jeeves was suddenly in the doorway, his palms bracketed against the paint-chipped frame in a double-jointed display. "Or me, perhaps?"

"I—bloody hell Jeeves. Didn't see you there. Give a girl a little warning, would ya?"

"Sorry to startle you, honeybun." He took the bottle of whiskey from her, setting it down on the table. He brushed a stray piece of hair behind her ear and whispered, "Something to take your mind off the pain, eh? You know that'll only make things worse."

"Maybe in the long run, but it sure as hell makes it bearable now." She tilted her head to the side and crossed her arms, a challenge on her face.

The maestro held a clever twinkle in his eye, a slow grin growing on his lips. "You need a distraction, ey girly?"

He stepped into her space, wrapping his arms around her neck and leaning in as if he was going to kiss her.

The liquor coursing through her veins making her stupid and brave. "Why the hell not?" She pulled him in, tilting her head towards him. "Show me what you got, daddy," she said, letting her eyelids flutter closed.

Jeeves grabbed her by the chin in one narrow hand, forcing her to open her eyes and stare into his. Then he released her, dropping his arms to his sides and laughing as he shuffled away from the young guitarist.

Kit's eyes narrowed in an instant. "The fuck was that about?"

He draped himself sideways against a chair, bony hips and elbows sticking out at odd angles. "S' really that bad, love? Even mad ol' Janus's a good enough distraction, 'cause anything's better than what you're feeling? Hurt, betrayal, failure, confusion, twisted lust you'd misdirect just about anywhere?"

"Fuck you," she said, grabbing her whiskey bottle from the vanity table and placing it against her lips.

"Ah ah ah," Jeeves shook his finger back and forth, chiding. "I'm trying to look out for you. For all of you," he said, tisking at her some more. "Sex, drugs, and rock n' roll. It'sss not the 20th century anymore, baby. It's a brave new world. Bigger than all of us—you, me, Sammy boy, Sailor boy. Now, we've got some fallout. With Sam gone, some of the kiddies are losing touch. The show tonight gave them the reassurance they needed. You know how fans are—they'll turn on you in an instant, but when they love you, they love hard, and they'll defend you without question."

Kit stared at the menagerie of beads and booze on the countertop, at the ugly purple fringe lamp near the door, the jagged crack in the ceiling, anywhere but at Jeeves. At first she welcomed the distraction. Now she just wanted him to leave.

"You're a part of it now, in the thick of it whether you like it or not," Jeeves said. "You gave them something to believe in that put them on the right track. They can't do it all by their little lonesome selves—no one ever taught them how. Never knew not to buy and sell their tender little hearts to the greedy cold profit and loss diamond desert mecca that only knows how to steal."

Kit set the whiskey bottle back down on the vanity with a clunk, avoiding Jeeves' gaze as she headed for the door. She was sick of this. She heard music playing outside in the hall and it sounded far away.

She turned around on her heel, finally lifting her eyes to meet his. "Was it worth it?" she asked.

Jeeves shook his head slowly back and forth. "Not up for me to decide, girly. It's up to them. For time to tell. For each to make in their own image." Jeeves squinted, regarding her quizzically. "What do *you* think, eh?"

Kit hesitated for a moment. "I wanted the revolution," she said firmly. "I was willing to pay a price. I just didn't know it would cost this much."

Jeeves smiled almost sadly as Kit turned and walked out of the dressing room, the heels of her black boots clicking against the linoleum.

"See you at the next show?" Jeeves asked.

Kit flipped him the bird over her shoulder, but her voice echoed back at him from down the hallway. "Always got more music in me," she said.

Jeeves watched her go, then noticed the abandoned bottle of whiskey sitting amidst the ruins of cigarette butts and glitter on the table. "Ah, hell," he said, and took a swig.

"I love him too, baby," Jeeves said solemnly, picturing the perfect dream. "I love him, too."

Kit took the long way home, walking past closed shops and down alleyways where it was dangerous for a girl to walk alone at night, or so people said. She didn't much care. Anyone who was dumb enough to try something would get the heel of her boot where the sun don't shine.

I'll walk the streets at night, to be hidden by the city lights.

"Love is Like Oxygen" by The Sweet played in her head as she walked past dozens of people without seeing them. *Love is like oxygen, you get too much you get too high.*

Not enough and you're gonna die.

She was tired. Maybe Jeeves was right. Maybe he was always right and she was always wrong. Or maybe it was she who was always right, but spoke up just a second too late for it to matter. Jeeves was careless, impulsive, brave, idealistic, the man himself more of a fever vision than a flesh and blood person. Her little encounter with him in the dressing room didn't even register, like a riff she'd scribbled out then abandoned once she realised it didn't fit anywhere, and was derivative to boot.

Sam was like a song she'd been working on for years and could never finish. Lyrics she'd written and re-written but failed to get the meaning across. Notes that danced along the edge of something important but didn't make your heart soar and then plummet the way a great song is supposed to. Her Sam song was a song forgotten after a year or two.

So forget him, she told herself. Know a lost cause when you see one. They were no Sid and Nancy, though considering how that story wound up, she should be grateful. Anyway, it wasn't like she loved him, it was just the comfort and familiarity of it. They had spent too much time together. It was the persona, she realised, the image of him that she wanted. Like Jeeves himself, Sam projected a dream up on the stage, possessed an energy, a magnetism no one could keep up 24/7 once they were behind the curtain. Like a naïve young woman before the storm of life hits, she thought she could save him, make him better than he was, keep him from self-destructing. No one can save anyone from themselves. She knew that now.

Kit turned down a path where the breeze was cut off and the street lamps were out. A horn blared. What time was it? Late. So late that only fog and demons and lost children were out at this hour.

Letting go is never really letting go, she thought. You tell yourself you're moving on, you're a different person now, but all it takes is one little thing to set you back. A scent, a scar, a bent dinner fork, a song, a song, a song, ones he gave you, ones you gave him, ones you'd written together.

Love gets ya high.

Long live the revolution, long live GGcoin. If the country had awoken from their slumber just enough to put the tea kettle on, it was worth it. If layers of greedy, ugly darkness had been torn down and were now crystal-clear glass thin as a pin, transparent and shatterproof, then it was worth it. A little heartbreak was worth it, getting caught up in the storm. The mistake of making a man in your own image, building him from cardboard and feathers and E strings, when behind his eyes, he was really just the cardboard.

They should be trying harder to find Sam, should have heard something by now. Just continuing the band without him, reveling in each small triumph while god knows what was happening to the real Saint Fox—it wasn't right. If he was in danger, there was nothing she could do about it.

I can't shake off my city blues

Every way I turn I lose

She reached her building, climbing the stairs with heavy feet, exhausted from the show, exhausted from everything.

She would have to begin writing a new song. A whole album maybe. One she would sing herself, no one else telling her what to do. In her flat alone, in a dingy little nightclub to an audience of ten, to a stadium full of thousands, she would crash through her strings however she wished, sing whatever her heart desired.

As she had wanted in the beginning.

Chapter Thirty-Seven

INVISIBLE MAN

Some people are natural born killers, they say. Not so for Sam Numan.

Sam was, in fact, born rather decent, someone who was always willing to lend a hand to his fellow man. A diamond in the rough, ready to be chipped at and moulded.

Now, they had chipped away until there was nothing left.

Alone inside his cell, Sam Numan tried to feel something, anything decent. Tried to remember former lovers, great nights out with mates, but when he looked inside, there was only bile. Only desire for vengeance upon those who had done this to him. Those who had delivered him into the fires of hell, delivered him to faceless men with cruel grins and heavy fists. Those who had never delivered him—from evil. Those who had broken their promises.

The promise breaker of all promise breakers was Janus Jeeves.

When Sam pictured his narrow, silly putty, crocodile-smile face, it felt like a bolt of lightning shooting down his spine, and then his blood would run cold. His eyes would tear and burn, his hands clenched into fists at his sides.

Janus Jeeves was a liar. He had promised a revolution. He had practically delivered a massacre.

Sam lay back against the thin, stink-infested cot and closed his eyes. He pictured wrapping his wiry, calloused hands around Jeeves' wiry, callous neck, and squeezing tighter tighter tighter. Each time he imagined it, it produced an increasingly comical result. The first time Sam had the fantasy, Jeeves' neck had snapped like a too-taut guitar string. The second time his head popped like a great red balloon. After that, Sam moved on to more colourful delusions, facsimiles of techniques that had been used upon himself. He pandered to Jeeves' love of dramatic eye makeup by painting around his eyes in blood-red streaks, cutting wide holes around those beady mismatched peepers. He followed up this butchering by submerging the maestro's head in water, red liquid from the cuts on his face bleeding into the tub in swirling patterns. Sam would pull Jeeves' head up as he gasped for air, begging for mercy when he found his voice again, his cries blending into a soothing, syncopated, babbling cacophony that was music to the frontman's ears.

Sam's eyes flashed open. He leaned over the side of the cot and vomited once, twice, suddenly appalled that he could ever conceive of doing such a thing.

When daybreak came, two of Simsworth's dog men came into the room, sidestepping the pool of sick and hauling him up by the shoulders.

They dragged him through a long, cold alleyway to a garage where Simsworth was waiting, flanked by a dozen or so uniformed slaves to the Crown.

"You're a free man," Simsworth said, the unreadable grin of the soulless upon his face.

The garage door groaned open as they pushed Sam unceremoniously into the daylight. Blinding light—white, with hints of blue and red.

Stage lights, Sam thought.

The uniformed men who were all the same shoved him into the back of a van. They drove for a time in silence. He might have fallen asleep.

When he awoke, he was alone. He blinked frantically, eyes attempting to adjust as he tried to determine where the hell he was.

Beige buildings, scene kids, street lamps filtering through smoke in the night air. A dingy little club across the street. Broken beer bottles along the sidewalk.

He was back in South London.

The passersby seemed to take no notice of him. Just another skiver on the street, like the good old days. An advert flew past him, a flyer printed on neon-green paper from a home instaprint.

The flyer advertised a show for a local band. A grainy, black-and-white image in which none of the band members' faces were recognizable, and fat words in some obnoxious font stating the venue, time, and date. The club was one he knew well—The Independence had played there many times before in the early days. The date on the flyer...what was the date? The show could have been days ago for all he knew. Sam stared at the grainy faces on the flyer, almost familiar. Some kid must've thrown this together all unofficial-like, else this band is really shyte at promoting themselves, he thought.

He tucked the flyer into his jacket.

~

Prime Minister Harold Waterman turned up the volume on his Dolby 11.1 5D surround soundsphere system so that he could properly enjoy the nuances of Johann Sebastian Bach's Concerto for Two Violins in D Minor. The two cubes of ice in his glass were perfectly square, and his drink was the perfect temperature. The electronic fireplace was at a measured 20 degrees, and no one had called to bother him for at least an hour.

Everything was perfect. And then his wife entered.

Amelia waved her hand, turning down the stereo volume. She positioned herself so the holo display she held was directly in front of Harold's face. He couldn't make out what it said—she was standing too close and he didn't have his reading glasses—but it appeared to be some news article about the latest military action. An unflattering 3D image of him with his mouth open mid-speech accompanied the article.

"So, you're a murderer now? Is this who I'm married to?" Her voice pierced through Bach like a laser beam.

"Amelia, please," he said, leaning forward in his chair.

"Don't you 'Amelia, please,' me. Your men are out there killing innocent civilians."

Harold sighed. "Look around you. Look at this house. Look at your clothes. You do your own shopping; you know what these things cost. How do you expect us to pay for all this without restoring our already precarious financial system to its former disglory? We're protecting a way of life that has been successfully in operation for decades. A way that has allowed you, me, and our children to live comfortably. It's not as if I derive any pleasure from what has to be done—I don't like it any more than you do."

"Of course, you've got it all figured out as usual. You're doing what's best for the country. Well, if you expect me to just sit by and let this happen, you're dead wrong, Harry." Amelia's lips were set in a thin line, something like regret on her face. Something like it, but not quite. More as if she had encountered a question on an exam she didn't know the answer to, in a requisite class she'd never wanted to take in the first place.

"You don't seem to understand, Amelia. We are at war. With war comes casualties. Now, whether this is a revolution or an anarchist uprising that must be quelled, I don't properly know. No one is truly capable of judgment until a godforsaken mess such as this is where it belongs—in the past. But I do know that it is my job to orchestrate the fight for the side that I'm on, for as long as I'm required to. And it *will* come to an end. Perhaps sooner than you think. The fact is, whatever military action we've taken doesn't seem to be working. People aren't scared unless they're face to face with the barrel of a gun, and we simply don't have the arms and the manpower to keep this up. It's not a physical world we live in anymore; you can't kill a digital virus with 20th century weapons. You adapt, or you die out. For goodness' sake, Amelia. Maybe you should go out there and open up a GGcoin account for yourself."

"Very funny. Spin it any way you like—you're still a killer and a coward." Her short, perfectly manicured nails gripped the back of the cream-coloured leather sofa, one they had bought just before the chaos began.

"You also realise I don't care what you think." Waterman turned away from her and faced the fireplace, taking a sip from his drink before it got too warm.

"No. You don't care what anyone thinks. Just doing your duty, is that it? Well then, you won't mind if I leave. You won't mind if I divorce you, take Felicity and Stephen— one sick with fear, the other infected with that awful virus— and go to Windermere to live with my parents."

"I won't mind if *you* go," Waterman said. "As for the children—they aren't as fragile as you think. I have my doubts about Stephen's illness... the boy's symptoms are practically non-existent. Nevertheless, considering the circumstances, perhaps it would be good if they spent some time away." Waterman waved his hand to the left, turning the sound back on.

Amelia's eyes were colder than usual. "You'd say anything to silence whatever's left of your conscience, Harry."

She left, then, carrying with her the scent of her subtle woodsy perfume, and all her accusations of the things he just could not get right, no matter how he tried.

He would miss her, a little.

Waterman smiled, as much as a man like him ever did. He gazed into the crystal ball of his expensive drink. He had done the right thing.

He would play it on their terms. In the present, in the future, not the past. The Crown would acquiesce, let the hippie-geek uprising think they'd won. Tell the world that they would no longer hold back progress, that it was okay to come out of hiding.

Of course, the best plan of action had been to set the fox free. The lad had proven himself a useless source of information, so they'd done what they had to do, and now his indoctrination was complete.

He is a wild fox now, intent on destroying his little movement's key players, Waterman thought to himself. He'll do all the work for us, and then—then we will get back to setting things right.

It's hunt or be hunted, now.

Chapter Thirty-Eight

KING OF KINGS

Saint Fox and The Independence will come alive again. Just life Frampton, Jeeves thought, smirking.

Tonight. They would come alive tonight. Now that they had won.

He sat in his plush velvet chair, facing the window as the morning sun filtered in through the jewel-toned curtains, and replayed the video on his holo display. The broadcast they had been waiting for. The beautiful new song they all wanted to hear.

The British government would allow GGcoin as an alternative form of currency.

"Only as a secondary form of monetary exchange," said the overly polite news anchor on the screen. The official currency of the United Kingdom would still be the pound. Backed by a universal standard, they said, which wasn't true.

"GGcoin will be recognised as an allowed method of payment, but is only expected to circulate on a small scale," the announcer repeated in a patronizing tone, his plastic face

taking on a scolding demeanor. *"It will phase out soon enough; its use will return to the fringes, but for now, we must find a way to continue."*

Jeeves grinned and slapped a palm against his knee, shooting a glance over at Benson and the others who were slinking in through the front door, like lizards coming out from under rocks once it had cooled down enough.

The kids were returning.

Jeeves waved his hand, sending the video feed from his cleverband display to the large main screen in the Morden flat. A modest screen by the standards of most, and secondhand, but it was plenty big enough. The driftwood rascals of the Arcana gathered round.

"Stores nationwide will accept GGcoin," the man on the screen continued, *"but don't expect a paradigm shift. We plan to give everyone back their dues in due time, and will revert to transactions via cleverband, the predecessor to the Dot. No more swiping and risking infection.*

This is not acquiescence to terrorism. This is damage control. Now is a time for peace, a time to put down our arms and work to repair the harm that's been done. All infected P.O.S. terminals will be destroyed, and retroactive technology set up in its place. Resources nationwide will be available for Dot removal."

Jeeves held up his index finger to the room, showing them the scar where the Dot had been. It was almost completely faded. One by one, others raised their fingers in the air, showing similar small pinkish circles on the pads of their fingers where once there'd been pieces of metal with too much power.

The announcer went on to tell people when they could expect to resume commerce as usual, *hopefully within a matter of weeks*, and where they could get their Dots removed, *the same places they had them installed.*

Benson Bridges sat on the floor, leaning back on his hands. His hair was flat against his head, washed and anti-static for the first time in a long while.

"They're wrong about the pound," Benson said. "It ain't gonna make the comeback they think it is. Even with them reverting to old tech."

"Aha! That's exactly right," said Jeeves. "And why is that, my economic wizard?"

Benson smiled a little, mouth lifting in a slight curve. "They've lost faith in it. In the pound. The government has the power to declare anything legal tender, but they don't have the power to give it any value. The people decide what has value, not the government. The government still doesn't realise that, but now, the people do."

"Gold star for you!" exclaimed Jeeves. "All we needed was bodies, I told you. GGcoin's been in operation long enough for everyone to recognise its superiority. The peer-to-peer transaction model has spread like a fire in the desert. People keep what they make; their finances are plain straightforward with GGcoin exchange rates. We did the maths—or rather you did, Bezzy Bez—and folks have helped each other figure it out, like the kind and caring members of the *communiteee* they should have been all along. It's all about making them feel like they're a part of something. Connected. The previously rich will try to return things to the old paradigm, but they will fail. We *are* the majority."

Jeeves turned the large screen off with a wave of his hand, facing the room.

"Now, we celebrate! Sing and dance to our victory march," he announced. Faces around the room lit up as members of the Arcana congratulated one another with high-fives and hugs.

"The Independence will play a comeback show tonight," Jeeves said. "Out in public this time. Where everyone can see."

～

385

Sam awoke in the bed of his old flat, his former flatmate hovering above him.

"Fucking hell, Sam. I weren't even sure it were you. I've seen you look a lot of things, but you've never looked quite this shyte before," Sailor said. He wore a jumper with a big old rifle printed on the front, and a red taffeta skirt.

"How'd I get here?" Sam asked. The words formed slowly, sticky and bitter like marmite.

"Hell if I know. Imagine my surprise when I walked in and found you."

"C'mere and give us a cuddle," Sam said.

Sailor rolled his eyes. "Oh alright, you."

Sam reached his arms up and around him, squeezing tight.

A car alarm sounded. Sam opened his eyes.

The harsh glare of the sun reflected in dirty pools of rainwater. Cardboard boxes and other bits of rubbish. Not in bed, then. No Sailor here. Sam's arms were wrapped tightly around himself, curled up in an alleyway that smelled of piss and vinegar. His torn shirt stuck wetly to his skin. The swirling mass of clouds above him made patterns in the sky, orange and violet.

He didn't remember, but he knew he'd just had a fix. He felt too good to be anything other than high.

Sam closed his eyes and saw himself on a dancefloor. Beautiful boys and girls bathed in aquamarine light moved in slow-motion liquid love, their eyes shining brightly. Sailor was amongst them—Kit too, both shimmering gorgeous, eyes smeared with shadow, lips glistening, painted in reptilian leather. They waved at him, smiling.

Then, he saw him. On the edge of the dancefloor, the sinister, phantom form of Janus Jeeves. His eyes were black and bloodshot, his teeth metal spikes. A white flame surrounded him as he cackled like the demented maniac he was.

When Jeeves waved his hand, the people danced. They squirmed and twisted, leapt through the air. They kissed, they tore off all their clothes. They laughed and cried.

When he waved his hand a second time, everyone froze.

Another wave and they were dancing again.

Sam made his way through the vast crowd of bodies towards his former mentor. When he reached his target, Janus Jeeves grinned at him with all his teeth.

"So, the prodigal son returnssss," he taunted, clasping his bony fingers together.

"I ain't your son," said Sam. "You ain't nothing to me."

Jeeves only shook his head, tisking at him like a child.

Sam looked down and noticed a six-inch blade held tightly in his right hand. The blade was thick and sharp, the handle enameled in black glitter.

He lashed out, two quick slashes. X marks the spot across the body of a man who should never have existed in the first place.

But Jeeves did exist, and he bled like a stuck pig.

He didn't scream, just looked down at his open wounds, as if now that Sam could see his insides, he could really see him. He smiled and snaked out an arm, grasping Sam's wrist in a vice claw. "I'm not the enemy," Jeeves gritted out through eyes of stone. Or were they eyes of light? Sam couldn't properly tell.

Jeeves let go of his wrist, then vanished. No cloud of smoke, no flash of light, but as if he was never even there.

The boys and girls on the dancefloor kept right on swinging.

Sam was left amongst the disco-blind. The knife fell from his shaking hands.

He opened his eyes, and found himself back in the alleyway, cold air biting his wet face. Had he been crying?

I would never do that to Jeeves, he thought. He don't deserve it, not really.

His jeans pocket beeped. He was surprised to find a cleverband inside, its navy blue plastic shell a little worse for the wear.

Where'd this come from? he wondered. Is it even mine? Didn't have one with me back there in the pen. Didn't have nothing. Shyte but my feckin' head hurts.

Sam activated the cleverband. An alert appeared on the display:

Rejoice! We have TAKENBACK what is ours. Come see Saint Fox and The Independence play their comeback show at Wembley Stadium.

Why would they be playing out in the open like that? Sam wondered. And how are Saint Fox and The Independence supposed to play without Saint Fox?

Sam scratched at an itch on the back of his neck, an itch he'd felt since Simsworth had set him free into the harsh light of the city.

He checked the display again to make sure he'd actually seen what he thought he'd seen. Maybe he just wanted to see his band's name, wished they were playing again, to a crowd of adoring thousands who all believed in them.

He squeezed his eyes shut tight, then opened one eye to stare at the tricky holographic words.

Saint Fox and The Independence, the display said. And the concert was tonight.

It was a show he wouldn't miss.

Chapter Thirty-Nine

SONG OF SONGS

The lights had never been so bright back when Sam had fronted the band.

It seemed as though there were millions in the crowd tonight at Wembley Stadium, thousands upon thousands of jubilant faces bathed in blue and red light, singing along to words they knew by heart, some of which they'd written. They got high on the music, spirits soaring as the notes climbed.

It scared him. That huge mass of people, all thinking as one.

Saint Fox and The Independence roared into the next song, led by one of Kit's dazzling guitar licks that left Sam feeling hungry and slightly sick. The song was one he'd barely played a part in creating, music by Kit and Muzzy, lyrics by an eighteen-year-old girl in Suffolk via the FoxDen app.

Hold my hand, 'cause you're not alone
Together we will fight
Hold my hand, hold on to someone, anyone
Help me make it through the night
Whisper to me dear, and tell me
That what we did was right
Fight! Fight!
We'll put up a good fight
Hope we make it through the night

It blared across the loudspeakers, a live recording from a previous show, and Sam barely recognised his own voice. He'd recognise Saint Fox anywhere, though. That swagger and fey jut of his hips could only belong to his former flatmate.

The frontman wore a red and gold suit of flames, face done up in iridescent makeup to match, his red shock of hair moulded into rebellious spikes. Like a fuckin' gay outer space Joan of Arc, Sam thought. His arms spread wide like the proverbial sacrifice, radiating with the high of being the center of attention in a stadium packed to capacity.

No one in crowd seemed to realise it wasn't him. No one could tell. The audience stared at the stage enraptured, surging forward to get closer to the band, taking Sam right along with them.

His fans didn't know him from a minute or a mile away. He'd been nothing more than another manufactured ticket. And yet, Sam found that he didn't really care whether or not they knew him.

All he felt was hatred towards Janus Jeeves. The more he thought about it, the more the back of his neck itched.

Up on the stage, Saint Sailor strode over to Kit as they entered the second chorus of the mid-tempoed "Money Dance." He was bending, spinning, writhing, tarting it up proper-like, more than Sam ever had. He should have been Saint Fox all along, thought the former frontman. And Kit's guitar solo is rubbish. She's playing too fast, missing notes. S'not like her.

No one appeared to notice this, either. The audience screamed their approval at the frantic screeches she wrought, hair a tangle of electricity, fingers flying across the strings. Cleverband cams went off like fireworks in the night.

Muzzy and Seth played like perfect machines, not a beat out of sync, their faces painted with energy.

Where is he? Sam wondered, as the band glided seamlessly into the next song. Where's big daddy, the maestro, the puppet master?

The song was a ballad, now.

I'm a lonely, lonely man
I just do what I can
Can't face the day
Without you, baby
Gotta keep hangin' on
If we stop, it all goes wrong
I'm drowning, and you
Are drowning now, too

This song was one of the few he'd written all on his own. Just an acoustic guitar and brushes ghosting softly against the drums. The vocal track playing over the PA system was familiar to him, a recording from a half-packed Wednesday night show at the Wormhole, that little club in Brixton they'd played at almost every week when they first started. He'd been happy to play then. Just a few people really paying attention, people whose eyes met his and held his gaze, if only for a moment.

The acoustics are all wrong, thought Sam. A vocal cut from a little dive bar laced with too much reverb played back through an enormous stadium. Can no one hear that it sounds wrong?

Sailor, of course, knew the words by heart. Sam had played it for him before anyone else. His performance makes it believable. Hell, I almost believe it's him up there singing. Maybe it always was.

So fuckin' tired, he thought. I'm so fuckin' tired. I feel good though. Feel high now, all the time. How do I feel this good and this pissed off at the same time?

Sam slid snakelike through the crowd, making his way towards the front of the stage. In a raggedy grey pullover and black jeans he was unrecognizable, eyes sunken in and vacant, looking just like any other scene kid.

One skinny bloke by himself can successfully navigate his way through the swarm of bodies that is the general admission section of a rock show, pressed together like the rear of the stadium was on fire. He wormed his way through gaps in the crowd—lulls in songs made for lulls in waves of bodies, and Sam knew how to read a crowd like a favourite book. Before long he made barrier, standing right at Saint Sailor's feet.

They locked eyes almost immediately.

Sailor paused his lip-syncing. He stood still, looking wide-eyed and other-worldly. Something like guilt, too, underneath the shock.

The band stopped playing. Muzzy spotted Sam next, letting the deep echoes of his strings fade out. Kit and Seth followed his lead and silenced their instruments, puzzled looks on both their faces.

"Sam..." Sailor said into the microphone.

The sound of Sam's plaintive, out-of-body voice still drifted from the speakers. Whoever was operating the PA cut the vocal track.

The bewildered audience craned their necks to try and see what was happening. Most figured there was some sort of malfunction with the sound system.

For a moment, the stadium was silent.

Standing in the wings watching the band play their audacious comeback show, Janus Jeeves felt both proud and ashamed. Proud of the Arcana's success, proud that they'd managed to pull this together tonight given the short notice and the technical challenges, but sorry that in their finest hour, they'd had to resort to deception.

But the show must go on—and would, if necessary, go on without Saint Fox.

Or at least, that's how it had gone at first.

"Go get him," Jeeves said to one of the security crew. "Bring him to me."

Below, the crowd grew restless. Jeeves shook his head as he watched Sailor, his new Saint Fox, standing before them alongside his silent band, opening and closing his mouth like a landed fish. Meanwhile, it seemed Kit had not yet spotted Sam amongst the crowd. She began fingerpicking a slow tune to try and diffuse whatever unnerving situation was unraveling. Seth, a.k.a. Zephyr, started rat-tat-tatting on his drums in accompaniment, a cautious, steady beat.

Down on the floor, Sam was seized by two well-built security guards who dragged him away from the railing and up the webbed metal stairs towards the stage. The way they roughly manhandled him and commanded that he move forward was oddly comforting, reminiscent of his previous role as the Crown's prisoner.

The security guards soon brought him face to face with Janus Jeeves.

Both men appeared barely human as the lights and shadows from the stage flickered across their bodies. Jeeves' face was green-toned, whether from the stage lights or his natural pallor it was impossible to tell. His head and shoulders appeared almost disconnected from his body, which was clothed in a flowy, black-violet suit, making him appear watery and boneless.

Sam struggled in the security guards' grip until they released him. He stood jagged like a broken statue, his hands balled into fists.

Jeeves took in the former rock star's unshaven face, sallow cheeks, and the black emptiness in his eyes that said he was gone, gone, gone. No Sammy left here, he realised grimly. No Saint Fox, either.

"Sammy, listen…" he began, hands open in surrender.

"Don't you…wrap your snake words around me," Sam spat out, his breath coming in shallow puffs. "I'm done with you. Done with your lies."

Jeeves reached out to him, placing a silver-ringed hand on his shoulder. "We won, Sam," he said in a quiet voice, taking on an unusually calm demeanor. "Because of you. Couldn't have done it without you. I'm so happy to see you, I—"

Sam wrenched himself away from Jeeves. He took two steps backwards towards the stage, his face ensconced in shadow, his eyes on his former mentor's mismatched ones, before turning around and breaking into a run.

Back on stage the band had started up another song, a fast-paced jam to get the audience's energy roaring again. There were only a few in the crowd who'd noticed the brief seconds when Saint Fox's voice rang through the stadium independent of Saint Fox's lips moving. A few were belligerent that their beloved Saint Fox was apparently a lip-syncer. The rest made excuses to themselves—a delay in the sound system, a one-off where they had to use a recording to produce a vocal effect, a backing track turned up too loud, a mistake made by the sound guy. Now, the silver electric squeals entering their ears drowned out all other thought. They wanted only to shout and dance, to be carried away. Their energy continued to rise. A small mosh pit had begun front and center, fans jumping high in time with the beat, crashing into one another.

Sam ran out onto the stage. He happened to do it just as the stage lights went black at the end of the song, the last wails from the guitars fusing with the audience's screams.

When the lights came up again, Saint Fox in costume was standing beside Saint Fox in street clothes.

The audience came to the same shocking realization in the exact same moment, or so it seemed. They stopped singing along, lowered their cleverband cams. Hollow, absolute silence filled the stadium.

Then, they turned.

Shouts rose up from the crowd, slurs and curses. They threw anything they could find at the stage—cups, glow-sticks, shoes. Fights erupted in the pit, in the stands, as they sent their anger in every and any direction. Friends and strangers connected fists with jaws and feet with shins, punching, pulling, wailing, getting into the bloody war with unabashed enthusiasm, a 90,000-bodied screaming whore who could not get enough of the violence. Wembley pulled and surged with the weight and the sound of it.

On stage, Sailor numbly handed over the microphone. He gazed dazedly back and forth between Sam and the crowd, his face an apology laced with fear that slowly engulfed him.

Sam stared back at Sailor, then looked away, out into the crowd where angry bodies swarmed en masse, just like in his fever dreams. He looked at the mic in his hands like it was a foreign thing, then lifted it to his lips. He doubted there were any words he could say that would have any effect. Maybe there never were. Words didn't make any difference.

"Stop," he said into the microphone, dully, quietly, without conviction.

The weak protest was swallowed up in the din. The fighting continued. Sam imagined he could hear every shattered bone, every tooth smashed, every echo of that sickening squish-splat sound that blood makes as it sluices between fingers.

He dropped the microphone cord, letting it hang limply at his side.

It was picked up by Janus Jeeves.

"Ladies and gentlemen, and those both or neither..." he began.

And was not allowed to finish, for Saint Fox had pushed him into the crowd.

Chapter Forty

DIAMONDS AND RUST

When Charlotte Piebald watched the broadcast announcing the nation's plan to rebuild their broken economy, she broke down in tears. But they were not tears of joy.

All will be fine now, back to business as usual, she thought.

As long as you're not infected.

Some would come through this unscathed, the whole gruesome disaster fading into watery memory. And those who'd been brave or stupid enough to go to those wackos for the cure while it had been available could forget about it, too, just go on their merry little ways.

Some of us aren't so lucky, thought Charlotte, her mind reeling. She thought back to her last visit from Dr. Wender. *I surmise it's only a matter of time before you move on to Phase II*, he'd said, face drawn and solemn. *The symptoms being reported are most alarming. If you feel this poorly now, you'll find the discomforts that await you unbearable. I wouldn't wish that on you, Miss Piebald, wouldn't wish that at all.*

The dear man had prescribed her three more medications to try and ease her pain. The name of one of them, she noticed—iFixor—matched an engraving on the doctor's cleverband.

All I can do is try to stave off the inevitable, he'd said, entering her new prescriptions into the system.

Inevitable?

I'm afraid so, he said gravely.

Over the past several weeks, Charlotte had received an endless slew of invite alerts via her cleverband. DWD: The Final Hour. DWD: Countdown to Extinction. DWD: The Last Reich. DWD—Death With Dignity, the latest fad to arrive on the scene in response to the Dot virus's merciless rampage. Rather than suffer the slow decay of the virus, proponents of the cause advocated the right of the infected to take their own lives, and before long, the idea of beating the virus to the punch had spread as quickly as the virus itself.

Charlotte could just picture it. Gruesome drunken orgies, free-flowing narcotics, deafening heavy metal raging while overgrown teenagers dressed in black with hideous gobs of makeup on their faces indulged in one last hurrah before the final whimper. Death With Dignity indeed. Unlikely.

The title of one invitation, however, caught her eye before she could touch Delete.

DWD: Whispers on the Wind

Ladies and gentlemen, we somberly invite you to join us on the Twelfth of May, Eight o'clock p.m., in this dark year of our Lord. Let us end our suffering with dignity, and bravely embrace whatever awaits us on the other side.

The invite ended with a quote from Charlotte Bronte, her namesake.

Liberty lends us her wings and Hope guides us by her star.

Last night Charlotte's fever had reached 37.6 degrees according to her cleverband. Her hands shook when she lifted a glass of water to her lips. Her poor legs shivered despite layers of woolen blankets piled atop them.

It had become unbearable, she decided, the weakness, the insomnia, the hopelessness of it all. The fear of what awaited her as the disease grew worse. Despite the countless medications she was now on, it seemed the virus was progressing at a merciless rate towards its inevitable conclusion. Each day it seemed some new symptom appeared.

Charlotte felt as if she was going mad. Lying in bed, her mind raced constantly with the things in life she had not done. She'd never been to South Africa. Never rode one of those ultra high-speed trains. Never had children. Not that she wanted any, of course. She was a businesswoman first and foremost.

Charlotte had never been in love.

She glanced around her bedroom, made dark by curtains drawn to block out the daylight that her eyes were so sensitive to. Only the artificial ghost light of the television illuminated the room, currently playing a popular soap opera. Her gaze lingered over piles of purchases she had made from the Ideal World shopping channel, things she would never use. Speed-presto crock-pots, smartbot alarm systems, a waterproof plastic terry cloth sheet that was both a blanket and a shower curtain.

This was no way to live. Fantasizing of things to come, things that would never be. I can't take another day alone in this dark room, she thought.

Charlotte scrolled to the bottom of the invite, where the options Yes, No, and Maybe appeared. Before she could second-guess herself, she touched Yes, sending her promise to attend this somber event through the invisible network in the sky.

When the appointed evening arrived, Charlotte was in utter torment. She'd tried on at least nine outfits, and still could not decide what to wear. It would be her last soirée, after all, and everything must be perfect. If she did not pick an outfit soon, she would be late.

Eventually she decided on a modest cream-coloured cocktail dress with delicate beading stitched in floral patterns across the bodice, and a pair of cream-coloured pumps to match. She fastened the 24k-gold cross pendant encrusted with small diamonds that her father had given her on her twenty-first birthday around her neck. Delicate pearl drop earrings. A satin clutch that matched the dress. Somehow she had managed to find the strength to take a curling iron to her hair for the first time in ages, styling it in loose waves.

Charlotte felt better than she ever remembered feeling since she contracted the virus. Almost like a normal, healthy person, she thought. A little peach-coloured blush had livened up her complexion. Her eyes held some of their old sparkle once they saw how lovely she still managed to look once all dolled up, and how slim her illness had made her too—the dress had slid on with ease.

One last glance in the mirror and she was ready to go. Almost.

Charlotte tiptoed quietly into the sitting room. All the staff had been given the night off so the place was empty, save for two.

Curled up together in a corner of the plush, mauve-coloured sofa were Joxer and Edward III, her two precious, prize-winning Corgis. When Charlotte entered the room, their ears perked up and they gazed at her expectantly. It had been a while since they'd seen their mother up and about.

"My gorgeous darlings," Charlotte cooed. "You're all I have in this world, you know that? You do know that, don't you?" She scratched their chins and continued to heap praise upon them, to which they responded enthusiastically with short barks and wagging tails.

"Mommy's so sorry she has to leave you. So, so sorry. It isn't my fault though, darlings. There is evil in this world. No, you wouldn't know anything about that, would you? Sweet things," her eyes began to mist over, but she managed to keep her tears at bay. "I've left you to Talia. The poor girl isn't used to dogs of your caliber, so you must be patient with her. But I believe she'll take good care of you. She's taken good care of me."

She fed them each a treat. Truth be told, she was close to calling off the whole thing in the face of their affection, but it was a testament to her character than she remained resolute. She exited her lovely house in Holland Park for the last time, locking the door and descending the cobblestone steps.

The house where the event was to take place was located in her same neighbourhood. Charlotte rang the doorbell, wondering if she would run into anyone she knew, and if so, would she feel proud or ashamed to be here?

Charlotte decided that she would be proud. She would be brave.

A slender woman with grey hair and coral beads around her neck answered the door. She's probably only a few years older than I am, but doesn't wear it quite as well, thought Charlotte.

"Hello, come in," the hostess said. She took Charlotte's coat and showed her into the main room, where guests were sipping martinis and glasses of champagne, conversing quietly with one another or listening attentively to the young woman skillfully rendering Chopin on the baby grand piano in the center of the room. Charlotte was pleased to note that the sitting room was decorated not with black candles and upside-down crosses, but with tasteful bronze sculptures and oriental art. A large mosaic portrait of the Hindu god Vishnu hung on the far wall. The furniture was cherry wood and the fabrics were warm patterns in red, brown, and gold. Charlotte admired a rust-coloured satin pillow with leaf patterns embroidered in gold thread that sat in the armchair closest to her. Would that she lived past tonight, she would have asked the hostess where she'd purchased it so she could acquire a set of her own.

"We're very pleased you could make it," the hostess said. "What is your name, dear?"

"Charlotte. Charlotte Piebald."

"Charlotte Piebald, as in *Charlotte P.* handbags?" she asked enthusiastically.

"The very same."

"A shame. Such a shame," the hostess said. "That the disease has claimed such talent, I mean. At least we can help you end your suffering. You're amongst friends. My name is Mikhaela."

"Thank you," Charlotte said. "One really needs friends at a time like this. Those who aren't infected just aren't capable of understanding."

"I know, I know," said Mikhaela. "Come, meet some of the others. Would you like something to drink?"

"Some champagne would be lovely, thanks," said Charlotte.

She spent most of the evening sampling hors d'oeuvres—the seafood tarts were her favourite—and meeting other guests. Two businessmen from Amsterdam who had caught the disease while in town for a convention. A pleasant couple in their sixties who owned a string of hotels. A dour-looking man with a splotchy beard and a vast original book collection who apparently lived two doors down from Charlotte, and they had never met.

She was speaking to the hotel owners about her award-winning corgis when Mikhaela tapped a fork against her champagne flute.

"Ladies and gentlemen," she began in a somber tone. "As our night here draws to a close, so ends an important chapter in all our lives. We're going to start proceedings shortly, and I would just like to thank each and every one of you for coming here tonight. For choosing the path of bravery. For fighting the good fight with strength and dignity. Let us not succumb to mass chaos and manipulation. Let us live our every breath joyously, and end these breaths that are our own without fear, without apology. Let us not look backwards, only forwards, into opportunity, into the light."

The guests applauded her steadily.

"Now, as I believe that every individual possesses the right to end their own life when they determine such action is necessary, I also believe they have the right to speak their last words when they are of sound mind. If you would please come forward and form a semi-circle, we'll go around the room, and everyone will get a chance to say whatever it is they feel they need to say. We'll pass around this cherry blossom branch, which will be used as a talking stick. Please try and keep your speeches under five minutes each."

Charlotte froze. She had no idea what she wanted to say.

Before she knew it, the man beside her was speaking, saying something about his dear, departed mother and wars he'd never voted for. It would be her turn next.

The man finished, passing her the branch. The room turned its attention towards her. Charlotte politely cleared her throat.

"I'm not sure what to say, really. But I've always believed in living one's life to the fullest—an option those bastards stole from me. And the pain, recently, it's just become too much. I can hardly get out of bed, most days. All this not knowing," she said, shaking her head, "it just drives you mad. With everything that's been happening these days, it's as if life is a dream. Nothing seems real anymore. It isn't like when I was young, playing on the beach without a care in the world, running into daddy's arms…That was before cleverbands, even," she stated. "Life made sense then."

The woman beside her, the elderly hotel matron, touched her arm sympathetically.

"I just want peace," she said. "At long last. That's all anyone really wants, isn't it?"

She passed the talking stick to the next person. The room gave her a round of applause.

"You're so brave, dear," the old woman next to her said, before launching into a long speech about her esteemed family and all its generations, which only ended when Mikhaela cleared her throat.

When the speeches were over, each guest received a ruby-coloured beverage in an ornate crystal cordial glass.

Mikhaela lifted her glass to the room. "See you on the other side," she said.

They closed their eyes and drank the crimson liquid, Charlotte taking one tentative sip, then downing it all in one go.

If you could have asked her what dying felt like, she would say it felt like dreaming she was watching herself on a television programme, a soap opera where the heroine is accidentally shot by her true love. It felt like tasting the sweetest, most delicious trifle in the world, only to have it turn bitter and green before your eyes. It felt like a children's nursery rhyme that you had once loved, but now couldn't remember the words to no matter how you tried.

She thought about these things, and how they felt. And then she felt no more.

Chapter Forty-One

DEATH OF A DISCO DANCER

Jeeves plunged headfirst into the fray, into the blurry crowd of limbs, blood, and angry faces.

A metal-encrusted fist impacted his face immediately, striking him in the jaw, shattering his two rows of unnaturally-coloured teeth. Hits to his blue and yellow mismatched eyes followed.

He saw only red, and did not have time to cry.

Two youths, one a tattooed punk, the other clean as a baby, grasped him by his long arms, wrenching them from their sockets.

A knife stabbed him in the back, and Jeeves bled and bled. Enough blood for all his lives thus far.

He tried to think of his good work, his dreams fulfilled, but there was only pain. Higher reasoning failed, and he gave up the fight.

His spirit left his body, then, before the body was torn to shreds, into unrecognizable particles of red and black.

But the spirit, the spirit lives on. It becomes a bulldog working construction in Mississippi, it becomes a neglected daughter, it becomes an alien farmhand at the tail end of a star system light years away. It becomes a lithographic press, it becomes a balloon, it becomes a message in the television screen, it becomes the man that always was and would always be.

Later, he would look down and watch the mad children from somewhere—from up in the clouds, from the seventh dimension. The riot was already beginning to die down.

He wondered if the price of this life was worth it.

He decided that it was.

~

Kit's eyes had not left Sam. He seemed far away, standing at the front of the stage bathed in light, an angelic ghost.

Save them, she thought. Do something. She didn't know if she was talking to Sam, or to herself.

Then, as if in a trance, Sam lips parted, and he began to sing. A soft, sweet tune. A new song. The words he sang were something about rebirth, about leaving things behind.

Zephyr backed him up almost immediately, his drums beating a steady rhythm. It was picked up by Muzzy, strumming a soothing bass line that began to calm frayed nerves.

Kit held the neck of her guitar in a death grip as she watched Sam in a paralyzed daze. In time she began strumming accompanying chords without even realizing it.

Slowly, like an encroaching wave, the chaos abated as the soft melody bled from the sound system into the sweet pleasure paralysis centers of the brain.

The crowd grew quiet.

Adrenaline and carnage soon gave way to tears and regret. They hadn't meant it. Were slaves to mob mentality. That frenetic, contagious venom that short-circuits reason.

Saint Fox stood at the pinnacle of the stage, glowing with electric energy. His old guitar, taken from Sailor's frozen hands, was slung across his shoulder.

When he finished singing, Kit watched as he crumpled to the floor and folded over his guitar, like a mother protecting a child. He stayed like that for what felt like hours, maybe days.

The crowd thinned out in wounded intervals. Had there been casualties?

They would tell themselves stories to try and forget, to banish the guilt, to shape the present and the future into something that looked more like how they'd imagined it all along.

Kit took steps in the opposite direction she wanted to go, backing away towards the stage exit. She watched as Sailor untangled Sam from his guitar, pulling him to his feet.

"C'mon, Sam," Sailor said, his voice a shaky, broken thing. "Let's go home."

Sam followed him with bleary, vacant eyes, hanging onto him like a lifeline. They walked right past Kit, Sailor not noticing her at all, Sam looking at her like some precious thing he no longer recognised.

Then they were gone. She barely noticed as others around her, one by one, walked off into the wings.

Soon, she was alone on stage. No one with her except her guitar.

Just as it had always been.

She would play it again in her mind, over and over on repeat, like an irritating chorus that was stuck in her head. All she wanted was for it to stop, to leave her alone and go bother someone else.

What good am I? she thought. She'd witnessed the whole horrendous nightmare and hadn't lifted a finger to try and stop it. I'm no better than those government bastards who gave the order to fire. Just stood there and watched. So damned useless.

She had wanted to run to Sam, to tell him how glad she was that he was alive, to assure him that everything would be okay, though she had no way of assuring anyone of such. But she'd frozen every time she tried to make a move towards him; her body would not cooperate. She'd let out a scream that no one heard when Jeeves went careening over the edge of the stage and into the vulturish crowd, had started blindly plucking at chords when Sam began to sing.

Kit never did know what exactly to do with herself, except when she was playing.

I'll forget in time, she thought. Wash myself of the whole bloody massacre.

But whether she drowned herself in alcohol or scrubbed herself clean under fire-hot water, she could not get clean enough and could not forget, as long as she remained looking upon the same grey skies.

The lights inside the vast buildings of Heathrow airport were too bright. People ambled back and forth wearing grey suits, grey sweatpants, grey raincoats to protect them from the grey rain. Paper cups of tea clenched in one hand, their cleverbands the sole focus of attention. Grey suitcases rolled on grey wheels and were loaded onto silver planes.

Kit stared down at her black boots, which were scuffed. She lifted one foot and gazed at the dirt underneath. Blood, hair, and mud, she noted. She would have to walk many miles to get them clean again.

Her cleverband trilled, alerting her to the last thing she expected—a text from Sam. It probably isn't even from him, she figured. Sailor using his device, Sam resending an old message by accident.

Kiss me, little Miss Rock n' Roll, it said.

Bet he doesn't even know what he's saying, she thought. Just like always. Kit lifted her hand to reply, not knowing what she wanted to say back. The scar of the Dot on her index finger was faintly purple underneath the callus made by steel strings.

The cleverband trilled again. Incoming file transfer: "Songs we never finished." Accept. Decline.

She touched Accept, but then minimised the display and switched the device to silent, not waiting for the file containing his scrawled lyrics alongside her scribbled riffs to download. The others waiting inside the terminal stared at their displays, their personal 3D worlds, texting and transacting freely.

Now boarding, Flight 723 to New York, the gate agent announced.

She boarded the plane, looking back almost the whole way, as if the greatest hits of un-merry England was the only thing playing on the viewscreen that shimmered across the headrest in front of her.

It was only when the clouds parted and the aircraft started to descend that she decided to look forward.

Chapter Forty-Two

SMOKE MACHINE

London hospitals were sick to death of the endless stream of patients showing up at their doors with claims of contracting the Dot virus. They began turning people away unless they could easily spot or scan some life-impeding symptom—a tumor, a rash, a fractured limb, a goddamn broken nose or black eye, at least. Every day new cases of the Dot virus continued to surface, despite the fact that the Dot was now barely in operation. Some patients claimed to have contracted it from means other than swiping at a terminal. They believed it was airborne, they believe it was passed through blood, semen, spit, contracted from toilet seats, from riding the Tube, from food in restaurants, from door knobs.

It was a visiting Swiss doctor, a Doctor Birchmeier, who first proposed the theory.

Birchmeier's own wife and sister-in-law became infected shortly after their arrival in London, the temptations of Oxford Street shopping too strong to ignore.

In them, the doctor found two willing subjects upon whom he could test for a cure outside the confines of the legal process. He conducted a series of double-blind studies testing various treatments, all to dissatisfying results, until the last and final one. His wife appeared to have a positive reaction to prednisone, with numerous symptoms including fatigue, constipation, and muscle stiffness subsiding after administration of the drug.

His assistant then revealed that it was the sister who'd been given the prednisone, and she, if anything, seemed to be getting worse. His wife had been given a placebo.

Birchmeier was then able to validate a hypothesis which till now had only been vaguely speculated upon in hushed tones.

The Dot virus was psychosomatic.

Birchmeier proposed that those who had supposedly progressed to Phase II of Dot virus syndrome could be diagnosed with any number of previously catalogued disorders. And those with Phase I, well, they could be diagnosed with a case of mass hypochondria, their symptoms the result of stress, age, allergies, bad diet, lack of sleep.

Days later, the Arcane Society confirmed the hypothesis via their website.

The TAKEBACK virus was benign, a program designed to pirate the terminals' displays, then spread across the network. Widespread paranoia, however, was not only highly contagious—there existed no cure for it.

Thousands were outraged, having keenly felt losses too close to home. Others marveled at the concept, the audacity, laughing in triumph at the revolution that had used the people's own foolishness against them. There was no unity of mind regarding the situation; everyone seemed to have their own spin on it, vlogs going mad with rants on both sides of the equation, news stations reporting all manner of disturbances, people dressed up like big plush P.O.S. terminals chasing pretty girls down the streets.

Harold Waterman watched the latest report of Birchmeier's discovery on BBC News, and was appalled.

"My, my," he said to no one at all. "That spidery geezer certainly had a pair, didn't he? Too bad he didn't live to see it all the way through. I accomplished that much, at least." He felt smug and disgusted at the same time.

It seemed the Arcane Society was no more, at least as far as he was concerned. His pawn had eradicated the blasted movement's ludicrous leader during some outrageous riot at Wembley. Waterman grinned ever so slightly, picturing the startled look on the madman's circus face when, during his own celebratory rock show, a feral mob tore him limb from limb.

But, it hadn't been enough.

That damned digital currency was the real virus—it had gotten in everywhere, it couldn't be stopped, it seemed the British were more in love with it than lager. People have minds like fruit flies, Waterman thought. Although the Arcane Society had deceived them time and again, GGcoin, their ultimate product, was here to stay. Waterman was positively through with trying to help the common people when they did not want to be helped. There was nothing more he could do, and nothing more he wished to do.

Harold Waterman sat alone in his very comfy chair in front of the fireplace, sipping the last of his imported brandy. He had not been able to procure a number of his favourite libations lately. Many of the fine establishments that he did business with now only accepted GGcoin. His outdated currency was useless. When he at last accepted his fate and acquiesced, converting to GGcoin, he would find that his accounts held merely a percentage of what they had once retained. Years in office had provided him with a heavy dosage of kickbacks, and now, it had all been for naught.

At next year's general election, to no one's surprise and to Waterman's relief, he was voted out of office, the people scattered somewhere along the spectrum between disappointed and furious at his handling of the Dot crisis situation.

The former Prime Minister cut his losses and moved to Cardiff, where he could live by the sea, and no one would bother him about the past.

Two years, four months, and twenty-seven days after Harold Waterman left Downing Street, he received a phone call.

"Harry," a gruff voice spat out his name in between coughs.

"Lucas. I almost didn't recognise you. You sound unwell."

"No shit I'm unwell, Waterman. Try to contain your shock. I've always been healthy as an ox."

"Whatever is it?" Waterman asked tiredly, gazing out of his cottage window at the rainfall. "Wait, don't tell me...you've caught a latent strain of the Dot virus. It lay dormant inside you for years, kept at bay by the fact that you had so much money at the time, it was afraid to fully manifest itself..."

"Shut up, Harry. I'm sick, obviously, but not with that goddamn phony scare crisis. I've got lung cancer, you miserable bastard."

"And you decided to use your last breath to phone up your old university chum and call him terrible names? I'm chuffed, Lucas. How thoughtful."

"Hah hah, Harry. Always a kidder. If only your humor didn't fall flat every time. You know there's only one reason I'd call you up."

"You need a favour."

"See? Your mind hasn't entirely rotted."

"And what a good start you are off to, Norcoford. I'm already completely charmed and will give you whatever it is you ask of me."

"Would you cut the snark for just one damned minute? You owe me. I backed you. Used practically everything I had left to finance your 20th century rifle war against those bloody techno-charlatan hippies."

"Oh, Lucas. You know it was just a number in a spreadsheet somewhere out there in the cloud, all it ever was—we didn't have a real dime to stand upon. The foreign banks we borrowed from with our smoke and mirrors came after the Treasury with furious vigor once they found we couldn't pay them back. But that's someone else's problem, now."

"I need money, Waterman. Money for treatment, for whatever's left in this bloody walking corpse of mine. All my hard-earned cash is now only worth a fraction of what it used to be. What I have left, that is."

"And just what precisely do you think happened to my bank accounts, Lucas? That terrorist-socialist attack hit me as hard as anyone. I don't have a secret stash piled up somewhere. Not anymore."

"So, your son was never infected," Norcoford pointed out. "What was wrong with him?"

"He too wanted money," Waterman replied emotionlessly. "Stephen went on and on about this revolutionary—no pun intended—treatment therapy center up near Abingdon. Probably spent it all on weed." He sighed almost wistfully. "I suppose you and I are both alone now."

Lucas Norcoford leaned back in the one designer armchair he had left, rubbing at his forehead and swearing up a storm. He now lived in a one-bedroom flat, and had been forced to fire most of his staff. Not even Michelle, his ginger vixen, had stuck around when the going got tough.

He sputtered and spat, blood and phlegm, a rusted machine on its last legs. Norcoford stared at his cuticles. He'd not had a manicure in months, and his skin was flaky and dry. He would be having another microwave meal for dinner tonight. How do people live like this?

"I'll see you in hell, Harry," he said. And hung up.

Waterman unwrapped his cleverband from his wrist, setting it down on his modest oak desk.

He did not feel guilty. He had done what he could, after all.

Chapter Forty-Three

SKY IS A LANDFILL

Benson Bridges sat in front of his domain of monitors in the Morden flat that now appeared to be his because no one else had claimed it. He was oblivious to the unsteady stream of Arcana who trailed scents of sandalwood and ribbons of colour throughout the flat, fewer of them now than there used to be.

Benson leaned back in his chair and watched the infoboards flood with new posts. The truth about the Dot virus was out.

He thought it was only fair to let them know. After all, it'd been Jeeves' backup plan—as soon as GGcoin was in high enough circulation. His original plan had been to 'cure' everyone through GET CLEAN, of course, but that plan failed as soon as the military armed themselves with 20th century weapons, sending the Arcana's troops scurrying underground.

"Oi, Bezza," Jack-of-all-Trades called from the kitchen, staring forlornly into an empty fridge.

"Curry's gone," Benson said.

"Aye, not that," Jack-of-all-Trades said, entering Benson's tech domain. "What's the latest over the 9G waves? Things I've heard make it sound like our old man's some made-up creature straight outta Greek mythology. Like he's got horns and a tail, like he can make folks sick and well. Like he weren't even at Wembley Stadium that night."

"Maybe he wasn't," Benson said. "How would I know? I stayed here to clean things up like I always do, while everyone else is out there playin' and singin'."

Benson shut down one display after another, leaving only a single tablet on that illuminated his pale face in blue.

"From what I hear, they're making Sammy out to be the hero-slash-victim, an' Jeeves is some sort of venomous villain. Some folks gots to keep things tidy and simple like that," Jack-of-all-Trades said, trying to get Benson to make eye contact with him. "They're saying things like he came up with the traitorous notion to hijack Sam's band and replace Saint Fox with someone he could control better. Handed Sam over to the government himself to be tortured and all. Didn't mean for TAKEBACK to be benign at first, only came up with the smoke and mirrors idea after he were unable to make people sick for real."

"Craziest one I've heard is that Sam is Jeeves' son, and Jeeves manipulated him all whaddyacallit? Codependent-like. 'If you love me son, you'll do thissss for me. Lead my revolution. Help your daddy make the world a better placcccce.'" Benson's impersonation of Jeeves was alarmingly accurate, yet lacked a certain flair that only the ringleader himself could have mustered.

"Saint Fox really being made a Saint, eh?" Jack-of-all-Trades sat on the edge of the table, his long legs dangling. "So, what do we do now?"

"Scripts have already been executed, converting old accounts to GGcoin on a sliding scale. A *fair* sliding scale, which means some people lose *big time*, and for everyone else, not much is gonna change from where they started."

"Damn. Is it really up for us to decide that?"

"We're just resetting the balance. Someone's got to do it. After that, it's up to them. Anyway it ain't me, it's the numbers, stuff Jeeves had me started on a long time ago. Can't please everyone, just have to aim for statistical averages that make sense given how much money's in circulation, data from economic trends, stuff like that."

"Yeah, yeah. What he said." Jack-of-all-Trades grinned, looking over his shoulder for his brother James, who wasn't there. He kicked Benson lightly against his shin, earning an irritated look from the programmer. "Think they'll stick with it? GGcoin, I mean. After Wembley, after the virus, after everything that's happened?"

"How long did they stick with the pound? And why? Just 'cause it was there, that's why. Doesn't matter how it got there or what happened to it along the way. Now, GGcoin's here. It's everywhere. There's people rebelling against it of course, but they're the minority. Fancy that, *they're* the rebels now. And they're operating on who knows how many conflicting stories about what happened with the virus, what happened to Sam, to Jeeves. We're living in this over-information, misinformation age, and people's memories are short. It's not the cleanest method, way messier than we ever predicted, but it got us where we wanted to be."

"Getting into other countries, too," said Jack-of-all-Trades. "Australia, New Zealand, Iceland, all using GGcoin or something like it, something compatible. Trade's getting back to normal."

"E.U.'s testing the waters of conversion...still bickering about it of course, but they'll figure it out eventually."

Jack-of-all-Trades sighed. "The U.S...."

"Is still laughing at us. But my ear to the floor tells me an underground movement's gaining a foothold there."

Benson smiled, placing his hands behind his head and leaning back.

"Oh?"

"They're called the Arcane Society 2.0: Extreme Makeover edition."

"Jeebus. I hope so." Jack-of-all-Trades inhaled sharply through his nose, leaping down from the table. "How long before the fat cats destroy GGcoin, too? Make everything just as bad as it was?"

"That'll happen…" Benson said, standing to leave, "just before Jeeves comes back. Just before he's mad enough to strike again."

"Don't know whether or not I hope to be around for that. You gonna stick around? Gather up what's left of the Arcana, help us maintain?"

"I can maintain from anywhere in the world," Benson said, slinging his black backpack over his skinny shoulder. "When you stop by the hospital later, make sure to give James my best. How's he doing?"

"He's doin' alright. Might be a little uglier, but I always was the better-looking twin." Jack-of-all-Trades half smiled. "He was only on the fringes of the riot; he'll pull through just fine. When he gets out, we're going back to film school—we can afford it now."

Benson nodded, making his exit through an annoying tangle of beaded curtains.

"Hey, Bez?"

"Yep?"

"I know you don't get a lot of credit 'cause you're not the guy covered in glitter and feathers and all. But hell, it was all about you, man."

Benson schooled his face to expressionless, almost robotic, though he was not.

"Thanks," he said.

~

The citizens of the United Kingdom were a little bit freer, now. A bit smarter, a bit savvier, a bit more aware of how easily things come and go. England was home to pleasures hard won, to spoils that tasted sweeter when they remembered what they'd gone through in order to acquire them. They were a people of ideas, of words, of poets and philosophers and the electric guitar. They were proud and ashamed, joyous and sorrowful, cold and kind and fiercely loyal.

And, as with all revolutions, though lives were lost and lies had been told—

The people forgot. Made up myths and legends. Moved on to the next crisis, the next scandal.

GGcoin was king, embraced by all whose arms and pockets had too long been empty. The alternative currency became the currency. With the exchange of goods and services no longer crippled by the remittance of the VAT and other fees, small businesses and sole proprietors flourished. There began a resurgence of hand-crafted goods—individually-made clothing and jewelry, furniture and furnishings. People's flats and houses began to look more homey and unique, and less like digitally-rendered catalogue adverts. After having lived so long inside boxes, a trend towards things less uniform was more than welcome.

But nothing is perfect. Those clever and heartless would keep scamming those trusting and naïve. Wars would keep raging. Innocents would keep dying in the crossfire. Hearts would keep breaking.

Janus Jeeves was born into his fifth life broken-hearted. He arose one sunny orange morning on American soil, a young man with such a large heart in so many pieces. This Jeeves had curly brown hair and coal black eyes. He was always a head taller than his classmates, was brilliant at English and history, bad at maths, and loved American football.

He grew up and kept his head down, working the plow. He worked in a cubicle at a mid-sized corporation at a satellite office in Albuquerque, a city that was all brown and turquoise and bright lights advertising fast food, suburban housewives who liked the jut of his chin. Lads in peacoats were now bros on skateboards, Nuvo glam rock was now Nuvo hip-hop—entirely computer-generated, the vocals and the rhymes, too. Jeeves worked as a copywriter and his name was John Little. He wrote clever copy that would help sell heaters and air conditioners. Keeping people the right temperature was important.

He would wait until his next life to try and save the world again.

Next time—it would be better. Things would run like clockwork. The next time, the next time, the next time, the next.

Each time a little closer to perfection.

Epilogue

TURN THE PAGE

Sam and Sailor lived in a flat on the South side of London. Today, some Londoners would set off to work before the sun rose in the sky, hurrying underground to wait for the train. Others would work from home, some would sleep in, some would go to school, some would walk the streets looking for new work and new adventures.

Not so for Sam Numan.

"C'mon Sammy, it's suppertime," Sailor said.

Sam, in bed in the middle of the day, yawned, stretched, and opened one eye, squinting suspiciously at his accoster.

"Hope it's not kidney pie again," he said.

"Nope. Seafood pie. Mostly fish, but you like it better." Sailor leaned against the side of the bed, waiting for Sam to be ready. Sam signaled as much by raising his arms above his head. Sailor leaned forward and gripped him around the middle, lifting him to stand. Sam rested his head against Sailor's shoulder, content with the embrace for a moment till he extricated himself and wandered off towards the living room with his flatmate a few steps behind.

"Do I?" Sam asked. "I can't remember. Is seafood pie what they eat in Buckingham Palace?"

"Probably these days. They eat some good food and some bad food, just like the rest of us."

"I won't eat any bad food. Only the quality stuff for me," Sam said over his shoulder.

"You should eat whatever's given you. Look how damn skinny you are. Not even rock star skinny. Just...never mind." Sailor cocked his head to the side, clicking his tongue against the roof of his mouth. He thought about how Sam used to look, all rough edges and fire up on the stage, embodying everyone's fantasies like some glitter acid love demon.

"I look good," said Sam. "My picture's plastered all over the place. On buildings, on trains, in the bottom of yer teacup. Look everywhere; I'm there."

They went into the kitchen and Sam sat down at the table. Their kitchen was sparsely decorated in shades of white and green, much like their old flat, only a bit colder, both in temperature and love. Sailor had tried to pep it up with some summer flowers, but they had such a short life span. A makeshift bouquet of blue and orange wildflowers sat in the center of the table, bent over and decaying, but he hadn't the heart to throw them out yet. They still held wisps of sweet fragrance mixed in with the rot.

In his wardrobe he kept some of Sam's old outfits from his Saint Fox and The Independence days—feather boas with most of the feathers missing, skintight jeans with holes in them, ruffled, bizarre-patterned shirts that were torn and frayed. The leather jacket that had once been Montreal's was there, too, hanging in the back of the wardrobe like an apparition. It smelled of stale sweat, old cigarettes, and days when they'd been on top of the world.

After the Wembley massacre, Sailor and Montreal had done what they could to try and help Sam, taking him out to the quiet countryside until things died down, giving him time and space to rest and detox. Montreal had managed to find and retrieve the time-released capsule that had been injected into Sam's neck near a ready and willing vein, releasing a psycho-sweet mixture of opiates and amphetamines, a tactical maneuver Montreal recalled having come into contact with during his MI-5 days. Sam's sudden energy surges and anger that clashed with the glassy look in his eyes and spiked approximately every hour on the hour had tipped him off, and it didn't take long for him to figure out the risky move Waterman had taken, banking that

Sam would wind up either killing himself or someone he had been programmed to hate.

Sailor stayed with Sam in the country for a few weeks to take care of him, as he always would, before moving them back to London. Montreal had cursed a few times, then retreated to the post-war post-rock-star lizard lair from whence he came.

Now, Sam seemed incapable of harming a fly. He slumped in his kitchen chair, staring blankly ahead. "S'cold," he said.

"You're always cold. I keep turning up the heat but it don't seem to make no difference," said Sailor. He took off his own denim jacket and put it around Sam, threading his uncooperative arms through it.

"There anything to drink?" Sam asked.

"There's some leftover wine from last night."

"Pour me some?"

"Fine," Sailor shrugged. "Just one glass though." He poured the last of the pink rosé into a glass for him.

"Just one glass," Sam repeated, laughing to himself a bit.

Sailor sat down next to him at the table, his own glass of wine in hand. "Have you heard about Bez?" he asked.

"Bez. Bez is dead," Sam monotoned.

"No, he ain't. At least I don't think he is. Rumor has it he's in Seoul now, working on some virtual reality game where the user never has to disconnect. Seriously, the console, like, takes care of feeding you, pissing and shitting, a sleep cycle, all that. Sounds fucking horrible."

"Not so bad," Sam said. Sailor wasn't sure if he was talking about Benson's game or something else entirely. He never was sure these days.

Sam stared into the bottom of his empty wine glass. "Kit used to drink shyte like this," he said.

"I used to...I mean, I still drink shyte like this. Stuff like this," said Sailor. "You're getting mixed up again."

"*You're* getting mixed up." Sam scratched his stomach, looking off in the distance. "Have you heard from her?"

"Can't say I 'ave. But I don't need to, what with the ol' electric grapevine and all. That girl's doing alright—better than us, I'll tell you that. She's pretty big in the States now."

"Flying solo?"

"Flying high."

"Music," Sam said, clattering a spoon left on the table against his glass to a beat in his head. "Music's her lover."

"Actually, she's dating some architect now." Sailor looked down at his hands, eyebrow raised. "Last week it were a supermodel."

"Blimey." Sam pushed himself away from the table and stood up. "M'tired," he said, heading back towards his bedroom.

"How's your neck?" Sailor called out to his retreating form.

"S'fine. Itches though."

"The wound will heal up."

"No it won't," Sam's voice echoed softly from the hallway.

"You don't want yer supper?" Sailor hollered after him. No response. He sighed, tossing the empty wine bottle into the recycling bin. "Guess I'll feed yours to Binky then."

Sam retreated to his room, one that was a close facsimile of the room he'd once slept in, with posters of his favourite musicians on the walls and navy blue sheets lining the bed. Modest and unfussy, but he couldn't remember having had or having wanted anything else.

He lay down on his back, singing one of his old Saint Fox and The Independence songs softly to himself before drifting off to sleep.

Come closer now, my darlings and hear me
I am the face of what you ignore
No more protests, and the songs will be few

In his first dream of many that night, Sam met Janus Jeeves, face to face and alone in a vast wheat field. The wheat was green and the sun was high. Janus Jeeves was wearing a farmer's hat and held a shiny, black scathe.

"Don't cut me with that thing," Sam said.

"Never did mean to," Farmer Jeeves said. "You know I'm sorry, don't you, Sammy? My intentions were good. I never wanted it to play out that way. Did I thinks it was a possibility? Yeah, I thought it was a possibility. Thought I could wager a victimless war, a war of peace. Wasn't so. There were casualties. There was you."

"Just feels like I can't get it right, no matter how hard I try," Sam said.

"Keep trying. That's getting it right," said Jeeves. "You and I...we're alright."

"I don't feel alright most days." Sam blinked hard against the pounding light of the sun overhead.

"You will," said Jeeves, casting his gaze at the land around him, the stalks of wheat high and low. "Give it time. Maybe another life or two."

Sam exhaled a loud breath, something like a laugh stuck in his throat. "So, this life…this plan. Was it worth it?"

Jeeves shielded his eyes from the sun with one hand. "Hard to say. The world turns in circles. It'll go back to the way it was eventually. Sometimes you're called upon to reset the balance—somebody has to. And there's always a price to pay. But I'm proud of us. At the end of the day, I'm proud of what we did. Proud of you," he said, grinning so that a sliver of white teeth shone through.

"Next time, leave me out of it," Sam said. The breeze blew his hair back, hair that was long and perfectly tousled again. "I just want to sit and watch the clouds go by."

"Okay, Sam," said the farmer. "Next time." Jeeves made no promises for the time after that. He walked away then, towards the horizon with scathe in hand, whacking unripened stocks of wheat left and right as he went.

About the Author

CORIN REYBURN drifts through Southern California teaching a bit of this and coding a bit of that, and enjoys transmuting cosmic energy, cats more than people, and the use of unconventional instruments in rock n' roll music. Corin holds a degree in Creative Writing and Critique from Oregon State University, and has had work featured in places such as *M-BRANE SF*, *Subtopian Magazine*, *The Molotov Cocktail*, *Jersey Devil Press*, *The Gateway Review*, *Free Focus*, *Silicon Valley Debug*, *Clutching at Straws*, and *Quantum Muse*. Reyburn co-produces and curates the speculative fiction podcast SubverCity Transmit.

Find more of Corin's work at corinreyburn.com.

About the Press

UNSOLICITED PRESS is a West Coast independent publisher that focuses on literary fiction, creative nonfiction, and poetry. Our team has expanded into a group of talented editors, marketers, producers, graphic artists, and the occasional lawyer here and there. We work hard. Unsolicited Press started off an idea, "Who better to publish books than writers who know how to write?" We decided that we would do it. That we would bring back the literary love of books--

Our motto: No **bullshit**. Just **books**.

Learn more at www.unsolicitedpress.com.